When the Need Is Great

Gail P. Robertson

When the Need Is Great

ISBN: 978-0-9921203-5-1

This book is dedicated to
my late husband, Peter Graeme Robertson,
for his endless support, patience and love.

Background photo by W. John McDonald,
modified and added-to by Gail P. Robertson.
Thank-you to Judy Desrochers for being
the face (and personality) of the heroine, Jan.

CHAPTER 1

Jan Brody projected her focus across the light-years separating herself and her telepathic penpal, Ablakan. Conversations with the Shalaian youth were usually the highlight of her day, but this time something felt very wrong. Her pulse quickened. Jan mentally 'tasted' the sensation, but was unable to put a name to it. Whatever it was, she didn't like that feeling at all. She was about to withdraw when Ablakan completed the connection.

Greetings, Jan.

The now-familiar lilt echoed through her mind, and she responded with her best effort at the reply in Shalaian, *Greetings to you, Ablakan.*

Do I find you well? You are different today.

I might be coming down with a cold, she fudged, not wanting to worry her friend.

Jan's husband Tom was sitting beside her in what she had dubbed the 'Reading Room', her own little sanctuary in their Maine hilltop retirement home. Tom leaned forward to decipher her shorthand scribble, then touched her extended arm in a tactile query.

She opened her green eyes long enough to wink reassuringly at him before asking Ablakan, *How was your first day in Learnmore? Did you make any friends?*

I am befriending two bodies. They are boy and girl of a family.

His self-image was of a lanky, beige, sparsely-furred youngster sprawled on a multi-angled couch which conformed well to his shape. A bank of eyes glistened at Jan good-naturedly, each black pupil moving independently of its brethren. Beneath them in Ablakan's horizontally-oblong face were four small breathing slits which rhythmically opened and closed in pairs. From this angle, Jan couldn't see his cream-colored mane which she knew formed a vertical ridge down the back of his head to end mid-spine. It would turn golden as he matured, she'd been told. Her best guess placed him around 10 years old, in human terms.

1

A frisson of foreboding impinged on Jan's mind. She struggled to subsume it, along with the thought 'What the heck is going on?'. Ablakan didn't notice, as he enthusiastically talked about his school chums.

Do you plan to visit them? Jan asked.

They not live far. Maybe I go.

Reading this, Tom gave her arm a quick squeeze and she nodded in agreement. They'd been afraid their talks were keeping the child from making other friends. After his father died, Ablakan and his mother had moved to coastal Tabix on Pantai, Shalaii's largest continent. That was nearly three months ago (Earth time) and this was the first interest Ablakan had shown in meeting others of his age. Or species.

"What else should we ask him?" Jan wondered aloud.

Tom stroked his tidy salt-and-pepper beard. "It would be interesting to know what kids there do for fun. Is hide-and-seek and tag universal, so to speak?"

Jan relayed his question, wishing Tom could do it for himself. Not that he hadn't been trying. He was spending hours in his little observatory lately, eyes closed, brow furrowed in concentration. So far, his only success had been to pick up Ablakan's emotions during these sessions the few times they had been strong enough. And, Jan realized, chances are Tom was getting those through her, rather than directly from Ablakan.

Plenty things, their telepathic penpal now transmitted, interrupting her reminiscences. *In warm time, youngers stand on swimmers to run far fast best.*

Reading the shorthand symbols, Tom murmured, "I think he means when it's warm, they race on the water, though I don't know what he means by 'swimmers'."

Swimmers make big plate on water, youngers no fall down under. Ablakan had no trouble 'hearing' Tom's words as he spoke to her, easily picking them up from Jan's mind.

YoungSSters, she enunciated. *Is it your warm time now?*

Yes. It is Earth's?

2

Well, on this continent it is.

During the brief pause that followed, Jan felt another spurt of apprehension. Quickly, she covered it with a feigned cough. Was it her imagination, or did whatever was bothering her seem more imminent, somehow?

Deliberately, Jan redirected her thoughts to the first time she and Ablakan had 'met'. Technically, it had been Tom who 'found' Shalaii. Night after night, he'd trained his telescope on the same star, some 140 light-years away. Intrigued, Jan had cast about mentally in that direction, and almost instantly been contacted by Ablakan.

Jan surrendered to a dollop of smugness. SETI hadn't found intelligent alien life, she had. Well, Tom and her. Too bad she could never tell anyone about the child and his beautiful Cassiopeian homeworld.

From Ablakan's description, it was surprisingly Earthlike. Their level of technology was also similar, running the gamut from commercial aircraft to nanotechnology. But socially the two worlds were quite different. Most telling was the fact that they had no word for 'war'. Must be nice, Jan thought wistfully.

It is. Killing bad.

AIIIEEEIIIAA –

Jan yelped and clapped her hands over her ears. She doubled over, reeling from the mind-piercing scream. Alongside it, she heard Ablakan's cry of pain and her husband's gasp.

"What was that?" Tom's face had gone white.

"I don't know." *Ablakan, are you all right? That wasn't you, was it?*

Nonononono, he groaned.

Jan didn't know if he was answering her or trying to scrub the ghastly shriek from his mind.

Someone pain fear cry. Not here.

What do you mean, not here? Where?

Out there.

Not on your planet? Jan asked, incredulous.

Yes, yes! Big scary pain.

Jan spoke slowly. *Ablakan, do you know of any other peoples besides yours and ours?*

Do now. Mind hurt.

"Whose mind?" Tom wanted to know, when he read Jan's notes. "Yours or – whoever that was?"

Both, Ablakan replied candidly.

"What direction did it seem to come from?" Tom asked, ever the scientist.

Jan stared at her husband. "You heard it, too?"

"Mostly I felt it, but yeah, there was sound, sort of." He grimaced at the memory. "And it sure had a kick to it. About the direction?"

"I don't know. It happened so fast, and all I wanted to do was block it."

"I can imagine."

"What about you? Where did it seem to come from?"

Tom faced north, then pointed north-northeast.

Jan bit her lip. "Hmm. Now that you mention it, it felt more to the left and up a bit."

Tom slowly moved his outstretched arm.

"There! Right there! Well, that way, anyway. I think." She blinked, no longer certain.

My here cuts your here . . . here, Ablakan offered, sending a mental image of a line slicing across their trajectory. Jan silently thanked Tom for his persistent (and often annoying) requests for monthly star charts of what Ablakan saw in his night skies. Translating them to paper from mental images was no fun at all. But now, using the latest one, they soon had a fix on the region.

Tom did some quick calculations. "I'd hazard a guess the source is some 117 light-years from us, and maybe 110 from Shalaii."

Jan could feel Ablakan's eagerness to search that sector.

Maybe I should scan it first, Jan said, not looking forward to the prospect. Whatever had happened was not going to be pretty.

No, I closer. I go first, okay?

If you wish, but please be careful, Ablakan. Much as she wanted to, Jan knew she must temporarily break contact. Otherwise, he would just pick up on her, instead of on – whoever.

During the silence that followed, Tom reached over to give her hand a reassuring squeeze, mouthing 'I love you'.

"I love you, too," Jan said. She winced as she caught sight of herself in the antique mirror on the opposite wall. The fear she felt for an unknown being was starkly etched on her face. Not wanting Tom to know how badly it was affecting her, Jan straightened her five-foot-one-inch frame. She had been hunched over in a subconscious effort to protect herself – from what, she didn't know. At the moment, she looked every one of her 54 years, from the graying hair to the tiny lines at the corners of her mouth. But right now, Jan didn't care. She might have just heard some poor soul's dying cry.

Ablakan's thought presence reappeared beside hers. *Mind busy, not asleep, not awake. Body quiet,* he reported.

"He's alive!" Fleetingly, she wondered how she knew the alien was male.

"That's a start." Tom gave her a faint smile of encouragement.

She asked Ablakan, *Do you mean that he's unconscious?* She transmitted an image of a head hitting the ground, then the body lying motionless but still breathing.

Yes. Hurt.

Could you see him?

No. Just feel. Fall hit hard, maybe. Jan look now?

I will.

Jan composed herself to change focus, less afraid now of what she might find. At least the person wasn't dead. She followed the 'line' she had been given. Unlike contact with Ablakan, in which mental joining was immediate, Jan had to sense her way along. She had no way of knowing how far she had to go, or how far she had gone.

Come on, she urged. Just a little hint. Jan cast around until, quite suddenly, she felt his presence. Unaware he was, but beneath strained a consciousness roiling with fear and pain; a nightmare afraid to awaken and find it all true.

Snippets of the crash flashed in her mind's eye, then blinked off moments later. She 'saw' his hands fighting the frozen controls, the planetoid's surface hurtling towards the capsule's nose, the explosion of light and heat and pain, then blackness. The images repeated again and again, the being's subconscious locked in an internal loop.

Caught up in the horror of his situation, Jan tried to think of some way to help. She couldn't just leave him like this, but what could she possibly do? Abruptly, Ablakan parked his focus beside hers. Jan could have hugged him.

We tell him he not alone? I do first, Ablakan said, not waiting for an answer.

The crash images slowly faded as Ablakan poured in calm and reassurance. Even unconscious, the injured being responded with a flicker of hope. Surely that was a good sign.

Now you, Ablakan said.

Jan flushed. She'd been so caught up in what he was doing, she hadn't thought out what to say, or even how to project to the alien.

Mind open. Just put in, Ablakan instructed.

Cautiously at first, then with more confidence, Jan implanted an image of herself. As yet, she had no picture of the being, save of his arms and hands as they wrestled with the malfunctioning controls. Allowing her feelings to flow through, Jan mentally took one hand and held it between hers, then pictured Ablakan beside her. She surrounded the alien with a feeling of well-being and friendship before withdrawing.

He sleeps better, the boy reported. *I cut mind, keep open with him.*

You can do that? Split your focus, I mean?

Easy, like English, Ablakan teased. *You tire; you rest now. We talk when he awake?*

Good idea. That took it right out of me, Jan realized. *Thank you, my friend. Please let me know the minute you feel a change.*

I do. And with that, Ablakan was gone.

Jan opened her eyes to find Tom leaning forward in his chair, concern in every line of his face.

"You okay, hon?"

Jan realized her cheeks were wet with tears.

"Yeah, I'm fine." The words came out in a dry croak.

Tom gestured for her to stay put. "Don't try to talk. I'll be right back." He disappeared down the hallway, and returned less than a minute later with a large glass of juice.

Jan took small sips, and let the cool fluid trickle down her throat.

"Better?" Tom was still watching her closely.

"Much." And her voice sounded it, too. "Thanks."

"You found him, then?"

"Yes, poor thing." Between sips, Jan described the encounter and Ablakan's timely intervention.

Tom nodded. "I saw you stiffen and your face go white, and then you started to weep. I didn't know what to do, so I held you and worked like the dickens to get through to Ablakan, to let him know you needed help. I guess I succeeded." He tried to look humble, and failed.

"You're remarkable, you know that?" Jan stretched upward to kiss him.

"Mmmm. Remind me to be remarkable more often." His expression sobered. "So, what happened then?"

"We both gave him a message that we were there, in mind anyway, and that somehow we'd try to help." Jan felt the fear come flooding back. "But how? We don't have the technology, and neither does Shalaii. Unless his own people can rescue him, he's as good as dead." Tears welled up in her eyes again. She did *not* want the alien to die.

7

"I know." Tom drew her to him again. "But if he does survive, we'll give it everything we've got."

"Which is what?"

"I've no idea. But as my dad used to say, when the need is great, even if you don't know enough, you somehow find a way."

CHAPTER 2

Amazing how refreshing juice is, Jan thought. For some reason, it made her feel more optimistic. It was nearing lunchtime. Neither of them was hungry, but Tom insisted they have a bite.

"It'll be a long day," he predicted.

As she perched on a kitchen stool, Jan watched her husband deftly prepare a salad for them. The gray in his hair reinforced the air of intelligence so obvious to her in his eyes. Intelligence and resourcefulness, she amended, marveling at how he had contacted Ablakan. What had he said? 'When the need is great, you find a way.' If the stranded alien survived, they would sure be putting that one to the test. She wondered if whatever communication equipment he might have had with him would still be intact. Or maybe he had an emergency transponder, like planes do.

His mind moves, Ablakan stated without preamble.

I'm on my way. Jan hopped off the stool. "Ablakan says the alien is starting to come around."

"You get going. I'll be right there." Tom pulled out a box of plastic wrap.

Jan sprinted for the Reading Room and plopped herself down in her chair. Almost immediately, she felt her eyelids flicker as her mind sought out the stranded being. She was marginally aware of Tom easing himself onto his chair, and of the pen she held poised above the notebook.

Jan's heart went out to the castaway as he struggled to regain consciousness. Disoriented, he at first did not notice Jan and Ablakan's mental presence. But as memory of the crash flooded back, he panicked. That was when his telepathic visitors make their presence known.

"Thelqtouweht ertuwoty stqhei?" he shouted.

Easy, fella, Jan urged, taken aback by the force of his reaction. Once again, it was Ablakan who poured in a sense of calmness and safety. Fear downgraded to suspicion, and finally blossomed into wild hope.

"Tehoqtewt qou fjaytupoqe?" he begged.

9

Though of course Ablakan couldn't see it, Jan made an open-handed gesture. *You're better at images. Can you find out his status?*

Status?

If he's hurt, if he has a way to contact his people – that sort of thing.

Ablakan projected a nod. *Okay. Will take time. You listen through me, yes?*

Yes, I will. Jan carefully withdrew from the alien's mind to moor her focus beside the Shalaian's. Funny, she realized, I don't think of Ablakan as an alien any more.

There began an exchange of images that frankly astonished her. Both Ablakan and the being (his name was Moohri) 'think-talked' at a rate she could never have matched. Only by concentrating mightily was she able to glean a sense of what topic was being covered. It's we who must seem like children to Ablakan, she thought ruefully.

Her mind must have wandered, for she found Ablakan describing how they had met. By then, Moohri had been told, as gently as possible, that neither Shalaii nor Earth had the technology to rescue him. Jan was almost reduced to tears again, as she felt Moohri face the realization that he was truly, hopelessly marooned.

I will ask why fall, Ablakan said to Jan. *Maybe way to help.*

A long visual conversation flashed by her mind's eye, and presently Ablakan broke off to translate the images for Jan.

The space department on Moohri's planet, Orowa, had recently completed its first unmanned voyage around their furthest moon, Shyr. The moon had an atmosphere and water, and was widely forested. As head of the agency, Moohri had undergone rigorous training to become their first astronaut. His mission was to slingshot around Shyr and to record as much information as possible before returning home to splash down in the ocean.

All had gone perfectly, from liftoff to trajectory towards Shyr. The flight was so uneventful that Moohri had felt let down somehow.

But as he hit the moon's gravitational well, the thruster rockets he deployed failed to fire. Nothing he tried would bring them to life. When the time by which they had to fire was past, he reached for the safety-off lever, to ensure they would not catch. If Shyr's gravity swung him around to the other side, facing towards home, and if he could then get the rockets to fire, he might still have a chance. He pushed the safety-off lever, only to have the thrusters burst into full power and catapult him away from Shyr. He could only guess that some techno had wired the controls backwards.

Now he had no way to return home. Even voice contact was denied him, for his angle of departure kept Shyr between him and Orowa until long past the transmitter's limited range.

Moohri had reviewed his situation, praying it wasn't as hopeless as it seemed. His capsule was not equipped to land. Its steering mechanism was more of an afterthought, because steering was not part of the mission. A prototype, it represented the pinnacle of Orowan space technology. They had nothing to send out after him. He was on his own. His only chance lay in the remote possibility of finding a habitable planet before he ran out of oxygen. Moohri used the thrusters to reach maximum speed, then cut them to conserve whatever fuel was left.

He supposed he should be delighted to have found someplace to land, the odds against being what they were. On the thirteenth day, out of food and water and with oxygen reserves almost depleted, Moohri spotted an atmosphered planetoid off to his right. Rapid calculations confirmed he would pass close enough to have a shot at it, if there was enough fuel left in the thrusters. He had no way to check the composition of the atmosphere or ocean. For all he knew, he would be plunging into an acid sea.

With this his only choice, Moohri turned towards it. He dove in, thrusters at maximum, till he felt the capsule hit the atmosphere. He fought the controls to increase the angle, but they chose that moment to seize up. Now at the mercy of his fates, he could only watch helplessly.

The capsule arrowed into a bog, but it felt like hitting rock. The hatch was ripped off its fastenings and Moohri's restraints snapped. As he hit the controls, his right shoulder was pulled from its socket.

That must have been when he screamed, Jan surmised. At least, he doesn't sound too badly hurt. *Ablakan, how many legs does Moohri have? Is he able to get up and move about? Can he leave the capsule?*

I ask. Rapid-fire visuals flashed in Jan's mind, then Ablakan reported, *Two arms, two legs. Moohri can walk. Capsule is broken. He will check water, plants. Air okay, heat okay.*

How is his shoulder?

Moohri says shoulder is big, hurts.

Is it still out of place?

There was a brief pause. *Go out, go in,* he said.

Good. What about his ship? Is there anything in it he can use?

Seconds passed. *Some little things, not much.*

A long shot occurred to her. *Your people don't know how to teleport, do they?*

Teleport?

Move people or things from one place to another with their mind. Jan flushed, feeling foolish even mentioning it.

Ablakan perked up noticeably. *No. Your people do?*

I don't think so. Although, I have heard stories of people teleporting spontaneously – uh, without meaning to – when something terrible was happening.

This terrible. You can teleport?

Jan's color deepened, realizing Tom would be reading this. *I don't know how true those stories were. It may not even be possible.*

Moohri will check new place. I check with Moohri later. I go do Learn-more work. Jan go eat. Body makes sounds.

Jan shook her head in amazement. He didn't miss much. *When you're finished, Ablakan, can you ask him to give you a visual – um, a mental picture – of himself, his capsule inside and out, and anything else he can tell us about the planetoid he's on. You never know what details might be useful.*

I ask. Then we think, maybe find something.

We'll sure try. Jan signed off and returned her focus 'home'. Tom was staring at her, eager for an update. Jan glanced at the page in front of her. She had not recorded a single word.

"Oops. Sorry, hon. I'll fill you in while I eat. I'm famished, for some reason." Her stomach rumbled agreement. Making a mental note to write down the details while they were fresh in her mind, Jan made a beeline for the refrigerator.

* * *

Eating triggered an unexpected side effect. No sooner had Jan stacked the dishwasher than Tom noticed her eyelids begin to droop. Despite her protests, Tom soon had her snuggled beneath the covers. She was asleep in moments.

"Sweet dreams," Tom whispered. He turned off the ringer on the phone beside the bed before tiptoeing out of the room and easing the door shut behind him.

He paused briefly. Never much of a risk-taker, what he had in mind fairly made his skin crawl. And it would have to be played just right.

Tom headed for the kitchen phone and dialed a number from memory. Soon his old boss was on the line.

"Tom, how are you doing?" Young Rick Mallory's jovial manner erased the age difference between them, as it always had. "I thought you'd forgotten us slaves."

"No, I think of you every time I cash my pension cheque."

Mallory groaned eloquently. "And me still decades from retirement! How's the missus?"

"Fine, great. In a way, that's why I'm calling. I need a favor. Do you still play poker with that fellow from NASA?" Tom frowned in annoyance. Real smooth intro, he chided himself.

"Jack Foxworth? Occasionally, why? You joining the space race?"

Tom winced. That hit too close to the mark. "No, but I do need to talk to him, if you can arrange it."

"I suppose so. Seen a UFO, have you?"

"No, but something has come up, and it's time-sensitive. You wouldn't have his number handy, would you?"

Mallory remarked, "You really do have a bug in your craw!" There was a lengthy delay. "Okay, I've reached him a couple of times at this number."

Tom scribbled it down, as his former boss started to backpedal. "I can't promise he'll talk to you. As it is, he'll be sore at me for giving out his work number, so this better be important. Say, you're not writing a book or something?"

"No, nothing like that. I owe you dinner. You and Jacklynne. I'll brief you as soon as I can. Don't be too hard on the crew. And Rick – thanks." He hung up before Mallory could ask any more awkward questions.

The number he'd been given rang twice before it was answered. The girl sounded young but efficient. She took his message, and assured him Mr. Foxworth would call him back in a short while. All Tom could do now was wait and hope he wasn't making a big mistake. He had no desire to let official types know what had been going on in their little hilltop retreat.

They had chosen the two-bedroom rancher in Maine for their retirement home, with its flowerbeds and open skies, mostly to let Tom fulfill his lifelong dream of having a small observatory. He had converted the loft into a dome for that very purpose.

Tom had thought it fitting that Jan have a secluded spot of her own to pursue her hobby – psychic skills development. Which was how the den ended up being repurposed as what she euphemistically dubbed the 'Reading Room'.

His woolgathering was cut short by the phone. Jack Foxworth's voice was pleasant but neutral.

14

"Good day, sir," Tom began, as he perched on the edge of the counter. "Thanks for returning my call. I had to practically mortgage my soul to Rick Mallory – he was my boss – to get your number, but as I told him, time is critical. I just need to know how close to light-speed our present spacecraft can attain."

"You a reporter?" Foxworth's tone instantly had an edge to it.

"No, sir, and I'm not writing a book either. I just need to know how long it would take our fastest ship to go 117 light-years."

A snort greeted that statement. "You're kidding, right? Rick put you up to this?"

"No, he didn't. Look, I know how it sounds, but a rough estimate is all I need."

Foxworth grunted. "You probably heard about that new propulsion system we've been working on with the Russians, the Brits and the French. It's too early to tell if it'll even work, but the press have been calling it a done deal. Don't you believe it."

"Theoretically, though. If it were successful, how long would it take to go 117 light-years at maximum speed?"

Foxworth sighed. "I'll have to work it out. I'd really like to know what this is about first. They don't pay me to sit around answering hypothetical questions over the phone."

"I wish I could explain, sir, I really do. But I just need that one question answered. I could call back in a while, if it suits you."

"We're not that broke – yet. I'll get back to you." He hung up before Tom could thank him.

Tom sighed. He'd almost forgotten what a trial it was, dealing with scientists. You were one, too, he reminded himself. Tom frowned, wondering if he had ever grilled callers who requested information.

With nothing to do but wait – again – Tom went to check on Jan. She was sleeping soundly, her breathing slow and regular. Satisfied, he returned to the kitchen and turned his attention to Moohri's plight. No matter how he looked at it, the prospects were grim. He went over what little he knew of space travel. His thoughts were still casting about dispiritedly when the phone rang. He grabbed it.

"Hello?"

"Mr. Brody? Jack Foxworth. I've got your answer, for what it's worth. Even with the new propulsion system, assuming it got built and worked properly, you're still looking at around 700 years. Obviously, we'd be talking cryogenics or a generational ship which, incidentally, we don't have and aren't likely to have for a long time, if ever."

Tom's shoulders drooped. "That's about what I figured. Thanks for indulging me, sir."

"Okay, now why don't you tell me why you wanted to know?"

"It was just a long shot. Sorry I bothered you. And please don't blame Rick. I really did twist his arm."

"Yeah, well, after we talked I gave Ricky-boy a call. He assured me you had your head on straight – or did while you worked for him. Somehow I don't think you're the kind of guy to cry 'wolf', Tom."

So it was 'Tom' now. Red flags sprouted like weeds in Tom's mind.

"I figure you're onto something you want to keep pretty close to your chest, am I right? If you'll forgive the cliché, you don't have to be a rocket scientist to come up with an idea we can use. Why don't you run it by me, let me decide if it has merit?" Foxworth was speaking quickly, as though afraid Tom would hang up, which was exactly what Tom wanted to do.

Hearing the eagerness in Foxworth's voice, Tom hesitated a long minute. He could either come up with some cockamame notion to satisfy Foxworth or enlist his help. The former was by far the safest, and probably wisest, plan. But Tom knew in his heart they had no chance of saving Moohri on their own. All he could hope was that they wouldn't pay too dearly for his decision.

"You still there?" Foxworth asked.

"Yes. I was just thinking."

"And?"

Tom inhaled deeply. "Before I tell you . . . what's your title? How much of the whole space travel picture do you know?" First rule is, know who you're dealing with, Tom remembered.

Foxworth's voice turned frosty. "I know enough not to answer a question like that over the phone. Look, Tom, I've played straight with you, and you know I didn't have to. Now it's your turn."

Tom inhaled deeply. "Alright – Jack – but this has to stay between us, for the time being."

"*What* does?"

"A crashed alien. That's all I can tell you now."

"Where? At your place? Is he alive?"

Tom's grip on the phone tightened in alarm. "*Not so loud!* Is there any way you can come out here on the q.t.? I know it's asking a lot, but a life is riding on this."

Foxworth hesitated, but not for long. "Yeah, I've got some vacation left. But if this is a wild goose chase, you're gonna pay for a lot more than my plane ticket, buddy."

"Look, I can understand your skepticism. Hell, I was a scientist, too. But think what my wife and I are risking here. You know better than I what happens to people who become of interest to 'officialdom'. If you want in on this, you've got to come here, alone and soon."

"Alright, how do I get there?"

Tom felt almost weak-kneed with relief. He gave Jack directions from the airport to the village, three miles from their house.

"It's a bit hard to find," Tom lied. "I'll meet you at the gas station. We only have the one. It's at the light on the main strip. You can't miss it."

This would give Tom a chance to size him up before bringing him home. But so far he'd been impressed by Jack's forthrightness, and he had always considered himself a good judge of character. If Jack could be convinced of the existence of Ablakan and Moohri, he might just be the ally they needed.

17

For the first time since Jan had her emergency appendectomy, Tom paced the floor.

CHAPTER 3

Men in space suits were walking on the moon, looking for something. They heard a terrible cry and went rushing off in all directions. Then someone was knocking at a door. But there were no doors on the moon. The cry came again, but this time it seemed further away, and again the men searched in vain for the source.

Knock, knock.

Would someone *please* answer the door!

Jan sat up, still dull with sleep. "Come in." No one entered. "Tom, it's okay. I'm awake."

Then she heard the knocking again, inside her head, and understood. Ablakan was calling.

Jan sleeps. Sorry. Moohri checked new place. Enough drinkwater, no food.

That brought her to full wakefulness. *Did he say how long since he last ate? And how long he can survive without food?*

He ate little food a day for 10 of your days, now no food for two days. Needs food before two tens and five days to stay awake.

To stay conscious, you mean? Jan asked.

Yes. He eats small tree peel. Not food, but stops body rumble.

Jan felt her stomach twist. People on Earth die of hunger too, she knew, but she had never before known someone who was facing starvation.

Moohri give mind pictures for you. I show now?

Yes, please, but slowly. Vivid images, some stills, some panoramic views, filled her mind. At times, she asked Ablakan to return to a previous one, or to repeat a current scene. Faster than she had ever done before, Jan described in shorthand, on the pad she always kept beside their bedside, what she was seeing. At length, the visuals ended.

Thanks. You never know what bits might help. Have you or Moohri thought of any way we can help him get home?

No. Ablakan sounded despondent. *And Mother does not believe I think-talk. Shalaians believe they are only peoples, so no space travel.*

I know, but I was thinking about your mental skills. I didn't know anyone could split their focus two places like you do. There may be other things you can do that we can't and don't even know about. Like maybe teleport. If I can read up on it, would you be willing to try? Unlikely though it was, right now it seemed Moohri's only hope.

You tell me, I try.

Good lad. I'll see what I can find.

Okay. Ablakan's mindprint disappeared.

It took Jan a half hour to complete the rest of her notes, as she had to include those from her previous session. Then she freshened up and went looking for Tom.

Jan halted at the sight of him pacing the kitchen floor. "You look like an expectant father."

"Oh, hi, hon. How're you feeling?"

"Better," Jan yawned. "Ablakan woke me with a report. Moohri's got water but no food. I feel guilty saying this, but I'm hungry again." She relayed the rest of their conversation between munches on the salad Tom had prepared. He, of course, wanted descriptions of the visuals.

Jan winced. "I'll have to redo my notes, because I'm remembering things I didn't write down. But I can give you the condensed version:

Orowans walk on all fours or upright. They use the all-fours position to cover a lot of ground quickly. Anytime else, they walk like us. The skin – it's pearl-colored – looks like a cross between skin and the hide of a lizard, but there's nothing lizardy about Moohri. His head's sort of roundly tubular, with pairs of eyes on three sides. He's got a mouth like ours, but I couldn't see any lips, and his teeth are definitely omnivorean – is that a word?" Jan paused as other details surfaced.

"Oh, yeah. On each hand, he has four fingers and two thumbs – one on either side. His fingers are flattish, not round like ours, and much stubbier. Same with the toes. Small, squashed-looking ears, no nose that I could see, no hair or fur anywhere. At a guess, he's about six feet tall standing up, and maybe 130 pounds. But he's half-starved so who knows how much he should weigh."

Tom reached for a second helping of salad. "What about the capsule? Anything he can salvage?"

"Nothing much, and I have no idea what the things Ablakan showed me are for. I'll draw them as best I can when I redo my notes. Moohri is awful upset that a small container was destroyed. I think it held a picture or hologram or something of his family. Ablakan said Moohri has a 'wife-mate' and three kids." Jan shook her head slowly. "They must be just frantic. I wish we could at least let them know he's alive – but for how much longer?" The thought gnawed at her. Jan took a deep, trembling breath.

"It might be kinder if they never know," Tom said gently. "Did Ablakan show you anything about the planetoid?"

"Oh, right, the terrain . . . What his capsule bounced off of was like a peat bog. He just missed the big body of water. I don't know if it's a lake or small ocean. Anyway, what he hit was pretty small; he was lucky he didn't plow into the ground. I gather there's not much soil on top of the rocks, at least where Moohri is.

Moohri figures the planetoid is roughly in the same orbit and going the same speed as Orowa. But it's on the opposite side of their sun, so they never knew it was there.

The plants are mostly little bushes and mosses – at least that's all Moohri has seen so far. I couldn't tell much from the visuals." Jan studied him hopefully. "How about you? Did you come up with any ideas while I was sleeping?"

Tom waffled a hand. "Maybe. I made a couple of calls. I sure hope we won't regret this." He described the conversations. "When Foxworth gets here, I'll have him come in first. If I shake my head, let me do the talking. You just seem embarrassed whenever I speak, okay? If I can't convince him I've lost it, there'll be hell to pay."

"And if he's okay?"

Tom gave a lopsided shrug. "Then it'll be up to you and Ablakan. I doubt there's anything he can do, but right now, I think he's our only hope." He sighed and lapsed into silence.

Jan pointed her fork at Tom. "I've been thinking about that. You know, we're both good at playing hunches, and most of the time they pan out. Moohri already broke the bank, oddswise, by crashing where he did and not getting killed in the process. We've got as good a chance of lucking into something as he has of still being alive now."

Tom blinked, momentarily lost in her reasoning. Then he chuckled. "That's one way of putting it."

There were no further calls from Ablakan, so Jan used the time to research teleportation on the Internet. It took several hours, and in the end she new little more than she had when she started.

Jan stood up to stretch her cramped muscles and glanced at the wall clock. It was 7:32 p.m. Just enough time to make a no-progress report to Ablakan and tell him about Foxworth's upcoming visit. The boy's mother insisted he be in bed by 8:00 (Jan's time) on school nights.

She plopped herself back down in the chair, then sent out the doorknock signal.

Greetings, Jan, Ablakan opened to her mind. *Have you found help?*

Well, nothing helpful on teleportation, but I have a couple ideas of my own. And there's a man from our space department coming here – to our house, I mean – tomorrow morning. Tom will decide whether he can be trusted. If so, I'd like to introduce him to you and Moohri. Would that be alright?

Yes. YoungSSters go to old-dead-great-ones' home at Wifafi tomorrow. Mother said I stay home. No – money – for visit. I can talk to space man. I think Moohri can talk through me. Can your space man help?"

Jan smothered a grin at Ablakan's pronunciation of 'youngsters'. Nothing wrong with *his* memory. *I don't know. We're just casting about, really, but sometimes that's how you find the answer. Which reminds me: when you talk to Moohri, see if he knows anyone on his planet who can 'think-talk', or at least receive a message. If he does, maybe Moohri could send a message through you.*

Ablakan considered this. *I will check. Maybe he feels pain talking to home but cannot go there.*

I know; I was thinking that, too. But at least it might give him hope, and his people will know what is happening to him. Maybe there's some craft he doesn't know about that they could send out after him. Or someone who can teleport.

Then why build ship? Ablakan asked reasonably.

But Jan wasn't about to discount the idea just yet. *For now, all Moohri needs is food. Even if no one can move a ship about, maybe they could teleport him something small like that. I'd much rather someone there send him stuff than either of us. What we eat might poison him.*

That is true. I will ask Moohri tomorrow. You said you have ideas on teleporting?

To Jan, Ablakan's mind felt sleepy. His grammar always improved when he wasn't concentrating on it.

I'll talk to the 'space man' tomorrow. He might have some ideas of his own. Then, if mine seem worthwhile, I'll tell you, okay?

Okay. Goodnight, Jan.

Rest well, Ablakan. They severed the connection at the same time.

Tom was coming down the hall towards the Reading Room as she emerged. "I just had a thought."

"You poor baby!" Jan teased, then inhaled deeply. A wonderful aroma emanated from the kitchen.

With a knowing smile, Tom shepherded her to their small dinette. Jan clapped her hands in delight at the sight of her

23

favorite Chinese food delicacies. Thank goodness he freezes portions for hectic times, she thought.

"Thanks, beloved." Jan planted a kiss on his lips before digging in. "Luscious! Now, about this thought of yours?"

"If Foxworth turns out to be a 'good guy', chances are he'll have to bring others in on this . . . people with specialized knowledge we need. Which means we may not be able to keep a lid on it."

Jan sighed. "Yeah, I know. We're taking an awful chance. I don't relish the idea of becoming a lab rat. But Tom, you didn't touch Moohri's mind like I did. He's a kind, decent sort. If there's any way at all –"

Tom reached over to squeeze her hand. "Don't fret, love; I'm with you. But if things *do* get hairy, we might still come out okay. I made a strong contact (I wouldn't call him a friend exactly) in the media when I made that little breakthrough in mind-health correlation."

"There was nothing little about that breakthrough," Jan declared. "It was brilliant."

Tom smiled away the compliment. "Anyway, I'm going to get his number tomorrow, make sure I can reach him. If worse comes to worse, we'll give him the whole story, maybe even let him talk to Ablakan and Moohri. If it becomes a media event, it *should* make it a lot harder for us to be spirited away."

Jan shuddered. "Let's hope it never comes to that. Being hounded by reporters is not much better than being a lab rat."

"Except the attention only lasts till the next big headline," Tom pointed out. "And personally, I prefer microphones to electrodes."

Jan stifled a yawn. "Me, too. How long has today been, anyway? Three years?"

"At least. So much for a nice, quiet retirement."

"Woah! I just realized something." She gazed at Tom, feeling almost giddy at the thought. "We've been preoccupied with getting Moohri home and us not ending up under a microscope. But what if we were to succeed?"

"If we did . . ." The look of awe on his face spoke volumes.

"Exactly. We could have three planets mentally sharing knowledge, technology, all sorts of things. But you're right; either way, you can kiss your quiet retirement goodbye." She pecked his nose playfully.

"I'd rather kiss you," Tom stated, returning the favor. "And before you become too hot a commodity and find yourself a younger stud –"

"I'll never –"

"– I suggest we call it a night, early."

Jan batted her eyelashes at him, looking more like a pixie than a temptress. "Are you propositioning me?"

"Yes, ma'am."

"Good!" And with that she headed for the bedroom, dinner forgotten, with Tom right behind.

CHAPTER 4

Night on a strange world, a land on which he was probably the only living thing. In the warm twilight air, Moohri shivered convulsively. Everything was so silent. For the first time in his life, he missed the *crxxxkkk* of the kheepik bug which abounded everywhere on Orowa. Less than 15 days away, his beautiful lavender planet spun gracefully in her orbit. Less than 15 days to his wife-mate, Shira, and their three scampering, hyperactive blanas.

Moohri felt an almost unbearable longing. Perhaps it would have been better to die in peaceful oblivion in space when the oxygen ran out, he thought morosely. Space that Orowans shared with at least two other advanced species.

"How sad," he muttered to himself. "That I should be the first Orowan to learn of them, to talk with them and share deep, empathic feelings, and have to die here alone, taking that knowledge with me."

* * *

Sunshine on his face eventually roused Tom long after his usual wake-up time. Jan continued to slumber peacefully beside him. Memories of the night before produced a tender smile. It reminded him of their wedding night, and he vowed to invoke that magic more often.

Careful not to wake her, Tom picked out his clothes and shoes and tiptoed from the room. He was feeding the coffee-maker when Jan wandered into the kitchen, grinning like a Cheshire cat. She stretched luxuriously.

" 'Morning, honey," Tom smiled, "Need I ask how you slept?"

"Yummy," she purred. "How about you?"

"Dead to the world. Now, I wonder why that was?"

Jan stood on her tiptoes to kiss him soundly. "If you find out, I want the recipe. Did Foxworth say when he'll be here?"

"No. Just that he's catching a flight out this morning. He'll call from the village. Have you caught up on your notes?"

Jan nodded. "All typed out except for yesterday's. I figured if he believes us, he'll want a copy."

"No doubt." Tom rummaged around for a pen. "I'd better find that reporter's number, just in case."

Jan felt herself tense. "Do you really think it'll come to that?"

"Probably not, but you never know. Think of it as insurance."

At 10:40, the call came in. Jan sprinted from the Reading Room, where she had just finished printing the last of her reports, but Tom got to the phone first. Foxworth was calling from the gas station. Jan felt her stomach flutter. This was it; no turning back now.

Tom hung up. "That was him," he confirmed. "Wish me luck. And remember, if I shake my head –"

"I know, we make like you're gaga."

"See you in a bit." Tom picked up the car keys and headed for the door.

"Yup; it's show time." Her eyes strayed to his manly buns and her mind to the night before. Too bad they'd soon have a house-guest. An unknown quantity of a house-guest, she reminded herself. Jan returned to the Reading Room to make sure all was in readiness. The typed transcripts were neatly stacked on the desk, each 'session' dated and stapled. If Foxworth branded her a fraud, at least she'd be an organized one.

Ablakan must have been waiting, for he responded before she finished her knock. There followed the usual exchange of greetings.

Has the space man arrived? he asked eagerly.

Tom has gone to meet him. They should be back in a few minutes. Did you talk to Moohri this morning?

Jan felt worry flood into the boy's mind. *Yes. He think-talks quietly, but his mind has much fear. Shoulder not big now and not hurts. Stomach hurts from no food. So weak, so alone.*

Jan felt tears sting her eyes. Get a grip, she told herself sternly.

I hold mind-feelings softly, Ablakan assured her.

27

Jan grimaced. *Sorry, I was talking to myself. Did you ask Moohri the questions I gave you?*

Yes. He visited mindtalk man –

Actually, we call them telepaths.

– Telepath on Orowa one time. Telepath said great danger coming, alone time. That was all. Moohri can think-talk through me with your space man, Ablakan added, switching subjects abruptly.

Great. How?

Ablakan told her what he had in mind. It sounded promising.

Maybe later you could try to put Moohri in contact with that Orowan telepath.

Yes. He must talk to home. Too alone.

Empathy sent an echoing twinge of loneliness through Jan, but this time she was able to control her emotions. *I know. Somehow, we'll find a way to rescue him,* Jan promised, hoping it wasn't a lie.

Have to. Ablakan transmitted a surge of warmth before breaking the connection.

* * *

Tom took his time driving to the village. He prided himself on his ability to read people, but never had the stakes been so high. He mentally replayed the two conversations with Foxworth, looking for hints to the man's inner nature. There was precious little to go on. He could only hope that, one way or the other, the next few minutes would tell him what he needed to know.

As he pulled onto the lot, Tom spotted a rental car parked at the far end. It was compact and practical-looking. Tom wondered if Foxworth had put it on his expense account or was paying for it himself.

The man casually leaning against the car was shorter, stockier and perhaps two decades younger than Tom, with the unmistakable build of a man who works out regularly. His suit was casual but looked expensive, and he sported a trimmed moustache a shade darker brown than his neck-length hair.

28

As Tom approached, their eyes met and held. Tom saw the forthrightness he had heard in Foxworth's voice mirrored in the man's grey eyes. They shook hands silently. Tom realized he was being sized up every bit as much as he was evaluating Foxworth.

"Thanks for coming, Jack. How was the flight?"

Foxworth shrugged. ""Uneventful, the way I like 'em. What would you like to know?"

"I beg your pardon?"

"You're trying to decide if I can be trusted before you take me home." Foxworth's eyes never left Tom's.

The gloves were off. "And can you be?" Tom asked, equally forthright.

"Depends. If you're harboring a disease-ridden alien – no, you can't count on me to keep my mouth shut."

"Fair enough," Tom nodded. "And no, he's not here."

Foxworth's eyes narrowed, but Tom raised a hand. "You'll get all the evidence you could want; I assure you he's very real. But let us present this to you in our own way, alright? You've come this far – literally. Now give us a chance to show you what we're up against."

Foxworth eyed him mistrustfully, then gave an abrupt nod and climbed into his rental car.

Tom returned to his own. The guy must be one helluva good poker player, he thought. This was the third time they had spoken, and he still didn't have a make on Foxworth.

* * *

Tom opened the front door and motioned for Foxworth to precede him. Jan smiled at them pleasantly, but when she glanced at Tom, all she got was a shoulder shrug. She'd have to 'wing it'.

Jan strode forward with outstretched hand. "Please come in, sir. I'm Jan Brody. Thank you for coming."

"Glad to meet you." Foxworth's grip was strong, but not crushing. "Nice spot you have here. Very private. Just the sort of place I'd expect an alien to aim for, if he had to put down suddenly."

"It isn't that sort of contact, I'm afraid. But I've kept detailed notes. Would you care for a coffee while you read them?"

Foxworth glanced over her head. "Would the evidence be close by? I'd just like a quick peek first."

"Not in that sense, no." Jan motioned for him to follow her down the hallway. "My notes are not that long, and they'll prepare you for meeting him – actually, them."

"*Them?* How many are there?"

"Two. About the coffee?"

"Thanks; just milk," Foxworth acquiesced.

Tom turned toward the cupboard. "I'll get it, hon. You two go ahead."

Soon they were all seated around the desk in the Reading Room. From her chair behind the desk, Jan tried not to blush as Foxworth's gaze took in the bookcases which were stuffed with novels and anecdotal reports on telepathy, levitation and the like. She regretted not having dusted the old computer in front of her. Several chairs in varying states of comfort and repair dotted the spacious room. Foxworth had opted for the one on the far right. His back was to the windows which looked out on a small grove of young evergreens that disappeared from view down the slope.

No one spoke as Foxworth read Jan's transcripts. From time to time, he glanced at one or the other, as though trying to decide if this was an elaborate hoax. The coffee, after the first sip, sat forgotten on the desk.

At length, he looked up. "Forgive my bluntness, Jan, but this is remarkable, *if true.* Can you prove any of it?"

Jan inhaled nervously. Here we go, she thought. "Ablakan is standing by. With your permission, he will link with you through me. After you've chatted with him, he'll merge with Moohri and reconnect with us. Ablakan will have to translate for Moohri, as he knows no English."

Foxworth regarded her for a long moment. "I'm not telepathic. Are you sure I'll hear them?"

"Tom did, as you read in my notes, and he isn't telepathic. But he was touching me at the time. Ablakan thinks physical contact with a telepath is what makes the connection possible." Jan nodded at her husband. "If it works with Mr. Foxworth, you'll be able to get in on the 'conference call', too."

"Great!"

They both looked at Foxworth expectantly. Their guest took a deep breath and squared his shoulders. "I'm ready."

"Okay, I'll get Ablakan first." Jan shut her eyes and sent out her call. The youth responded instantly.

We're ready at this end, she told him. Then to Foxworth, "Sir, when you're ready, just place your hand on my arm."

"Alright." Foxworth hesitantly reached across to where Jan's arm rested on the desk. His jaw was set. Jan gave him a reassuring smile, remembering her initial experience. First contact was not for the faint-hearted.

All yours, Ablakan, she transmitted, then kept her mind as quiet as possible not to interfere.

Foxworth gasped, and his free hand raised halfway to his head.

Greetings, sir, Ablakan said formally. *I am happy to speak to you.*

Jan beamed at Tom. The link worked! She extended her other hand, and Tom clasped it.

Jack turned to Jan. "What do I do?"

"Just think what you want to say. He'll pick it up from your mind."

"Okay." *I am happy to speak to you, uh, Ablakan – did I pronounce that right?*

Yes, sir, Ablakan projected approval.

"It was pretty nerve-racking for us, too, the first time," Jan assured Foxworth. "You're doing just fine."

Uh, am I speaking too fast?

No, I listen fast, too, Ablakan replied drolly.

Foxworth chuckled, and Jan felt his hand relax a bit on her arm. *Ablakan, I read the transcripts – uh, notes – of how you two*

31

met. I was wondering, is anyone else you know of on your planet telepathic? Could they just tune in to us any time they wish?

I know no others here. And I only listen after 'knock' answered.

That's very thoughtful. Did Mrs. Brody explain I work in our space agency?

Yes, Jan *did.* Ablakan emphasized her first name. *But she said you cannot go get Moohri.*

No, though I sure wish we could. How about your people? Are you sure your planet does not have space travel?

Ablakan projected negation. *They do not know of other peoples. Why go out there when they think only peoples here?*

What about overpopulation? Foxworth asked. *Maybe your planet has too many people on it and not enough room. That would be another reason for space travel, wouldn't it?*

The youth imaged a head shake. *Many people, but much room, too. Shalaii is home.*

I understand they have something akin to television, Jan injected. *If they were involved in space travel, Ablakan would probably know of it.*

Does sir feel much better now? Ablakan asked solicitously.

That caught Foxworth off-guard. *What do you mean?*

Afraid before. Think maybe Shalaii attack Earth.

The thought had crossed my mind, yes, Foxworth admitted. *But I don't think that now.*

I am glad. 'First contact' scary time.

Yes, it is. My hat's off to you both, for having the – uh, heart – to ever try this.

Jan could feel Ablakan's confusion.

Hat's off?

That means, it took courage. It was brave.

In the interests of letting them getting acquainted, Jan parked her mental presence on the sidelines of their awareness. She was careful to keep her own thoughts quiet. As expected, Foxworth soon forgot she was there and became increasingly at ease with Ablakan.

At length he said, *There's a lot more I'd like to know, but perhaps that should wait. I understand the real purpose of letting me in on this is to see if I can help Moohri.*

Yes, sir, Ablakan said.

You are really worried about him, aren't you?

He is alone, afraid and very hungry. If we cannot help, he will die. Moohri is good person. Must not die.

Foxworth's mental voice was gentle. *He is most fortunate to have you three on his side.*

Are you 'four'? the youth asked bluntly.

Jan held her breath for the several seconds it took Foxworth to decide.

I am 'four'. And my name is 'Jack', to those who matter to me.

Jan opened her eyes momentarily to grin at Tom.

Do we matter?

Yes, Ablakan, you all matter to me.

A wave of Shalaian joy washed over them all. *Thank you, Jack. You matter to me, and to Moohri. We hope for your help very much.*

I will try my best, but I don't know if it will be enough.

To her dismay, Jan felt tears roll down her cheeks. She released Tom's hand to hastily brush them away before reconnecting. She hoped Jack hadn't noticed, either physically or psychically. She needn't have worried. If he had, he was gallant enough not to let on.

Wait, please. I will bring Moohri, Ablakan said.

It took some time to detach everyone, then reattach them with Moohri now in the loop.

After introductions all around, Ablakan said, *Jack, please talk slow, use small words. I make words into mind pictures for Moohri.*

I understand. To Moohri: Our planet is still at the start of learning how to travel in space. We also have lost courageous

33

people. I will do everything I can to find a way to return you to your homeworld.

Ablakan sounded puzzled. *Your lost people – did you find them?*

Jack's tone saddened. *No, I mean they died. The shuttle – that's a kind of space ship sent up by a rocket – exploded.*

I also am sorry. I will tell Moohri. Strange words and images flashed by their minds' eyes at light speed.

Jack stared at Jan in amazement. "I thought you said he's a child."

"He is, but a very special one."

"No kidding!"

Ablakan's lilt filled their minds. *Moohri said thank you for caring. I tell him your shuttles do not reach him. But maybe you can teleport?*

What? Me? No. Anyway, that's just speculation – uh, guesses. Nobody on Earth knows how to do that on purpose, if at all.

Can you learn? Ablakan pressed.

Jack snorted. *I can't, that's for sure.*

Then maybe you talk to Jan. Jan has ideas.

She does? Jack's eyes opened briefly to give Jan a searching gaze.

She felt her cheeks pink in embarrassment. *I was reading a bit about it on the Internet. I noticed the few accounts of someone spontaneously – sorry, Ablakan – suddenly teleporting had one thing in common: The person had an almost hysterical – uh, very, very strong – need to be somewhere else. Or, they felt such an intense break with where they were that the compulsion to be anywhere else catapulted them out of there. Either way, the feeling seems to have been the key.*

Theoretically, yes. That gels with what I've read, Jack agreed. *Sorry, Ablakan, did we go too fast for you there?*

I think I understand. If Moohri wants home very much, maybe he goes home?

34

Well, not exactly, Jan waffled. *I'll explain later. I was just wondering if there was some way to create that feeling and maybe use it to send food to Moohri. I wouldn't suggest he try to teleport home right now, no matter how strong a feeling he can generate.*

Jack agreed. *But that reminds me: A contact of mine – he's a physicist – once told me he was working on atomic translocation. I didn't pay much attention at the time, but he could have meant teleportation. I'll see if I can track him down.*

Thanks, Jan said. *We need all the help we can get.*

A feeling of growing confusion seeped into their collective minds. *Moohri asks me what you said, but I do not understand it all,* Ablakan said. *Please say again slowly, another way.*

Jack grimaced. *Yes, of course. Sorry about that. Please tell Moohri we have some ideas about teleportation. I will talk to a man I know who may be able to help. Maybe you and Jan could work on her idea, see if you can use it to get food to Moohri.*

Oh, and another thing: Ask Moohri to tell you – and you describe to Jan – plant food he ate on his homeworld, if any. Then find out about the plants around him. I have a botanist friend – a plant man – who might be able to tell from that what Moohri could safely eat where he is now.

I will ask him, Ablakan replied eagerly. *Wait, please.*

There was another burst of images. *Moohri will do. He eats plants on homeworld. He is afraid to eat plants where crashed because he is weak. If he gets sick, he maybe die faster. He said there are not many plants.*

I understand, Jack said. *Please tell him I will call the people I mentioned as soon as we are finished here.*

Maybe finish soon? Moohri tiring.

So am I, actually, Jack admitted. *Can we talk again later?*

Yes, Jack. I am happy to talk any time. Moohri says thank you, and please try to help fast.

Jack's lips pursed in determination. *I'll do my best. He can count on that.*

Thank you. Goodbye, Jan and Tom and Jack. The connection ended there.

"Whew, I'm wiped," Jack remarked as he leaned back in his chair. All the shields were down, and Jan knew they'd passed the test with flying colors.

"I've been known to need naps after some of these sessions," Jan confessed, with a wink at her husband.

Tom shook his head ruefully. "I didn't say a word, and I still feel pooped."

Jan wriggled in the chair to loosen some of the cramped muscles. "I must ask Ablakan sometime if he finds it tiring. He's never mentioned it." She peered into Jack's cup. "Can I freshen that for you?"

"Please."

"How about you, Tom?"

"Thanks." Tom stood up and stretched as well. "We might be more comfortable in the sun room."

Jan got out from behind her desk. "Good idea."

They converged on the easy chairs strategically placed between shrubs and fragrant hyacinths in large ornamental planters. The room offered a panoramic view of the forested valley below, with Tom's prized rose bushes in the foreground.

Jack exhaled deeply. "Of course you realize the significance of what's happening here, don't you? How we handle this – how we're *able* to handle this – could affect the course of three world histories."

"We know," Tom assured him. "But for now we're concentrating on the grassroots problem. The bigger picture will have to wait awhile."

"I'm used to thinking out the consequences first, but in this case . . ." Jack stopped there, lost in thought. "Alright, let's see what I can get from those two eggheads." He extracted his cellphone.

"Do you need something to write on?" Jan asked.

36

Jack pulled a thin, dog-eared pad from his pocket. "No, thanks; I've always got one with me."

"Shout if you need us," Tom said, as he and Jan headed for the kitchen. Once there, Tom turned to Jan. "What do you think?"

"I trust him. Did you pick up his feelings when he was talking to Ablakan?"

"Yup. Wide open, and if his compassion wasn't genuine, I'll eat my hat."

Jan gave him a quick hug. "Thanks for calling him." Then she straightened, remembering. "Oh, I promised to explain to Ablakan what Jack and I were saying. Back in a bit."

* * *

When the others departed from his awareness, Moohri felt Ablakan's mixture of hope and confusion. What could the aliens – no, he mustn't think of them that way. Whatever species they were, those 'people' were his friends. But they had no spacecraft that could rescue him, so what could Ablakan be so cautiously excited about? Moohri imaged his question and Ablakan explained what little of it he understood.

How is it possible to mentally transport a body?

I do not know, but humans think differently than we do. Abruptly, Ablakan said, *Mother is coming. I will call you later.* The connection between them dissolved.

Left to his own thoughts, Moohri wondered if Ablakan's optimism was just the wishful thinking of a child. But the Shalaian certainly didn't act or sound like any child Moohri had ever known.

The stomach cramps were again becoming too sharp to ignore. Reluctantly, Moohri removed another strip of bark from the little scrub-bush that abounded here and, softening it with a bit of water, chewed it as best he could before swallowing it. His mouth shriveled from the bitter taste, and he carefully washed it out with more water before taking the next bite. Presently, the pain in his stomach eased, and he lay down on the soft ground cover. He would just rest a while, then prepare the plant lists Jack had asked for. With an image of his wife-mate Shira in mind, Moohri closed his eyes and fell into a fitful sleep.

* * *

Jack frowned as the Brodys left the room. Just what did he think he could do? Earth was no more equipped to rescue the alien than was Shalaii or Orowa. Moohri was as good as dead. All they could do was stir the pot and hope for a miracle. Jack didn't believe in miracles, but he had to admit one would sure come in handy about now.

He pulled out his cellphone, found the number and tapped on it.

A tenor voice said, "Carstairs here."

"Hi, Jeremy. It's Jack Foxworth. Got a minute?"

The voice warmed by several degrees. "Hey, you old stargazer! I was sure they'd've spaced you by now. How're you doing?"

"Fine, no problem. I've got a little job on the side for you, if you're interested. It'd be right up your alley, and I'm paying."

"I like it already."

"Figured you would." Jack leaned forward in the chair. "It's like this: I'm working on a story about this guy who gets marooned on an atmosphered planetoid. He's an alien, so he doesn't eat what we do, and he doesn't know what plants are edible for him where he crashed. I've got to make this sound plausible, and I'm no botanist. If I come up with a list of plant types he ate at home, can you extrapolate what he could safely eat where he is, if I describe them for you?"

Jeremy snorted. "Fat chance, without them being real and me able to test them. But since it's fiction, yeah, I guess I could fake it. Throw in a description of your character as well. You know, teeth, what sort of digestive system he has, et cetera. Also, I'll need a rundown on this planetoid you have him on. Soil conditions, whether the plants get much water, heat and light – that sort of thing. You figure botanists'll be reading it?"

"Most likely. Why?"

38

"Just ego. Sounds like fun. What's my cut?"

Jack hesitated a moment, not wanting to sound too eager. "You come up with something your colleagues would buy – no pun intended – and you've earned yourself a couple hundred and dinner at Tibelli's for you and Diane. I won't even wait till it's in print, but I will run it by some of your colleagues at NASA, so make it good."

"Done," Jeremy said at once. "Tibelli's, eh? Diane will be thrilled. When can I get the list?"

"Day or two, I should have it done. Oh, and keep this quiet, will you? I don't want anyone to know I'm writing a book till it's published. I take enough ribbing as it is."

"No problem. You got my home number?"

"Not on me." Jack copied it down. "Thanks, buddy. Call you later."

He hung up with a grunt of satisfaction. Perhaps things weren't as hopeless as they seemed. Long shots had paid off for him too often to dismiss their chances now. If Moohri had food and water, it could buy them years to find a way of rescuing him. Might even spur Congress to loosen its purse strings. Not that he was eager to have this get out. At least, not yet.

Now for the physicist. Jack hesitated, thinking out what to say to Dr. Black. It had been half a decade since Jack had seen him, though the man's name seemed to crop up in the news a lot lately. His theories were being proven right with impressive regularity.

Jack drummed his fingertips on the pad. Black was not a gullible man. He would never buy the book yarn. Once he reached a decision, Jack phoned Information and got the number for the Martina Institute and asked for Quantum Physics. Turned out, Ryan Black had moved on and, not surprisingly, upward. Two more calls, and he was speaking to the Great Man himself.

Jack cleared his throat nervously. "Good day, sir. You may not remember me. It's Jack Foxworth, from NASA. We met at the space conference in Vienna."

39

A vitriolic growl emanated from the phone. "Oh, I remember you alright! You skinned me of over 300 bucks in draw poker. If you're looking for a rematch, you're out of luck. I gave up the game."

"Pity. I could use the money," Jack said, unable to resist needling the man.

"Do you have something on your mind besides insults?"

Jack hesitated slightly.

"Oh, it's one of those, is it?" Black snorted in derision. "A 'how can I make him swallow this one?' type of call."

"In a way, you're right. If we can't pull this off, it'll be a mighty bitter pill to swallow."

"So? Is it illegal? I'll turn you in if it is."

Jack was glad Black couldn't see his hand tremble. "Far from it. I got a call from a man with a cockeyed story that turned out to be bang-on true. I want to cut you in, but I don't know if you can shake the media. They seem to be camped out on your doorstep these days."

"That's the price of fame." Black sounded quite undisturbed. "What makes you think I'd be interested in some guy's story?"

"All I can tell you right now is it concerns sentient life outside our solar system. And sir, it's authentic and conclusive. I've verified it myself."

"You serious?"

"Very."

There was a long pause before Black said, "And you want this kept quiet."

"For now, yes."

"Can you come here? Bring your proof with you?"

"That would put it right under the media's nose. They could hardly fail to notice." Come on, man, Jack urged silently, we need you here.

"I suppose not. It'll have to wait; this Physicists' Roundtable runs all week, and I'm keynote speaker. Supposedly, they've got some award for me." Black sighed. "Well, give me your number, anyway, and I'll get back to you when I can." Jack complied, and was about to thank him, when Black added, "I'm assuming you're still the Jack Foxworth I knew. You do realize, if you're playing me, you're career is history." With that, the physicist hung up.

Jack repocketed the cellphone, sweating profusely. And he knew it had nothing to do with the temperature.

CHAPTER 5

Ablakan was explaining to Moohri what Jan had meant when his mother walked in on him. He bade a hasty goodbye to Moohri and looked up.

Epash accordioned down beside him on the couch – usually a sign of trouble. "Ablakan, I spoke to your disseminator. He said you have trouble concentrating, that you dream at Learn-more like you do here. He thinks you should see a mind analyzer."

Ablakan stared at her in horror. "But Mother, I'm just thinking."

Epash looked sternly at her son. "You told me once you were think-talking to someone on another world. That is not a sign of a solid mind, Ablakan. I have made an opening for you with Plaka. I am told he is kind."

"No, please, don't!" Ablakan begged, shivering in reaction. "I am not mind-ill."

"We will let Plaka tell us. Do not worry, my child. I will be there with you. We will care for you together." She leaned over and squeezed his trembling body, then left the room.

Ablakan's mind reeled in terror. To be subjected to a mindprobe was unthinkable to his young psyche. He folded himself into a tight little bundle, hugging his legs and rocking back and forth in anguish. He didn't even hear the 'knock' until it became quite loud in his mind. He yearned to ignore it, but knew it would upset Jan even more than finding him like this.

Ablakan, what happened? Jan cried, as soon as he opened to her. *I felt such fear. Are you alright?*

Mother will take me to a mind analyzer, he sobbed, unable to contain his grief and shame.

Oh-oh. It's because we talk, isn't it?

Yes, Ablakan said. *But I will not stop. Moohri needs me.*

Jan's mental voice was laden with regret. *I'm so sorry, Ablakan. I never meant for this to happen. It's all my fault.*

Not you; Mother! Ablakan was becoming angry now. *I do nothing bad.*

No, indeed you don't. And the sad thing is, she thinks she's doing the right thing. Jan blinked suddenly. *And maybe she is!*

No! I am not mind-ill!

Jan harrumphed. *Of course not. But this might help us rescue Moohri. If an analyzer is a person.*

Yes, he admitted, wondering how analyzing his mind could possibly help Moohri.

Good. When is your appointment?

Mother did not say; just she made an opening with Plaka.

Jan nodded. *When you go, put him in contact with me. Just because your mother won't believe there are other peoples in the universe, doesn't mean no one else on your planet will.*

Ablakan jumped to his feet. *Right! You are right, Jan, this might help!* He hesitated. *Maybe you talk to Mother, too?*

I think it would frighten her too much. Besides, she is more likely to accept it if it comes from the analyzer, don't you think?

The youth said reluctantly, *Yes, that is true.*

By the way, your English is becoming very good indeed. Congratulations.

Thank you. I work hard to learn fast. You are a good friend. I go now before Mother comes back.

Jan added quickly. *Oh, and Jack is making those calls he promised. Unless it's urgent, I'll wait till you call me, so your mother doesn't get upset. Is that okay?*

Very okay. Thank you for talking. It helped a lot. Goodbye.

'Bye, dear.

* * *

Poor little guy, she thought, it's not bad enough he has to bear the burden of another's life or death. Now he's being called unbalanced for it. She felt a stab of anger towards Ablakan's mother.

As Jan refocused in the room, she struggled to quell the resentment she had worked so hard to suppress while trying to calm Ablakan. Tom and Jack were standing there, looking at her.

43

"Is everything alright?" Tom put a gentle hand on her shoulder. "You tore out of the kitchen like the hounds were after you."

"No. Ablakan's mother lowered the boom." Jan described what had happened.

Tom grimaced in dismay, but Jack's eyes were flashing. "Somebody should muzzle that woman," he fumed. "The kid's trying to coordinate a three-planet rescue effort – and she calls him crazy?"

"I know." Jan held up a placating hand. "But like I told him, this could be a bad for a good, if the psychiatrist is openminded. What we really need is to enlist the help of the scientific community on both Shalaii and Orowa as quickly as possible."

"Did you reach your contacts?" Tom asked.

"Yeah." Jack waved dismissively. "No problem with the botanist; he thinks I'm writing a book." He described their brief conversation. "But the physicist is another story. You may have heard of him; he's been in the news a lot. Dr. Ryan Black."

Jan shook her head, but Tom nodded. "He seems to be the golden boy these days."

"Yeah. And from what I've heard, he intends to stay that way and doesn't much care how."

Jan didn't like the sound of that. "Meaning we can't trust him?"

Jack made a face. "Meaning we can trust him as far as our mutual interests are served. Past that, he'll serve his own. That also gels with the impression I got of him at a space conference we both attended a few years back. The last evening, a bunch of us played poker half the night. You'd be surprised how much you can learn about a man's character from how he plays cards."

"You lost, huh?" Tom smirked.

"No, actually, I won. Once I realized he'd try to deek us out every chance he got, and would play as dirty as the rules permitted, or even dirtier, it was easy to beat him at his own game. He still hasn't forgiven me." Jack scowled. "I wish we didn't need him."

"Specifically what do we need him for?" Jan wanted to know.

Jack pulled up a chair and straddled it, facing them. Tom occupied the chair next to Jan.

"We've already got some of the best minds on the planet – this planet, anyway – working on propulsion systems. But even our most optimistic projections put viable near-lightspeed travel 20 years out of reach. Long-shot though it is, figuring some way to transport food to Moohri, or teleport him out of there, is going to be his only hope.

We need Black for two reasons." He checked them off on his fingers. "First, I want to find out what this 'atomic translocation' business is about. Second, Black earned much of his reputation by being extremely accurate in pinpointing locations on other planets. That's how we got a probe onto Ganymede within a few feet of our target – with his calculations. If we're ever able to teleport Moohri to his homeworld, we'll need that kind of precision."

Jan twisted her hands. "I was supposed to give Ablakan ideas to try re teleporting, but with this 'analyzer' stuff looming over him, he'll have to keep a low profile." She shook her head and said bleakly, "I sure hope Moohri finds something there he can eat."

"Me, too." Jack's face was a study in frustration. "And I can't do anything till I get those lists. Keeping Ablakan from talking to Moohri and us couldn't have come at a worse time."

"No kidding," Jan muttered.

The quizzical expression on Jack's face heralded another change of topic. "I've been meaning to ask you. Why can't Moohri talk to you directly? Why through Ablakan?"

Jan nibbled her lower lip, thinking about it. "Several reasons. Moohri tires quickly, and not just because he's starving. Remember how exhausted you felt after talking with Ablakan, and then through him with Moohri? The mental process itself is draining."

Jack nodded.

"That's because Moohri's not a true telepath – well, not a deliberate one, anyway. You saw how rapidly he and Ablakan exchanged mental images. It would take me forever to say what they can in a few seconds."

Jack's eyes had attained a faraway look. "That'll be a problem, too, if – when – we make formal contact with Orowa. Later on, could you practice, see if you can speed up talking in images?"

"You saw that exchange between them. How much of it did you understand or remember?"

He looked sheepish. "Virtually none."

"Exactly," Jan said, trying not to sound defensive. "Maybe if they slow it down the way Ablakan did when we first 'met', I can pick up my end a bit. But even so, I'm not sure I could translate those images."

Tom patted her arm. "Give it time, hon. You didn't understand much Ablakan was saying at first either, as I recall." He turned toward Jack. "And speaking of time, how long can you stay?"

"Indefinitely," Jack replied without hesitation. "I'll take a leave of absence if I have to. I feel very sorry for Moohri, and I'll do anything I can to get him home. But you have to realize – and I have to keep in mind – this is a lot bigger than just Moohri. What we do now could forge a three-planet alliance. I'm here for as long as it takes, or as long as you'll have me – whichever is shorter."

"Then you're here for the duration." Jan looked to her husband for confirmation.

Tom nodded. "'Four', as Ablakan put it. I took the liberty of moving your luggage to the guest room while you were on the phone."

"Thanks!"

Tom rubbed his hands together. "Okay, so what's next?"

"Lunch," Jan stated. "I, for one, think better on a full stomach."

During the meal, Jan and Tom gained a greater understanding of their guest. Not surprisingly, Jack shared Tom's fascination with telescopes, and after consuming the ample leftovers, the two men retired to Tom's little observatory. There was nothing more they could do until Ablakan transmitted Moohri's plant lists.

Jan returned to the Reading Room. Now was as good a time as any to give her theory on teleportation a try. Though she imagined someone would have done it by now, if it was that simple. Still, it was a place to start.

If feelings are the 'fuel', she reasoned, there should be two sets: one to draw you to a place, and one to cut you away from where you are. But no sooner did Jan try to produce feelings than she ran into the first hurdle. Deliberately-generated emotions tended to be too objective, having been conjured up and then watched from the outside. But the kind of emotions she needed were deeply subjective, intensely personal and likely spontaneous. Perhaps it would help if she were to revisit some traumatic experience . . . .

Her mind latched onto Moohri's terrifying plunge towards the planetoid, the crash itself, and his psychic scream. Jan felt her throat constrict, revisiting his raw fear and pain which was now indelibly etched in her memory. Drawing upon it, Jan transferred the focal point to a ball-bearing she had enlisted for the purpose. It rested on a tea cozy, so it wouldn't roll away.

With the thrust of the fear/pain/denial coursing through her mind like an adrenaline rush, she mentally banished the tiny orb from her presence. The sensation faded quickly, and with a sigh of relief, Jan opened her eyes.

And stared. The tea cozy hadn't moved, but the ball-bearing was gone. She checked under the desk, then searched the whole room. It had disappeared, but to where? She hadn't specified a location beforehand; she had just felt an overwhelming urge to get it away from her. No, that wasn't quite right. She had wanted to get it *as far* away from her as she could.

With the emotional thrust fading fast, Jan grabbed a pen and repeated the experiment. This time, she chose the observatory as its destination. But try as she might, the pen wouldn't budge. Finally, she accepted defeat and put the pen away. Still, one question had been answered: It was possible.

Jan hurried to the observatory. She was thrilled by her unexpected success, but unsure whether the others would believe her. After all, what proof did she have?

Tom and Jack returned to search every inch of the Reading Room, but the ball-bearing was never found. Jan was gratified that both men seemed to take her account of the experiment at face value.

"Are you sure you did it exactly the sameway the second time?" Jack asked.

"Yes, absolutely."

"What felt different, if anything?" Tom tapped just above his heart.

"Hmm. Now that you mention it, the feelings were the same, but not nearly as intense. It's like something that surprises or scares you. The next time, you're prepared for it."

Jack rubbed his nose absently. "Does it have to be a strong *negative* emotion?"

"I suppose not. But those are usually the ones that get your full attention. Offhand, I can't think of any that do so on the positive side."

Tom grinned at her lecherously. "I can."

Jan laughed. "True, but I wouldn't want to try teleporting something then."

"I wouldn't recommend it, either," Jack chuckled. "Now, about your experiments: Could the weight have made the difference? A pen versus a ball-bearing?"

Jan thought back, savoring the experience. "I don't think so. The feeling I had when I banished the ball-bearing was like the tiniest surge of energy. It felt effortless. I'm just guessing, but I don't think weight matters. It'll either work or it won't, based on the feeling. I could be wrong, of course."

"Since you're probably the first person to teleport something deliberately, you're the resident expert," Jack pointed out. "I suggest you make detailed notes while it's fresh in your mind."

"Good idea."

Jack and Tom returned to the observatory.

"Is she always like that?" Jack asked mildly.

"Like what?"

"She tries to do psychic exploration and ends up in contact with an alien first time out. Decides to learn to teleport something – and presumably does. Don't get me wrong; I'm delighted. But I have to wonder: Is it that she knows so much? Or knows so little she doesn't realize how wildly impossible it is and so just goes ahead and does it anyway?"

Tom shrugged. "I've been wondering about that since this whole thing began. Maybe too much knowledge gets in the way."

Jack wagged a finger. "Whatever you do, don't ever tell her something can't be done."

"Don't worry; I won't," Tom grinned, adding, "She'd never believe me anyway."

* * *

Jan had completed her notes and was considering what to do next when the familiar 'knock' came in her mind. She winced, realizing she'd forgotten about Ablakan in her excitement about teleporting the ball-bearing.

How are you feeling, dear?

Mixed emotions filled her mind, as the boy said, *I am well, but I feel bad. I told Mother I am sleepy so I can call Moohri and you. This is a 'lie'?*

Sort of. There are times when we have no choice, and this is definitely one of them. How is Moohri?

Not strong. Needs food soon. He told me lists for Jack. I tell you now?

49

Yes, please. Jan's pen flew over the page as she recorded descriptions of Orowa's bounty of edible plants. But the list from the planetoid was alarmingly short.

Even if there are no sea animals there, might there be sea plants he could add to the list? Jan wondered.

I asked. He said not at deep he could go.

How far has he explored? Can he keep looking, maybe walk farther each day? There was still a chance the Orowan could find something edible if he kept searching.

Moohri said he walked much today, but getting very not-strong.

Weak, Jan corrected.

Yes, weak. Now a long time of little or no food.

The worry she could feel in Ablakan struck a similar chord in Jan's heart. She swallowed painfully, struggling to keep her own emotions in check.

I'll give these lists to Jack right away and call you when he has an answer. If you're not free to talk at the time, just give me a 'busy signal'. She imitated in her mind the appropriate telephone tone. *I'll understand and wait till you call me, okay?*

Thank you, Jan.

Oh, I almost forgot. I teleported something today!

You did? To Moohri? Was it food? Eager questions tumbled into her mind at lightspeed.

Whoa, slow down, Ablakan! It was just a tiny thing, and I was only able to do it once. But at least now I know it can be done. Jan described the process she had used, concluding, *We've a long way to go before we can send him food that way. Even if – when – I learn to do it right, we can access Moohri, but I can't send food to his mind.*

No, Ablakan said, understanding the problem. *Must find the place in our minds, and where Moohri is in that place.*

Exactly, Jan nodded. *And I mercifully have only a few really terrible experiences to tap into like that, and even fewer exciting ones. I'll have to find some other way to fuel the actual teleport.*

I will think also, Ablakan promised, then added sheepishly, *But later. I feel sleepy.*

Jan smiled. *Rest easy, my friend.* This time it was she who broke contact first.

Clutching the precious lists in her hand, she booted down the hall and up to the observatory. The men stared at the thin sheaf of paper, and she nodded.

"Here they are. Ablakan had to pretend to be asleep to get the lists from Moohri and send them to me. He's feeling pretty guilty, so I hope they're worth it." The headings identified which list was which.

Jack sprung to his feet. "Thanks. I'm on it." He headed for the sunroom and some privacy.

"Our home, the interplanetary command center. Who'd have thought?" Tom quipped, as he gave Jan an affectionate hug.

"I always wanted to be an interpreter," Jan chuckled. "But I never expected this."

They could hear Jack's voice down the hall, talking in short spurts.

"Looks like he got through," Tom remarked. "Would you like some coffee? I don't know how soon you'll be needed to send back the results."

"Hmm, good idea." Jan would need it to shake off the weariness that was encroaching on her mind. She stifled a yawn, and gratefully reached for the steaming cup Tom placed in front of her. "I've been drinking a lot of this lately."

"I'm way past my limit, too," he admitted.

They both looked up expectantly a short time later, as Jack appeared in the doorway.

"Sorry, folks. Jeremy took one listen to the list of what's on the planetoid, asked a few questions about soil conditions that I didn't know the answer to, and suggested I rework the list, as he's reasonably sure none of the plant types would be edible. Even if they aren't poisonous, they might fill the gut, but they'd likely have no food value. He recommended changing the list, 'for the book'."

Jan suddenly felt cold all over. "What do we do now?"

The phone rang, causing all of them to jump. Tom was closest. "Hello . . . yes, I'll get her." He covered the mouthpiece, wrinkling his nose. "It's Ariana."

Jan tensed. Ariana was her supervisor at the bank where Jan worked part-time. Dictatorial and with a hair-trigger temper, Ariana ruled the staff with an iron fist. Jan put up with it because the added income made the difference between comfort and just getting by. But what was she doing calling now? Jan was supposed to be on vacation.

"Jan, Beatrice called in sick. She got chicken pox from her nephew and won't be in for at least a week. We need you full-time till she gets back."

"I'm so sorry, but I won't be able to. We've got . . . a situation here, and I can't get away."

The voice on the phone became insistent. "I know it's short notice, but I need you, starting tomorrow."

"I might be able to get a way for a couple hours a day," Jan said doubtfully.

The voice turned crisp, the words clipped short. "That won't do. It has to be full-time, that's all there is to it."

"But I can't –"

Ariana cut her off. "Look, I haven't time to argue. You agreed when you started here that if I ever needed you, you'd be here at a moment's notice. That's why I hired you. I needed someone I could count on in a pinch. Well, this is a pinch, and you've had your moment's notice. Whatever you're doing will just have to wait."

Jan felt her face go beet red. There was a moment of stunned silence.

"Well?"

With an effort, Jan controlled her voice. "Ariana, you just don't know what –"

"And I couldn't care less!" Ariana exploded. "I will see you in my office tomorrow at eight o'clock sharp. Is that clear enough for you?"

Jan looked at her husband, and he drew a finger across his throat. Her knuckles were white as she clenched the phone. "I'm sorry, Ariana –"

"Sorry my crabgrass! You're here tomorrow or you're out the door. Make up your mind."

"I won't be there."

"Then you're fired! I'll see you never work in this town again!" The woman slammed the phone down at the same time Jan did.

Tears of outrage stung Jan's eyes. "What a *bitch!*" she spat. "Why did she have to call now, of all times?" Jan knew the answer, of course, but the shock of getting fired, on top of all her other worries, was just too much.

A strange light appeared in Jack's eyes. "Forgive me, Jan," he whispered.

She stared, uncomprehending, as he grabbed a large bowl from atop the refrigerator and rapidly tossed in every fruit and vegetable he could find. Jack slammed the bowl down in front of her.

"Jan," he roared, inches from her face. "Send this to Moohri! Don't argue; *JUST DO IT! NOW!*"

Understanding dawned. Jan pulled from the tidal wave of emotions drowning her and almost savagely sought out Moohri's mind. She felt his gasp as she punched through. Like a lightning rod, she traveled from his mind into his body, down to where his feet touched the ground. Marking a spot about a foot in front of him, she blasted the bowl and its contents out of her life with all her might, and simultaneously felt it appear in front of him.

Someone must have pulled the plug, for she found herself squatting on the floor, arms wrapped around her knees. She began to sob uncontrollably, and then it morphed into giggles. Before long, all three of them were swept up in gales of laughter.

When at last she could speak, Jan wagged her finger in Jack's face. "If you think I'm going to get myself fired every time we need to teleport something, you've got another thing coming."

"Oh, well, alright," Jack pouted. Then he shook his head, looking mystified. "I was watching that bowl closely. It never moved or glowed or anything. It just vanished like that." He snapped his fingers. "Darnedest thing I ever saw. Question is, did it get there?"

"Yes, I saw it appear in front of him. We did it – thanks to you." She stuck out her hand, and he gave it a solid shake.

"*You* did it; I just supplied the fuel." He grinned boyishly. "In case you didn't know, that's what I do for a living. I'm a propulsion engineer."

Jan gave a hoot of laughter. "That figures. I sure hope Moohri can digest what we sent. I went in there like gangbusters. I'd better apologize." She struggled to rise.

They both helped her to her feet.

"Right now, I suspect he'd forgive just about anything," Tom said. "Why don't you give him time to ease his hunger?"

"You're right; apologies can wait. When Ablakan awakens, though, I've got to tell him the good news and ask him to find out what Moohri could eat. If he is an omnivore, he might be able to digest most things we can, though I don't know if he could stomach our animal proteins. And there's still the matter of getting it to him."

She glanced at Jack, noting the bland look on his face. It suggested he was cooking up a 'Plan B' to help her teleport. Now I know how prey feel, Jan thought as she stretched taut muscles. "I need a nice, brisk walk. Any takers?"

"There's a idea," Tom agreed.

"It's all downhill from here," Jack quipped. "But coming back up would sure keep you fit."

Tom nodded vehemently. "It does indeed. Care to join us?"

"Thanks, but I think I'll unpack and do some thinking. At NASA, things don't usually happen this fast."

54

"If this ever gets out, they will," Tom predicted.

* * *

Moohri was digging under the ground cover with his fingers, stopping repeatedly to catch his breath. The weakness was becoming so pronounced now that every little exertion taxed him to the limit. Still, he had to try the one place he hadn't yet looked for food. The thought of eating bugs nauseated him, but it had to be better than that horrible gnawing pain in his stomach.

Doggedly, he ignored the exhaustion that rolled over him, wave upon wave, and continued digging. Just one little wormbug, he implored his fates. But all too soon, he was trembling so hard he could no longer control his hand movements. For a long moment, he remained hunched over, panting hard and sweating profusely. Even if there were insects underground, Moohri realized he no longer had the strength to reach them.

His back ached savagely from the unaccustomed effort. Moohri stood up slowly to stretch. It was at that moment that he felt a *presence* knife through his mental shield – an angry, irresistible presence.

Jan? Moohri gasped, feeling like he'd been struck by lightning. Then he stared in disbelief. In front of him – a mere hand's-breadth away – was an enormous container of . . . *FOOD!*

With an ecstatic cry, Moohri dove for it. He began stuffing anything and everything into his mouth, often forgetting to chew in his haste to swallow. Wildly unfamiliar tastes and textures blended in a celebration of flavorful sensations, and his desperate stomach begged for more. Wisdom suggested he eat sparingly, but his body, having been deprived for so long, firmly overruled him. The only way he could temper the binge was to gulp quantities of water between ravenous bites.

At length the frenzy eased and Moohri lay back against a rock, spent but comfortable for the first time in ages. *Jan,* he said fervently in his mind, *I thank you forever.*

Presently, he slipped into his first restful sleep since leaving Orowa.

CHAPTER 6

At a quarter to four, invigorated and relaxed by their trek, Tom and Jan were preparing dinner when she heard the familiar 'knock'.

"Ablakan's awake," she announced, and hurried down the hall to the Reading Room. As she opened the mental door, she was almost bowled over by a flood of warm pleasure.

You called Moohri first, did you? she surmised.

Yes, Jan. He – and I – is so happy! He ate many things, then felt better. He said thank you, thank you. Can you take him to Orowa or Earth?

It's not that easy, she said, hating the letdown the boy was bound to feel. *Let me explain what happened.*

When she finished, Ablakan, much-subdued, asked, *So maybe you cannot send more food?*

I don't know, dear. I think Jack is working on a way. But he can't tell me what it is if he needs to take me by surprise to make it work.

You are afraid, Ablakan observed.

Well, nervous, that's for sure. But getting food to Moohri is the most important thing, so whatever it takes, I'll do.

Ablakan projected approval. *That is good. I will tell Moohri you will maybe send more. If you can, you will send much?*

Jan nodded. *Yes, that's what we were thinking, too. Please tell him I'm sorry about the way I sent it. Oh, and could he describe anything that wasn't good for him or he didn't like. Also, if we are able to send more, does he need other things, like blankets or an axe or matches?* She imaged their use.

I will ask. There was a brief pause. *I hear Mother coming. I will split focus. Please stay.*

Okay. Jan waited tensely, hoping his mother would not be dropping any more verbal bombs on her friend. Presently, he spoke again.

Mother said if I sleep long now, I do not sleep tonight, so I must get up. I asked when is opening with Plaka. It is tomorrow.

Jan felt Ablakan's sadness as he admitted, *I think Mother fears me.*

On this planet, many people who have special talents are feared at first. One day, your mother will be very proud of you for it. How Jan hoped that was true. *When you see Plaka, I will send him that first message I sent you. That should convince him, shouldn't it?*

Ablakan's mood lightened. *Yes. We could never think up a person that looks like a human. Sorry – humans look nice, but – so different.*

Jan smiled indulgently. *I know what you mean. It was the same for me, when I first saw you. Now I couldn't imagine you any other way. Oh, one more thing: When you talk to Moohri, ask him who that Orowan telepath is, and where you might find him. I think it's time we get Orowa in the loop.*

Loop?

You, Moohri, Jack, Tom and I are in the loop now, Jan explained.

Loop. I understand. Must get up now, but I will call first time I can. And thank you for sending Moohri food.

I am very happy about that, too, Jan smiled. *Take care.*

Goodbye, Jan.

As she expected, Tom was there when she opened her eyes. Jan looked down at her notebook. This time she had recorded the session. It had become so automatic she no longer noticed, while she spoke mentally. Is this a form of 'split focus'? she wondered.

Tom's eyes twinkled as he looked up from the notebook. "I'd love to be there when you transmit to that 'Analyzer'. Is he in for a surprise!"

"Yeah, but it's *how* he'll respond that worries me. Humans react unpredictably when their beliefs are shattered. We have no idea what a Shalaian will do."

But Tom waved that away. "All you have to do is convince him you're real. Then if Ablakan can connect him with Moohri,

I'm sure the response to a marooned person would be the same there as here – a desire to help."

"You're probably right. Shalaians seem to value life more than humans do, if Ablakan's right in what he's been telling us."

Tom's eyes glistened with mirth. "By the way, I looked in on Jack. Would you believe he's asleep?"

She raised her eyebrows, and Tom nodded with a smug grin. "Yup, snoring and all. I think that emotion he blasted you with drained him as much as it did you. What say we take the evening off? No Ablakan, no Moohri – just us relaxing? I vote we put the chicken back in the fridge and call Peregrin's. I fancy a pizza, for some reason."

"Now that you mention it," Jan's tastebuds cast their vote.

They turned on the TV, snuggled on the couch and caught up on the news outside their roost. Around 5:30, Jack emerged from the guest room, yawning hugely. "Sorry about that, folks. But I haven't slept so well in weeks. Guess I needed it."

"It's our clean mountain air," Tom informed him.

Jack jerked a thumb towards the hill. "You call this a mountain? Why, in Colorado, from whence I hail, this would be considered a –"

"Yeah, yeah, we know," Jan interrupted. "But let us keep our happy delusions. Tom is treating us to pizza, delivered *all* the way up here, no less. What would you like on yours?"

"Everything – and lots of it, if you're buying. And just to be contrary, *now* I feel like a walk."

Tom said, "We'll get it delivered in about an hour. Think you'll be back by then?"

"If you're not, we'll eat your part," Jan warned.

"Bully!" Jack opened the door and, whistling, started down the winding driveway that led to the road just beyond the crest of the hill.

Jack and the pizza delivery van arrived about the same time. Jack staunchly denied hitching a ride in it to avoid the uphill trek. During the meal, the men traded stories of university highjinks until Jan pronounced them barely reformed delinquents. Neither hastened to deny it.

Eventually, the conversation turned to Moohri and Ablakan. Jan told Jack about the conversation she'd had with the Shalaian youth while Jack was asleep.

"Hang on; that can't be right," Jack exclaimed, frowning. "That food should have been frozen solid. I mean, think about it. It traveled well over a hundred light years through space to get there."

Tom's eyes widened. "You're right!"

Now it was Jan's turn to be confused. "What are you guys talking about? I just moved it from here to there. It didn't go through space at all."

"As in 'translocation'?" Tom asked Jack pointedly.

"Well, what do you know? Looks like Black might be on the right track with that 'atomic translocation' business after all. And it certainly opens a whole new set of possibilities for getting Moohri home."

Several hours later, they called it a night, and the small house became silent.

* * *

A pleasant childhood dream of playing with the hounds was banished by the ringing of the phone on Jan's night stand.

Tom stirred as she reached for it. "Who'd be calling at two a.m.?"

"I don't know. I hope it's nothing serious." If they weren't 'wrong numbers', in Jan's experience, late night calls usually meant a crisis.

"Hello?" A nasal voice hollered in her ear above the din in the background.

"Hello. Who's speaking, please?

"Let me speak to Foxworth."

"It's past two in the morning," Jan informed the caller, wondering if Jack might have left their number in case of emergency.

"Tell him it's Dr. Black."

Jan frowned at the phone. "Very well," she replied. "It may take a minute to wake him up."

"Well, he'd better make it quick. I'm calling long distance."

Jan didn't trust herself to reply to that, so she scooted down the hall to Jack's room. It would seem Jack's low opinion of Black was justified.

After two sets of knocks on his door, a muffled voice responded. "Yes?"

"I'm sorry, Jack. Dr. Black's on the phone and insists on talking to you immediately."

There was a groan. "What a jackass! Sorry about this, Jan."

"It's not your fault. Looks like you were right about him."

Jack grunted. "I'll be right there."

"Okay." Jan returned to their room and delivered the message. There was no response.

"Are you still there?" she asked.

"Yes," was the laconic reply.

Resisting the urge to slam down the phone, Jan tightened her dressing gown and waited till she heard Jack pick up the kitchen extension before hanging up. Tom had already gone to the kitchen, and Jan hurried over.

Jack's part of the conversation was, of course, disjointed and gave few hints, other than that Black would be coming out. At length, Jack hung up and turned to them.

"What was so urgent?" Jan asked.

"Nothing." Jack's lip curled in disgust. "He just wanted to save 60 percent long distance charges by phoning after 11:00 his time. I'm surprised he didn't call collect."

Tom stifled a yawn. "So he's coming here?"

"Yes. He's still in San Francisco at the conference. But three of the main players decided to go somewhere when they broke for

60

dinner. On the way back, their cab got hit head-on by a drunk. The driver's dead, and all three scientists are in the hospital with various broken bones. Nothing life-threatening, but they definitely won't be at the conference, so the chairman's decided to postpone it. Black is quite put out; calls it a 'darned nuisance'. He's a busy man, you know." Jack added with heavy sarcasm.

"An empath he is not," Jan agreed. "What time will he be here?"

"Tomorrow around two. Or I guess that's today, now."

Jan glanced over her shoulder towards her den. "I'm not sure where we can put him. All that's left are the Reading Room and the observatory."

"There's always the potting shed," Tom suggested with a nasty smile.

"Don't I wish."

Jack shrugged. "I'm sure he'll make himself comfortable. He'll just insist on having my room."

"Well, he's not getting it," Jan said hotly.

"You need your office for linking," Tom told her, referring to the Reading Room. "I'll just convert the observatory back into a loft. He can use the hide-a-bed."

Jack turned hope-filled eyes on Tom. "Is it lumpy?"

"Unfortunately, no."

"Pity. 'Night, folks."

"Sleep well," Jan called to Jack's departing back, then followed Tom to their bedroom. Despite the interruption, the Brodys were both soon asleep.

* * *

Morning brought rain-washed sunlight. Coffee in hand, Jan was standing on their patio, enjoying the fresh-tasting air, when her husband joined her.

"Another day, another scientist," Tom quipped as he sampled the fresh brew Jan had just handed him. "I'm willing to bet this Black character won't be nearly as pleasant to Ablakan and Moohri as Jack was. You might want to forewarn them."

61

"Good idea. I suspect Ablakan will be kept out of school today, to go see Plaka. He's taking a big chance, and there's not much we can do to help him," Jan worried aloud.

Tom placed a reassuring hand on her shoulder. "He's got you riding shotgun. He'll be okay, love. Still, that makes two unknown quantities to deal with today. I'm glad we've got Jack in our corner to handle Black."

"Me, too." Jan sighed gustily. She disliked Black already, and she had not even met the man.

Ablakan called at 8:25. He seemed in good spirits, despite the ordeal he faced. A talk with Moohri had greatly improved his outlook.

Moohri is much stronger. He has some food left. Only long half-around trunk with funny leaves –

I think that's celery, Jan offered.

– celery he cannot eat. Moohri said please send anything you can; he will eat everything he can. If you can teleport, added Ablakan.

If. That, of course, was the burning question. *We will sure try. Does Moohri need anything else besides food?*

No. It is warm there; does not need covers. Not much to burn, so no food he must warm to eat.

That simplified things. *Fair enough. If I can send anything, I'll include items to eat with and off of, and a cleaner to wash them with. Tell him if I attach a piece of paper to something, it's not for eating, okay? We'll include pictures of what it's for and how to use it.* She'd better tell Jack, too, in case he was cooking up another emotional thrust for her.

Good. The Orowan psychic is Shownae. If I am allowed today, Ablakan said, uncertainty creeping into his mental voice. *I will look for him.*

How will you do that?

Moohri showed me in his mind where Orowa is, and where they met. If Shownae is like us . . .

Telepathic, you mean? Jan supplied.

Yes. Then I should know his mind from Moohri remembering their talk, Ablakan said with aplomb.

Jan nodded. *That makes sense. Now remember, dear. I will keep myself available to you at all times today. So no matter what happens, I'll be there for you, and I'll do whatever it takes to make sure you are believed.*

A tidal wave of relief broke over her. *Thank you greatly, Jan. I go this morning.*

Good. The physicist is not coming until this afternoon. Please warn Moohri that Ryan Black is not very nice.

Maybe I cannot talk to him, the Shalaian fretted. *If Plaka does not believe.*

If I have to, I will explain the need to Plaka myself. Jan wondered how she would do that using just imagery. Well, one problem at a time.

Ablakan sighed. *So many people now.*

It is getting complicated, that's for sure. And it's bound to become more so. But we mustn't let anyone forget the most important thing right now is helping Moohri.

Yes, Moohri comes first. We make sure.

Jan infused her mental 'voice' with as much confidence as she could. *And don't worry about a thing. We'll all come through this just fine. I'll talk to Jack and see if he has ideas for getting things to Moohri more easily.*

He will help. Jack is kind. But you will be waiting? Ablakan could not quite hide his dread of the upcoming interview.

Yes, dear. I promise.

Thank you. Goodbye, Jan. The link was severed.

* * *

The morning seemed interminably long to Ablakan. Epash kept smiling at him reassuringly, which only made him more nervous. The last time she had done that, his brakitiks had been removed and his neck had hurt for a week. Epash busied herself with nothing in particular, humming a non-tune. Ablakan fought

63

the rising terror within him, reminding himself repeatedly that Jan would be there when he needed her.

At long last, Epash looked at the timemometer and said, "We will leave now. Bring your wrapover. There are strong winds today."

Ablakan retrieved the threadbare garment from his trunk. The transit ride to Plaka's office, which was on the other side of the city, seemed to take days. He thought about Jan's assurances and her suggestion that this might help Moohri. But what if he were too frightened to concentrate? If he froze up, all would be lost. What would they do to him? He shuddered, remembering stories of unbalanced people and the procedures they sometimes underwent. He began to tremble, feeling the onset of panic.

Suddenly, there she was, beside his mind.

I'm here, Ablakan. I won't leave you. All you have to do is touch the Analyzer with your hand or foot or whatever will reach. I'll get through to him. I know how; you showed me with Jack. You're not alone.

Th–thank you, Jan. I am so afraid, he wailed in his mind.

Listen to me, dear. Jan poured calmness into her mental tone. *We need you to be strong and to use your powerful mind the way you have been doing since this thing with Moohri began.* Moohri *needs you to be strong. You have to do this for him, Ablakan. He's counting on you.*

He latched onto the thought like a lifeline and felt his courage grow. *You are right. Moohri needs me; you need me. I am young, but I am strong,* Ablakan reminded himself.

No one on our planet can do some of the things you can, Jan assured him. *When you go in there, don't be forceful. Just be your normal quietly-strong self. I'll be right there with you, every step of the way. I will not leave till you tell me to, okay?*

Thank you, Jan. I think we are here. Yes, we are stopping.

Don't waste your focus on me. I'll wait here quietly. When you want me to do or say something, just tell me.

I will. We go in now.

* * *

On Earth, Jan withdrew to a quiet corner of his mind. It was frustrating to not be able to tell what was happening. Each time his fear threatened to gain the upper hand, all she could do was project reassurance.

Several minutes passed during which his emotions were relatively neutral. Probably reciting the Shalaian version of name, rank and serial number, Jan thought.

Next came a roller-coaster of emphatic emotions. Most likely he was detailing his psychic experiences with her, Moohri and Jack. If she was correct, Ablakan would soon be calling on her to replay for Plaka her first-contact message. Quickly, she reviewed it. Had it only been two months since she sent it to Ablakan? It seemed impossible, in light of recent events.

Jan, Plaka wants to meet you, please, Ablakan said in her mind. His 'voice' was quiet but tense. So much rode on what happened next. *I am touching his arm.*

Jan took a deep breath and cleared her mind. She followed Ablakan to where his hand grasped another body. It was surprisingly easy to find the mind attached to it. She 'knocked' on an imaginary door and imaged herself retreating a step with her hands clasped behind her back while she awaited an answer. Presently, she felt the other open the mental door.

Jan 'presented' the Analyzer with a bowl of fruit. But unlike Ablakan, Plaka did not invite her in. In fact, there was no response at all.

Ablakan, did he get the message?

Yes, the boy said bitterly. *But he will not believe. He says I project mindsickness to others. He will have me put where I cannot hurt others.* His courage crumbled. *Jan, do something!*

An icy terror clutched Jan's heart. No, this must not happen! Not now, not after all they'd been through; not to Ablakan!

Without thinking, Jan grabbed the closest thing at hand, which was a box of old floppy disks for her ancient computer. The door to Plaka's mind was already closing. She savagely pried it open, pouring hers into his body and down to where his feet touched the floor. With every ounce of mental force she could muster, Jan made his eyebanks look downward, then flung the box into the room. It crashed against the floor, sending broken shards of the box and disks flying across the room.

At the same instant, Jan felt Ablakan's mind rejoice and Plaka's shocked amazement.

Now do you believe? she demanded in English. She followed it with an image of herself seated at her desk, placing a disk from a similar box into her computer. She showed the disk icon appearing on the screen, opened it and double-clicked on the document it held. The photo it displayed was of the Statue of Liberty, with the harbor in the foreground and a panoramic view of New York City stretching majestically into the distance.

Ablakan, who had been tracking both minds, reported jubilantly, *He holds one of your pieces. We have nothing like this. He is touching the writing on it. Jan, he believes!* He believes!

Wonderful, Jan said, almost giddy with relief herself. *But be very calm around him, like this is an everyday event for you. We have to make him see you're in control of what's happening.*

I will, Ablakan said, quieting down internally as well.

It was quite some time before Ablakan spoke to her again.

Plaka asked to meet Moohri, he explained. *They think-talked through me. Now Plaka wants to talk to you, please. I will put him beside your mind now?*

Certainly. But remind him to send images slowly, and explain it may take me some time to make the right images to send back.

There was a brief pause. *I have.*

Jan felt Plaka's focus being parked beside hers. The Analyzer began imaging slowly and with considerable respect. He presented her with a mental container of a grapelike fruit. Jan bowed and said in his language, *Greetings, Plaka,* the way Ablakan had taught her to pronounce it.

In return, she 'saw' him bow and conjure up a picture of himself introducing Ablakan to someone who looked important.

This was followed by a scene with Ablakan in a large office with fancy furnishings, seated at an enormous desk-of-sorts. Obviously, he was being offered an important job. He had his head tilted to the side, his eyebanks looking skyward, and he alternately listened and wrote on the writing-board in front of him. Then he pressed a button and a servant bowed into the room, retrieved the board and replaced it with a fresh one before bowing out again.

A sense of query filled her mind. Was he asking for her approval? It wasn't hers to give; it was Ablakan's.

Have you been following this? she asked Ablakan in English, knowing Plaka wouldn't understand.

Yes. He seemed overwhelmed by what was being proposed.

Jan reviewed the images uncertainly. *Is he able to make good on such an offer? I didn't realize an Analyzer had so much power.*

I do not know, Ablakan admitted. *It feels real, but – not real.*

Like bribery?

What is that?

When someone offers you something if you do something else for them, Jan explained.

Ablakan pounced on the definition. *Yes, yes, it feels like that.*

So what's in it for him?

I will ask.

Be tactful, dear, Jan hastened to add. *He can help you or hurt you.*

Yes. Moment, please. Again there was a lengthy pause. *Person in image is his litter-brother, who Plaka said can help me, because litter-brother is the most important person on Pantai. And Plaka would become important Analyzer.*

Jan sighed. *Looks like politics and nepotism are universal.*

Say again?

It means they will help you as long as they also can gain from it.

Yes, he agreed. *But if this, I can think-talk when I need to. I do not have to play asleep. And Shalaians maybe will try to help Moohri.*

You're right. It is what we want, regardless of how it helps someone else's career. A thought occurred to her. *Has Plaka talked to your mother about all this yet?*

No. Plaka wants me to say 'yes' first, then he will talk to Mother.

I suggest you insist on being present when he does, so you know what he tells her and how she takes it.

Ablakan owed it to himself to watch his mother's skepticism dissolve in front of his eyes.

I will. Can you stay longer? I know you are tired. Concern for Jan and his own personal need battled for dominance.

She was feeling fuzzy at that. Jan honed her focus as best she could. *I'll stay as long as you need me.*

My friend, I thank you deeply.

There was nothing more to tune in to for some time. Jan assumed the mother was being told of her son's credibility and upcoming status. From time to time, Jan discerned a glimmer of satisfaction or pride, but aside from that, Ablakan stoically held his emotions in check, as she had recommended.

Mother does not understand all, he said at last. *But the pieces you sent –*

Disks, Jan informed him.

– disks have her much disorganized. She is excited I will be important, and as mother of important person, that she will be important, too. Plaka said there would be nice things, but did not say what. She asked for room near mine, but Plaka said I must not be – I think you say, 'distracted'. Plaka understands Mother. That was said with as close to a smirk as Jan had ever heard from Ablakan.

So what happens now?

Plaka said we live tonight at his house – big house, much room, the boy transmitted animatedly. *I have room so I can think-*

68

talk any time. Tomorrow we meet Plaka's litter-brother. That is all I know. Plaka says 'goodbye' to Jan and Moohri, please.

Jan felt her focus waver. *And give him our thanks back. Do you need me still for a while?*

No, dear friend. You go rest now. A feeling of gratitude flowed into her, and she sent back a wave of pleasure and pride in Ablakan.

Call me any time you need to.

Thank you, Jan. Sleep well, he added knowingly.

As the connection ended, Jan sagged against her desk, exhausted. Two pairs of hands instantly propped her up, as she foggily returned her awareness to the room. A glass of juice was put to her lips. She drank greedily. Somehow, it helped her focus improve.

"Do you know how long you were 'away'?" Tom asked, himself looking haggard.

"No idea," she croaked.

"Over an hour-and-a-quarter."

"Is that all? It felt like a month." She swallowed more juice to lubricate her parched throat.

"It's straight to bed for you, lovey," Tom ordered. "Just tell us one thing: Did it turn out okay?"

"Yes. Ablakan is to get a big office in which to 'think-talk' and be served by underlings." Jan's voice slurred a bit as she added, "There's a small matter of bureaucratic nepotism, but that'll probably just keep them in line out of self-interest."

"Mighty well done, Jan," Jack said warmly, as they helped her to her feet. "By the way, how did Plaka like your little gift?"

Jan stared at him, uncomprehending. "Oh, you mean the disks? That turned the trick." She walked unsteadily down the hallway, using Tom's arm for balance. "Don't know why I'm so rocky."

Tom said, "Well, when you consider that the longest telepathic conversation you've had before this was a half-hour . . . need I say more?"

"Oh." Jan didn't remember her head touching the pillow, nor the blankets being tucked in around her.

* * *

The gentle sound of slow breathing told Tom she was already asleep. He looked down at her with fatuous pride, then quietly left the room. Jack waited just outside the door.

"Dead to the world," Tom reported in a low voice as they headed for the kitchen. "I wish Black wasn't coming today. I don't know if she or Ablakan will be ready by then, and I won't let *anything* overtax her like that again." He held up a restraining hand. "I know, it couldn't be helped – this time. I got exhausted just watching her."

"Tell me about it! But . . ." Jack regarded Tom for a long minute.

"What?"

"I had a plan, but it'll depend on how it goes with Black and how Jan is feeling."

Tom raised a staying hand. "Whatever you have in mind, make sure it doesn't drain her."

"It shouldn't." A wicked grin spread across Jack's comely face. "But if Black disappears, check the potting shed."

* * *

While Tom did the rounds of the plants, inside and out, which had been neglected over the past couple of days, Jack drove down to the village grocer. He emerged some time later with a cartful of bags and one enormous flattened box.

Next he located the hardware store. Satisfied at last, he returned 'home' and began unloading the car. He could hear the mild whine of a weed-eater around the other side of the house.

So, where to stash all this stuff for now? With a grin, he settled on the potting shed. It took four trips to cart it all over. It would all end up in the one big box, but to carry it all in one shot would have been suicide.

Jack hoped he hadn't forgotten anything crucial. Easy-to-open tins of vegetables, fruit and veggie pasta soups made up the majority of the grocery items. He had included plenty of fresh foodstuffs which would last well without the need for refrigeration. Eating utensils and cleaning agents, labeled as Jan had suggested, rounded out the list.

From the hardware, Jack had purchased vegetable seeds. It being August, his first preference – potting plants – were no longer available. Bags of fertilizers, topsoil and nutrients, plus a few strong, lightweight implements and a watering can would let Moohri make a small garden, just in case. Jack knew from hard experience how reassuring a little self-sufficiency could be.

The weed-eater sound died away. Before long, Tom came around the corner of the house, wiping his brow on his sleeve. He halted at the sight of Jack's smug face.

"What have you been up to?"

"See for yourself."

Tom came over and surveyed the bonanza stuffed into his potting shed. He whistled appreciatively. "Well thought out. That must have set you back a pretty penny. Care to let me chip in?"

"Naw, I gave away your first haul; I'll get this one."

Tom smiled. "Alright then, and thanks. But that's gonna weigh a ton. I know Jan said weight wasn't an issue, but I don't know."

"Me neither. But if she's right, better we send as much at a sitting as possible. I don't know how many orgies of emotion I can whip up to help her teleport."

"Speaking of which, what *do* you have in mind?"

Jack outlined his plan and cautioned, "Whatever you do, don't let on, okay? And we'll have to do some fancy footwork to fill the box quickly and have it ready for her to send once she's properly primed, so to speak."

"I think I can help you there."

Their scheming was interrupted by the phone.

"Black." Jack sprinted for the patio. He picked up the phone on the third ring.

"I'm on approach," Black said, obviously using a cellphone. "Meet me at the airport in 20 minutes."

71

Before Jack could reply, Black hung up.

Jack swore imaginatively. "How long does it take to reach the airport?"

"About half an hour. Why?"

"I'm to pick him up in 20 minutes."

Tom shook his head in disgust. "A real winner, isn't he? I'll rouse Jan."

"Thanks." Jack grabbed the keys to his rental car. "Don't let her go near the potting shed."

"No problem there. She hates gardening."

* * *

A freshly-awakened Jan groggily stumbled into the kitchen and poured herself yet another cup of coffee. Though bleary-eyed, she began describing the meeting between Ablakan and Plaka, filling in the details she'd been too fuzzy to provide earlier.

"I'm hungry again," she realized, stifling a yawn. "What time is it?"

"1:40. Jack's gone to fetch Black. There's a lot of pizza left, and some salad. Will that do?"

"Perfectly."

They spent a pleasant few minutes devouring their lunch. It had the desired secondary effect, helping her feel more alert and energized.

"How are we doing for time?" Jan leaned over to peer at Tom's watch.

"Fine. They won't be here before three."

"I'll just go check on our Boy Wonder."

An overwhelmed Ablakan opened to her. Mental words spilled out at breakneck pace. *Jan, Plaka gave me* big *writing-board and shining writer, and I have big, big room to think-talk in with beauty everywhere to see, and Mother keeps coming in and hugging me, and –*

Not so fast, Ablakan, Jan laughed. *I can barely keep up. So you're at Plaka's house?*

Yes. I talked to Moohri, told him Black is not nice but needed. Does he come?

Jack has gone to get him. If you have time, please tell Moohri I think Jack is cooking up a plan to help me send him more food. But if it takes strong emotion, I may come in hard again. I just want him to be prepared.

I will tell.

Remembering a previous conversation, Jan asked, *Have you found Orowa and Shownae yet?*

Orowa, yes. Shownae is not where Moohri met him. But now I know Shownae's mind-feel from Moohri, so I can look for him on my own.

Excellent. Jan marveled once again at Ablakan's mental versatility. *I'll probably have to put Black in touch with you in a little while, so please don't tire yourself out trying to do so just yet.*

She felt the boy's mind turn wistful. *So nice here. I wish we could stay.*

I suspect from now on you will always live in nice places, Jan said. *But don't let it go to your head, okay?*

Go to –?

That means, become not-nice like Black.

I do not, Ablakan promised solemnly. *Will humans give you and Tom a nice place, too?*

Jan blinked. *I never thought of that. People here are, more likely to try to learn what you know, then throw you away.* She felt the boy recoil in alarm. *Don't worry, dear. We won't let anyone hurt us. And who knows? You may be right.*

Privately, she hoped nothing would take them away from their present location. It might be small, but it was home. Her reassurances seemed to ease Ablakan's fears for her, and he proceeded to describe in great detail the wondrous beauty around him.

At length he said sheepishly, *I chatter like forest child in play store.*

73

It's music to my ears. I love knowing you're happy.

For the first time ever, Ablakan transmitted to her a mental hug. *I love you and Tom and Jack.*

We love you, too. Jan felt the sting of tears. What a mush I am, she thought, as Ablakan 'hung up'. Wiping her eyes but feeling wonderfully warm inside, she beamed at Tom.

"That good, huh?" he smiled back.

Jan explained, noting with pleasure that he also became a bit misty-eyed.

"That's our boy," he said. "Well, so to speak."

"He does feel like the son we never had." Abruptly, Jan shook herself. "I'd better ditch the 'warm and fuzzies'. Black will be here any minute, and I bet he eats that type for breakfast."

Tom grimaced. He glanced out the window as they heard a door slam. "No doubt. And speak of the devil, I do believe they're here. Are you ready?"

"I'd better be." Jan checked her reflection in the mirror, and started down the hall to greet their new guest.

". . . and bring in my bags."

Black came into view, and Jan didn't know whether to laugh or cry. To call his outfit flamboyant would have been a gross understatement. From the obscenely loud-colored silk shirt he wore unbuttoned halfway down his chest to the tightest Spandex pants Jan had ever seen, the body swaggering into the room looked like an overstuffed sack that someone had desperately tried to rein in with a thick black belt. In front, an enormous buckle, with an over-endowed nude female etched on it, hinted of sexual conquests. Jan couldn't bring herself to look at his shoes. What she'd seen so far was making her eyes hurt.

With her best 'company's here' smile, she looked into his eyes. They were watery and bright, and she noted the nose beneath them seemed uncommonly red. Presumably, he had had a well-oiled flight.

"How good of you to come, sir," she said, keeping her distance.

74

"Yes." Black looked around him in distaste. Anger flared, but Jan was determined not to give in to it. Tom and Jack staggered through the doorway, both laden with suitcases. Black's hands were notably empty. Without a word, the men carried their burdens to the loft.

"So, what is this evidence Foxworth insisted you have?" Black was asking Jan.

"Two people from other worlds."

"I wish to see them."

"They are resting now, but should be available in a while," Jan replied evenly. On his way back outside, Tom grinned at her for the misdirection.

"I want to see them now," Black stated, his gaze frigid.

"Now is out of the question. They shall be available in a half-hour or so. That is their timetable, not mine. May I fix you some coffee?" Jan firmly dismissed the mental image of adding arsenic to the cup.

"Oh, very well. Black."

How appropriate, Jan thought spitefully, as she reached in the cupboard for a coffee mug. And where had Tom and Jack disappeared to? Surely there wasn't still more luggage to be trucked in.

"Your –" he waved a deprecating hand at the room. "Place is not very accessible, is it?"

"We like our privacy."

"If this is all you can afford," he sniffed, leaving the sentence hanging.

Jan could feel her hackles rise. It felt like he was deliberately trying to get a rise out of her, but she was determined not to give him the satisfaction.

"Here is your coffee. I don't know where Tom and Jack have gotten to, but they should be joining us shortly."

Black shrugged insolently. "Whatever." He took a sip of the brew and wrinkled his nose. He put it down with enough of a push to slop some of the coffee onto the countertop. When he showed no signs of wiping it up, Jan did, gritting her teeth to keep herself from commenting on his boorishly bad manners.

The physicist leaned against the fridge. "On the way here, Foxworth told me some ridiculous yarn about you teleporting something. I assumed he was joking." Black looked her up and down until her cheeks began to flame.

"As a matter of fact, I did. Twice."

Black snorted in derision. "Oh, come, now, madam. The finest minds in the world are working on it – mine included – and I'm supposed to believe a frumpy little undereducated housewife on some backwoods molehill *teleports*? You must take me for a fool!" He turned his back and walked out onto the patio, stopping to light a cigarette.

That was the last straw for Jan.

"Black, face me!" she yelled, furious. But her tormentor studiously ignored her, and carelessly flicked the still-smoldering match onto the tinder-dry grass.

"*BLACK!*" Jan roared, just as Tom and Jack arrived beside her. Both were puffing from recent exertions.

"*No, Jan! The box. To Moohri. Carefully!*" Jack hollered. Only then did she notice the huge carton six feet to her right.

With almost negligent ease, Jan felt her mind fuse into a laser beam of focus, and the box disappeared.

Black allowed himself a small grunt. "I assume it arrived?"

"Yessss," she hissed.

Black turned to Jack. "I've fulfilled my part in your little charade. Now, get out of my room."

Jack nodded, and turned towards the stairs.

Jan gaped at him. "What is he talking about?"

Jack gave Black a withering scowl, of which the other took no notice. "Sorry, Jan. I agreed to give up the guest room in exchange for Dr. Black 'fuelling' that 'port. But I didn't expect him to lay it on so thick."

Jan scowled at the new arrival. "You don't even seem surprised."

Black's baleful eyes regarded her contemptuously. "Why should I be? Either Foxworth was a charlatan and a liar, or he was telling the truth. I will expect full details on your procedure later. But *now* I want to see your aliens."

"Didn't Jack tell you?"

"Tell me what? He said you could teleport to an alien, but to see it I'd have to get you hopping mad. It was so easy." His smile made her want to kill.

Tom stepped toward Black, fists clenched, but Jack intervened.

"Enough!" He glared at Black. "If you want to meet these aliens, you'd better behave yourself. They won't stand for that kind of crap, especially towards Jan." Not taking his eyes off the physicist, Jack half-turned his head toward Jan. "Forgive me for bringing him into this. And if he gets out of line again, you have my blessing to send him anywhere you wish. And now, *Dr. Black*, I'll show you to *your* room. My things will be out of there in five minutes, and I will bring down your luggage. By the time you've unpacked, the aliens should be free." Without waiting for an answer, Jack started down the hall. Black followed with an indifferent shrug.

"Ooh! I never knew I could hate," Jan said, her voice trembling. "But *I hate that man!*"

"Easy, love." Tom massaged the taut muscles in her neck. "Let's get him settled in, have him meet Ablakan, at least. I don't know if we should trouble Moohri with him just now. Then I'd like the three of us 'human good-guy types' to do some brainstorming, even if we have to do it mentally so he can't listen in. You could set that up, couldn't you?"

Jan thought about it. "Yes, but I'd need to be touching you both, and that would be more revealing than the three of us just sitting down and talking."

"We could go for a walk or something, but I wouldn't put it past Black to search the house."

"I expect he will, anyway," Jan muttered. "But I'll tell you one thing for sure: He isn't getting my notes about teleporting, and I most certainly won't teach him how, either."

Tom grinned at the ferocious determination on her face. He leaned over and kissed her nose. "Then you'd better make a copy and remove the original from the drive. I'll lock the disk and your notes in the car. It'll be cool enough for them in the carport, and I'll keep the keys with me at all times."

"Tom, I say we send him packing, right now. We can manage on our own; I'm sure we can." The thought of having Black under their roof made Jan's stomach turn.

"Maybe so, but don't we owe it to Moohri to use the best resources we have? Unfortunately, those resources include His Highness over there," Tom gestured toward the guest room.

"You're right," Jan sighed in frustration. "But Tom, you don't know how close I came to hurling him to the ends of the Earth. I would have, if Jack hadn't stopped me. I've never teleported anything alive before. I could have killed him. Not that it would have been much of a loss."

Tom squeezed her shoulder gently. "Let's table this till we can get the three of us together, okay? Black will be trouncing out soon, demanding an audience with Ablakan." At that moment, a panting Jack came into view carrying the last of Black's baggage. "So let's get the physical evidence under lock and key."

"Alright."

The job was no sooner completed than Black appeared in the kitchen, his jaw set uncompromisingly. This time he would not be diverted from his goal.

Jan glanced at him, made a point of looking at the watch she had retrieved from her bedstand and, nodding, marched toward the Reading Room. The others filed in behind her.

"So, where are they?" Black demanded.

"They are not physically present. As close as we can determine, they are, respectively, 140 and 117 light-years from Earth. We converse with them telepathically."

Black regarded Jan in silence. Finally, he said, "Madam, if I had not seen that carton disappear, I would deem you mad. Under the circumstances, I shall accord you the benefit of the doubt."

"How big of you," Jan replied acidly, letting her eyes focus on his bulging belly.

They glared at each other until Black shook his head. "This will get us nowhere. I have expertise you require. You have information I want. We do not have to like each other to – cooperate."

"Agreed." Jack's chin jutted out belligerently. "But civility wouldn't hurt."

"As you wish. I assume I can communicate with them directly?"

Jan waffled a hand. "With Ablakan, through me, yes. He's fully telepathic and his English is impressive for the short time we've been 'think-talking', as he calls it. With Moohri, you'll be watching them speak in images." Jan was careful not to mention the speed of those exchanges. Perhaps their skill would humble Black a bit. "Like Tom and Jack and, I presume, you, Moohri is not a full telepath, so we will converse with him through Ablakan, who will translate the images for us."

"And you believe his translations? You just blindly take his word for it?"

Tom and Jack both started to object, but Jan held up a hand.

"Let me briefly explain the circumstances. Then ask *them* anything you're not satisfied about. Okay?"

Black nodded, a judge waiting to pass sentence. "Proceed."

As quickly as possible, Jan described what had led to her meeting Ablakan, on through to the present situation.

It seemed to placate Black for the moment, for he sighed, "Very well. Put me through to Ablakan."

Jan quieted her mind and projected her focus. Ablakan responded immediately.

Greetings, Jan, he began as usual. *Is the not-nice man there?*

Yes, and he is the 'not-nicest' man I've ever met. Please remember, Ablakan, you don't have to answer any question he asks or do anything he tells you to. If he is rude – not-nice – just tell him you will not put him through to Moohri unless he behaves himself, alright?

I will do. And thank you, Jan. Moohri said you sent him big lot of food, and other things he does not understand but is very happy to have. Ablakan mentally heaped warm approval on her.

Actually, I have no idea what was in that box. I think it was from Jack. After Black is finished, I'll ask Jack to explain what he had me send.

Okay. We talk to Black now, so we can finish talking to Black soon? Ablakan suggested.

Jan smothered a chuckle. *Well put. Stand by.* She turned to Tom and Jack. "You guys know the drill, so I'll just concentrate on getting Dr. Black attached."

"What do you mean, attached?"

"Ablakan needs non-telepaths to be in physical contact with me, so they also can have access to his mind," Jan explained. She didn't mention that Ablakan could pick up the thoughts of someone close to her without physical contact. No point in promoting paranoia.

Black scowled. "How much of my thoughts and memories will he have access to?"

"Ablakan does not pry without permission, except in an emergency, like when Moohri was unconscious and in shock. He's waiting now, but he can't stay 'open' forever."

"Very well." He reached out to touch her arm. It was all Jan could do not to pull away.

"I suggest you close your eyes. It'll help you concentrate." She shuddered involuntarily as contact was made. Tom gave her hand a little squeeze, and she smiled at him gratefully before closing her eyes and opening up to Ablakan.

The 'conference call' unfolded much like the one they had had with Jack the day before. Jan was relieved that Black actually

80

behaved himself and did not talk down to the boy, at least initially. Of course, his main interest was in determining what Shalaians knew of physics, especially things outside his own knowledge. Black found Ablakan sadly lacking in that department.

My dear young man, surely you understand at least the basic theory of –

Dr. Black, please remember you were not a world-famous physicist at age 10, either, Jan intervened, effectively putting an end to that line of questioning. *Would you like to meet Moohri now?*

I might as well, Black said, making no effort to hide his disappointment. No physics plums for him today.

When the group had reconvened with Moohri in the link, Black tried to converse directly with the Orowan. To his embarrassment, even with Moohri slowing down the images to a fraction of the speed he used with Ablakan, Black was unable to translate them into human terms. Even more humiliating, Black found himself to be a thoroughly inept imager.

None of us can talk to Moohri directly, Jan pointed out, wondering why she was helping him save face. *Shalaian and Orowan images have a lot more in common with each other than they do with ours.*

So why can Ablakan talk to us so well? Black demanded, still smarting from his failure.

English is easy, Ablakan explained. *But I do not know Orowan, so Moohri and I talk in mind pictures. I understand most, but not all.*

Black muttered something under his breath, then demanded, *Say something in Shalaian, then repeat it in English. I want to compare.*

You'll be sorry, Jan warned.

I'll take my chances. A moment later, Black winced, as did the others. Some of the tones were virtually hypersonic, others so low they felt like an earthquake in Jan's mind. Embedded in the

81

sounds were complex phrases delivered at varying emotional intensities and decibel levels.

Black gasped. *What was that?* All the others, with the exception of Moohri, shook their heads to stop their minds from ringing.

I said, 'I am happy to meet you, Dr. Black', Ablakan translated, but Jan suspected Ablakan had expressed a far less complimentary sentiment.

Now you know why he finds English easy, Tom said.

Emphatically. I am ready to disconnect now.

Jan tried to hide her relief. *Just remove your hand and that will release you from the link.*

Black promptly let go of her arm.

"Jack," she said aloud and in the still-linked minds. "Moohri needs you to explain a few of the things you had me send him, if you've a minute."

"Sure thing."

Jan quieted her thoughts while they discussed the items through Ablakan. At length, a grateful Moohri took his leave, and Tom and Jack released Jan's arm. That left only the Shalaian and Jan linked.

How are things going for you at Plaka's house?

It is quiet, no sounds. I concentrate very easy. But I am afraid a little to see Plaka's litter-brother, the boy admitted.

Did Plaka say when the meeting is set for?

No, just 'tomorrow'. Jan, be careful with Dr. Black. There is more than 'not-nice' in him. I felt it.

Jan suppressed a shudder. *I know. He only opened up for a second, but it was enough. I, too, felt his greed. It's very important, Ablakan, that he never learns to teleport.*

Never.

When Jan's focus returned to the Reading Room, she found only Tom and Jack present. Black, having gotten all he could from the session, had simply walked away.

Jan shivered. "This room feels stifling, just from him having been in it. Let's go to the sun room."

"Good idea," both men said almost in unison.

Tom raised the window as high as it would go. "This should air it out."

On the way to the sun room, they spotted Black in the kitchen, rummaging through the refrigerator.

"Makes himself right at home, doesn't he?" Tom commented, deliberately positioning his chair next to the door so he could keep a lookout for Black.

"Someone should teach him some manners," Jack snarled. "And I'd love to be the one to do it. He's gonna be real trouble. I shouldn't have brought him into this. Not yet, at least. If I had waited till we were ready to try sending Moohri home . . ." Jack shook his head in regret. "I'm sorry, folks."

Tom said, "My guess is we'll need his expertise long before that." Then he turned his head towards Jan. "You've done a wonderful job getting supplies to Moohri, hon. But that's from home base to 'elsewhere'. What we're looking to do is send a living being from 'elsewhere 1' to 'elsewhere 2', and have him get there in one piece and still breathing. Unfortunately, I suspect we'll need Black for that kind of precision placement."

"I suppose so. But first I have to learn to send things without my blood pressure going through the roof."

Jack leaned forward in his chair. "I've been thinking about that. You've 'ported – what, three times now?"

Jan nodded.

"Emotional thrust helped you overcome your self-doubts about 'how-to' and to just go ahead and do it. But now that you've gotten a 'feel' for it, you might not need the 'feather' anymore."

"It was more of a 'boot' than a 'feather'," Jan noted.

"Yes, but if Jack's right, you may be further along than you think. Why don't you try it right now?" Tom picked up a bookend, and the row of plant books promptly leaned over at a rakish angle. "Put this, say, on the floor in the bathroom."

Jan reached for it, her mind filled with uncertainty. So far, she had just blasted things out of her presence and into the presence of another. Here, she'd have to send it where there was no one present, using just her memory of 'there' as a destination.

"Don't think about it, Jan. Just let your mind do it for you. You don't want it here any more; you want it 'there'," Jack prompted.

After placing the bookend on the edge of the stand, Jan made the necessary mental adjustments. Then she gave a small 'push'. When she opened her eyes, the object was gone. Tom glanced down the hall to make sure Black wasn't around before scampering to the bathroom. He strode back in, triumphantly holding the bookend aloft. Tom's eyes gleamed with pride as he presented the item to Jan with a bow.

"To the victor go the spoils. Your trophy, milady."

She accepted it with a small curtsey. "Thank you, sir. I never realized how easy it is. I don't know why I was making such a big deal of it."

"Everything's hard when you think it's beyond you," Tom pointed out. "Once you know it isn't, it's just practice."

"It sure seems that way. Boy, we'd better not let Black find out how easy it is. Oh, while we were on that 'conference call', was there anything you picked up about Black that we didn't already know?"

Both nodded.

"He's in it for what he can get, not to help Moohri," Jack said.

"Yes, definitely greed. But there was something else underneath." Tom tapped the bookstand. "I can't quite put my finger on it . . ." His voice trailed off as he looked, unseeing, into the distance.

Jan frowned, trying to put the nebulous feelings into words. "It's strange, but I got the feeling he wasn't particularly impressed with meeting people from other worlds. It was like it was just a small diversion to him, while he waited for the main course – whatever that is."

"That's it!" Tom slapped his knee before pointing a finger at her. "Jan, he's waiting for you to become expert at teleporting, then he'll try to learn it from you and discredit you so it belongs to him. *That's* what I was feeling!"

Jan stared at Tom in confusion. "But why? Okay, sure, it would be a boon to mankind. You could use it for search and rescue, sending relief supplies to places that just got hit by a flood or earthquake or something."

"No, don't you see?" Tom leaned forward, his voice trembling with emotion. "Look at what you're trying to do: get someone from one planet to another."

Jack moaned. "Oh, man, have I been blind! You're absolutely right, Tom."

"Will you guys stop talking in riddles and just tell me what you're seeing that dumb little me isn't?"

" 'Am not'," Tom corrected absently. He leaned forward. "Jan, for 'planet' think 'real estate'."

Jan felt her mouth open in a soundless 'O'.

"Precisely," Jack said. "With his ability to calculate precision drops – and pick-ups – he could claim, colonize and rule whole planets. Can you imagine him as a dictator? I sure can. And if Earth tried to interfere, what would stop him from 'porting a few well-placed nukes or whatever?"

"Surely not?" Jan whispered, aghast.

"Do you want to take that chance? I don't," Jack said with feeling.

Tom looked from one to the other. "So what do we do about it? We still need him, for now. But he's not the type to help us unless there's something big in it for him. Have we something else to trade? Because he's not getting taught to 'port, no matter what."

"I would die before I'd teach him," Jan said, her eyes flashing. "And since I have no intention of dying, let's find another solution."

Jack noted, "Well, he won't do anything until he sees you've successfully 'ported Moohri home. So we should be okay until then."

"Jack's right," Tom said. "I'll do my best to keep him out of your hair, Jan. And in the meantime, I suggest you practice bringing things *back* from that planetoid – empty cans, that sort of thing. When you're ready – when you're *sure* you're ready – I'll buy a mouse from the pet store and you can send him back and forth."

Jack raised a finger of caution. "I'd recommend getting a large, airtight glass cage and scrub it down with heavy disinfectant before we send it, and have Moohri do the same before we get it back. We can't risk the transmission of nasty viruses. For that reason, I wouldn't suggest 'porting back the empty cans."

"Good point," Tom agreed. "Do you NASA types have an appropriate disinfectant? Preferably one you can get without calling in on your 'vacation' to have it sent to you?"

"Hmm, I'll have to think about that one." Jack pulled on his lip reflectively. "And by the same token, we can't send Moohri home till we're sure he won't be infecting Orowa."

Jan sighed. "Poor Moohri. But I agree; for now it's one-way traffic only. Speaking of which, how long would you estimate that box will keep Moohri going? What-all was in it, anyway? I got a glimpse of handles like on shovels and such."

Jack looked at the ceiling, calculating. "I'd say a month at least." He produced the itemized receipts from his pocket, and handed it to her. The prices and totals had been torn off.

"That was a good notion. A garden will keep him occupied, so he won't worry so much." Jan estimation of Jack went up yet another notch. "Though I hope Moohri won't be there long enough to eat the fruits of his labor."

Tom waffled a hand. "I don't know. It depends how soon you learn to fling people about intact between planets, and how long it takes us to get around the 'potential disease' angle."

Jan grimaced. "This is getting so complicated. Let's table it for later. I could use some lunch."

"Me, too," Tom agreed. "If there's any food left. I'm surprised His Nibs hasn't stuck his nose in here to find out what we're doing. But 'gift horses', and all that."

Jack nodded. "Does seem out of character, doesn't it? But I'm with you; let's eat."

Black was no longer in the kitchen and his door was closed. They made a meagre lunch from what little was left in the fridge. Jan gritted her teeth when she saw that once again Black hadn't cleaned up after himself. A scoundrel not even his mother could love, she bet herself.

When they stepped out onto the patio for a breath of fresh air some time later, Black quietly snuck into the sun room. He returned in less than a minute, quietly closing the guest bedroom door behind him with a malevolent smile.

CHAPTER 7

The garden beyond Ablakan's window had been beckoning to him all morning. Finally, the temptation became too great. He timidly opened the door and stepped out into it. He longed to remove his footwear and feel the soft magical moss between his toes, but dared not. It was bad enough he had ventured here without permission.

Guilt quickly gave way to wonder. Never had Ablakan touched such velvety flowers or smelled such delicate fragrances. His mother found it hard enough to feed and clothe them; luxuries such as flowers and gardens and mosses this ornate were unheard of in his young life. For one brief moment, he allowed himself to dream that one day, beauty such as this would be his to behold. Then he withdrew the wish, appalled at such a thought.

A sound behind Ablakan made him duck. If Mother caught him here –

"Do you like flowers?"

The boy turned guiltily towards the speaker. "Yes, Plaka. They are so beautiful. I am sorry. I should not be here."

"Of course you should. What good is beauty if no one will enjoy it?" Plaka came to stand beside him, and placed a hand lightly on Ablakan's shoulder. "Why don't you pick a bouquet for your mother?"

He recoiled as if bitten. "If I pick them, they will die."

"In time, yes, but others will grow in their place. Look here." Plaka indicated a brilliant emerald-and-lavender bloom. "I picked two blossoms just like this one from this very branch four days ago, and now another, even larger one, has opened in their place."

Ablakan could only stare in wonder.

"Go ahead," Plaka urged him. "And perhaps this one to adorn your mother's mane."

Hardly daring to believe this was happening, Ablakan snapped off several multi-hued flowers, his hands trembling with excitement.

"I think we will find a suitable container in here." Plaka stooped to slide back a panel under one of the many benches strategically placed among the flowers. Inside were a row of receptacles, differing not only in size and shape, but in color and texture as well. Ablakan's mother did not own even a modest vessel. To see so many casually kept inside a bench took the boy's breath away. Such opulence was unimaginable to him.

The one Plaka chose was softly iridescent. He bade Ablakan add water from a half-hidden spigot, then placed the blossoms in the container. How they sparkled as the sunspray bathed the flowers, the water and the vase!

Ablakan looked up at his host, eyebanks radiant. "Thank you, Plaka," he breathed. "Mother will be ecstatic."

"Then, do not keep her waiting."

Ablakan hurried inside, after carefully wiping his footwear.

Plaka remained in the garden as his protégé departed. He shook his head sadly. Whatever the future might hold for the bedraggled boy, at least he would have these few moments of pleasure. Tweno, Plaka's litter-brother, was unpredictable. How would he react on learning there were other planets with life on them? People who could travel in space and – what did Ablakan call it? – teleport. Plaka was beginning to regret his haste in contacting Tweno. By tomorrow, they could either be heroes or dead.

* * *

Moohri sat on the flat-topped rock facing the quiet waters. A soft breeze pleased his skin, and the sunbeams reflected off the strange implements the humans had sent. Tools and soils with which to make a garden awaited his decision. A wise precaution, in case he must remain here. But surely, with Jan's skills growing every day, she would soon be able to send him home. Or perhaps it was harder to transport people than food.

Moohri gazed into the distance at his broken spaceship. Perhaps someday, another unfortunate might become stranded on this silent world, someone who would need self-propagating foodstuffs for survival. At least, he hoped they were self-propagating. Moohri knew little about gardening, and nothing about Earth produce. Still, it was a great improvement over sitting here helplessly, feeling sorry for himself.

Moohri stepped down and grasped the spade. He chose the flat top of a small rise beside the saltless ocean on which to prepare his first garden on, and with, alien soil.

* * *

Jack and the Brodys returned to the sunroom to continue their discussions. There was little else to do until certain decisions were made. Comfortably seated, this time with iced teas in hand, they took up where they had left off.

"What if we sent Moohri a healthy rat in a large cage, with lots of rat food?" asked Jan. "Then, when we're at the point where we could 'port Moohri back to Orowa, we could first bring the rat here and have it tested for diseases."

Tom opened his mouth to comment, but Jan held up her hand. "I know, we want to keep a low profile – for now. But at some point we'll have to get governments here involved, so they can interact with those on Shalaii and Orowa."

"That's true. But I wouldn't recommend getting a rat from a pet store. A lab rat would be better – one we know doesn't have any diseases to start with," Tom supplied.

Jack agreed. "I think I could get you one without giving the cat away, so to speak. The trick will be to keep it quarantined till we can get it to Moohri. And that need won't be easily explained away."

"You could say your nephew is in quarantine with some godawful disease and is pining for a pet," Jan offered.

Jack shook his head. "Too unusual and too easy to check. Keep it simple. The more ordinary, the more believable."

"There's nothing ordinary about needing to keep a rat in quarantine," Jan pointed out. She took a sip of the pleasantly chilled liquid.

Tom leaned forward. "Wait a minute. What about the Brendant Research Center in Portland? I hear they often sell off their excess young rats."

"And we could say it's for our grandson," Jan suggested. "I'll pretend I'm neurotic about Bubonic Plague or some such, and insist we keep it in an airtight cage till we get it to his home."

Jack waffled a hand. "I don't know. It'd take an awful big cage to have enough air to get the rat back here alive."

"Who says we have to bring it here?" Jan said. "I should be able to 'port it from the car. We just have to find a quiet spot to stop for a minute. We'll also need to send Moohri something to pen it in with, so it doesn't just disappear on him."

Tom shrugged. "I doubt that'd be a problem. If he makes a pet of it and feeds it, and there's nothing else there it can eat, it'll stay close by."

Jack rubbed his hands together. "Okay, that gives us a starting point. Jan, can you call Ablakan now?"

"Sure. Why?"

"We need him to gently explain the disease angle to Moohri, and see if he'll accept the rat. And remind him through Ablakan to keep his own food out of reach."

Jan was about to place the call, when she spotted a slight frown appear on Tom's face. "What's wrong?"

"Oh, I was just wondering what Black is up to. I expected him to be breathing down your neck to teach him to 'port, but he hasn't said a peep. Does he even know what we wanted him here for?" Tom asked Jack.

"All I told him is we need him to find coordinates on another planet."

Jan glanced towards the open doorway and shivered involuntarily. She hated the very sight of the man, but at least when he was there you knew what he was doing. "But you're right, it is odd that he isn't bugging us. I'll bet he's waiting till we go to bed to search the place, figuring I kept notes. After all, who

91

wouldn't, under the circumstances? Keep notes, I mean," she clarified.

Jack looked from one to the other. "He can't get at them, can he?"

"No, they're locked in the car," Tom said. "And if he breaks in there, I'll personally wring his neck."

Jack pursed his lips. "No, that's not his style. Personally, I'd expect something much sneakier from him."

Jan rubbed her bare arms. "He gives me the creeps. Even Ablakan said he's a bad one." She walked to the door to check the hall. Black was nowhere in sight. With a shrug, she returned to her chair, closed her eyes and sent out her 'knock' signal. It took a few moments before the Shalaian responded, and when he did, his mental voice shook with excitement.

Plaka let me pick big, big flowers from his garden for Mother! he said, forgetting for once to precede it with a greeting. *They are sooooooo beautiful!*

Jan smiled. It was delightful to feel his joy, after all the stresses he had been subjected to of late. *That's wonderful, Ablakan. I bet your mother was pleased.*

She almost woozed, he projected a happy grin. *She has not had flowers since Father –.*

Jan felt the boy's mood flatten.

He would have been very proud of you, dear. But now you and your mother can start to have a better life, with – flowers and things.

He brightened somewhat, and Jan quickly changed the subject. *And I have good news, too. I practiced teleporting something just within our house, but not using strong emotion, and it worked.*

Jan, that is great! Will you send something to Moohri with no emotion?

Yes, we'd like to. But there's a problem we hadn't thought of before. She explained the possibility of there being disease-causing pathogens on the planetoid, and the fear of Moohri bringing them back to Orowa.

Poor Moohri, Ablakan sighed. *He will be very sad.*

I'm not saying he can't *go home,* she temporized. *Just that we have to be sure he doesn't bring any illnesses with him when he does. He could be a 'carrier', you see – the germs riding on him and getting other people sick, even if Moohri remains well. But we think we have a way of finding out if there are any nasty germs there. Would you ask Moohri if he would agree to a rat? Please be very gentle when you explain about possible diseases.*

I will.

Jan was about to take her leave when she remembered something. *By the way, have you caught up yet with that Orowan psychic?*

Not yet. I will call Moohri now, and then try again to find Shownae. It would be best that Moohri and his wife-mate speak before I meet Plaka's litter-brother tomorrow, he added quietly.

Jan could feel the tension in his mental voice. *Why?*

Plaka cannot hide his mind well. He is afraid of litter-brother. His thoughts speak of death.

Jan gulped. *Surely your people wouldn't react that badly to finding out they are not alone?*

I do not know. Litter-brother is very strong person in government. He added in a small voice, *I wish you could come here.*

Oh, Ablakan, I wish I could, too. And Jan meant it with all her heart. *But I've only sent things; I've never gone anywhere myself. I don't even know if I could. And there's the same problem as with Moohri going home, except I know that on Earth we have terrible diseases. I wouldn't risk inflicting them on Shalaii for anything in the world. Not even to save you, dear friend.*

Ablakan sounded morose as he said, *No, we must meet litter-brother, but apart.*

I will send him a gift; that should help. But I'll clean it with disinfectant, just in case. I didn't think of that when I teleported the disks or boxes of food, she said regretfully. *I sure hope there was nothing nasty on them.*

You are not sick, Ablakan pointed out.

No, but Moohri or your people could get ill from things that don't bother us.

The youth projected a nod of understanding. *I will call Moohri. Thank you for the news – all of it. It is better to know.*

Take care, dear. Jan signed off. So compassionate and wise for his tender years. How she wished she could meet Ablakan in person, but the same deterrent applied.

How will interplanetary travel ever happen, she wondered, if no one dares set foot on another world for fear of disease?

* * *

Ablakan sadly took his mental leave of Moohri. To his relief, Moohri had quickly understood the problem and approved of Jan's caution. The rat would, in time, tell them whether or not the Orowan could return home.

Moohri was ecstatic at the prospect of a psychic reunion with his wife-mate, and Ablakan pretended not to notice the tears which bled from the astronaut's eyes. Moohri was so very lonely.

With his focus now hovering above Orowa, seeking Shownae's mindprint as he had felt it from Moohri's memory, Ablakan was more determined than ever to arrange a telepathic reunion between Moohri and Shira. And it had to be done before his meeting tomorrow. He firmly dismissed the fear which threatened to pull his focus away from what he was doing.

Ablakan opened his mind as widely as possible, holding strongly to that mindprint. He let his awareness roam across the planet at will. At length, an answering echo on the same frequency reached his awareness. Quickly, he zeroed in on the source. The person wasn't even on the same continent where Moohri had met him, but the corresponding memory was there. Ablakan had found Shownae.

Ablakan watched in his mind as Shownae, feeling the contact, backtracked it. There was a hiss of alarm as the Orowan realized the focus he touched was not of his world. Ablakan remained silent and mentally open, allowing Shownae to access any memories he wished. And the Orowan would be able to read them all for, like Ablakan, he was a true telepath.

Slowly, Shownae's fear subsided and acceptance grew. A tentative image was placed in his mind.

What is a 'rat'?

I don't know, Ablakan imaged back. *Jan forgot to send me a mental picture.*

There followed a series of questions about Shalaii and Earth which Ablakan fielded as best he could. Eventually, Shownae appeared satisfied.

How can I help? he asked simply.

Can you contact Moohri's wife-mate? Moohri so needs to talk to her. But she is on the continent where you met Moohri.

Ablakan felt guilty asking Shownae to take on the expense in making such a trip. For all he knew, Shownae might be unable to afford it, even if he was willing.

It is not a problem, the Orowan imaged back, effortlessly picking up Ablakan's concerns. *I do not have to be there in person. Many times I have performed mental contacts on the listen-far. And I was planning a trip back there anyway.*

'Listen-far', Ablakan presumed, was akin to his own 'hear-other' or the humans' 'telephone'. *That is good to know.*

I will contact you when I find the code for Moohri's wife-mate.

Ablakan thanked him and broke off. He now had a true telepathic mind-friend on Orowa as well as on Earth. Somehow, it made him feel more optimistic than he had all day. Humming quietly to himself, Ablakan returned to the garden to love the flowers.

* * *

Moohri surveyed his handiwork as he wiped his furrowed brow. Eighteen long rows now stood where before there had only been the thin ground cover. He had painstakingly mixed the alien soil into the native earth, and added plenty of fertilizers. By the time the seeds were planted and liberally watered, the sun was near the horizon, casting long shadows from everything in its path.

Moohri washed his hands in the ocean, using as little of the precious cleansers as he could and still become clean enough to eat of the bounty Jan had sent. It had been a remarkable day so far. Shownae had reached him and promised to seek out his wife-mate. Moohri dared to hope that once more he might speak to his beloved Shira.

Homesickness washed over him as he ingested the delicious foodstuffs. Why had he ever risked being parted this way? How foolish to wish to travel in space. And yet, to see the stars in all their magnificence, out in their native element . . . surely that had a place in the hearts of his people?

His musings were cut short by a 'knock', and he quickly opened his mind to allow Ablakan in. But it was not Ablakan who entered.

Shownae! Moohri's heart leapt in wild hope, for he was not alone.

A voice soft as flower-petals spoke in his mind. *I bid you joy, my life-love.*

"SHIRA!" he cried aloud. *My Shira, can you ever forgive my folly?*

Do not grieve, my One, she said, pouring her love into his mind like a healing balm. *Shownae tells me in time you will return to me, and to our blanas. They will be overjoyed when I tell them you live. I begged your fates to keep you safe, and I am so grateful.* She broke down then, weeping tears of relief and of fears finally at rest.

Shira, I have missed you more than life itself, he whispered.

Please tell me, my Only, how I can help you.

Moohri wiped a teary eye and tried to clear his emotions enough to think. *If Jan – she's the human who sends me Earth items – can pick up food from you and send it to me, I can eat what I know feeds me best. And, it will help Jan get ready for when she can send me home.*

I will prepare a container with all your favorites, Shira vowed. *And I will send your sampi chair and fresh clothes and –*

Moohri laughed for the joy of her enthusiasm and the bliss of having her love, despite the distance between them. *No, cuddle-cumby, just the food and clothes. You don't want me to get too comfortable here.*

Please tell – Jan – I will await her 'call' with happy impatience.

She cannot understand our words, Shira, Moohri cautioned. *Ablakan translates between us, as he will have to between Shownae and the humans. Please be patient with them; they try very hard to help, and they have already done so much.*

I shall revere them always. I must go now, Onliest. Shownae tires. I sleep blissfully tonight knowing I have not lost you. Be well, Moohri.

And you, Shira. Tell our blanas my love protects them this night.

Gentle though the parting was, it left a ragged tear in Moohri's heart. How he longed to feel Shira in his arms, smell the fragrance of her skin, bask in the glitter of her eyes. Pushing away the meal he had been eating, Moohri dropped his head onto his forearms and wept.

* * *

Black came out of his room at the same moment Jan exited the sun room. Evidently, Black thought she was looking for him, for he grunted, "About time you get around to me. You have completed your notes on this morning's transport?"

"No, not yet. I've been quite busy."

"This takes precedence. I assume you want me to research the whereabouts of Orowa, and where on it to deposit your alien, in case you ever learn to teleport without first having to throw a tantrum." His eyes bored into Jan's, and she felt her face turn crimson.

97

"Yes, we will require that," she agreed, controlling her tone with an effort. "But why would you need to know how I 'port things?"

He snorted contemptuously. "Madam, you teleport through rank hysteria. To mold it into an efficient technology requires a disciplined, scientific mind. Teleportation is far too important to the future of humanity to remain in the hands of a dabbler. Surely even you can see that."

Tom emerged from the sun room and spotted Black looming over his wife. He marched towards them, his jaw set.

"Can I help you, Black?" he said, a challenge in his tone.

"That's *Dr.* Black. And no. Your wife is about to finish her notes on teleporting, as I require them."

"I am not!" Jan denied hotly.

"Oh, but you will, if you wish me to provide what you need." Black whirled to face Tom. "I agreed to keep your little secret quiet *for the time being.* No time frame was set, and it is up to me to decide if and when the press are to be notified. Do we understand each other?"

Jan's voice rose in outrage. "You would stoop to blackmail?"

"Call it what you will, madam. I have not come all this way to be your pawn. Provide me detailed – *and accurate* – notes on your procedure, and I shall research the coordinates you require." His pitch became softly persuasive. "You must realize how unwise it is for only one person to develop a new technique. If something happened to that person, the technology would be lost. *Moohri* would be lost," he added with insincere concern.

"Perhaps you are right," Tom conceded blandly.

Shocked speechless, Jan could only gawk at her husband.

"However, who says *you* have to be the other person to learn it? I think Jack would be the natural choice. He's part of the space program, and traversing space would be the prime use of teleportation, wouldn't it? Let's ask him if he'd like to learn." Tom turned toward the sun room, but Black stepped over, blocking his path.

"Foxworth has not been researching teleportation. I have."

"And you still don't know how, do you?" Jan challenged. How she hated the man! She raised her voice. "Jack, would you come out here?"

Black glared at her. "We are to stand in the hallway like savages?"

"Very well," Tom said. "Join us in the sun room."

Jack appeared at the door. His face darkened at the sight of Black. He stepped back coolly to let the physicist enter, then returned to his own chair. Not surprisingly, Black claimed the plushest seat in the room.

"Jack," Jan said, her voice raspy with barely-suppressed emotion. "*Dr.* Black proposes trading coordinates for sending Moohri home in exchange for my notes –"

"And training –" Black added.

"*And* training," Jan amended acidly. "On 'porting. He believes it must be removed from the realm of my 'hysteria' and brought into science. He also thinks it's unsafe to have only one person know how to do it; ergo teach him. Tom has proposed *you* be the 'other', since it is more properly a space technology."

Jack hesitated, taken aback. "Yeah, that makes sense. But I'm not sure I can learn it."

"Precisely my point," Black pounced. "It is a function of physics, regardless of the uses to which it is ultimately put. And I assure you, this is not open to debate. I shall exchange the coordinates you seek for your rudimentary notes. Those are my terms; take them or leave them. But know this," he glared icily from one to the other. "If you refuse, I no longer have an interest in your little venture. And I shall provide the authorities with full details. I wager they would take a dim view of you negotiating with these aliens without their knowledge. Perchance exposing Earth to attack. Treasonous, I would call it."

He stopped then, surveying the effect his words were having on his audience. They stared at him in mute dismay.

"I shall have your decision within the hour." With that, he departed.

The trio looked at each other helplessly. Before anyone could think what to say, Ablakan 'knocked'.

"Ablakan's here." Jan's throat was so constricted with tension, she had a hard time getting the words out. The two men waited silently while Jan linked them with the Shalaian. Jan then told Ablakan what had just transpired.

The boy clucked sadly. *Black is cold inside. Can you send Moohri home later without coordinates?*

I've been wondering the same thing, Jan said. *And I have an idea. Have you been able to find Shownae?*

Yes. He is good person, and remembers Moohri. He found Moohri's wife-mate and let them think-talk.

Forgetting the immediate problem, Jack exclaimed, *That's great! Maybe she can get a box of Orowan food together, and then, Jan, you can try to send it to Moohri.*

She will get it ready, Ablakan confirmed. *Shownae said she will put in clothing, too.*

Jan smiled. *Excellent. That'll give me practice sending non-living things to him from Orowa. And when we've solved the disease angle, maybe I could use Shownae as a location focus to place Moohri on Orowa. You know, like I did to put the bowl and box near Moohri. Then we wouldn't need Black's coordinates.*

Jan could feel Ablakan's pleasure as he said, *That would be wonderful. Shownae's mind is easy to find. He is telepathic, like us.*

That's a help. Jan peeked at her watch. *Now, what are we going to do about Black? Any ideas?*

For some reason, when Jan opened her eyes it made her realize she was becoming uncomfortable in the wicker chair. She squirmed, trying to adjust the thin cushion under her. In so doing, the notepad on her lap tipped and her pen fell onto the floor. Naturally, it rolled under the coffee table.

With a grimace of annoyance, Jan bent over and fished around for it. A low hum caught her attention. Jan looked up and froze in shock. Attached to the underside of the table was a miniature tape recorder.

That son-of-a-! Careful not to make a sound, Jan picked up the pen and returned to her seat.

What's wrong? Jack asked.

I just found a really high-tech-looking tape recorder stuck to the bottom of the table. I'll bet there's one in the Reading Room, too, Jan told them mentally. She was not going to say anything aloud until that thing was turned off.

Tom groaned. *Oh, no! Remember all we've been saying?*

Including about teleporting, Jack added tensely. *He may already know all he needs.*

Jan shook her head. *I don't think so. Otherwise he wouldn't have given us that ultimatum.*

Don't bet on it, Jack said. *He might have just wanted to watch us squirm. He's that mean, you know.*

Ablakan's mental voice took on a peculiar quality. *Black listens and learns. So maybe you give him something you want him to learn?*

Feed him false information? There's an idea. Jack brightened at the thought.

The emotion in the Shalaian's mental tone became carefully neutral as he said, *I will speak to government person here, and I will ask Shownae if he can talk to high space person on Orowa. Maybe you can talk to Earth government person now? Then you do not have to give Black information.*

Jan felt like a coward, as she hedged, *I don't think we can yet. Some government people here would hide us away and try to get information for themselves only, just like Black is trying to do. We don't know which ones to trust and which are like Black. They might call it treason.*

That is bad? Ablakan asked.

Very, very bad. Everyone involved can be put to death here for that.

He sighed dispiritedly. *Maybe I die tomorrow, too. It is wrong. We try to help Moohri go home; that is all.*

I know, dear. But too many people are frightened or greedy. And we're caught in the middle. Jan tried to clear her mind. *Let's work this out, one step at a time. Right now, we have half an hour to decide how to deal with Black so he doesn't turn us in yet. I have to be free to talk to Plaka's litter-brother tomorrow, otherwise you could be in big trouble.*

Yes, Ablakan agreed in a small voice.

Jan mentally addressed the group. *So what could we offer Black that would buy us some time?*

Jack snorted. *Compared to teleporting? Nothing.*

Hon, what if you 'ported Black someplace where he couldn't get to a phone? Just put him on ice for a while.

Jan bit her lip. *I've never 'ported anyone before. What if he dies? That would be murder. I hate the man, but I don't want to kill him.*

Jack stated the obvious. *And we can't exactly run down to the pet store, get a mouse or something for you to practice on, without it being noticed. Especially not in the time that's left.*

Tom gestured toward the coffee table which hid the recorder. *I say, to hell with practice. Desperate times call for desperate measures.*

Jan felt her stomach twist at the thought. *At minimum it's kidnapping. That's a federal offence. No, there's got to be a better way.*

Does 'other thing' you offer to Black have to be true? Ablakan interjected.

No, Jack told him. *But what would be an even bigger plum than 'porting?*

Tom said, *An M-class planet. What's the point of being able to go anywhere you want if you've no place to go?*

Perfect! Jan agreed.

But if he can't 'port himself there, what good would it be to him? Either way, he'll want to learn 'porting, Jack said.

Jan waffled a hand. *Maybe I could teach him how, but the wrong way. While he practices, it gives us time to get things sorted out a bit. By the time he decides he can't do it, or realizes I mistaught him –*

– we may already be in jail, Tom finished drolly.

Jan elbowed him in the ribs. *Ablakan, do you know of such a planet – an uninhabited one?*

No, but some of Shalaii has no people on it. I could show him that, then tell him where it is, somewhere else.

It's worth a try, Tom agreed.

They discussed various options, but none seemed as viable.

All too soon, Tom said, *I hear Black coming.*

Wish us luck, Ablakan, Jan said by way of goodbye.

Right on cue, Black stepped into the room, tapping his watch. "Time's up, people. Your decision?"

Jan said, "We've been in touch with Ablakan. He offers something else in trade. He knows the location of an M-class planet, uninhabited and pristine."

Black favored her with a look of contempt. "What good is it to me if I can't get there?"

"Look. I can't either – yet," Jan reminded him. "But in a few days I might be able to get you there, let you claim it for yourself, send you supplies. You'd have to buy them yourself, though. We don't have that kind of money. And I'd need to practice sending living things back and forth first."

"Not good enough. I must be able to move myself between planets. I will not be dependent on you or anyone else. You will teach me, and now."

"I'm still too new at this," she countered. "You can't expect me to teach you what I can't even do myself."

Black sneered, "Your incompetence doesn't mean I can't. You will show me your technique now, and give me that planet's coordinates, or I give the authorities an earful. " He withdrew his cellphone, finger poised as though to dial.

"You greedy scum!" Jan spat.

"Last chance." Black's eyes flashed dangerously. "You give it all to me, right here and now, or face the consequences."

Abruptly, Black found himself squinting in full sunlight. Something was terribly wrong. He stood in a large meadow ringed by dense forest. A clear brook meandered to his left. A variety of berries abounded within sight, and some of the trees bore strange-looking fruit. Dead ahead, a lavender planet filled the horizon.

"Brody, you'll pay for this!" he screamed.

On Earth, Jan stared numbly at the spot where Black had been.

"Wow!" Jack whistled, greatly impressed. "Where did you send him?"

"I didn't," Jan said unsteadily. The hair stood up on the back of her neck.

There was a stunned silence as the significance of her words sunk in.

At length, Tom asked, "Then who did?"

In the beauty of his garden sanctuary, Ablakan smiled in quiet satisfaction. He had picked up on the physicist's intention to kill them once he had what he craved. Black would be safe on Shyr, and Ablakan's friends would be safe from Black. It pleased him to have become Jan's 'other'. What was it Tom's mind had held not long ago? *'When the need is great, you find a way.'*

CHAPTER 8

Sunbeams streamed through the windows, but the solarium felt icy cold. *Could I have 'ported him without knowing it,* Jan wondered dully.

No, Jan, Ablakan's mindprint appeared beside hers without preamble. *I did.*

You? Relief flooded into her, and the room seemed to warm instantly.

I have become your 'other'. It was needed. Ablakan explained the fate Black had planned for them all, and Ablakan's decision that Black was too dangerous to leave in their midst.

I don't know how you did it, but I thank you with all my heart. Jan's gratitude mingled with amazement that this, Ablakan's first attempt at teleporting, had been so spectacular. *Where did you send him?*

He is safe. There is much food and water on Shyr.

Jan grinned. *Perfect choice; I love it. Would you hang on a bit? I want to tell the others. They're still in shock that I didn't 'port him.*

"Guys," Jan spoke out loud. "It was Ablakan. He picked up that Black was going to off us as soon as he learned to 'port, so our Boy Wonder banished him to Shyr. That's the moon Moohri was trying to go around before he crashed, remember? Ablakan says there's plenty of water and food there."

Tom's mouth fell open. "Just like that. He 'ports a person first time out."

"*And* between two distant worlds," Jan pointed out. "This opens up a whole heap of possibilities. He's still 'on-line' so let's discuss them."

Moments later, the men were thanking the Shalaian, both talking at once.

We help each other, Ablakan said with aplomb.

We sure do. Jan relaxed back in the chair. *But I was thinking: You're a full telepath, and so am I, and we both can teleport. So I'm guessing you could teach Shownae to do so as well. It would be simpler for him to send food and supplies to Moohri, since he's right next door, so to speak.*

That is true. I will call him when we finish.

Another thought occurred to her. *Could you show us where on Shyr you put Black?*

Why? Jack asked.

Tell you in a minute. An image of the location, at present *sans* Black, appeared in their collective mind's eyes. *Thanks. Here's what I suggest: If a planet becomes too dangerous, I propose using the other side of Shyr as a safe haven. It'd have to be a last resort move, though, for the same reason we can't yet send Moohri home. Also, I suggest we not let anyone else know Ablakan can teleport.*

Good idea, and I agree – respectively, Tom smiled. Jack and Ablakan added their vote in favor, if there was no other alternative available.

Jan, if it is bad tomorrow, can you also send Plaka and Mother? Plaka is good person, and Mother is – Mother.

Jan chuckled at his wording, but sobered quickly, as she realized what she was being asked to do. *I'll do my best, if it becomes necessary. But I'll need to practice first. Are you certain Plaka is trustworthy?*

Yes. His mind is open and I read a little, Ablakan confessed.

Jan projected approval. *Under the circumstances, I think you were wise to. I suggest you tell him about our 'Plan B' for tomorrow – what we'll do if things go too wrong to repair. But unless you have to, don't tell even him that you can 'port, okay?*

I will not, Ablakan promised, adding, *Maybe we get foods that stay good long, like you sent Moohri, and send to Shyr.*

Stockpile, Tom approved, then snapped his fingers excitedly. *Moohri! We can't send him home, but why don't we send him to Shyr? He'd be self-sufficient there, even if nobody sent him food. And he'd at least be able to see his homeworld.*

Jack said, *That would double the chances of him contracting some local disease. But for that same reason, we may not be able to let Black come home, after this is all over. Wouldn't that be a shame?* He grinned evilly.

I may weep, Tom snickered. *We'd better try to find safe havens on our respective planets and hope we are never forced to use Shyr.*

Jack's eyes twinkled. *And I know just the place. I've got an uncle in the Ozarks. He's a real maverick and just loves to snub his nose at bureaucracy. He'd take us in, no questions asked.*

Not even why we're on the run? Jan raised skeptical eyebrows.

Oh, he'd wonder, alright. But he was never one to pry, so long as you kept your nose clean.

Jan turned to her husband. *What do you think, Tom?*

Sounds good to me.

How about you, Ablakan? Do you know a place you and your mother and Plaka could go where you would be safe?

No, but Plaka might.

Jan added. *And we'll have to see where each person would be, so we can find them easily, or in case we have to 'port them there instead of them doing so themselves.*

Maybe no time tomorrow, so we should do that now, Ablakan suggested. *Jack, can we see your uncle's house, where it is?*

Uh, okay. Jack closed his eyes in an effort to create the image.

Jan murmured, *Think of the things you did together there.*

As the visuals began to form, the location coalesced in Jan's mind. *Hang on, everyone,* she said, and projected her focus along Jack's memory-line until they saw it.

The rustic cabin was reassuringly large and sat in the center of a sizeable clearing in the forest. A brawny, sunbaked man was splitting wood on a huge stump.

That's Uncle Daven! Jack exclaimed.

Jan stifled a yawn. *One down. Ablakan, let me know when you've found a 'safe haven', okay?*

I will ask Plaka, he said. *Can you come see it before tomorrow?*

Sure. Call as soon as you're ready and I'll follow you there. And just to make sure I can do it, I'll send something from Plaka's house to 'there'.

That seemed to satisfy the youth. *I will call soon, if Plaka knows a place.*

And Ablakan, thanks again for handling Black for us. Jan projected a hug to her 'second'.

I am glad, too, he stated, and ended the contact.

Jan yawned again, then shook off the weariness as best she could. There was one more thing left to do.

"Jack, hand me that flowerpot, would you?"

He did so, a silent query in his eyes. Jan refreshed her memory of Uncle Davin's cabin, and projected the flowerpot to a spot just behind the house.

Now for the test. Carefully, she positioned their group focus above the house, and indeed, there at a rakish angle leaned the flowerpot. Jan 'ported it back home, and returned their awareness to the sun room. The flowerpot lay on its side, soil spilling onto the carpet.

Jan grimaced. Apparently some fine-tuning was in order.

"Shall we adjourn?" she asked the others.

They all hastened to agree. Obviously, she wasn't the only one feeling the strain.

Once disconnected, Jan let out a "whuf" of relief. "If this is 'dabbling', I'd hate to see what real 'porting and 'pathing are. I hope Ablakan doesn't call for a while. I'm bushed."

"You and me both." Tom's expansive stretch produced audible sounds from taut muscles.

Jack said dreamily, "Right now, I could be sitting in my nice, peaceful little NASA office, playing with figures and eating a sticky-bun, instead of mentally booting all around the galaxy. This is taking space travel far too literally for an old country boy like me."

"What are you griping about?" Tom wanted to know. "*I'm* supposed to be retired, remember?"

Smiling to take the sting out of her comment, Jan said, "And I'm supposed to be an airy-fairy type. A *hungry* airy-fairy type, at the moment," she added.

"We've already polished off what little Black left," Tom observed.

Jack pursed his lips reflectively. "I saw a Chinese food place in the village. Are they any good?"

"Mindy's? Great. Why? Are you buying?"

"Tom!" Jan admonished, but not too firmly. It sounded like *such* a good idea.

"I will if you give me the number."

Tom recited it by heart. With a grunt of satisfaction, Jack reached for the phone.

"Thank you, Jack." Jan dragged herself to her feet. "Before I zonk out for a bit, I want to know how many of those little tape recorders Black has stashed around the house."

Tom crawled under the coffee table and dislodged the one Jan had found. He pressed the 'stop' button, then rewound it briefly before pressing 'play'.

"– recorders Black has stashed around the house," emanated from the device with impressive clarity.

Jack was ordering Mindy's 'dinner-for-four' and a few side items, but his eyes were glued to the object in Tom's hand. When he hung up, he stuck out his hand and Tom passed the device over to him.

"I'd love to know where he got this baby," Jack murmured appreciatively. "Tiny as it is, it's good for six hours continuous use. Definitely not your chain-store variety."

"I'll bet there's one in the Reading Room," Jan said over her shoulder on her way there. She returned to the sunroom carrying an identical unit.

Tom called from the kitchen, "Here's another one."

Jack found the last recorder in the living room. Black had been taking no chances. He would have heard anything of significance that was discussed in the house's common areas.

Jack's eyes flashed. "Shyr's too good for that varmint. Ablakan should have thrown him into the sun."

"Well, at least he's out of our hair." Jan suppressed a tremor. "Let's hope Plaka's litter-brother doesn't turn out to be the same sort of cuss."

A gentle knock reverberated in her tired mind. "Ablakan's back," she told the others. They had all migrated to the kitchen by then, so Jan settled herself onto a chair at the table and closed her eyes.

Plaka knows a place, the Shalaian reported. *Are you strong enough to look with me?*

I think so. Is Plaka certain it's safe?

He said it is a field inside an empty mountain. There is water, and caves to sit in if it rains. Plaka found it when young. Caves are forbidden places, but he looked anyway, and found this field. I could send much food in there tonight, for if we have to hide tomorrow. Plaka said he has a lot of food.

Good plan. Let's go.

An overview of Plaka's modest estate visually dopplered to a remote, ancient-looking mountain range. A couple of the peaks appeared to have collapsed. Cloud cover obscured the higher elevations. Then they were on a grassy plain, surrounded by towering cliff walls. Several dark holes, presumably caves, could be seen in the distance.

This is good, Ablakan said to Plaka in Shalaian. It was one of the few phrases Jan understood. Plaka's response, painful to her mental hearing, was mercifully brief.

Can you find this place? Ablakan asked her.

I believe so, yes. Let's see if I can 'port something of Plaka's here.

A lengthier dialogue assaulted her mind before they returned the group focus to the Analyzer's home. Plaka pointed to a peculiar-shaped object – a paperweight, perhaps? The experiment completed without a hitch.

After Ablakan disconnected Plaka from the link, Jan said, *I suggest, if you have to escape tomorrow, that I send you first, and while I bring Plaka, you get your mother.*

That would be safest, Ablakan agreed. *Because then they will not know I can teleport.*

Exactly. Have you practised 'porting anything or anyone else?

The youth nodded. *Yes, a few things. No other people.*

I'd better practice with someone tonight, just in case, Jan reminded herself with great reluctance. She signed off, again feeling like a coward compared to Ablakan who, based on the necessity at hand, had made his first teleport that of a person, from one world to another, and neither of them his own. Perhaps a little backbone was called for, but the thought of maybe losing Tom or Jack scared her cold.

* * *

For the fourth time, Black replayed the snippet of conversation on the tape he had fortuitously retrieved from the sunroom before that bitch teleported him onto this godforsaken moon. The new tape in the recorder would eventually run out, but it was of no use to him now.

– getting supplies to Moohri, hon. But that's from home base to 'elsewhere'. What we're looking to do is send a living being from 'elsewhere 1' to 'elsewhere 2', and have him get there in one piece and still breathing.

Black fast-forwarded the machine to the next noteworthy segment. *– Why don't you try it right now? Put this, say, on the floor in the bathroom.* There was a pause, then, *Don't think about it, Jan. Just let your mind do it for you. You don't want it here any more; you want it 'there'.*

The final section of interest was most encouraging. *To the victor go the spoils. Your trophy, milady.*

Thank you, sir. I never realized how easy it is. I don't know why I was making such a big deal of it.

Everything's hard when you think it's beyond you. Once you know it isn't, it's just practice.

111

"Then practice is what I will do," Black said with soft determination.

After returning the recorder to his pocket, he picked up a rock and focused on it with all his might. As with his previous efforts, the wretched thing refused to budge. A few more tries later, Black threw the rock at the ground in disgust and stalked away.

* * *

It was late evening before Ablakan was able to reach Shownae. Orowan's days were shorter than Shalaii's. Ablakan had had to call during Shownae's night. He apologized but Shownae graciously invited Ablakan to discuss now, rather than later, whatever he was calling about.

The boy informed Shownae of the day's events, and proposed showing the Orowan the 'safe havens' on both worlds. That way, Shownae would be able to find Jan or him more easily if they had to go into hiding.

After wiping the sleep from his eyes, Shownae mentally followed his host and committed to memory both locations. That done, Ablakan astonished the Orowan by offering to teach him to teleport.

It took some time before Shownae developed the feelings-and-projection technique Ablakan had used, and considerably longer to practice under Ablakan's tutelage. But in due course, Shownae succeeded twice in a row in teleporting a small object between two places in his sleep chamber. Satisfied that the Orowan had grasped the basic concept, Ablakan recommended secrecy about their abilities, and took his mental leave.

He wished his mother and Plaka a peaceful night, and took himself off to bed. No matter what might happen tomorrow, each planet now had a 'porting telepath. And as one, he must ensure he stayed alive, if only to help Moohri, Jan and Shownae. Despite his misgivings about the coming day, Ablakan was soon asleep.

* * *

"I've got to lie down for a while," Jan said. "Call me when the eats arrive, would you?"

"That depends how hungry we are," Tom stated.

Jack added, "And how good it tastes."

"Gluttons!" she rebuked them. Jan kissed her husband and admitted, "I'm nearly cross-eyed with fatigue. I feel like I could sleep for a week."

"Then you'll definitely miss the grub," Jack smiled.

"Couldn't have that, I guess. But really, boys, don't let me sleep through, okay? I promised Ablakan I'd practice 'porting one of you someplace, just in case I have to do it tomorrow with Ablakan and Plaka."

Jack's voice cracked in consternation. "One of us? You're kidding, right?"

"Nope." Jan weaved a bit as she headed for the bedroom.

"Which one?" Tom's voice called after her, his voice unnaturally high. But Jan gently closed the bedroom door without replying. She chuckled as she climbed into bed and soon became dead to the world.

The irresistible smells wafting from the kitchen awakened Jan four hours later. The men had postponed the order until late evening, to give her a chance to recover from the day's activities. At least, that was the excuse they used. Jan suspected they had merely put off as long as they dared her 'porting one of them. Like Jan, they realized the necessity of it, but being first in a test of this sort was not for the squeamish. Right now, they both looked exceedingly squeamish, and she felt the same way.

Throughout dinner, which seemed to last a lot longer than usual, talk remained animated, with much banter and camaraderie and a significant avoidance of the event still to come. But as the meal finally came to an end, the tensions in the room increased until they were almost unbearable.

"So who's it gonna be?" Jack finally blurted out. Both men eyed Jan as one might his executioner.

Jan bit her lip gently. "I guess the only fair thing to do is draw straws. But I will make darned sure whoever it is will arrive where he should and get back here in perfect health."

"Well, come on, then," Jack motioned to Tom. "I'm gonna have kittens if we don't get this over with."

Tom opened a cupboard door and pulled a drinking straw out of a box. Carefully, he cut it in half and then halved again one of the pieces. Silently, he handed the two mismatched straws to Jan. She turned her back to them while she made sure the ends protruded evenly. To ensure total fairness, Jan's eyes were shut tight when she again faced them.

"You first," Jack nodded towards Tom.

"No, you're our guest. You choose."

Jan heard Jack swallow noisily as he pulled one straw from her clenched fist.

When she opened her eyes, she saw that he held the longer piece. Jan's heart skipped a beat as she gazed at her husband, whose life she must now risk. Tom's eyes held hers steadily, helping her to be strong despite the potential cost to him. It made her love him even more, though she would have sworn that was impossible.

"I'll just practice a bit first, okay?" Jan kept her voice as nonchalant as she could manage.

"Take your time." There were multiple meanings in the simple reply.

The stand-up freezer fitted perfectly in the corner of the kitchen. Jan unplugged it and took a deep breath. "Where would you like it?"

"Eventually, back here." Tom smiled weakly at his own joke. "But for now, how about the driveway?"

Jan carefully performed the mental gymnastics. Reassuringly, it was within inches of the spot she had chosen for it and, even better, it was right-side up.

Tom nodded encouragement, and Jan mentally repositioned it in the exact location it had originally occupied. When they went inside, there it was, right where it belonged.

Jan felt at once pleased and dismayed, for now there was no excuse to postpone the real test. Her throat was so tight she was

114

afraid to swallow. When she looked up at Tom, he took her hands in his.

"In a few minutes, we will look back on this little practicum and laugh. Jan, you've demonstrated time and again that you know your stuff. And I haven't doubted you for a minute since this crazy adventure began. I'm not about to start now. You can send me anywhere you like, as long as you bring me back home to you."

The mist in Jan's eyes were mirrored in her beloved's. How she adored this man! The 'backbone' she had been seeking took its rightful place.

Tom saw the change in her and smiled bravely. "Let's do it, then! Send me to the sunroom."

Jan's mind enveloped him, then reduced him to a needle-point of focus. In an instant, she saw and felt him where she had chosen, standing in front of the full-length windows, looking out at the roses he nurtured with such tender care.

A delighted, if relieved *"You did it!"* came from the solarium, followed by "Home, James."

Jan suppressed a giggle and sharpened her focus. Once again, her husband stood in front of her, this time his eyes shining with joy. He picked her up in his arms and twirled her around, as Jack let out a whoop of delight.

"Piece of cake," she grinned, pink-faced. "May I faint now?"

"Don't you dare," Jack admonished. "You'll spoil your image."

Tom purred smugly, "And I have an image of you getting spoiled. Jack added a little something to the dinner order." He opened the fridge and withdrew a bottle of champagne, which he handed to Jack to do the honors. "Okay, so Jack made a special trip in to get this."

"I figured we'd either use it to celebrate, or to toast the memory," was Jack morbid rationale.

Jan didn't know whether to laugh or take offence. "Thanks a heap for the vote of confidence."

"At the time, I didn't know which of us would be 'it'," Jack reminded her as he extracted the cork. "And if I was to be a dead duck, I wanted it celebrated properly."

"And celebration it is," Tom pointed out. "Just half a glass for me, though. Tomorrow's going to be another interesting one, and I don't want to be foggy."

Jan sidled up to Tom. "I'll just have a sip out of yours."

When the requested amounts had been poured, Jack raised his glass toward Jan. "Care to make the toast?"

"How about, 'May saner minds prevail'?"

"Saner than whose?" Jack wanted to know.

"Black's," Tom said firmly.

Jack nodded. "I'll drink to that," and they all did.

Tom raised his glass aloft in the general direction of Shalaii. "And to our unbelievably resourceful friend, Ablakan."

"Too true!" Jan took another sip of Tom's meager supply. "And let's not forget the reason for this whole escapade, Moohri."

By the time Shownae and Plaka had also been saluted, Jan had the giggles, despite the small quantity of alcohol she had consumed.

"Sorry about this, Jack," Tom hammed a long-suffering sigh as he steered his wife back down the hallway towards their bedroom. "I'd better get this boozehound to bed before she breaks into song."

"How dry I am –" Jan belted out, deliberately off-key.

A hand was hastily clamped over her mouth. "Oh, no, you don't!" Tom unceremoniously frog-marched her down the hall, as they both dissolved in laughter.

CHAPTER 9

Moohri awakened feeling surprisingly refreshed. The emotional turmoil of the previous day had been swept away by a good night's sleep, and he eagerly awaited the promised supplies from home. *Home!* It had become the most revered word in his personal vocabulary, second only to the names of his family.

"I love you," he intoned in Orowan, wishing fiercely that they could hear him.

Moohri took his time with his first day-meal and went to check on the progress of the little garden, knowing, of course, that there would be nothing visible yet.

A gentle knocking in his mind alerted him that he had a visitor. Or visitors? But Shownae was alone. Moohri tried to hide his disappointment as he greeted the telepath. Shownae told him of the wondrous gift from Ablakan, and what it would mean in terms of Moohri receiving regular packages from home.

I have a large carton from your wife-mate here right now, Shownae said, doubt coloring his mental tone. *But since this will be my first time sending anything off-world, maybe I'd better start with something else. Something small, in case it falls on you.*

Moohri resisted the urge to crouch down. Jan had used him as a locator, to put the foods she sent close to him, so Shownae would probably need to do the same.

For what seemed like an eternity, nothing at all happened. Then he noticed a child's braklam-ball a few feet in front of him.

I sent a ball. Did it arrive? Shownae asked.

Yes, I'm holding it, Moohri exclaimed with growing excitement. *Can you put the box in the same place?*

I will try.

More time elapsed, and Moohri was beginning to fear they had lost contact when a large box appeared, slightly further from his location than the ball had been.

Thank you, Shownae, it is here. Moohri rushed towards it. A package from home!

Be heartened, Moohri, Shownae said, and left him to enjoy in private.

Feverishly, Moohri pulled the flimsy lid off the box and reached inside. He felt like a child receiving his Pelama-day gifts from his relatives on turning four. One by one he unpacked delicacies he never thought he'd taste again. Familiar aromas filled the morning air. In a large, separately-wrapped container was comfortable clothing, soft bedding, covers and his own headrest. "Thank you, Onliest," he murmured. He breathed deeply of her scent, which lay upon the pillow like a talisman of hope.

The balance of the large box held miscellaneous toiletries and pleasantries, a recorder and multiple pictures of Shira and their blanas. For the longest time, he stood there, basking in the warm smiles on their faces before reluctantly placing them to one side. At the very bottom of the box was what he had most hoped to find: a message from Shira. He held it to his chest in gratitude a long moment before opening it. Moohri began to read, adoring every word that she had written because it came from her. All else was forgotten in his need to feel her presence, if only in words. Love, compressed into symbols, for him.

* * *

Ablakan awakened early, despite having retired late the night before. He checked the timemometer and realized no one in the house would be up yet. But Moohri should be. Ablakan decided to call before whatever the day would bring happened. At the thought, fear poured over him with a vengeance, but Ablakan forced it back. Today of all days, he must be strong.

Ablakan cleared his mind and contacted Moohri. The Orowan was in such an emotional state that at first Ablakan thought another calamity had befallen him.

No, I am well, Moohri imaged. *But Shownae sent me a box from Shira, with a message. I need so much to see her, and to see my blanas.*

A wave of homesickness worse than anything he had ever experienced washed over Ablakan. Gagging in reaction, Ablakan accordioned over and clutched his stomach. He fought desperately to gain control over rampant empathy.

Moohri hurried on, unaware of his effect on Ablakan. *My department, Spacefarers, has an isolation chamber. If you could get Shownae to send me there, maybe they could find out if I am contagious. At least I would be home on Orowa and could see Shira and my blanas, even if just through the windows. I could speak to them on the listen-far. Can you call Shownae for me?*

I will ask him, Ablakan promised, straightening up with an effort. *Goodbye, Moohri.*

He broke the connection as quickly as he could. Almost immediately, the symptoms subsided. He sat on the edge of the bed, shaking. *Breathe deeply,* Ablakan instructed himself. With time so short, he could not afford to be sidetracked.

For Moohri's idea to have any chance of success, Shownae would have to convince the Orowan space department that their astronaut was still alive.

It is not that easy, Shownae imaged regretfully, when Ablakan outlined Moohri's request. *I am feared and hated by many in our government.*

That surprised the boy. *Why?*

Several years ago, I was overcome with a feeling of doom for a dignitary who was visiting our city. In my haste to save him, I broke through the guards and told him he was about to have a massive heart attack. And he did, right then and there.

That is bad, Ablakan agreed.

Yes, and the doctors could not say whether he died from heart ailment or from my telling him he was about to die. Eventually, I was found blameless, but my reputation in the eyes of the ruling body is ruined. I could never get an audience with the new leader of Spacefarers, no matter what I might say, the Orowan concluded miserably.

Ablakan was silent for a time. *Shownae, would the leader accept a visit from Moohri's 'widow'?*

Of course. It would be shameful not to.

Good. If you and Moohri rode quietly with Shira, you would feel the Leader's mind when she speaks to him, wouldn't you?

Shownae's mental voice became animated as he finished Ablakan's thought. *Yes. Yes, we would. And if Shira touched him, I could let Moohri speak to the new Lead Spacefarer through me. He would not have time to disbelieve before he'd know it was indeed Moohri. Ablakan, you are most wise – and crafty.*

Ablakan projected a crooked smile. *I am learning it is how adults survive.*

Shownae nodded. *Sadly, that is often true. Thank you, my friend. I will begin at once. May the fates be kind to you this day, in your meeting.*

I hope so. Goodbye, Shownae.

The kitchen was permitted to him, so Ablakan made himself a light meal of leftovers. His stomach fluttered nervously, so he dared not overfill it. For the third time in quick succession, he checked the timemometer on the wall, wishing it was later. He longed to call Jan, admittedly to get her assurances all would be well. There were times, he realized, when he felt very young indeed, and this was one of them.

A gloomy hour passed before Plaka joined him. The sickly smile he offered Ablakan did nothing to ease the boy's fears. Small talk soon petered out to a fretful silence. Presently, Ablakan's mother arrived, chattering excitedly of the improved social status they would soon enjoy. Neither male had the heart to inform her of the other possibility.

As soon as Ablakan could politely leave, he headed for the garden to gain strength from the beauty around him. He noted with relief that it was finally late enough to contact Jan. He closed his eyebanks and projected his mind across the light-years between them.

* * *

They were having a leisurely breakfast when Jan got the call. "Ablakan's awake," she said.

120

"Be gentle with him," Tom advised. "He's bound to be pretty scared about now."

"I sure would be," Jack agreed.

Good morning, dear. Are you well rested?

Yes, but I have much fear.

Jan said confidently, *I'll be right there with you. Remember how frightened you were when you first met Plaka? And that turned out great. So will this.*

But Plaka is afraid of his own litter-brother! Maybe he is a bad person, like Black.

Not necessarily, Ablakan. I was afraid of my sister, too, Jan lied, hoping she could hide it from him. *I was sure she hated me. I found out years later she thought I was so much smarter than her that she avoided me so she wouldn't feel stupid.*

I think *I understand.*

You just go to that meeting being strong, like you did to meet Plaka. Don't forget, just because Plaka is afraid of his litter-brother doesn't mean the litter-brother is bad, just powerful. Probably, he'll want to believe what Plaka tells him, and I'm sure that box of disks I sent will help with that.

Ablakan gulped. *I think he will believe. But he may be afraid your people will attack Shalaii.*

Oh, Jan said, as understanding dawned. *That's what our people might think, too. And why we've been keeping it quiet here.*

Ablakan and Shownae were in the same situation, on their respective planets, but they were taking chances. Once again, Jan felt like a coward. After all, she thought, could our own kind be more xenophobic than Shalaians and Orowans, considering so many of us believe in alien life and theirs do not? It took her a nanosecond to reach the cynical conclusion: Yes.

If we can find one high-ranking 'good guy' on each planet to talk to each other, we should be alright, Jan observed. *How high up is Plaka's litter-brother?*

Very, I think. Is Jack?

She sighed, wishing it were otherwise. *Not high enough, I'm afraid. Will Shownae be contacting anyone in power on Orowa?*

He will talk to new leader in space department.

Jan took a deep breath, not liking the obvious next step. *Once your high-level person is in the loop – assuming he's reasonably accepting of what's going on – we'll see about finding one here on Earth.*

That is good, Ablakan said, and Jan had the feeling he considered it long overdue. *And Jan, Shownae now can teleport like us. He sent Moohri food and other things from his wife-mate.*

Excellent! At least now we can be sure Moohri's getting the kind of food he needs.

The youth projected a nod. *Yes. Now if anything happens to me, at least Moohri still has someone who can understand what he is saying and can help him.*

Nothing bad will happen to you, my friend, Jan promised. *I won't let it. But you're right; precautions are always a good idea. When is the meeting with Plaka's litter-brother?*

His workers said they will call us when it is time to go. Litter-brother works in Tabix not far from Plaka.

Do Plaka and his litter-brother visit often?

No, never, was Ablakan's discouraging reply.

Jan digested that bit of information. *Alright, then, we'll have to handle it as it comes. Is your mother going along?*

Ablakan leaked annoyance, as he said, *She refuses to stay here. She wants important people to know she is my mother.*

As Jan had expected she would. *Please call me just before you leave. I'd like to travel with you, so I can get a sense of what's happening as early on as possible.*

Thank you. I will.

Jan disconnected then, determined to save her energies for when they would be most needed. Tom and Jack eyed her pointedly, and she synopsized the conversation. On this occasion, she hadn't bothered to take notes.

"And just who have you got in mind as this 'high-ranking good guy'?" Jack wanted to know.

"I was hoping you could suggest one."

Jack grimaced. "Are you sure you want me to? Remember, I'm the one who brought Black into this."

"Think of it as a chance to redeem yourself."

"You know your problem?" Jack shook his finger at her. "You're altogether too trusting."

* * *

Oblivious of their comments about him, Dr. Ryan Black was summing up in his mind the results of the past several hours he had spent exploring Black Moon. He assumed it was the Orowan moon, Shyr, but since he was the first person to set foot on its surface, he claimed it as his own, in its entirety. Too small, of course, for his base of operations, but it would make an excellent leisure destination. Already he had found many local foods highly edible and quite to his liking. The forest held an abundance of small creatures with no fear of man, so they were easy to catch. The two bodies of water he had found so far – one a wide creek and the other a shallow lake – teemed with fish, one upon which he was presently dining. Burnables were in abundance everywhere, but he would soon need a replacement for his lighter. He shrugged, unconcerned with that triviality.

Mastering teleportation was his only real challenge. Once he had that, he would take care of Foxworth and the Brodys permanently and have the universe at his disposal. He smiled as his imagination conjured up a vision of Jan Brody staring in shocked amazement as he appeared in front of her. Then he would gently place her on Earth's moon. She would have ample time to contemplate the error of underestimating him before she died a most satisfyingly unpleasant death. He regretted the others would not be there to watch her die, but he couldn't leave her mentally unattended until she was well and truly dead. Then they would join her in final defeat.

With his goals firmly in mind, Black focused on a nearby pebble and continued to practice with single-minded determination.

* * *

The high-pitched tone of the hear-other brought Plaka running. He spoke briefly into the instrument, then disconnected, gulping.

"It is time," he informed his guests.

"Finally!" Epash hurried to her room to gather her few belongings. As he went to retrieve his wrapover, Ablakan told Jan they were on their way. A shuddering breath escaped him. Jan bolstered his courage with an image of him standing tall, with her shadowed form beside him.

Ablakan followed his mother to Plaka's rider, a modestly-luxurious vehicle which had thrilled him the day before. Now all he could think about was the spectre of the all-powerful litter-brother waiting at the other end of the trip.

Epash gushed incessantly, pointing at outrageously expensive items in the shop windows they passed, intimating they would soon adorn her dowdy body. Plaka drove in silence, his fingers gripping the shaft with unnecessary force. All Ablakan could do was regret having eaten at all.

Ghastly though the trip was, they arrived at their destination much too soon. Ablakan stared up and up at the skyzone tower. How long would it take them to get to the top floor where Plaka said his litter-brother worked, he wondered.

Ask him what the brother's name is, and what title he holds, Jan suggested, and Ablakan numbly complied.

His name is First Tweno. He rules this continent for our Primary.

Does your Primary run the whole planet? Jan asked.

Of course, Ablakan said, forgetting she'd have no way of knowing that.

At the door, they were provided a temporary permit and escorted by two uniformed minions to the tube which would take them to Tweno's private floor. The journey took close to a

124

minute, and Ablakan's ears popped painfully twice before they reached the top. When the tube came to a halt and the door lifted, Epash exited first, her chest stuck out like a Primary. But the worker who collected them motioned to Plaka to follow him, and Epash was forced to take second place in the procession.

Understated opulence was everywhere, and despite his fears, Ablakan found himself gaping in awe. Not even in pictures of the ancient halls had Ablakan seen such magnificence. The underling led them around corners and down passageways that seemed without end, till they turned one final corner and halted before an exquisitely carved door. Tweno's name and official title were emblazoned onto it in a shiny material Ablakan did not recognize, but which he found both impressive and intimidating. They were told to remain there until summoned. Then the worker trotted off to attend to other business.

For a few minutes, they all stood there. Not even Epash seemed inclined to speak. Ablakan glanced at Plaka and was horrified to see the Analyzer's legs tremble violently. One look into Plaka's eyebanks and Ablakan wanted nothing more than to bolt down that hall and away from this place. The door was suddenly opened from within, and another uniformed attendant ushered them into the presence of First Tweno.

"You wished to see me, Plaka," the golden-maned patrician behind the endless desk said. His voice was devoid of emotion. The chair upon which he sat was on a raised platform, and Ablakan suspected he used it to advantage, looking down upon those who sought an audience with him.

"Yes, First," Plaka croaked, bowing his body. "It is good to see you again. You look most well."

"I am. You said you have important information?"

Plaka swallowed hard and, reaching behind Epash, pulled Ablakan to stand beside him. "This boy has an amazing story, and we have brought proof as well." The Analyzer turned imploring eyebanks on the youth. "Go ahead. Explain it to him."

Just tell it like it is, dear, Jan whispered in his mind. *Save the disks for last, just before you introduce me.*

"First Tweno," he began in a quavering voice, then cleared his throat. "My name is Ablakan."

To her credit, Epash tried to go stand beside her son, but the attendant warned her back.

"Two months ago, I received a mental image message from a person on a planet 140 light-years from us."

Tweno's eyebanks enlarged, but he remained silent.

"We have been talking every day since then. Her name is Jan. She is a human being. The name of her planet is Earth." He stopped to take a breath, realizing how unbelievable what he was saying must sound to their ruler.

"Four days ago, while we were talking, we heard a mental scream. We found out that a person from another planet – his name is Moohri and he is from Orowa, about 110 light-years from us – had crashed on a planetoid while trying to pilot a rocket ship around their furthest moon. There was no food for him to eat there, and Jan has since learned how to send him food from Earth. Jan may be able to return him home now – she is becoming quite good at sending things – but we are afraid he may bring some disease from where he is back to his world if she does." Ablakan found himself panting. He paused to calm down a bit, and at the same time realized he had given their First old news, in that now Shownae was the one sending food to Moohri.

He was wondering if he should correct it when Tweno leaned forward in his seat. "That is quite a story, boy. Is that how you met Plaka – you were sent to him?" The inference was obvious.

Ablakan nodded miserably. "Yes, sir," he said, forgetting he was using an English term. "And Plaka didn't believe me either. But Jan was mentally with me and she threw this into the room." He produced the wrecked box and disks.

"Approach me," Tweno instructed, holding out his hand.

Ablakan walked toward him, weak-kneed, and handed him the 'evidence' before returning to stand with his companions.

126

Tweno turned the objects this way and that, scrutinizing the strange lettering on each item. Several times, he glanced up at Ablakan while ignoring the others. Ablakan found it increasingly difficult to remain tranquil, despite soothing input from Jan.

Presently, Tweno called his attendant over for a second opinion. They discussed it in low tones. Then the attendant left the room, taking the pieces with him.

Now Tweno focused his unblinking gaze on Plaka. "By what method did those arrive in your presence?"

"I am told it is called 'teleportation', First," Plaka said, bowing again. "May I explain?"

"Yes."

"When Ablakan came to me with this story, it sounded so foolish I did not believe him. Then he had Jan speak to me, but I thought he was just leaking mindsickness. That was when I felt her yell in my mind in a language I did not understand, and my eyebanks were made to look at the floor. Then that container crashed there from – nowhere." He raised his hands in supplication. "I know how it sounds, but I swear on our mother's heart that it is true."

"You may not speak of our mother that way." Tweno fixed Plaka with a frosty glare.

"Forgive me, First," Plaka quaked, bowing so low his forehead scraped the tiles.

Tweno turned his eyebanks on Ablakan. "This 'Jan' you talk about . . . Is she with you now?"

"Yes, First."

"What manner of being is she?"

Ablakan's face softened. "She is the kind of person to weep when she thought she could not help an alien being she had never heard of, but who was stranded without food. She is a person who taught herself a way to send food that has never been done before on purpose, so Moohri would not die. And she is my best friend."

"You have spoken with her since?" Tweno directed at Plaka.

"Yes, First."

127

"What is your opinion of this 'Jan'?"

For once, Plaka did not bow, but replied simply, "She is kind."

"And she is listening to what we say?"

Ablakan shook his head. "She only understands a few of our words, although I speak hers pretty well now. It is an easy language to learn. But she can understand if you speak in very slow images."

Tweno was silent for a moment, regarding the trio.

"You two," he gestured at Plaka and Epash. "May wait in the outer-room. You," he beckoned toward Ablakan. "Shall come with me."

He arose and separated the curtains behind his chair, moving beyond them. Terrified though he was, Ablakan had no choice but to follow.

They entered a short corridor which led to an elegantly-appointed sitting room, furnished with the softest seats Ablakan had ever beheld. Tweno arranged himself on one and motioned for his guest to be seated on the adjacent chair. To Ablakan's surprise, Tweno unbuckled his sash and let out a long sigh.

"I hate these things," he confided. "But we must keep up appearances, mustn't we?"

"Sir?" Ablakan said, taken aback.

"Tell me, boy – Ablakan – what is this 'sir'?"

He felt his skin tone flush in embarrassment. "I'm sorry, First. It is an English term of respect. I use it when being introduced mentally to humans."

"You did not mention other humans," Tweno said, his eyebanks narrowing dangerously.

Ablakan gulped. "It was necessary to make them believe so they would help Jan and me try to rescue Moohri."

"These humans, do they also have space travel?"

"Just a little, First. They could not reach Moohri that way."

"Tell me, then, about this 'teleportation'."

Taking care not to seem too knowledgeable on the subject, Ablakan explained. Tweno listened attentively.

"You realize I cannot believe this until I see it with my own eyebanks."

"Yes, sir. Jan has chosen an item from her planet to send you as a gift, and to help you believe. May she send it now?"

"Will it crash to the floor?" Tweno asked. "This is expensive covering."

Ablakan failed to notice the twinkle of amusement in Tweno's eyebanks, and assured him hastily, "No, First. Jan has learned how to put things down gently."

"Then she may send it."

Ablakan said, "I will explain quickly to Jan and ask her to put it on this table, if I may."

"You may."

As rapidly as he could, Ablakan brought Jan up-to-date and asked her to send the gift she had chosen. He hoped it would be suitably impressive, since it was going to their First. Once the article arrived, they stared at it, uncomprehending.

What is it? Ablakan asked Jan.

It's a picture encyclopedia, showing people, places, animals – all sorts of things about our planet.

Pictures! That is perfect. Then Ablakan switched to Shalaian to explain what Jan had sent. They spent a few minutes marveling at the sights each new page revealed to them.

There is a strange smell to this gift, Ablakan told Jan at length, as tactfully as he could. *Is that what Earth smells like?*

No, dear, Jan laughed. *Remember, I said we'd have it disinfected for your safety?*

I forgot. Ablakan related that bit of information to Tweno, who seemed duly impressed by Jan's concern for their wellbeing. The patrician laid the book aside.

"I would like to meet her now, if she is ready."

"She awaits, First. But to hear her, you would have to clasp my arm, please."

Ablakan shivered involuntarily at having the hand of a First touch his unworthy self. His voice shook a bit as he continued, "It is easier to concentrate if you shut down your eyebanks, sir."

Tweno looked at him sharply, then shrugged and closed them. Ablakan immediately followed suit.

He's here, Jan, Ablakan said needlessly.

Thanks, dear.

As she had with Plaka, Jan replayed her initial message, after greeting Tweno in Shalaian. Ablakan, listening in, was relieved to see Tweno conversing in images simple and slow enough for Jan to understand and respond to.

Ablakan tells me you and he have been talking for some time now. Are you a ruler on Earth?

Jan laughed. *Heavens, no! Nor would I ever want to be.*

At times, neither do I, Tweno imaged with wry humor. *Has Ablakan told you much about our planet, our civilization?*

Some. And I have told him a bit about life on Earth.

Ablakan felt Jan's feelings base change abruptly.

First Tweno, I can understand your concern that I am somehow using Ablakan against your world's best interests. When we bring high-ranking government people into this on our planet – and we are about to do so – they will doubtless have the same worries. But between Ablakan and I, all it has been is building a friendship and hoping one day we may meet in person. And now, with Moohri stranded as he is, our main goal is getting him home in a way that will be safe for him and his planet. Ablakan has been risking his life to help Moohri, and –. Ablakan felt Jan swallow convulsively. *– My friends and I are willing to take the same chance here with our government.*

Ablakan sent a warm hug along a private beam of focus to Jan. This had been the longest speech she had ever made in images, and the sincerity had rung true as sunlight.

Apparently Tweno believed her, for he changed the topic. *Has the Orowan government become involved as well?*

Not yet. But I think Shownae is about to contact them.

Who is Shownae?

An Orowan psychic Moohri once met. Ablakan put him and Moohri in contact. He helped Moohri talk to his wife-mate. Moohri is terribly lonely.

Ablakan noted with approval that Jan hadn't mention Shownae's ability to teleport.

A sigh escaped Tweno. *I sympathize, but I do not see what we can do to help him. We have not even considered space travel, you know.*

With teleporting, that wouldn't be necessary anyway. What Moohri needs most is a way to be proven free of disease-causing germs, Jan explained.

Perhaps we can be of some help there, Tweno imaged. *We have very few ailments we cannot at least control.*

This was welcome news to Ablakan. He felt a rush of hope, but couldn't tell if it was his own or Jan's he was feeling.

Thank you, First, Jan breathed.

Tweno's tone became cautionary. *I can make no promises. I am but one voice. There will be others who must be consulted, including our Primary. But I will do what I can. Will you make yourself available, so others can speak with you?*

Indeed I will.

Then I look forward to our next meeting, sir. Tweno removed his hand from Ablakan's arm and the conference was over.

Ablakan felt Jan chuckle at being called 'sir'. Still, the intent had been most thoughtful, and Ablakan's anxiety dropped a notch.

I think I will be alright now, Jan. Thank you for coming.

My pleasure, Jan told him. *If you need me, just call.*

In his mind, Ablakan hugged an image of Jan, the closest he could come to doing so in person, and was gratified to be 'hugged' in return.

Be well, my friend, he said, and broke the link as Tweno addressed him.

"Do you tire now?"

131

"A little, First," Ablakan admitted. "But I am happy to serve."

"I would like to talk to your Moohri. Can he also speak in images?"

Ablakan nodded emphatically. "Yes, much more easily than humans can. He images the way we do, although there are some things I do not understand, because I am a child."

"Young, perhaps, but not a child," Tweno said kindly, and Ablakan blushed at the unexpected compliment. "Do you need me to touch you again?"

"Yes, please. But we will have to speak in my mind, because Moohri is not a telepath."

"Telepath?"

"It is an English word that means a person who can hear and speak to others mentally."

Tweno nodded. "Proceed."

"I must reach him and link up, sir."

"I have time."

Ablakan sent out the call, and Moohri answered eagerly. Ablakan realized the Orowan had been hoping it was Shownae and Shira. In rapid-fire images, Ablakan explained to him the morning's events.

"He is ready, First."

This time, Ablakan did not shiver as Tweno clasped his forearm. He kept to the background while they conversed in images. Tweno expressed sympathy for Moohri's situation, but had no immediate solution to propose.

I cannot act alone, Tweno explained. *And even if we can help, there would be much involved before we could guarantee you are free from dangerous germs. What would harm your people might be safe for us. It will be difficult to test for safety of a people with whom we have no contact.*

Ablakan shook his head sadly. Tweno was right. They had a long way to go yet.

An unexpected jolt came near the end of the discussion.

If all goes well with my counterparts and the Primary, perhaps I can act as a high-level motivator, should officials on your homeworld be reluctant to help.

Ablakan could feel how scandalized Moohri was by the suggestion. *Thank you, First. But why wouldn't they want to help? I am – was – Lead Spacefarer.*

Tweno projected a jaded smile. *I suspect people are much the same on any planet. Forgive me if I have offended you, but the offer stands, should it be needed.*

They parted with mutual respects.

"You look weary, Ablakan," Tweno said. "Rooms will be provided for you and your mother, and your needs shall be met at your request. I must now speak to my counterparts and the Primary. Keep yourself rested, for they will no doubt wish to interview you at length."

Ablakan swallowed, his eyebanks bulging in alarm. Him talk to the other Firsts, and the *Primary*? He began to tremble.

Tweno regarded him in surprise. "Calm yourself, boy. They are very powerful, yes, but they are people just like you and me. You are not afraid of me, are you?"

"Y-Yes, First."

Tweno accordioned down in front of him, making them virtually of equal height. Putting his hands on Ablakan's shoulders, he spoke softly, his eyebanks never leaving Ablakan's face. "You are afraid because Plaka is afraid, is that not true?"

Ablakan nodded woodenly.

"Then you must understand: It had been decreed at our birth that, when our mother died, one of us would become First. You remember this from Learn-more?"

"Yes, sir," Ablakan whispered. This aspect of his people's history bothered him the most.

"We were each given the three tests: The Test of Mind, of Body and of Heart. He who scored the highest would rule. The other would be destroyed, lest he seek to unseat his better."

Ablakan nodded, miserable.

133

"I repealed that law when I came to power. It will never happen again. But you see, Plaka still does not believe it. He fears for his life, and a fearful person will sometimes try to destroy the object of his fear, to feel safe. That is why I may not speak to him kindly, litter-brother to brother, but only as leader to citizen. Do you understand, Ablakan? I do not hate him, and I will not hurt him, *and I will not hurt you.*"

"Thank you, First." Ablakan bowed his head. "But the Primary may call it 'treason' and order me killed."

"What is this 'treason'?"

"On Earth, if a person helps someone who might try to hurt the government, they call it 'treason' and both people can be killed," Ablakan explained, his concern for Jan intermingling with his own.

"Have you done 'treason'?"

"No, sir, never!" Ablakan cried.

"Then you need not worry. I will speak to the Firsts and the Primary on our behalf. All will be well; you shall see." Tweno gave Ablakan's shoulders a tiny squeeze, then bade him accompany the attendant who would show him to his quarters.

* * *

By the time the attendant returned, Tweno was back in his chair behind the desk on the raised platform.

"The boy and his mother are installed, First," the aide reported. "Have you instructions about Plaka?"

Tweno considered, then looking down at his own, bade his attendant bring him a new sash. "The gold one will do."

Once it had been delivered to him, he placed it in the side receptacle, out of sight. "I will see him now."

Eventually, the door opened and Plaka was ushered inside. He was quaking uncontrollably.

"Come here, Plaka," Tweno beckoned. He pointed at a spot right in front of his desk.

It took an inordinately long time for his frightened sibling to complete the journey.

"Plaka, you have done your world – your people – a great service this day, bringing the boy to me. As you know, I may not award you a position of authority."

The Analyzer bowed his head in acknowledgement.

"However, it is my right to present you with the Sash of Safety." Tweno extracted the item and, leaning forward, strung the material across Plaka's shoulders with as much solemnity as he could muster. In ringing tones, he proclaimed, "From this day forth, none may harm you, on penalty of my wrath."

Plaka looked up in disbelief. "Then I am not to be killed?"

"No, my brother," Tweno smiled. "Continue your life of good citizenry. The sash will speak to others of your excellent character and help your practice to flourish."

"Thank you, my First! You are a most benevolent leader," Plaka enthused, evidently unable to believe his good fortune. He bowed and turned to leave, then hesitated.

"Yes?" Tweno asked.

"The boy – will he be made welcome, First?"

"He will by me."

"But will the Primary?"

Tweno sighed. "That I do not know."

Their eyes met in mutual concern, then Plaka lowered his in deference, bowed once more and left.

* * *

Shownae fretted as Shira was being escorted into Klyfin's spacious office, the office which until recently had belonged to Moohri. Shira had briefed Shownae beforehand on the rivalry which had existed between her husband and Klyfin ever since their training for the space program began. Both were equally qualified, and each longed to be the first one to travel in space. Klyfin had been particularly bitter when Moohri edged him out in their final anti-gravity test. Moohri was already head of the space department. To now have him also become first astronaut had goaded Klyfin to open animosity.

135

And now they would need the new leader's active assistance to bring Moohri home, with the help of a psychic Klyfin despised.

"Widow Shira to see you, Lead Spacefarer," his receptionist informed the figure seated with his back to an enormous star chart. Shownae involuntarily shrunk back further beside Shira's mind, as though fearing premature detection.

"Shira, how happy I am to see you," Klyfin said, waving her toward a chair. "I am honored by your visit. We all miss Moohri, you know. I owe him most of all. Had he not done so well in training, it would be I –" He stopped, perhaps realizing how tactless the observation was. "Please sit down. How might I serve you?"

Shira cleared her throat nervously. "I have a peculiar favor to ask. Would you come sit here beside me?"

"Certainly, if you wish." Klyfin relocated to the vacant seat next to her.

"Would you place your hand on my arm, right here?"

The Spacefarer regarded her uncertainly. "Why?"

"There is something I wish to show you. It will not take much of your time."

Klyfin hesitated before self-consciously clasping her arm.

Shira twisted her hand to grasp his as well. *Good fates, Shownae,* she said in her mind, and went silent.

In a flash, Shownae linked to Moohri.

You sit well in that office, Klyfin, Moohri remarked casually.

Klyfin gasped and tried to pull away, but Shira held on tightly and gave him a reassuring smile.

Yes, I am alive, and very much still in physical form. I crashed on a planetoid that's on the other side of the sun. Without going into too much detail right now, I have a way home, but dare not until I can be certain I would not be bringing with me some alien disease. I feel well, but I must be sure. Is the isolation room still sealed?

Klyfin did not answer for so long, Shownae began to think he would simply deny the evidence of his own mind.

Eventually, Klyfin said, *How is it possible for you to talk to me through Shira?*

Not through Shira. Through Shownae.

Shownae? *That fraud! It is a trick!* Klyfin tried to wrench himself free from Shira's grip, but she held on doggedly.

Then perhaps you will believe this, Moohri said. *Send it, Shownae.*

A stylized depiction of their planet appeared beside Klyfin. The object weighed many times more than Shownae and had, until that moment, stood outside the entrance to the Spacefarer complex.

What manner of magic is this? Klyfin demanded weakly.

It is the manner by which we can bring Moohri home, Shownae explained, speaking for the first time. *And yes, it is me, Shownae. I sit on the bench across from your window. See for yourself.*

Klyfin raised his head and glowered at the psychic, who acknowledged the scowl with a small wave of his hand.

We can continue to speak this way, or you can invite me inside to explain all that has happened since Moohri's rocket misfired.

Clearly, neither alternative pleased Klyfin, but eventually he gave Shownae grudging permission to enter. Only then did Shira release her hold on Klyfin's arm. He rubbed it, while glaring at her as though she was unclean.

Shownae walked in, having run the gauntlet of at least a dozen people who favored him with looks of scorn and disgust. By then, Klyfin had returned to his seat behind the desk. Without waiting to be asked, Shownae sat down on the chair he had just vacated and regarded Klyfin levelly.

"May I assume you accept that this is not trickery, and that we may proceed from here?" Shownae asked.

"For now," Klyfin nodded. "You have 10 fractions; use them well."

It took considerably longer than that to bring Klyfin up-to-date and to convince him of the existence of not one, but two other

137

inhabited worlds. Jan, with the help of Ablakan, tried her best to converse in images with Klyfin, but he stubbornly refused to send the visuals in slow motion.

"Why do you make it difficult, when you seek her answers to your questions?" Shownae demanded in exasperation.

"I will not stoop to talk as if to a baby," Klyfin rumbled. "If she cannot keep up, she is an inferior life-form and not worth my time."

"This 'inferior life-form' was the first being on any of our three worlds to learn to teleport," Shownae informed him coldly. "Surely that is more important than quickly deciphering our images."

"That is what she tells you. How do you know it is true?"

Shownae managed to keep his tone neutral as he explained, "True telepaths like we three cannot hide anything of importance when we speak to each another. She is worthy of our respect – and yours."

But in the end, they were no further ahead than before. Klyfin staunchly refused to let Moohri occupy the isolation room.

"We have no way to test for alien microbes. Until we do, I cannot allow him to set foot on Orowa. It is too dangerous."

"What were you planning to do when you sent explorers to Shyr?" Shira interjected. "Just leave them there?"

"We have a team working on the problem. Of course, we have no plans of landing anyone anywhere until the team's work is complete. Which won't be for many years to come. Until then, Moohri will have to stay where he is." Klyfin stood up facing Shira, pointedly ignoring Shownae. "I have been more than generous with my time, in deference to you, Shira. But this meeting is now over. Shownae may only teleport Moohri into the chamber when I tell him it is safe to do so. And he can get that sculpture out of my office, now. Good fates."

He pressed a button, and his office door opened. Shownae and Shira had no choice but to leave.

* * *

138

Is that what you call a 'dodge'? Ablakan asked after he synopsized the meeting for Jan. They had ridden along at the edges of Shownae's focus so Klyfin wouldn't know they were there.

Yes, but with enough logic behind it to make it stick. Jan sighed dispiritedly.

Shownae and Shira had returned to her mover, where the conversation was expanded to include Tom and Jack. Ablakan was kept busy translating between the two species.

Moohri, I think this is what First Tweno meant when he said important people on your world might not want to help, Ablakan remarked.

Jan nodded, remembering the comment as it had been described to her by the youth. *Yes. Look at what will happen when you get back: You'll be a planetwide hero and have your job back as head of the space department. Klyfin is 'top dog' now, and I don't think he intends to give that up.*

He will not let me come home, Moohri summarized it glumly.

Shownae waffled. *Not by the isolation room. But perhaps there is another way, one that he does not control.*

I know of no other, Moohri said.

Ablakan brightened, as he asked hopefully, *Not on your world, but perhaps on yours, Jan?*

I think we do. Trouble is, if we brought Moohri here, our people would use him and us as guinea pigs; you can bet on it.

What is a 'guinea pig'? Ablakan asked.

Jack said, *It's an animal which researchers often use as test subjects before they try something on a human.* Jan could feel him picking his way carefully toward the 'in context' meaning. *If certain people got their hands on Moohri, they might start testing him, and those 'tests' could be most unpleasant.*

Jan felt the gasps of horror as the non-humans viewed movie snippets brought to Jack's mind by his description.

But why? Ablakan wailed.

Tom grimaced. *Humans are a peculiar species. They can't stand not knowing something, and will violate almost any rule of decency to find out. They justify it as 'research' or 'for the good of the people'. But oftentimes, it's just overpowering curiosity, and maybe fear of the unknown. It's hard to explain.*

Ablakan translated Moohri's disbelief. *But I am a fellow astronaut. Humans travel in space, too, and they also could crash. Would humans not expect them to be treated well, if another species rescued them?*

Jack's 'voice' was filled with regret as he said, *The average person would treat them well. But some scientists and government officials can be very clinical and unfeeling. Believe me when I tell you, Moohri is safer where he is.*

Ablakan clucked sadly to Jan. *That is why you are afraid to talk to important people on Earth about Moohri and Shownae and me and teleportation.*

Yes, dear. We can be a kind and helpful species, but some of us are – well, like Black, only more powerful.

I am sorry. I did not understand.

Don't worry, Jan assured him. *We'll find a way.*

Jack piped up with, *Why not send Moohri a lab rat, like we discussed?*

Tom shrugged. *Even if our labs confirm it is safe to send Moohri home, what makes you think Klyfin or Orowa's public health department would accept Earth's findings? For all they know, we could be out to destroy them. Even if they took us at face value, put yourself in their shoes. Would you entrust the health and safety of your species to someone else's unknown technologies, just to let one person return? I wouldn't.*

Moohri sighed. *Nor would I.*

So we're back where we started. Jack shook his head in frustration.

An idea was forming in Jan's mind. *Maybe not. Look at what we do have: Earth has the technology to check for diseases – even if it means keeping someone in isolation for a long period of*

140

time, like they do with pets being imported from some countries, right?

Jack nodded. *Pretty well, yes.*

Okay. First Tweno said Shalaii has a good track record at curing their diseases. And Orowa has at least one isolation chamber, but not the needed disease-screening technology, at least according to Klyfin.

Tom leaned forward in his chair. *So what you're proposing is that we and the Shalaians teach the Orowans. That could work, right, Jack?*

Maybe. We have strong links to the Centers for Disease Control in Atlanta and elsewhere in the country. If we could have those guys teach their counterparts on Orowa, Klyfin might have to relent.

Tom added, *At least it would make it harder for him to refuse, especially since they'll need that technology if they get much further into space exploration.*

Jack raised a cautionary digit. *But there's a risk. If some disease did get by them, they'd be bound to blame us, directly or indirectly. We'd become the pariahs of the universe.*

What is that? Ablakan asked.

Jan explained, *It means we'd be mistrusted and hated. What we're figuring out here will either set the stage for travel between planets, or complete insularity – uh, everyone keeping to themselves.*

Jack summed it up. *What we need is an isolation chamber on each planet, where people from anyplace in the universe can come and be decontaminated before stepping out into the mainstream of that planet's population. Then they would repeat the process before returning home. We have rudimentary procedures for humans, but who knows if they'd be safe for Orowans or Shalaians – or anyone else, for that matter.*

Once he had been brought up to speed on the conversation, Moohri imaged to Ablakan, *Looks like I will be here a while.*

Wait a minute, Tom said. *This may sound crazy –*

Compared to what? Jack demanded with droll sarcasm.

Tom grinned. *No, seriously . . . why don't we get samples from Moohri and Shownae and Shira – you know, blood, DNA, urine, skin, whatever, and have those tested in our labs under quarantine conditions. If both Shownae and Shira are disease-free, they'll be the benchmark to test Moohri's samples against before he leaves the planetoid.*

Yes, of course! I should have thought of that, Jack exclaimed. *And we could use the lab rat as a secondary control test.*

Jan laughed. *You do like that rat idea, don't you?*

He ignored her heckle. *If both Moohri and the rat come out clean, it should be pretty conclusive.*

Ablakan asked, *But again, would Klyfin accept the results?*

Jan said, hating the need for it, *He might if even afterwards Moohri and his family agreed to stay on some isolated island or something for an extended period, purportedly to ensure they were remaining healthy. And if Moohri resigned as Lead Spacefarer, that should sweeten the pot enough to make Klyfin cooperate.*

Ablakan had been translating the conversation to Moohri as it unfolded. Now he added, *Moohri says yes to samples. It is a good idea. Moohri thinks Klyfin might agree. I think maybe First Tweno can help make Klyfin agree. He promised to try if needed.*

Shownae said, *I will talk to Klyfin when we finish, since we are still here. If he will let me back in.*

Shira spoke for the first time. *I will be with you; he will dare not refuse.*

Let us know how it turns out, Jan transmitted through Ablakan. The humans broke off then.

Jack stretched his arms as he stood up. "At the risk of being an optimist –".

"Perish the thought!" Tom grinned.

"– I could see this working. And once each planet has one of those chambers – *if* they do build them – we could have an exchange program going, so people in all specialties could share their knowledge."

Tom expounded with a grin, "An intergalactic bull session of gargantuan proportions."

Jan's eyes lit up. "We could actually *meet* Ablakan and Moohri and Shownae."

"And all we have to do is get three planets to work together as a team," Jack pointed out. "Realistically, what are the chances?"

That wiped the grin off Tom's face. "If they're like Earth? Slim to none."

"But you forget," Jan predicted. "It would appeal to two of humanity's strongest motivators: greed and curiosity. When you've engaged those two elements, you've got it made. And I'm banking on those traits being universal."

Tom regarded her with comic reproach. "That's the most depressing thing I've ever heard."

CHAPTER 10

Ablakan looked out the window of the elegant suite which had been assigned to him and his mother. The city of Tabix stretched before him. From here he could see parklands and play areas. Far beyond, the ocean glistened in the sunlight like a bejeweled aqua carpet.

"Come, Ablakan," his mother warbled for the third time in as many lengths. "We must discuss our future."

"Mother, we do not yet know what it holds. First Tweno will speak to the other Firsts and the Primary. They might not be as understanding as our First is." Ablakan did his best to hide his disgust with her greedy fantasies.

"Nonsense, child," she said, strutting towards him. "We shall be rich, and the envy of all Shalaii. I will attend the most exclusive events. Nothing will be denied us, you shall see." She chattered on in this manner for some time, but Ablakan had ceased to actively listen. When Mother got on a track, she was unstoppable, and would repeat herself endlessly.

Ablakan took stock of their situation, what little of it he could see. Tweno was a 'good guy', as Jan called it. He would do his best to persuade his counterparts and the Primary to help Moohri. Ablakan had heard that the other Firsts were well-thought-of, but when the Primary's name came up, for some reason people became silent and looked around them as though someone might be watching. Ablakan realized he had never actually heard any comment made about her – either good or bad. To him, that seemed strange, since people were always eager to talk about each another, at least in private.

His mind turned to the recent discussion with, and afterwards without, Klyfin. How sad that Moohri's best hope of getting home lay in quitting his job and basically going into exile with his family for a time, as though he had committed some terrible crime. After all, it was not his fault some techno had wired the controls backwards.

Something niggled in Ablakan's mind, and he tried to catch it. Something about Klyfin, but try as he might, it eluded him.

There wasn't much he could do right now. The suite included a wonderful music system, but Mother was already playing her Chan-Shor, which Ablakan disliked. She would not let him put on the Player-box because the sounds would interfere with her music. So Ablakan had to content himself with looking out the myriad windows and seeing how many places he recognized from the map and pictures of Tabix he had seen in Learn-more.

His boredom was interrupted by the servant who had been assigned to them during their stay. He entered, bearing a large bowl of fruit and sweets. He also produced an envelope which he presented directly to Ablakan, to Epash's annoyance. She tried to grab it, but the servant intervened, stepping between them with an apologetic bow to Epash. His instructions had been specific – the envelope was for Ablakan. The minion further infuriated Epash by remaining close by until Ablakan had finished reading it. Only then did he take his leave.

"Well, what does it say?" Epash demanded.

"It is from First Tweno," Ablakan said, hoping this sort of thing would not happen again. After all, she was still his mother, and he had to obey her.

"The other Firsts will arrive tomorrow morning, and we have an audience with the Primary tomorrow afternoon." Ablakan swallowed, as something in the note caught his eye.

Epash wailed, "But I haven't a thing to wear for such an occasion. First Tweno did say we could have anything we want. Surely he cannot expect us to appear before the Primary in these rags. We must call that servant back at once."

"Mother," Ablakan said, grimacing at the inevitable explosion. "The audience is for the Firsts and me. Perhaps it is a mistake," he gulped. "But you were not invited."

"*WHAT?* Not invite the mother of the world's most important child? Give me that. You must have read it wrong."

Epash snatched it from his trembling fingers and read it twice before throwing it to the floor in outrage. For the next many lengths, Ablakan was subjected to a tirade on how badly the manners of the ruling class had deteriorated in recent times. Ablakan knew enough to nod and say nothing.

The servant eventually returned to offer her the services of the body salon and to say that a modest account had been set aside for her use in the purchase of clothing and other amenities for unnamed upcoming social engagements.

"That's more like it," Epash declared, flouncing out the door. "Be a good boy while I'm gone."

To Ablakan's surprise, the servant gave him a conspiratorial grin before shutting the door behind them. Ablakan smiled to himself. First Tweno was not only kind, he obviously read people well, though he was no telepath.

Left to his own devices, Ablakan had just settled himself in front of the Player-box when a different uniformed attendant arrived.

"You are to be clad and groomed by Tweno's own staff," he announced.

Ablakan gaped. "But I am unworthy of such an honor."

"Not from what I hear – sir," the attendant smiled, carefully pronouncing the English term.

Perhaps I will die tomorrow, Ablakan thought philosophically as he followed the servant down the hall. But at least I will do so in style.

* * *

"Jack." Jan was trying to spear a grape in the bowl with her fork. "How hard would it be for you to get us an appointment with the head of NASA?"

"I couldn't. But my boss could, though I'd prefer not to bring her into this. She'd tear a strip off me for having gone this far solo."

"Could you get us in to see his secretary?"

He shrugged. "Oh, sure, but that's as far as we'd get."

"Depends how we arrive."

Jack stared at her in dismay. "You don't mean teleport in?"

"Why not? In for a penny."

"You scare me sometimes, you know that?"

Tom chuckled. "Now you know what I've had to deal with all these years." He ducked as a grape narrowly missed his left ear.

"So how much would you suggest we tell him?" Jack wanted to know.

Jan gazed at the ceiling in thought. "Might as well 'fess up the whole thing – except the part about Black. We'd better leave him out of this for now."

"Hmm, yes. You do realize there's a better than even chance we'll end up in the pokey, or guests of the FBI or something," Jack warned them.

Jan shook her head and said, with more hope than actual confidence, "Why should they lock us up, if we're handing them all the goodies? I think it's all in how we present it. If we go in looking self-assured, and point out that we've done all the preliminary work for them and are now bringing them into the loop with the high-levels on the other two worlds, what can they do? They need us to communicate with Shalaii and Orowa, and we're offering to do so for free."

"She does have a point there," Tom said.

"I hate it when I can't see the trap," Jack moaned. "But it's bound to be there, just waiting to trip us up."

Jan admitted, still feeling guilty about it, "We're the only ones in this galactic drama who have put very little on the line. I think we owe it to the others to at least try."

Jack sighed, "You're right, of course. But I sure don't like it."

"Either way," Tom prophesied. "We'll make it into the history books."

Jack pointed a finger at him. "Just remember, those books are full of people who met a messy end."

* * *

For Ablakan, most of the afternoon was spent in the dizzying pursuit of presentability. When the staff had finished with him, he stared at the reflection of a total stranger in the mirror. His new clothes felt stiff and unnatural. His mane shone with an unlikely luster, and where it had been straight this morning, it now held waves and curls. The thufts above his eyebanks were trimmed so close they were all but invisible. Ablakan was not at all sure he liked this 'new look' of theirs, but he resolved not to let on, lest they think him ungrateful. He was escorted back to his suite, after being treated to an enormous muchipans. Only once before had he feasted on this delicacy, and he polished it off with gusto.

Back in his suite, he found a much-transformed Epash admiring herself in the full-length mirror in her sleeping room. As he had feared, she made a big fuss over him and refused to let him change back into his comfortable old clothes which, she said, were destined for the recycler.

A gentle 'knock' in his mind rescued him from further gushings. He excused himself and hurried to his private chamber to accordion down onto the bed. Shownae was reporting in.

Klyfin had refused re-entry to him and Shira, claiming to have prior commitments for the afternoon. Something about an improved thruster unit. He had reluctantly scheduled a short appointment for them for the following morning.

Ablakan sat up abruptly, remembering what had eluded him before.

Shownae, he imaged. *Think back to when you were telling Klyfin why Moohri's rocket missed Shyr. Do not think about what Klyfin said then, just what his feelings were.*

There was a short pause.

He was not surprised. In fact, he was feeling smug, Shownae imaged back, astonished. *He* knew!

Yes, Ablakan confirmed. *I believe it was not an accident.*

Shownae's mental voice shook with indignation. *He wanted Moohri dead, so he could have his job. But how can we prove it?*

Perhaps Moohri can find the evidence if he checks the rocket.

I will ask him to do so at once. Thank you, Ablakan.

Before signing off, Ablakan urged, *Be well, and tread carefully.* The humans would need to know about this, too, he realized. His call was promptly answered, and he told Jan of their findings.

So that's what was going on, she said. *I felt something, but not enough to identify it. What a monster!*

Yes. Moohri must not give up his job. Klyfin cannot be left in charge of space travel.

Jan nodded emphatically. *You got that right. We're just working out how to get a meeting with the head of our own space agency. I don't know what will happen to us when we do so, but we've decided to teleport in, to make certain he'll see us. We plan to tell him everything – except about Black, and for now we won't say anything about you 'porting. Shownae has already let it be known he does, of course, so we can say about that.*

Be careful, Jan. When you need me, I will be ready if you have to go to 'safe haven'.

Thanks, dear, Jan smiled. His self-confidence had indeed grown since he teleported Black to Shyr. *How's everything going with you?*

Ablakan fidgeted. *First Tweno's staff made new clothes for me and cut my thufts and made my mane all shiny and wavy. They want me to look 'presentable' for the Primary. The other Firsts will be coming here tomorrow morning, then we all go see the Primary in the afternoon.*

Well, you know I'll be there for you when you need me.

Ablakan sighed. *So many people to see, and all of them dangerous.*

How true. But even if the very worst happened to all of us, we can still live on good old Shyr.

With bad old Black.

Shyr's big enough, we'd likely never cross paths, Jan reassured him before they separated.

To the relief of all concerned, the balance of the day held no further surprises or major events. Ablakan and Shownae took advantage of the respite to prepare for the morrow.

Jan decided it was time she learn to 'port herself, as well as others. It turned out to be relatively easy, and by evening she had bounced herself, sometimes alone and sometimes with one or both of the men in tow, all over their little hilltop. Satisfied at last, she did one practice 'port as far as the village and back, and pronounced herself ready for the coming day.

* * *

On the planetoid, Moohri painstakingly dismantled what was left of the thruster's wiring into the main console and found, as expected, that the wires had been cut and spliced onto their opposing controls. He was careful not to touch them, lest he remove fingerwhorls or other incriminating evidence he hoped would be there. After several hours, he had freed the panel, its casing and various attachments which would have to be brought to Orowa by Shownae as one unit for proper analysis.

Privately, he decided that Klyfin would pay dearly for the anguish he had caused Moohri and his family. Using the precious recorder his wife had thoughtfully included in her carton of supplies, Moohri taped a detailed report that would accompany the evidence. He addressed it to his loyal friend, Trikon, third-in-command in the space department. At least, he had been third when Moohri was there. Trikon would ensure the panel received a thorough inspection.

* * *

One other person enjoyed what he considered a well-earned rest. In a small meadow on Shyr, Dr. Black feasted on his favorite local berries, symbolically enjoying the fruits of his labor. He had just teleported a rock to the other side of the clearing.

* * *

Morning birds *cherree*'ed the birth of a new day, and Jan awakened refreshed and optimistic. Not that she had a reason to

150

think their plan was foolproof, but sometimes you just had to give it your best shot and trust that it would be enough.

Before long, it was 'showtime' (in Jack's lexicon), and he phoned the secretary's office. "Is the Chief in this morning?"

"Yes, Jack, but he's got a full schedule. Perhaps you should send him a memo, via your boss. You know he's a stickler for channels."

"Can you hold a moment, Diane?" Jack covered the receiver. "Have you got her?" he whispered to Jan.

She nodded, hand on Jack's arm and eyes out of focus.

"We'll just pop in for a minute, okay?" he said into the phone.

"If you insist. But you can't see him."

A moment later she stared uncomprehendingly at the strange man and woman who suddenly stood before her, along with Jack. All three had been holding hands and now released each other. The phone fell back in its cradle as Diane tried to make sense of the impossible.

"Are you sure the Chief can't see us for just a few minutes?" Jack wheedled.

Diane pressed a button on her telephone pad. They heard a muted voice respond.

"Please forgive the interruption, sir. Jack Foxworth and –". She looked at the others, who dutifully supplied their names. "– Jan and Tom Brody to see you . . . Yes, I realize that, but they just 'popped in'. . . No, I mean they *really* just 'popped in', from nowhere at all. The office was empty, and I was talking to Jack – Mr. Foxworth, on the phone. Then they were here in my office. I haven't even unlocked the door yet." Jan noticed perspiration had formed on the younger woman's brow.

From the intercom came another low-pitched murmur. Diane cocked her head towards the door, and said rather weakly, "He'll see you now."

"Shall we?" Jan asked the others.

"Might as well," Tom sighed.

An instant later they stood in front of Dr. Lesley Saunders himself. He regarded them, his expression deadpan.

Jack stepped forward and extended his hand. "Good of you to see us, sir."

After a moment's hesitation, Saunders accepted the gesture and briefly shook hands, doing the same with his other visitors. He waved them to chairs.

"Not a bad entrance," he acknowledged. "I assume there's a story behind this?"

"A beaut," Jack assured him. "But Diane told us you're quite busy. Do you want all of it, or just the high points?"

Saunders pursed his lips, sizing up the trio. Then he leaned forward and depressed a button. "Diane, please reschedule my 10:00 to this afternoon. And no further interruptions till I'm through here."

"Yes, sir," emanated from the box.

Saunders turned a quizzical eye on his visitors. "I assume there are no more of you coming?"

"Not physically, anyway," Jack said.

Saunders raised an eyebrow but made no comment.

"I'll turn the floor over to Jan Brody now, as it's primarily her story."

By morning's end, they had presented all pertinent details to Saunders, except any mention of Ryan Black or of Ablakan's ability to teleport. Saunders' requisite conversation with Ablakan was cut short when First Tweno's messenger announced that the other Firsts had arrived and wished to meet the youth. Fortunately, the chat had lasted long enough to answer Saunders' most pressing questions.

Efforts to converse directly with Shownae and Moohri ended in the usual confusion. Jan wondered how humans and Orowans would ever communicate on their own. Perhaps in time her Orowan colleagues would learn English, but Jan doubted that humans would ever master their language or imagery.

Saunders leaned back in his chair as he recuperated from his effort to decipher Orowan visuals. He fixed Jack with an unblinking glare. "You've been party to all this and never said a word. Meanwhile, we've been spending megabucks scanning the cosmos for just what you've found. Give me one good reason not to send you packing."

Jack swallowed. "May I speak frankly, sir?"

Saunders gave a curt nod.

"Right now our main concern is Moohri. Next time it could be one of our astronauts who gets stranded. We didn't know whether you'd help us or turn us over to the FBI or something."

Saunders grunted and directed his gaze at Jan. "So I take it what you want most is protection from such interference."

Three heads bobbed vehemently.

Silence reigned, except for the sound of Saunders tapping his pen-tip on the desk. Jan held her breath, waiting for him to reach a decision.

"Alright. As of now, you two –". Saunders pointed towards the Brodys. "– Will work in 'Special Projects' out at Ames Research Center. We'll figure out a title for you later."

Jan gulped. "Research Center as in a *lab*?"

"*Cognition* Lab. And no, you won't be tested. You're to carry on as you have been."

"Thank you, sir." Jan was almost weak with relief.

Saunders began making notes on a pad in front of him. "I'll arrange for the labwork on the Orowan specimens to be done there as well, once you get them."

"And a rat to send Moohri?" Jack put in, in such a hopeful tone that both Jan and Tom chuckled.

Saunders looked from one to the other. "Did I miss something?"

"Sorry," Jan explained between giggles. "It's been an, um, *pet* idea of Jack's, is all."

Tom groaned at the pun, but the others studiously ignored it.

Saunders' face relaxed into a ghost of a smile. "Very well, Foxworth, you may have your rat."

"Appreciate it, sir," Jack grinned back.

The pen was tapping again. "Are you working on anything that will fall apart if you're not there?"

"Not really, sir. I'm in Propulsion, which'll need a complete rethink, now that we've got us a resident teleporter."

"So it will. I'm reassigning you to keep these two in line and monitor interplanetary activities until I get a solid framework in place. Over time, I'll be adding to your workload and job description if this proceeds the way I hope. You are to report everything directly to me, for the time being – and I mean *everything*."

Saunders took a business card from its holder on his desk and scribbled a number on the back of it. He handed it to Jack.

"This is my direct line here. Use it only in an emergency. And you are to tell no one about this situation outside of Ames' management. I'll brief them myself before you arrive." He blinked. "At least, no one else on this planet."

Jack pocketed the card. "Understood, and thanks. Uh, before we go, may I have a private word with you?"

"Make it short," Saunders grunted. He made a show of consulting his watch.

Tom eyed Jack suspiciously before opening the door for Jan to precede him into the secretary's office. Diane watched them take a seat, her expression a mixture of awe and annoyance. Patently, she felt she might somehow be blamed for this breach of protocol. Jack walked into the waiting room less than five minutes later.

"What was that all about?" Jan asked.

"Oh, just boy-talk."

She glowered at him. "What are you cooking up now?"

"You'll see." Jack turned his smile on the secretary. "Thanks for everything, Diane."

They silently joined hands and an instant later, Diane was alone in the office. The intercom buzzed, and she hurried in.

154

Saunders seemed in good humor, and his only reference to the morning's events was to demand absolute secrecy.

* * *

When the attendant informed the youth that his presence was required in the meeting room, Ablakan hastily apologized to Dr. Saunders and broke the connection. He hoped he had not caused trouble for his human colleagues, but Firsts were not to be kept waiting. As Ablakan hurried down the hall after the attendant, he worried that his new clothes might be wrinkled from him having lain on the bed.

Ablakan found the three Firsts talking casually in the sitting room beyond the curtains. First Tweno smiled at him as he was ushered in.

"There you are. Come, let me introduce you to First Lisham of Tunan, and First Konapi of Enaxat. I have told them all about you and your great adventure."

Ablakan approached and bowed low before each First. He was motioned to a chair in front of the two new rulers and beside First Tweno.

"We are alone here, and titles can be cumbersome," First Tweno noted. "Why don't we dispense with titles and speak person-to-person?" The others murmured their agreement.

Lisham said kindly, "That includes you, Ablakan."

The boy gulped at the thought of such familiarity, but bowed in compliance.

Tweno turned to the other Firsts. "I am sure you have many questions for Ablakan."

Konapi raised his hand. "I think I understand the situation well enough. What I really want is to talk to these aliens."

"As do I," Lisham smiled. "Who would have believed it possible?"

Ablakan cleared his throat nervously. "Jan and Tom and Jack – those are the humans – are meeting with the head of their space department right now. I was just talking with them when you called," he added to Tweno. "And before that, I talked with the

155

Orowans. There has been a lot happening." Ablakan gave them an abridged version of his conversations.

"I see," Tweno said, on being told that Klyfin had sabotaged the thruster controls. He made no further comment, but Ablakan sensed there was much going on behind Tweno's natural mental shield.

"Would you like to meet Shownae and Moohri?"

The Firsts glanced at one another and nodded. While Ablakan put through the calls, Tweno explained in a low voice the procedure the others would have to follow to achieve mental contact.

Ablakan was again party to the get-acquainted ritual. He was becoming quite comfortable with this part of the process, since those involved were so focused on each other, they barely noticed Ablakan's presence.

With the pleasantries out of the way, Ablakan paid closer attention, for each meeting brought with it a fresh exchange of questions and ideas.

Lisham set the tone by imaging to Moohri, *What was it like, being out among the stars?*

Quiet. Everywhere there was silence. I have never felt so awed, nor so small and alone.

Ablakan could feel Moohri's present loneliness sharpen, and hoped they would soon change topic.

The moon you were trying to go around . . . would it support life? Konapi wondered. *None of ours has an atmosphere.*

That is what we were hoping, since it is widely forested. I admit, I have long dreamed of starting a colony there.

To Ablakan, Moohri sounded wistful and slightly embarrassed, the way adults do when they admit to fantasies Ablakan would consider perfectly natural.

Tweno leaned forward, his expression intrigued. *Is that what your trip around Shyr was for? A prelude to landing there?*

Yes, although as the humans pointed out, we don't yet know how to test for possible diseases, Moohri explained. *We can't land there till we do.*

Konapi cleared his throat. *Forgive me if what I am about to say seems indelicate, but perhaps your present circumstances will speed up that process.*

Klyfin does not want me back. He is the reason I am here at all.

Tweno nodded sympathetically. *Yes, we heard. But even as the Leader, it won't be easy for him to justify waiting, when the need is so obvious and urgent.*

Sirs, Ablakan interjected. *If Klyfin doesn't inform anyone else that Moohri is alive, he can just tell Shira and Shownae his staff are working on it. Who would know if they really are?*

Shownae growled, *I would. He has to let his shield down sometime, and I will keep checking till I know.*

Be careful, Shownae, Tweno urged. *Remember, he already tried to kill once.*

Moohri added, *And should have succeeded, by all odds.*

We will take our leave now, Tweno said. *But be heartened, Leader Moohri. You are not alone in this. We will help in any way we can.*

After a brief rest break, Ablakan checked on Jan. He was pleased to find they were now back home, packing, so at least they were not to be imprisoned. Since they were in a hurry, Ablakan explained to the visiting Firsts the need for this first meeting to be brief. The Firsts seemed happy about this as well, for the efforts of first contact with Moohri and Shownae had taken its toll. Ablakan could tell the rulers were in the early stages of fatigue.

Following the initial exchange of greetings, Konapi asked Jan, *Is your space department willing to help?*

Yes, to whatever extent they can. I suspect their main contribution will be in helping to find out whether Moohri is

157

medically safe to return to Orowa. From a human standpoint, anyway.

That would be most useful, Konapi agreed.

Ablakan smiled quietly to himself. Instead of relying on images, he was routing the Firsts' queries in Shalaian through his own mind and muting them to a level humans found comfortable before translating them into English for Jan.

Tweno offered, *As I had mentioned, we also have expertise in locating and destroying disease-causing germs. Perhaps after your people have run their tests, we could run ours on the same samples.*

Wonderful idea! Thank you, sir. Then Jan's voice turned apologetic. *Forgive me for cutting you short, especially after such a generous offer. My husband and boss are carrying out boxes, huffing and puffing. I can feel them looking at me pointedly.*

Lisham laughed good-naturedly. *It is usually I who am accused of being lazy. Thank you for meeting with us at such a busy time.*

They exchanged good-byes, and the Firsts removed their hands from Ablakan's arms.

Konapi yawned. "I would not want to do this every day. But it was a remarkable experience."

"We are not alone," Lisham beamed happily. "And our 'neighbors' are good people. Well, most of them," he amended, obviously referring to Klyfin.

And Black, Ablakan thought privately. He must remember to check in on him soon.

Tweno smiled down at Ablakan. "You have done well. But I can see you are tired, too. Go rest. We will send for you this afternoon. You will accompany us to meet the Primary."

Ablakan bowed and left the room. The Primary. The idea excited and terrified him at the same time. But then, he reminded himself, he had been nervous about meeting the other Firsts, and they had turned out to be as nice as Tweno. He should not 'borrow trouble', as Jan called it. The Primary lived in a grand palace on a majestic island, a mere 50-longs cruiser ride from the tip of Tabix. Never had he expected to set foot on such hallowed ground.

Ablakan followed a servant to his quarters. He was in high spirits. All in all, things were turning out well, just as Jan had believed they would. And as an added bonus, his mother was absent. A message informed him she was attending a luncheon.

He found a sumptuous meal of his own awaited him in the cook-keeper. Ablakan ate heartily from the platters decorously arranged for his pleasure. That kept him busy for a time. With nothing else to do, and realizing he was feeling 'snoozy' (he liked the feel of that English word in his mind), Ablakan carefully positioned himself on the bed and drifted off to sleep.

* * *

"I hate leaving home," Tom grumbled as he picked a box of books off the desk in the Reading Room. "Tommy never waters the roses right. They're always thirsty or half-drowned by the time we get back." Tommy was their housesitter of choice, as well as their paperboy.

Jan morosely sorted through the remaining books. "I know. Hopefully it won't be for too long."

Jack taped yet another carton shut. "I wouldn't count on that. I'd suggest boarding your indoor plants with someone in the village, if you can, and closing up the house as though you'll be gone for a long time. It could be years, you know," he added gently.

"I'm sorry, Tom." Jan sighed dispiritedly as she reached for the phone to find a new home for the plants in their sunroom. The men packed in silence while Jan made the arrangements.

"Look on the bright side," Jack said to Tom. "You've been drooling about a new telescope. Now you'll have access to some of the best equipment in the world – and it's all just a 'port away."

"You really think so?" Tom brightened visibly.

Jack favored Jan with a wicked grin as she finished leaving a message on an answering machine. "And I would guess, a much inflated bank account, as well. Just think how much that would piss off that witch, Ariana!"

"Jack Foxworth, does your mother know you have such a mean streak?"

"Where do you think I got it?" he countered, then sighed happily. "Yup, I'm a right mean cuss, alright. Not to mention – for the time being anyway – your boss."

"Boss as a noun or verb?" Jan wanted to know.

Jack raised both hands defensively. "Considering how easily you could send me to Shyr, most definitely noun only."

"That's good to know. So, where exactly is this lab?"

"Northern California. Specifically, Moffett Field; that's in Silicon Valley. Saunders is arranging digs for us – two later, if you'd prefer your privacy. Its usually kept for visiting dignitaries but, at least for now, we rate."

Tom glanced at Jan, and she nodded emphatically. "One will do for all of us, if you're willing."

"Love to! Where you folks are, the action is. I haven't had this much fun in years." He grinned boyishly at them.

"Thrill-seeker," Jan admonished him.

Jack looked smug. "That I am. But of course, there's a practical side to it, too. I'm supposed to monitor your communication with the offworlders, remember?"

Silence reigned for most of the next couple hours, as each set their hand to securing the house for an extended leave of absence. Jan's eyes were wet when the time came to lock the door and turn away. Tom held her, rubbing her back consolingly.

Jack tactfully became interested in a nonexistent smudge on his rental car. Mrs. Crickshaw, who had called back and agreed to adopt Jan's plants, had also kindly volunteered to pick up the Brodys' car from the airport and keep it at her home till they returned.

"Ah, well, onward and, uh, downward," Jack said, as they got in their respective vehicles. They had debated simply 'porting to Ames, but that seemed too flamboyant, so flights were booked

160

instead. Their precious personal effects would be sent to them later by rail.

As the short caravan started down the hill, Jan looked back, wondering sadly if they would ever see their home again.

* * *

While the trio jetted toward California, Ablakan and the Firsts jetted over the sea in a private ocean cruiser, towards the island estate of Shalaii's Primary. Nobody spoke much on the trip. Ablakan could feel the tension grow the closer they came to the island. Once again, he checked to ensure that Jan, nestled so quietly beside his mind, was still there. Something told him that he would need her help this day.

The island looked quite small from a distance, but as they approached it, he realized its magnitude. Uniformed guards met them at the jetty and escorted them, with deference, to the palace. If Ablakan had found Tweno's tower impressive, its opulance paled compared to that of the palace. He kept falling behind because one item or another of incredible grandeur beguiled him.

Finally, Tweno slowed till he was beside Ablakan. "It would be most unwise to keep the Primary waiting. She is not known for her patience."

"I'm sorry, First," Ablakan said, chastened. He was careful to not look around him as he followed the others down the massive hallway and into the throne room where she sat.

As each entered, they bowed deeply, continuing to do so until they had reached a dotted line on the floor a short distance from her throne. There, with heads bowed, they waited to be 'recognized'.

"You may rise, my friends," the Primary said in ringing tones. Slowly, Ablakan raised his head and looked, for the first time, upon the Primary. He had only seen pictures of her in her youth. It came as somewhat of a shock that she was exceedingly old underneath her face-colorings and majestic flowing robes.

"So this is the child you spoke of. Come here, boy," she beckoned with a bony finger.

161

Timidly, Ablakan approached her.

She looked him up and down, then turned doubtfully towards the Firsts. "He doesn't look like much. What is so special about him?"

Ablakan hung his head, deeply ashamed. He was unworthy, after all.

Tweno cleared his throat. "Primary, we dared not speak freely on the hear-other. We would now beg your indulgence in listening to his story. It is most remarkable, and we three have proven it true."

She turned her glassy eyebanks upon Ablakan with renewed interest. "A story, have you? We shall see. You may proceed."

In his mind, Jan cautioned, *Be very precise, Ablakan. I feel a deep imbalance in her.*

I know, he replied mentally, feeling trapped. There was no alternative but to go through with it.

"Most magnificent Primary, my name is Ablakan," he said, forcing himself to maintain eye contact as he spoke. He had only gotten to the part about meeting Jan when the old woman let out a guffaw and stamped her foot.

"You are a good storyteller. Most entertaining."

"No, Primary, it is true," Ablakan hastily assured her.

Tweno put a hand on Ablakan's shoulder. "He does speak true, Primary. We all have spoken to her."

"Yes, of course," she agreed. "Realism improves a good story."

Lisham spoke up. "Primary, she is here in mind, awaiting your pleasure, if you will permit it. But may the boy finish? He has barely begun, and there is so much more to tell."

"He may," the Primary intoned, then pointed a gnarled finger at him. "But make it quick. I am too busy for long entertainment."

Ablakan looked imploringly at Tweno. The First shook his head and murmured, "Continue, boy. Just the important parts."

Almost mechanically, Ablakan explained what led to Moohri's crash, and the efforts to date to rescue him. Black, and Ablakan's own 'porting abilities were, of course, left out.

When at last he finished, the old woman threw back her head and roared with laughter. The three Firsts exchanged glances of consternation. Ablakan noticed that her own guards were staring at the floor in obvious embarrassment for their monarch.

"Such a tale as I have never heard," she crowed. "You have done well, boy. I am not easily amused."

"But Primary," Tweno exclaimed. "It is all true. We have brought you proof." He bowed and handed her the picture encyclopedia.

Her laughter faded as she stared at it, flabbergasted. "What is this?"

Ablakan said, "It is a gift from Jan, Primary. If you look through it, you will see pictures of people and creatures and things from her planet, Earth."

She opened the book, turning page after page incredulously. At last, her eyes bored into Ablakan's and she said, just above a whisper, "Do you mean, it is all true? This 'Jan', these planets, teleportation – all of it, true?"

"Yes, Primary," Ablakan said, and the Firsts nodded solemnly.

She stood up with an effort and shook her royal reed at her Firsts. "How long? How long has this been going on under your nose slits?"

Tweno said carefully, "We informed you as soon as we learned of it, Primary."

Jan, it is turning bad. Ablakan began to quake.

I know. Just stay calm, and don't speak unless you have to. Let the Firsts handle it.

The old woman's voice rose. "And you let this boy *talk* to them? Even as we speak, this 'Jan' is talking to him, using him to learn about us – where we are, how to find us, how to destroy us?"

Konapi cried, "No, Primary, you do not understand –."

Ablakan's knees threatened to give way under him.

Easy, Ablakan, don't do anything to draw attention to yourself, Jan cautioned. *I've felt that feeling before. She is insane.*

Ablakan knew Jan was right, but all he could do was stare at the old ruler as her rage grew.

Tweno stepped forward to stand between her and Ablakan. "Most wise Primary, they are not coming here. They only wish to speak with us. There is much we could learn from them –"

"Fools!" she screamed. "They are invaders! They will destroy us. And you would let them come, and call them 'friend'." Spittle puffed from her mouth as she raved on, brandishing her reed. "I will not stand for it. You have betrayed us – you and that – that demon child!"

Ablakan's blood froze in his veins. He felt as though he was watching some other boy standing there, about to be struck dead.

Ablakan, Jan told him urgently. *Hold your mind steady. I'm here. No matter what happens, I'm here. I'll keep you safe; you know I will.*

"Primary!" Tweno's voice boomed, and Ablakan gasped, amazed at his daring. "You are making a mistake. We have a chance here to grow as a species, to exchange learning and technology –"

"How *dare* you raise your voice to me!" she thundered. "You who have doomed your own people. At least I shall have the satisfaction of seeing you die first – you and your collaborators. *Guards! Seize them!* Kill them all. Here! Now!"

Ablakan felt as though he had been rooted to the spot. He wanted to run and run, but Jan kept saying, *Don't move, dear. Not a hair. Keep absolutely still. Trust me on this. If it becomes necessary, you know I'll get you out of there in a flash. But right now, don't budge an inch.*

The guards, instead of rushing to behead him or run him through, kept looking at the floor in front of them, not moving.

"*NOW!*" the old woman roared at a decibel level that hurt the ear and made everyone in the room cringe. Then her eyes fastened on the book in her hands, and she flung it with all her might at the closest guard.

Before he realized what he was doing, Ablakan 'ported the precious item to his outstretched hands, just before it would have struck the guard's unprotected face. In stunned silence, all eyes turned on Ablakan.

The old woman screeched, "There, you see? He is bedeviled. *KILL HIM!*"

Tweno stepped forward then, and in an infinitely sad voice, said, "Primary, forgive me, but it is time for you to step down. My colleagues and I have seen enough. It is our unhappy duty to relieve you of your throne."

"You would not dare!" she rasped in a hoarse whisper, while looking at each First in turn. Lisham and Konapi nodded firmly.

In desperation, she pointed her reed at her guards. "You have sworn to protect me. Do your duty!"

For several agonizing moments, nobody moved. All eyes were on the guards, who continued to stare at the floor, motionless.

Then Tweno placed a gentle, supporting hand under the ruler's arm.

The old woman snatched it away. "No! You cannot do this. I am Primary. My loyal subjects will not stand for it." Her voice changed abruptly to a pleading whine. "I have many years left to me. Do not take my throne. I can be kind. Perhaps I was wrong. You may keep your lives. You may go now. Yes, go, go." She made shooing motions with her hands.

"I am sorry, Marinthias," Tweno said kindly. He firmly captured the Primary's hand. She seemed about to resist, but one final look at the others changed her mind. She lowered her eyes and allowed herself to be led from the throne she had occupied her whole adult life.

Tweno murmured soothingly, "I will introduce you to my litter-brother. He has a wonderful way about him, and I believe he will help you feel like your own self again very soon."

Marinthias followed him from the room like a child, moaning deep in her throat. She looked neither right nor left as she departed. Three uniformed attendants were waiting in the hallway. Each smiled reassuringly at Tweno. One of them took Marinthias' hand from Tweno and said, "We will care for her well until you are ready to leave."

"I thank you."

Tweno returned to the throne room with a heavy sigh. His counterparts were still staring, dumbfounded, at Ablakan.

Tweno frowned at the boy. "What did you do, just then?"

Ablakan's voice cracked as he started to speak. He cleared his throat, and tried again. "Forgive me, First, for deceiving you. I also have learned to teleport, and I taught Shownae to do so as well. It was necessary so he could send Moohri food from his planet, and so that later he can bring him home. I thought it wise that each planet have one person on it who could teleport."

"So no planet would have an advantage over the others," Tweno nodded approval. "And I suppose Jan would have rescued you, if the guards had attacked."

"Yes, First," Ablakan whispered. He looked up at Tweno beseechingly. "Sir, all we ever wanted to do is help Moohri get home."

Tweno gave his shoulder a reassuring squeeze. "I believe you, Ablakan, and it is an admirable desire." He turned to the others. "We have much to discuss."

"Indeed," Konapi agreed.

Lisham addressed the guards. "We thank you for your forbearance. Would you leave us now, that we may select a new Primary?"

As one, the guards bowed and left the room, single-file.

Ablakan looked at Tweno. "I should leave, too, while you choose."

"No, this concerns you also," Tweno said with a quiet smile. "Just wait at the far end of the room."

166

Ablakan bowed and trotted to the chairs against the wall. His mind was still reeling from the tragedy that had so narrowly been averted, not to mention the history he had just witnessed. It was only the second time that a Primary had seen deposed for mental incompetence.

He watched with interest the process of choosing a new supreme ruler. From his Learn-more, he knew that one of the three Firsts would become Primary by the simple process of each voting for the one they felt would best serve Shalaii's interests. Ablakan would have thought each candidate would nominate himself, but historically that had seldom been the case. After the new Primary had been selected, they would discuss candidates for the now-vacant position of First.

As Ablakan watched, the three leaders formed a triangle, back-to-back on an angle. Each wrote down his choice for Primary. Then they turned towards each other and simultaneously held their vote out towards the center of the triangle.

Had that been successful, the formation should then have been broken, but this did not occur. Tweno spoke quietly, his words too low for Ablakan to understand. The process was again repeated. This time, when they broke formation, Tweno motioned for Ablakan to approach.

"My colleagues have chosen me as the new Primary."

Ablakan beamed at him then, remembering his manners, bowed low.

"But there is more," Tweno said, his eyebanks twinkling. "You are to remain here with me, so that I may personally oversee your tutelage. You shall bear the title of Interpreter and Alien Ambassador. And you must teach me this 'English'."

Ablakan looked at his new Primary in utter confusion. "But a Primary has no time for teaching children; you have a planet to run."

"I also have a new First to train," the Primary smiled. He placed a hand on Ablakan's shoulder. "Once you have reached the Age of Arrival, you shall become First of Pantai."

And the boy who had set up communications between three planets and 'ported Black to Shyr fainted dead away.

CHAPTER 11

On Earth, Jan's initial impulse was to 'port him out of there. But moments later she felt Ablakan's body being gently lifted and supported, and realized those with him were rendering assistance, not causing harm. She remained at the edge of his mind, uncertain what to do next. Presently, she realized he was on his way 'up'.

As he awakened, Jan poured a sense of calm and security into his still-befuddled mind. He rallied around this nucleus, quickly regaining self-awareness.

Are you alright?

Yes, very alright, Ablakan replied. *I will call you later, please?*

Any time. Take care, dear.

Obviously, some other extraordinary event had happened. While he had been waiting in the bleachers, so to speak, Ablakan had explained to Jan how First Tweno had dethroned the old Primary. The process for choosing a new one was fascinating indeed, but just when she was about to find out who would hold the title, Ablakan swooned. Now her curiosity wouldn't be appeased till he called her back.

Ooh, I hate waiting, Jan thought, as she took her mental leave. No sooner did she open her eyes than her companions were upon her, eager for news.

"It's good – that much I can tell you. But the frustrating part is, I missed the ending."

"How could you miss it? You were right there!" Tom exclaimed.

"In mind only." She filled them in on what she knew.

Jack mused, "Tweno must have gotten it, what with Pantai being the largest, most populated continent. But I can't see Ablakan fainting over that."

"No, it was something unexpected. I'd give my first paycheck for just a little hint," Jan sighed wistfully.

"Maybe I was wrong about your salary," Jack teased. "Maybe we expect you to work for free, out of the goodness of your heart."

Jan eyed him pointedly. "*We?*"

"Well, symbolically-speaking."

Jan leaned forward, feigning great interest. "Just how much are *we* making, anyway?"

"I don't know," Jack admitted. "Not even my own. For all I know it could be a demotion."

Tom tapped Jack's shoulder to get his attention. "Am I supposed to be working, too, or just keeping you two company? Remember, I'm retired."

"Not any more, you're not." But when pressed for details, Jack refused to give them any.

Jan nudged Tom. "Looks like our boss was a busy boy while he was closeted with the big muckymuck."

"That I was," Jack agreed, looking insufferably smug.

Tom fixed him with a look of exasperation. "You mean to say you expect me to take on a job, but you won't tell me what it is or how much I'll be making?"

"Precisely."

Tom turned toward Jan with an nasty smile. "Hon, I've been feeling sorry for Black of late, up there all alone. I bet he could use some company."

"It's a thought," Jan admitted. "But to be fair, I suppose we *should* wait till we see what Jackie-boy here has cooked up."

Jack stated, a little too brightly, "Did you know there's an obscure clause in your Master Agreement which specifically prohibits the teleporting of one's boss without his permission?"

"Uh-huh," Tom said, then blinked. "With Jan on the payroll – presumably – they may just have to put in such a clause."

* * *

Ablakan peered at the anxious faces of the three Firsts – no, two Firsts and a Primary. He was reclining on a bed so large he couldn't see the other edge of it from where he lay. Noting their concern, he sat up and swung his legs over the side of the bed.

Tweno's face softened in relief. "Are you feeling better?"

170

"Yes, thank you, First – I mean, Primary." Ablakan looked an apology at his ruler. "Did – did you really become Primary? I wasn't dreaming?"

Lisham smiled and shook his head. "No indeed. Tweno is Primary, and you are to become – now, don't wooze again! – a First when you are old enough."

Ablakan knew he was grinning foolishly, but he couldn't seem to help it. Then another thought occurred to him, and he sobered. "Is it just because I can teleport and talk to Jan and Moohri and Shownae? Because I will always be glad to do that for you. You don't have to make me a First."

"That is part of it, yes," Tweno admitted. "But your skills alone would not have won you the post. You have shown great wisdom and resourcefulness in your dealings with the offworlders, Ablakan, and much compassion. These qualities above all others are necessary in those who would govern.

But understand: you will have to make sacrifices as well. There will be less time for play. You have a great deal to learn, and as you become capable in those areas, you will be taking on the duties of a First. Until then, I will remain First of Pantai, as well as assuming the responsibilities of Primary."

"I will learn as fast as I can, sir."

"I know you will," Tweno assured his protégé. "But on top of that, we will need you to represent Shalaii and her interests in all matters concerning other planets –". He held up a restraining hand, as Ablakan opened his mouth to speak. "– And to continue rescue efforts for Moohri. But I will want a full report of any conversations you have with your colleagues."

Though Tweno's expression now turned solemn, Ablakan noticed the twinkle had not left the Primary's eyebanks.

"Ablakan of Tabix, do you accept the role of office I have described, to learn and perform your duties to the best of your ability?"

"Yes, Primary, I promise always to do my best," Ablakan said, feeling his heart flutter just a little.

"Then I appoint you First-in-training." With that, Tweno pressed a button on the wall beside the bed. An attendant hurried in, bowing deeply. She looked barely older than Ablakan.

Tweno said, "I assume by now you know of my appointment?"

"Yes, most honored Primary. We are all eager to serve you."

He inclined his head slightly in acknowledgement. "Tomorrow I will return to Tabix to ensure the welfare of our former ruler, and to have my effects as First transferred here." Tweno put his hand on the boy's shoulder. "Ablakan will become First of Pantai at Age of Arrival. Kindly arrange quarters and amenities suitable to his station. And his age," he added with a smirk.

"With great pleasure, Primary." The girl smiled shyly at Ablakan before murmuring into a small hand-held device.

Tweno looked down at Ablakan. "Your mother will accompany me here on my return. But that will not be for several days. I suggest you spend the time getting acquainted with what is on the island, all of which, as you probably know, belongs to the Primary during his term. That means you can go anywhere you like, as long as you let me (once I return), or one of your attendants, know where you will be."

Ablakan bowed deeply, overwhelmed by his good fortune. "Thank you, sir, for everything. I would like to see if there are gardens here, and flowers and –" He stopped, embarrassed.

Tweno regarded him fondly. "You will find here almost anything that is beautiful." He glanced at his personal timemometer. "There is still much daylight before we dine, if you wish to explore a bit."

"Yes, please." Ablakan could actually feel his eyebanks shining with enthusiasm. "But first I must let Jan know I am alright."

"Give her our thanks for standing by you in the recent – crisis." He leaned towards the attendant to ask a question, then nodded. "Evening meal will be served in two achras. You have a timepiece?"

Ablakan beamed. "Yes, sir. Plaka gave me one of his."

The Primary nodded, as though he had expected no less. "One more thing: When we are at home and are not entertaining guests, I would prefer you call me Tweno. Or 'sir', if you are feeling formal."

Ablakan grinned sheepishly. "I am honored."

"Then off you go."

Ablakan gave the rulers a quick bow and followed the long-legged attendant out of the room.

* * *

Shownae sighed heavily. It was now late evening. Another crazy day had finally come to an end, and he was glad of it. Not that it hadn't had its moments. He'd taken an instant liking to Firsts Konapi and Lisham. As with Primary Tweno, they felt open and genuine, and very willing to help Moohri.

Shownae's mover slowed as it approached his tiny, temporary lodging. He turned off the engine, letting the last of the energy coast it into its spot before getting out. He had planned to be on this continent only long enough to finalize his affairs here and let Moohri speak to his wife-mate. But now that Shownae could teleport, he would be needed indefinitely to ferry supplies from Shira to the marooned Spacefarer. While he was glad to do so, it meant he would now need to find more permanent quarters.

As Shownae closed the mover's door, he froze in alarm. His awareness reached out in all directions in the gloom. He was not alone. Malevolence assailed his psychic sense and yet, there seemed no intelligence behind it, no intent. Just a timeless waiting.

Shownae could feel his heart pound, his breaths coming in rapid succession. But until he could identify the source of the danger, he dared not move.

'Port yourself out of here, his inner voice whispered urgently, but Shownae ignored it. From what little he could tell, there was no being attached to the danger. Then he remembered the means Klyfin had used to get rid of Moohri: sabotage. Klyfin believed he had gotten away with it once; why not a second time?

173

Shownae nodded quietly to himself. Whatever was waiting for him in the dark was technological in nature, no doubt rigged to look like an accident. Which still left a world of possibilities. Though 'porting elsewhere remained the wisest option, Shownae balked at being chased from his home by a lowlife like Klyfin.

He toyed with the idea of asking Ablakan to help him get a fix on the device, but rejected it. This was his fight; he would win it on his own.

Shownae leaned against his mover while he thought out his next step. The biggest disadvantage he faced was the darkness, but his only walk-light was in the eating area inside the house. His enemy would expect him to go directly from his mover onto the ramp and into the dwelling before turning on illumination. Presumably, somewhere during that short trip, the 'accident' would occur with sufficient speed and force to kill him. That narrowed it down somewhat, but not enough.

There were still lights on at Nagona's house next door. He had met her and her brood the day he moved in.

Shownae walked down his short driveway and onto the road before cutting across his neighbor's land to palpate the door-alert. Here was a scuttling sound inside, then the latch was released and Nagona stood before him, blinking in surprise. Her son, Winshap, held onto her tunic-flap.

"I'm sorry to bother you so late," Shownae said. "But have you a walk-light I could borrow?"

"Yes, of course." Nagona leaned over to give instructions to Winshap, who hurried off to fetch the light. "You look tired."

"I have been kept busy since I arrived."

The youngster appeared at her elbow with the light. He held it at arm's length toward Shownae.

"Thank you, Winshap," Shownae smiled, taking the precious item. "I will return it tomorrow."

"Sleep peacefully," Nagona said.

"And you." Shownae bowed slightly, and turned away as Nagona gently closed the door-flap.

174

Armed with the walk-light, he retraced his steps until he was again standing beside his mover. Shownae cast his beam over everything in his path before proceeding with infinite caution towards the house. The bushes were especially suspect, but there again, the light revealed no foreign object, no trip-wires or beam-breakers.

"Where are you?" Shownae muttered. By now he was almost at the ramp. Scrunching down as best he could, he played the beam under the ramp and through every crack. Gingerly, he put his weight on it. There was no response other than its usual creaking sound.

"I'm too old for this," Shownae groaned. He could feel the tension in his chest grow with each passing moment.

So whatever awaited him was likely inside the house. As a final precaution, Shownae tossed his mover key at the metal door latch, but there were no sparks. Again, his walk-light could find nothing more sinister than a lazy perla-moth resting on the shrub next to the house.

Shownae took a deep breath, and tried to slow his racing heart and steady his shaking hand. He used the end of a broken bough to key in the combination to the underlatch, taking care to keep his body as far from the door as possible.

"Up, up," he urged under his breath as the stick slowly raised the latch. The door opened a crack and Shownae pulled away, wincing in anticipation. But again, nothing happened. He pushed the door all the way open with a hard shove on the branch, and waited. There was silence from within.

Could I have imagined this, Shownae wondered. All he had had to go on was that sudden, overpowering sense of danger. He peeked around the corner into the darkened room. The walk-light revealed a trail of acid on the floor which leaked from the big storage batteries behind the cupboard wall. Had he stepped in it, the acid would have made short work of his footwear, and possibly his feet as well.

Perhaps a warning, then? Somehow, he had expect something more lethal from Klyfin.

In annoyance, Shownae flicked on the light toggle, and as he did so, a tiny green dot flashed in his peripheral vision. Shownae flung himself away in a panic 'port just as the blue-white bolt of electricity slashed through the spot he had occupied an instant before. Disoriented, Shownae started to open his eyes. As he did, something hit him with the force of a jana explosion, and the world went black.

* * *

Unaware of Shownae's plight, Ablakan followed his attendant down hallways that led to enormous rooms and more hallways. The attendant was speaking quietly into the communicator, flashing occasional sunny smiles at Ablakan. The palace seemed endless. Soon Ablakan realized he could be wandering around for achras if he didn't find some way to keep his bearings.

"Juneli, how do you keep from getting lost?"

"I still do, once in a while," she admitted. "You can have my vid-map for now; I have another."

She depressed a button, and an aerial representation appeared, with a red marker on it. The dot was moving slowly as they walked. "This shows you where you are, and where everything else is on the island. If you are inside the palace, press this."

Ablakan pushed it down and was delighted to see a similar map of the palace interior, and another moving red dot. That would certainly come in handy.

They were approaching a major junction, and he watched with interest as Juneli shepherded him into a gigantic kitchen. A score of cooks and assistants were preparing exquisite foods Ablakan had only seen on the Player-box.

The attendant clapped her hands for attention.

"Royalty in the kitchen," she sang out, eyebanks glinting impishly. Immediately, all present snapped to attention.

"First-in-Training Ablakan, may I present your kitchen staff." Those assembled in the great room bowed in unison and murmured assorted greetings.

Ablakan squirmed in embarrassment. He wasn't used to being treated with such deference. Everyone was watching him, waiting expectantly.

"I am very happy to meet you. I am honored to be here," Ablakan said lamely in what he hoped was an appropriate tone. His words sparked another series of bows.

The lead cook stepped forward, bowing yet again. "Any time you wish, come in and eat whatever pleases you. Or ask your attendant to bring it to you. It has been a long time since we have had the pleasure of catering to a young palate."

"Thank you," Ablakan blushed.

Juneli lead him to a large counter overflowing with sweets and fruits. "A banquet is being prepared to honor our new Primary and the Firsts, including you, sir." (Did everyone now know this English term, Ablakan wondered.) "So please do not indulge yourself too much beforehand."

An enormous muchipans caught Ablakan's eye. Noticing this, Juneli placed it on an ornate platter and presented it to Ablakan with a flourish and a hand-clean. Ablakan accepted it with thanks, realizing he was famished.

"We have every type of beverage as well." She lead him to a cooler twice his height. In no time, he was seated at a glistening table, shamelessly 'filling his face', as Jan would have put it. A mote of guilt attached itself to him at the thought of making Jan wait for his report while he ate, but it would also have been impolite to eat too hurriedly.

Juneli stood at a respectful distance from the table. To Ablakan, she looked thin and hungry.

"Will you please eat with me?" Ablakan asked.

"Gladly! Thank you, sir." Juneli quickly garnered a muchipans of her own and plunked herself down opposite Ablakan, her skin glowing with pleasure.

He regarded her, then slowly put down his treat. Seeing this, she followed suit.

"Juneli, I will become a First over time, but right now, I'm just a boy. Can you treat me less formally?"

Her eyebanks twinkled as she asked, "Like a favorite litter-brother, perhaps?"

"That would be great." If Mother heard him speak like this, she would be most annoyed. But Tweno had told him Mother would not be coming for a few days, and Ablakan intended to make the most of it.

When his treat had been dispatched, Ablakan expected they would be on their way, but Juneli seemed in no hurry to leave.

"It may take some time to get your rooms ready," she explained when he asked. "Did you wish to see more of the palace now, or shall we stay here and annoy the cooks?"

"If they don't mind too much," Ablakan voted. Already they were asking for his 'expert opinion' by tasting a number of wonderful dishes for the upcoming banquet.

To Ablakan, Juneli seemed completely at home in the palace. "Have you lived here all your life?"

"Yes. My family has served on this island for generations. I couldn't imagine living anywhere else. What about you, Ablakan? Where have you lived?"

Juneli was a wonderful listener and, little by little, he found himself telling her all about his early life and how tough things had been since his father died.

"He would be so proud of you," Juneli smiled softly. "Perhaps, in his wherever-place, he knows."

"Perhaps." It was not a subject to which Ablakan gave much thought, but the idea was comforting.

At length, the kitchen hear-other toned. Juneli picked it up and identified herself. She listened, then thanked the caller and hung up.

"Your rooms are ready when you are."

Ablakan and the cooks exchanged multiple good-byes and bows before Ablakan followed Juneli on their circuitous journey to his rooms. Considering how beautiful the suite Tweno had loaned him and his mother at Tabix had been, Ablakan felt better prepared for whatever was being assigned to them here. After all, it *was* a palace.

Or, he thought he was. The first room of the suite they stopped at looked like any boy's dream come true. Everything he had ever ogled on the Player-box seemed to have made its way there. Games were stacked like wood-fuels on a shelving unit in one corner of the room, along with a Player-box that took up half of one wall. A music system of epic proportions poured out its magical sounds. Someone had even correctly guessed his preferences, and there they all were, awaiting his pleasure.

Juneli led him from room to room, until he refused to budge any further.

"How many rooms do we have?" he asked, overwhelmed.

Juneli's laughter peeled softly. "These are all yours, Ablakan. Your mother has her own, *way down the hall.*" She grinned mischievously. "There are 18 rooms assigned for your comfort and entertainment, but more can be added, if you wish."

Ablakan sank onto a handy chair. He looked up at Juneli in disbelief. "Eighteen? Just for me? Why so many?"

"This palace was designed to handle five hundred royals and their servants. Nowadays, we seldom have more than five notables here at one time. So actually, you can have as many rooms as you wish. Would you like more?" Her eyes glistened with humor.

"No, please! I would get lost and never find my way out."

"Our tailors will create you a wardrobe for all occasions. Tomorrow, why don't you let them know your personal tastes?"

Ablakan said, his mind reeling, "Thank you, Juneli, but this is all happening too fast."

"Perhaps you would like to relax a bit? Catch your breath before the banquet?"

"I think I had better." Ablakan followed Juneli as she led him into yet another room. It held a massive bed that looked soft as a cloud. With a sigh of relief, he sank onto it.

"Your valet, Saymin, will attend you a half-hour before the banquet. If you need anything, at any time at all, just press this button. There is one like it in every room. Rest well, sir," she smiled and, bowing slightly, departed.

For a while, Ablakan did absolutely nothing. After the hectic pace of the past few days, it felt wonderful to not have to do anything or go anywhere. Perhaps tomorrow he would awaken and find it had all been a fantastic dream, but for now he would enjoy it all he could.

At length, Ablakan roused himself to search on Earth for Jan's mindprint. She would still be on an airplane, but by now he knew the feel of her mind almost as well as he knew his own. Perhaps more so, he amended. He found her easily enough, but was taken aback at the excitement in her mind as she opened up to him.

Quick! Tell me what happened. I can't stand the suspense!

Ablakan felt the laughter that accompanied the demand, so he knew she was not actually in distress.

I am – overwhelmed? he said, hoping he had used the right word.

Details, Ablakan. I want all the juicy details.

'Juicy' reminded Ablakan of the muchipans, but he realized this was not the type of detail Jan sought. It took a while to tell her everything that had happened since he sat on the bench while the Firsts chose a new Primary.

Oh, Ablakan! I'm so happy for you, I don't know what to say, Jan cried. *A First! You sure deserve it, my friend.* Then she chuckled. *I was telling Tom, I wish I could have been there to see the looks on their faces when you 'ported that encyclopedia in mid-air.*

Ablakan shivered convulsively, remembering. *I was so frightened, I did not know what to do. I am fortunate our new Primary and the Firsts are such good people.*

That they are, Jan agreed.

Ablakan squirmed a little, for there was something he had to do, and it frightened him a bit. *Jan, would you be angry if I told Primary Tweno about Black and teleporting him to Shyr? I think I must tell him.*

Not at all. Actually, now that we're working for NASA – our space department, that is – I was thinking we should tell our boss, too, Jan said. *It would be a load off all our minds, I think. I've always hated keeping secrets.*

I do, too. It feels bad. Ablakan heaved a grateful sigh.

If Tweno is upset by it, I'll speak to him for you.

But Ablakan mentally shook his head. *You are a great friend, Jan, but a First – even a First-in-Training – must account for himself, by himself.*

You're right, of course. I'm so proud of you, dear. We all are. I just want you to know that. Jan sent a hug over the light-years that separated them.

I do, and it helps very much, Ablakan smiled, as he returned the hug. *I will call Moohri now. He can tell Shownae the news for me, because I must get ready for the banquet soon.*

Enjoy yourself, dear friend.

Feeling wonderful all over, Ablakan repeated his news to Moohri. By the time he had finished, the giddy excitement had worn off, and Ablakan found himself thinking quietly about his future as a First. Tweno had pointed out it would mean long hours and a great deal of work to keep a whole continent running smoothly, not to mention relations between three worlds light-years apart. In the privacy of the room, Ablakan wriggled with joy. What more could a boy want?

* * *

Someone was moaning. As he struggled back to consciousness, Shownae realized that someone was him. A searing pain behind his frontal eye warned him not to open it.

"He awakens," a faraway voice reported. The air was tainted with an antiseptic smell.

"Can you hear me?" someone asked loudly, quite close to his face.

Shownae cautiously opened his left-hemisphere eye, then the right one. He was in a hospital receiving room. Medical staff bustled around the occupied beds, and ambulant injureds milled about.

"What is your name?" the medic asked, his voice dropping to a more natural level.

"Sh– Shildrop," Shownae lied. "I am a migrant worker from Weehaj Territory, vacationing here. What has happened to me?"

"You were hit by a mover. The driver said he came around a sharp turn, and you were in the middle of the road."

"I was thinking. I must have wandered over and not noticed. Am I hurt badly? Why can't I open my central eye?"

The medic touched his arm reassuringly. "You are fortunate, Shildrop. The surgeons micro-repaired it. The bandage must stay on for at least a subri. Your head injuries are not serious, but you should remain here overnight. You will be moved to your room shortly, and I will come by to check on you before I leave."

"Thank you." Shownae realized how fortunate he was that his injuries hadn't been worse. When he 'ported himself out of his house, he hadn't had time to specify a destination. Considering all the places in the universe he could have ended up, he was lucky to be alive.

* * *

Nearby in that universe, Ryan Black was admitting to himself what a wonderful training ground Black Moon had been. With no one around to ridicule his awkward attempts, Black had wholeheartedly thrown himself into the process of becoming a first-rate – no, *the* premier teleporter in known space. But now it was time to leave this little play-world behind and embrace his destiny.

Earlier today, he had effortlessly, almost carelessly, 'ported himself to the opposite side of the moon, then returned to stand in the exact spot he had previously occupied. The next step would be no different, he assured himself. A simple matter of focusing on that accursed hilltop in Maine, performing the usual mental gymnastics, and there he would be, ready to give those rubes the shock of their lives. Or what little was left of their lives.

Black smiled to himself indulgently. Really, he harbored no grudge against them. Unwittingly, Jan had done him a great service, banishing him abruptly as she had. He would send her to her death without a qualm, but also without hate. Unfortunate, but necessary that they must all perish. Black sighed, feeling good about himself for having purged the malice from his heart.

Almost with regret, he regarded his 'home away from home' for a long moment before sending himself on the instantaneous trek to land precisely where he had chosen. A frown crossed his face as he noted that the dwelling had been boarded up, as though the occupants expected to be away for a long time.

So they've run to ground, he thought. But how could they have known I'd be coming? Unless it was someone else they were running from.

Another possibility came to mind. With him gone, they would have needed another physicist, or at least some specialist who could tell them where to deposit their wretched Moohri once they figured out how to get him home. There were several pitifully inadequate substitutes for himself, but they were scattered all around the globe. Which meant that sorry trio could be almost anywhere. How like them to rob him of his just rewards.

Black's eyes fell on Tom's prized rose bushes, and a smile radiated slowly from the corners of his mouth. Purposefully, he marched to the potting shed. A hard kick made short work of the door latch. With a grunt of satisfaction, he picked up a sharp axe, then noticed something even more appealing: gasoline for the mower.

Armed with both, he proceeded to the house. First, he chopped viciously at the rose bush, then realized it was close enough to the abode to be destroyed in the blaze he would be setting. The axe demolished the glass patio door, and he proceeded to sprinkle the

183

gas liberally throughout the house. When the can was empty, he stepped out onto the patio. Nonchalantly, he lit his last cigarette while he considered where to begin his search for his Three Blind Mice.

Were he they – perish the thought! – where would he go if he was seeking a physicist? Well, Foxworth worked at NASA, so most likely he'd have contacts there, or through there. It was a reasonable place to start.

Black regarded the glowing end of his cigarette for a moment, then with an air of indifference, flicked it onto the fuel-soaked kitchen floor. The room became alight, and Black stepped back as room after room burst into flames. It was a most satisfying sight. He had no doubt that at some point, once they realized he was on their trail, they would head for home. It pleased him immensely to think of them finding nothing but ashes.

With a tight little smile, Black regarded the loaded snub-nosed revolver he had found in the Brodys' bedroom. He pocketed it, focused on the NASA headquarters in Washington, DC, and left the hilltop inferno behind.

* * *

For a scientist, Jack can be awful childish, Jan thought in annoyance. Instead of letting them peer out the windows of the limousine Saunders had sent to collect them from the airport, Jack had insisted on blindfolding them, of all things.

"Indulge me," he'd pleaded, smiling ingratiatingly at Jan and Tom. And so here they sat, seeing absolutely nothing of Silicon Valley.

Eventually, the vehicle slowed and turned in somewhere, before rolling to a gentle stop.

"*Now* can we take these damned things off?" Tom asked in an aggrieved tone.

"Not yet. Just stay put." Jack sounded like a puppy about to get a treat. They were helped out of the limo by Jack and, presumably, the driver. Jan could feel flagstones under her feet as she was led a short distance from the car. A click, and she heard the unmistakable sound of a sliding glass door opening.

"We're home," Jack sang, and the blindfolds were whisked off.

After such a build-up, Jan had expected a spacious bungalow in suburbia. What she saw instead was a sprawling rancher, at least 4000 square feet. They faced an indoor garden – it was much too large to be called a sunroom – which abounded with flowers, shrubs, hanging and standing planters, a rockery with a waterfall cascading down its face into a large pool that held koi. Jan had the feeling the floral amenities had been added very recently. When she spotted newly-transplanted rose bushes just outside the sunroom, she knew she was right.

"Do you like it?"

Tom's voice was husky with emotion. "How could we not? This was your idea, obviously. I'm much obliged, Jack."

Jan could only gawk in speechless amazement.

"Wait till you see the rest of it." Jack stepped back to let them discover its wonders for themselves.

Jan gazed around her in awe. " 'Suitable for visiting dignitaries', my eye! This is fit for a king."

"We don't get too many of 'em in these parts. But if we ever do, we'll be ready."

"I'll say!" Tom peered into the enormous sunken living room from the sitting room through which he had been strolling.

The building sported self-contained two-bedroom suites in each wing at either end of the main house – presumably to accommodate visitors without having them underfoot. Although the core of the house had two bedrooms of its own, the Brodys opted for one wing, with Jack taking the other.

To Jan's added delight, a vastly-oversized den had been set up as her new 'Reading Room'. Among other amenities, it featured a state-of-the-art computer, a speaker phone with built-in answering machine, a tape recorder and a printer/copier/scanner/fax machine. A cushy recliner invited her presence, set behind a magnificent oak desk with innumerable drawers, already outfitted with all manner of stationery items. Reference books were nestled between ornate bookends on one corner of the desk. Several comfortable-looking chairs radiated outward in a semicircle beyond. One entire wall was devoted to a star chart. Colored pins marked the approximate location of Shalaii and Orowa. Another wall with floor-to-ceiling bookshelves looked like it could accommodate a lifetime's accumulation.

Jan clasped her hands together ecstatically. "Jack, for a boss, you're the greatest!"

He picked up the recorder and held it out towards her. "Would you mind repeating that for the record?"

Grinning, Jan did.

"Anything you want or need within reason, I am authorized to get for you folks," he said. "Right now, you could do no wrong. Better order whatever you want while he's feeling generous."

Jan hesitated. "Um, before we get carried away, maybe we should let him in on the one, shall we say, 'Black' mark on our record."

"Yes, I suppose we'd better," Jack sighed.

Tom nodded. "I'd prefer not to have that hanging over our heads. Not that we had anything to do with sending him to Shyr. But we didn't exactly rush to find a way to get him back either, did we?"

Jan admitted, "I'd just as soon leave him there permanently. But I guess we can't have everything."

"The thorn in the rose bush," Jack agreed, reaching for the phone. "It's not quite five. Saunders should still be at the office."

They crowded around the speaker-phone. Diane greeted them warmly, and put them right through. Apparently, Saunders had been expecting their call.

"Hello, folks," he said cheerfully. "Getting settled in?"

"Yes indeed," Jan replied. "And thanks so much for putting us up in Heaven."

"Glad you like it. Have you heard from Ablakan? I understand he had a meeting with their – Primary, is it?"

Jan relayed the latest developments from Shalaii. Then she hesitated and took a deep breath.

"Oh-oh! Okay, give me the bad news," Saunders said.

"We've been keeping a dark secret from you, sir," Jan said. "Do you perhaps know a Dr. Black?"

"Ryan Black?"

"Yes, sir."

Saunders snorted derisively. "All too well. That egomaniac spent six months riding herd on our Computational Department. During that time, we lost three good people to stress and two others who just up and quit rather than have to work with him. Why do you ask?"

Jan told him, in detail. When she finished, there was silence at the other end of the phone. At length, he sighed. "I suppose we will have to get him back, eventually."

Tom smothered a laugh. "Yes, sir. Oh, by the way, Jack staunchly refuses to tell me what I'll be doing."

"Yes, he does like his little secrets. You'll be getting at least one hour a night on the Hubble Telescope –"

"Are you serious?" Tom blurted out.

"Absolutely. Your job will be to scan the stars, see if you get a 'feeling' from any others. If you do, in due course Jan will be asked to send them a message. Between the two of you, we have 'first contact in a can'."

Tom whistled softly. "The Hubble Telescope, no less. You've got a deal, sir."

"Foxworth's idea, again, and a good one, I think. Well, if there's nothing else –"

"No, that's all the confessions we have at the moment," Jan said airily.

"Good. Let's keep it that way."

After Saunders hung up, Jan remarked, "Well, that wasn't so bad."

"Funny man," Jack mused. "Sometimes he can be a real tyrant, and just when you think you've got him pegged, he turns into a pussycat."

Jan marveled, "Well, he sure had someone go all out on this place."

"I could really like it here," Tom deliberately understated.

Jan wandered into the spacious kitchen. "And how. They thought of everything else. I wonder . . . "

She opened the fridge door. Sure enough, it had been stocked for them with the standard items, plus a large platter of hors d'oeuvres and fruits. A bottle of champagne lay on its side, inviting celebration.

Tom stretched luxuriously. "You know what I could really go right now? A soak in that Jacuzzi I saw in the ensuite. Care to join me?"

Jan nodded. "And then maybe a nap. That king-size bed looked soft as a feather."

Jack headed for 'his' wing to unpack, and the Brodys prepared to soak in quiet splendor.

"By the way, what's so great about that telescope?" Jan asked as they were climbing in. Over the next half hour, she learned more than she had ever wanted to know about the Hubble Space Telescope.

* * *

Saymin, the valet assigned to Ablakan, was a chatty sort who seemed to have an opinion on just about everything. Almost as wide as he was tall, his chubby fingers were surprisingly nimble, and he shucked Ablakan out of his 'regular' clothes and into the shiny new outfit with practised ease.

"Forgive me, sir," Saymin smirked, as he adjusted yet another layer of clothing on Ablakan's spare frame. "But I feel like I am dressing a skeleton. Wait till the kitchen folk get their hands on you. They will fatten you up in no time."

Ablakan smiled, remembering that muchipans. "They've already begun."

188

"Did you really – teleport, is it? – the human's gift from the Primary's hand?"

"No, it had left her hand and was about to hit a guard."

"If I anger you, and you feel you just *have* to teleport me somewhere, can you make it Jinanak?" That private island paradise was much in demand for holidays, but visitors were allowed on it by invitation only.

"I would never teleport in anger. It would be very wrong."

Saymin said, "I can think of a few people I would love to teleport someplace."

Eventually, all the fussing with Ablakan's clothing and mane was over, and Juneli escorted him to the banquet. On the way, she gave him his own vid-map, accepting her old one in return.

Ablakan examined it while he followed her. It was a small box with a series of buttons and a prominent dial. It was far more sophisticated than Juneli's had been, but like most boys his age, Ablakan had a knack for gadgetry. He mastered it long before they reached their destination. A pocket in his leg-warmers was shaped differently than the rest and proved to be a perfect fit for the little box.

Tweno and the Firsts were already in the great dining hall, chatting quietly as they admired the view from the wall-across window. The palace was situated on a flat-topped hill. From this vantage-point, a vast network of small wooded areas, meadows, farmlands and ponds were visible. Even the farms looked pristine here, and Ablakan sighed with pleasure. He had never really liked living in a city. When he became First, he would have to do so again, but for the next several prilks he would enjoy this island to the fullest his free time would allow.

Tweno spotted him. "Come join us, Ablakan."

When he did, Tweno gestured toward the one sizeable lake within view, perhaps two longs away. "Do you like water sports?"

"Yes, sir, very much. In Tabix I ran on swimmers." Ablakan gazed at the shimmering expanse. It certainly looked inviting.

189

Tweno nodded. "Good. Until I return, you are on vacation. Many of the staff have youths around your age. I will have your attendant introduce you to them. There are hurrymaries in the stables for riding. We have cruiser and fisher boats, and plenty of swimmers, I understand." He smiled at the delighted expression on Ablakan's face. "After all, we must keep you fit, and pleasurable activities are the best form of exercise, especially for the young."

"I will be most happy to keep fit," Ablakan assured him.

"One small point, which I know will not be a problem for you, as it is already part of your nature. Here on the island, during worktime, each behaves according to their station. But when not at work, there is no rank distinction. The stableboy and you are on equal footing, as am I."

"That will make it easier; thank you, sir."

A small chime sounded in the room. They were being asked to take their place at the table, so that serving might begin.

It could have seated more than 100 people, but today there were only four, so they grouped themselves at one end. Despite their small numbers, a gala feast was laid out for them. Tweno had vetoed having live musicians attend, opting instead for soft recorded background music.

Lisham asked, as the first course was placed in front of them, "Tweno tells me you just moved to Tabix recently. Where did you live before that?"

Ablakan hastily swallowed a succulent pipa root before answering, "Omu, sir."

"To think I had a teleporter on my own continent, and didn't even know it."

"I hadn't even met Jan then," Ablakan pointed out. "Or heard of teleporting."

Conversation continued in a relaxed, informal vein, and over the course of the meal, Ablakan learned quite a bit about each of them. They had come from varied backgrounds, but shared similar plans for the future – a future in which Ablakan would play a prominent role.

Konapi enthused, "Someday soon, our three species may visit each other, exchange goods and technologies, maybe explore and colonize new planets together."

Lisham added, waving a utensil about dramatically, "And there are bound to be all manner of other peoples out there we do not know of yet. It is a most exciting time to be alive."

"I would suggest caution, in seeking out other peoples," Tweno said. "So far we have been very fortunate to find – or be found by – offworlders who mean us no harm. We may not always be so lucky." He turned to Ablakan. "Have you talked to your offworld friends today?"

"Yes, sir." Dutifully, he described his discussions, including reference to their joint decision to tell their bosses about Black.

Tweno nodded, looking at Ablakan with mock severity. "So there was more. I thought so."

"Yes, Primary – sir," Ablakan gulped. "I may have done a bad thing, but I do not know how to undo it. May I explain?"

"I think you had better." But Tweno's eyebanks twinkled a bit.

Ablakan explained all he had been privy to regarding the physicist, and about his 'porting of the blackguard to Shyr. "We cannot bring him back either, in case he has picked up a disease there."

Lisham asked, "Have you checked on him lately?"

"No, sir, not since yesterday. At that time, he was well and had much to eat and drink."

Tweno was watching him closely. "How sure are you that he planned to harm your friends?"

"I am certain. Jan was very angry, and when she is angry she does not read people well."

"I see." Tweno drummed his fingertips on the table absently, eyebanks narrowed in thought.

Konapi pointed out, "If he is a powerful human, and is brought back, he may try to damage our ties with Earth."

191

Lisham said, "I would not think so. If I understand what happened correctly, he believes it is Jan who teleported him."

"Which would make him determined to hurt Jan and her friends," Konapi insisted. "And one way might be to make trouble between Earth and us."

Tweno inhaled deeply, reaching a decision. "I am tempted to leave things as they are, but as I understand it, he had been working on learning to teleport long before he met Jan. If he were to succeed, Jan would be his main target, if he believes she is the only other person who can teleport. If he knows there are others who can, it may keep him from going after her. Let us see what we can do for now. Ablakan, please call him. I wish to speak with him."

"Yes, sir." Ablakan quieted his mind and sent his focus to Shyr. With only one human mind there, it should have been easy to locate Black. But this time, he was nowhere to be found.

Ablakan tensed. He could not have died, could he? Switching to a visual search, using his mind's eye, Ablakan set his parameters to scan for a human body, or any part of a human body. But there was nothing.

"Is there a problem?" Tweno asked.

"Yes, sir. Moment, please," Ablakan whispered. Twice more he scanned. Where could Black be? A horrible thought manifested itself, and Ablakan broke connection. His mane was standing up in a ridge.

Tweno leaned forward. "What has happened, Ablakan? You are pale as a parwoky."

"He – he is not there. I searched for his mind, then his body, then pieces of his body. He is just not there." He looked up at Tweno in terror. "He must have teleported to Earth."

Tweno grimaced. "If so, your friends are in peril. In fact, so may Earth be, if he carries some disease."

Ablakan nodded miserably, shivering in reaction.

"You must call Jan right away. But first, calm yourself. Breathe deeply," Tweno said, emulating for the frightened boy.

192

Ablakan drew in a couple shaky breaths, and found it helped. Then he closed his eyebanks and send out his call to Jan.

* * *

The happy trio were enjoying the tray of tasties from the fridge when Saunders phoned.

"Hold a minute, please," Tom said. He signalled Jack, who was closest to the den, to depress the speaker phone in that room. Tom hung up the extension and hurried over.

"Okay, we're all here, sir."

"Brace yourselves. I just now got an irate call from our Computational Department. Black was there looking for 'Foxworth and a couple of old geezers', as he put it."

"*WHAT?*" Jack and Tom cried in unison.

Jan placed her hand over her mouth. "He's done it. He's learned to teleport."

Saunders pointed out, "And we don't know what he may have brought back from Shyr. He has to be found and contained, and fast. I've isolated everyone we know of who has had contact with him. But if I'm right, contagious or not, you're in grave danger. I'm sending you a security team. Stay put till they arrive."

Jan said, "But nobody knows we're here. We haven't even gone to the office yet . . . No, scratch that. All the people who got this place ready for us know, and they're probably on NASA's payroll, right?"

"Right," Saunders confirmed. "We'll try to capture him if he's still here. But watch yourselves." He seemed about to hang up, then added, "And Jan, if he shows up and threatens you, do whatever you have to to protect yourselves, understand?"

Jan was aghast. "You mean like spacing him?"

"Listen carefully, all of you." Saunders' voice was deadly earnest. "You already know how badly Black wanted to learn to teleport. As far as he knows, you're the only other person who can do so. And the first thing he does when he gets back is goes looking for you. Maybe it's to get the coordinates of that M-class planet you conned him about. Or more likely it's to rid himself of

193

his one rival, the only person who could stop him. And a couple of witnesses. Remember, that's why Ablakan banished him in the first place." He waited a few seconds for his words to sink in. "All I'm saying is, don't underestimate him. It could cost you your lives."

"Understood, sir," Jack said. His jaw jutted out aggressively. "If he comes, we'll be ready."

Saunders sighed in frustration. "We'll try to corral him here, although how you stop someone from 'porting is beyond me. Any ideas, Jan?"

"Other than keeping his mind so drugged he can't concentrate, or doing a frontal lobotomy, I can't think of anything that would work. About the only advantage we have right now is he's not a telepath, which means he can't locate us mentally – at least, I hope not."

"But you're telepathic. Can you find him for us, without him knowing?"

Jan felt a bit sheepish. She'd been too rattled to realize the obvious. "I think so."

"Good. Do it. I'll contact Security at Ames now. Stay sharp – all of you. Call me when you have anything." Saunders hung up.

"Would you boys keep an eye out while I look for Black?" Jan blinked. "I just realized, it's the first time I've had to hide *and* seek at the same time."

Tom groaned, "Oh, Jan, not now!" But the levity did break the pall that had descended upon them.

Jan settled herself in the comfy recliner. She started at NASA's headquarters in Washington, but soon knew he was no longer there. She finally located him in an elite physics research institute in Los Angeles. He did not pick up her mental presence, which confirmed he had not become telepathic.

On returning her focus to the room, Jan told the others of her findings. Jack informed Saunders of Black's whereabouts and hung up to let their boss call that institute before the rogue 'porter 'jumped' again.

"I'd better warn Ablakan and the others, just in case," Jan said. "No telling what Black has in mind for later."

Ablakan opened to her quickly. *Jan, please wait with your news; this is more important. I just checked on Black, and he is not there. He is not on Shyr.*

I know, dear, Jan told him, hoping he wouldn't realize how frightened she felt. *I was just calling to tell you the same thing. He's on Earth, looking for us. Now that he can teleport, he's even more dangerous. Our boss said he has to be stopped, no matter how. If he can be captured and kept from 'porting, that would be best. But he could be contagious, and he's popping up all over the place.*

Ablakan's tone was crisp with tension. *Jan, this is very bad. How can I help you?*

Right now, just watch out for him. If he could get from Shyr to Earth, he can get to Shalaii or Orowa just as easily.

Ablakan sounded infinitely sad. *Teleporting should never be used to kill.*

No, it shouldn't. But he must be stopped, whatever it takes.

I understand. I will tell Shownae. Be careful, Jan, please.

I will. She voiced the guilt that was bubbling up inside of her. *Take care of yourself and your people. I'm so sorry one of ours might be a threat to you.*

Black is not one of anyone's, Ablakan said almost savagely.

Thank you, my friend. Jan disconnected and turned to the others. "Ablakan and Shownae will be on the lookout. Now, we'd better have a plan if he does show up here."

* * *

Shownae was laying in his small hospital room, trying to ignore the persistent throbbing in his head. He had repeatedly refused pain medication. At any time, Klyfin might locate him and try again. The Lead Spacefarer must know by now that no body had been found in whatever remained of the house. Good thing Shownae had had the sense to give the medic a false name.

Amid the pounding in his head, a secondary sound-feeling appeared. It took Shownae a few moments to recognise it as a gentle 'knock'. Gingerly, he opened to his visitor.

Shownae, you are hurt, Ablakan exclaimed. *What happened?*

Klyfin sabotaged my home. I barely got away in time, and then I was hit by a mover. And now I am in the hospital with a terrible headache and one eye patched.

A mixture of sympathy and anger flow into his mind from Ablakan, tinged with guilt.

And I bring you more bad news, he apologized. *Black has teleported to Earth and is looking for Jan and the others. I think he wants to kill them. Jan says maybe he will try to harm us, too. And if he has diseases, it could be even worse.*

Shownae sat up abruptly, the pain forgotten. *What can I do to help?*

Just be watchful – for both bad people. I will guard here and stay open for Jan at the same time.

I just hope I can still focus enough. Thank the fates he had refused the pain draughts.

* * *

Jan paced the room, wishing she could do more.

Tom's gaze kept switching from the doorway to the windows. "If he does come here with lethal intentions, think you can mentally subdue him, so he can't teleport himself or us?"

"I doubt it. Even though we're forewarned, he'd still have the element of surprise."

Jack was peering out the window towards the road. "But you located him. Can't you 'port him from where he is now?"

"Where could I send him he wouldn't just instantly come back from? And I can't just off him, even if I wanted to, which I don't. We've no proof he's out to kill us."

"Black might be infecting everyone he contacts with some incurable alien spore. He doesn't have to space someone to be a threat. Dead any which way is still dead."

196

Tom put his hand out to stop Jan's pacing. "How about 'porting those security guys Saunders is sending us to where Black is now? They could shoot him with stun guns or something, then just keep him drugged up." Of them all, he seemed the least rattled by the situation.

"Good idea." She turned to Jack. "Could you –?"

"I'm on it." Jack dialed Saunders' number again.

"Extra security is converging on the Morrisby Institute. What have you got?" Saunders asked by way of greeting.

"Tom suggests Jan 'port the security guys you're sending us over there with stun guns to subdue him."

Saunders grunted. "They should be at your place now, and I told them to go in loaded for bear. Do it." He hung up.

"They're here," Tom confirmed, as an unmarked van pulled into the driveway.

From the bullet-proof vests and the grim looks on the faces of the four occupants, it was obvious they were taking the threat seriously. Jack flashed his I.D. and briefed them. It was decided that two guards would be transported to Black's location, while the others remained at the house.

Jan wondered what it would take to get them flustered. They could have only just been told they were after a man who could teleport, and they were ready to take him on, and be 'ported to his location to do so.

Based on their new information, the guards each armed themselves with a handgun and a taser. Jan sent her mind to locate Black, only to find he had left the Institute. To her horror, he was now in Ames' main complex. Noting his exact position, she turned to the guards.

"He's at Ames. I can send you there now. Are you ready?" They nodded, but understandably looked none too happy about it. Jan placed them two yards behind where she had spotted Black.

A loud bang came from the kitchen area.

"Stay here," one guard ordered, and the two security officers fanned out, searching for the intruder.

197

The door to the den closed behind them and was locked by a gun-wielding Black. He grinned wolfishly at his captives.

"You three led me a merry chase; I must thank you for that. Challenges are so hard to come by these days. Oh, and I wouldn't even blink if I were you," he told Jan, pointing what looked like their own revolver at her. "Close your eyes or change your focus, and I'll kill you in a heartbeat."

From the other room, they could hear muffled words. Presumably, the guards realized they had been duped.

"You've already learned to teleport; you don't need us any more," Tom said. "Why make yourself a fugitive for nothing?"

Black shrugged indifferently. "I'm already being hunted in case I've brought some back some disease. I rather hope I have. Earth could use a few billion less people, starting with you three."

He walked to the bank of windows and drew the drapes across them, all the while keeping the gun trained on the trio. "We don't want any nosy parkers disturbing our fun, now do we?"

"I suppose you'll be wanting the coordinates of the planet Ablakan spoke of," Jan said, stalling for time. "Especially if you've infected Earth."

"How astute of you. Get him for me. Now." He waved the gun to emphasize his point, then shouted, "WAIT! Do it with your eyes open."

"I'm not sure I can."

"You will, if you don't want to watch your husband die right here and now." Black pointed the barrel of the gun at Tom's chest.

Jan gulped. She had thought she couldn't be any more frightened, but she'd been wrong. The thought of Tom dying galvanized her to glaze over her eyes and place the call, hoping desperately it would work. There was no way she could teleport Black without the necessary mental change being evident in her eyes, and by then Tom would be dead.

I'm here, Jan, Ablakan said tensely. *And so is Shownae. We are watching for a chance, and we will act.*

198

If *he gives us a chance. Right now he's demanding the coordinates of that planet we made up.* It was exceedingly difficult to hold her focus on Ablakan, with her eyes open and the gun pointed at Tom.

Ablakan recited a set of numbers. Jan had to write them down twice, her hand was shaking so badly.

Keeping the gun trained on Tom, Black ordered her to back away from the notepad. His eyes slid to the numbers. "In the Plaiedes Cluster?"

At that moment, an object of bizarre proportions narrowly missed Black's head. As he instinctively ducked, Jan realized this was the opportunity they had been hoping for. Before she could do anything, both men rushed Black. Tom was closest, and Black fired into his body, point-blank. Tom crashed to the floor in front of the physicist. Jack grasped the gun, and the two men tumbled over Tom's inert body, fighting ferociously for possession.

Jan grabbed a paperweight and tried to get a clear shot at Black's head, but the two men were thrashing about so frantically that she dared not strike. Tom lay beneath them, his blood pooling on the carpet. Jan prayed he was still alive, and stood back, hoping for an opportunity to 'port Black the hell out of there so she could get Tom to the hospital.

"Ha!" Jack yelled, as he wrestled the gun away from Black. In that instant, a bewildering number of events took place. Black 'ported himself back to Shyr at the same time Jan, Ablakan and Shownae sent him there. Unfortunately for Black, none of the four locations coincided. The physicist died in his body's vain attempt to occupy multiple places at one time.

Jan and Jack carefully turned Tom over. An ugly red stain was radiating outward from a hole in his chest.

Jan turned terrified eyes on Jack. "Where's the hospital?"

"El Camino on Grant Road in Mountain View. Two miles that way," he cried, pointing.

In a flash, she found it and 'saw' a clear area in the emergency room. Jan 'ported them into it, forgetting entirely about the guards still waiting outside the den.

All activity in the E.R. halted, as three people appeared out of nowhere.

"My husband's been shot," Jan yelled, wild-eyed.

Still no one moved.

Jack whipped out his NASA security card, and unerringly stuck it under the nose of the nearest doctor. "NASA, Special Projects. My man needs attention. Now! Get on it, Doctor."

That broke the spell. The surgeon barked orders, and Tom became the subject of intense medical efforts. Jan and Jack were herded out of the room, with promises to let them know as soon as there was any news.

Jack phoned Saunders to apprise him and to say that, surprisingly, there was no sign of Black.

"Stay away from people, and get into quarantine. If he's contagious, you've both been exposed."

Jack's face blanched. "Oh, God! I forgot."

I no time, they found themselves confined to a large isolation room, with armed guards keeping a constant vigil outside and through the window in case Black showed up again. Then the interminable wait began. Jan tried to come to grips with what had happened, but found she just couldn't. Dully, she wondered why Black had not followed them here.

A timid knock in her mind made Jan wince. She had forgotten to thank her colleagues for distracting Black.

What happened, Jan? Ablakan cried as soon as she opened to him. He sounded almost beside himself with worry. *I felt Tom explode.*

Black shot him, up close. We're at the hospital, and the doctors are with him now. I don't know if he's going to live. Despite her resolve to appear 'brave' for her young friend, tears slid down her cheeks. Jack silently handed over a handkerchief. He looked like he needed it himself.

"It's Ablakan," she explained, then returned her focus to the boy. She could feel him weeping.

I am so sorry, Jan. I thought I could help by throwing a miklaun at Black.

You did. We'd likely all be dead now if you hadn't. But watch out for him. He hasn't come back, so he must be up to something else.

Ablakan shook his head. *Black will never hurt anyone again.*

How can you be sure?

I checked. He is in many spots. We all sent him to Shyr, but not the same place.

Jan shuddered. *How horrible! But I can't think of anyone who deserved it more.*

When will you know how Tom is?

Jan could only shake her head. *I don't know. I'll call you as soon as I hear. I promise.*

Thank you. If you need me, I am always here for you. Ablakan closed the link between them so gently she at first wasn't sure he had left.

"What did he say?" Jack asked.

"Black's dead." Jan numbly recited the rest of the conversation before lapsing into a listless silence.

By again flashing his identification, Jack borrowed a cellular phone from one of the guards.

"Sir? It's Jack Foxworth. Black is toast, and Jan and I are in isolation."

"Good to hear – on both counts," Saunders growled. "The team working on Tom has been told they'll have to be quarantined, along with him if he pulls through. Everyone who's been in contact with Black are being isolated, so let's hope we've got this thing contained."

"Thank you." Jack hung up and joined Jan in miserable silence. There seemed nothing to say till they knew if Tom would survive.

A ghastly hour-and-a-half dragged by before the surgeon arrived. He was wearing a quarantine suit and helmet. The guards gingerly let him in.

He looked tired but relieved. "Your husband is a lucky man. The bullet narrowly missed every major organ and artery. Didn't even nick the spine. There was a lot of internal damage, of course; he took it right up close."

Life rekindled for Jan. "Then he'll live?"

"We believe so. Of course, there's always a chance with shock, but yes, he should come through it all right."

The doctor nodded toward the guard and was let into the room next to theirs. Jan didn't even notice him leave, so great was her sense of reprieve.

Jack was bouncing up and down. "He's going to live!" he cried joyously. Then he threw his arms around Jan and hugged her.

"I'm not sure I will," she said, her voice muffled by his armpit. "You're squashing me."

Jack's eyes were misty-bright as he released her. "Sorry. I'm just so happy, you know?"

"Me, too. I'd better tell Ablakan. He was in tears over it."

"He's quite the boy, that one."

"That he is."

A short time later, Jan said goodbye to the jubilant youth.

* * *

Tom will be alright!

Shownae let out a mental cheer as Ablakan reported the good news to him and Moohri.

But how are you feeling, Shownae? Ablakan asked.

My head does not hurt as much. But now that I can think more clearly, the attendants are pressing me for details I don't want to give.

Moohri said, *You might not be safe, even at a hospital. Are you strong enough to leave yet?*

I have been thinking the same thing. But it took everything I had to 'port Black to Shyr. I don't know where I'd end up if I tried to send myself anywhere. A wave of weakness washed over him, emphasizing the point.

I could send you to a 'safe haven' on your planet, Ablakan offered. *Do you know of one?*

Shownae squinted in concentration. With a patch over his eye, he would not go unnoticed, so it would have to be someplace uninhabited.

Yes, he said, and projected, albeit fuzzily, the image of a small rocky island in the southern hemisphere. Researchers flocked there during the winter to observe the migration of the sarfo birds. The island was unoccupied the rest of the year.

Moohri identified it readily. *Anxuri. I spent a season there once. You would have to live off the sea. How would you do that with your prime eye covered?*

As usual, Ablakan had a solution. *I could 'port you food, if there is someone you can trust to buy it for you.*

I would not put at risk the few people I do trust. And they are very few, Shownae admitted.

I know where to find a person who will offer you shelter, Moohri said. *But you're not going to like it.*

* * *

Spacefarer Trikon, Moohri's old third-in-command (now Klyfin's second) didn't like it, either. Trikon's back had been turned when Ablakan 'ported Shownae into his office, so he had missed Shownae's unusual entrance.

"Klyfin told me you were here earlier, stirring up Moohri's widow with some crazy story. And now you think you can fool me with another lie and that stupid bandage?"

Trikon's fists were clenched, but Shownae stood his ground.

"It is not a lie, and I can prove what I say. All of it." Shownae was getting very tired of being called a liar.

"Can you?"

Without his frontal vision, Shownae missed the lightning movement of Trikon's hand as the Spacefarer grabbed the edge of the bandage and ripped it off Shownae's eye.

Shownae yelped as light triggered searing pain. Both hands flew to his eye, desperate to cover it.

"By the fates! You *are* injured," Trikon gasped. "Here, let me put this back on."

It took every scrap of willpower Shownae could muster to let Trikon near his eye again, but mercifully, the bandage soon again blocked out the light.

"I am sorry," Trikon said rather stiffly. "But you still can't expect me to believe Moohri lives."

"I told you I could prove it," Shownae said in an aggrieved tone. "But I'm in no shape to force you to listen." His eye ached so savagely he wasn't sure he could make a connection with Moohri anyway.

"Alright. I suppose I owe you that much."

Shownae realized his body was trembling with fatigue and reaction. "Can I sit down?"

"Yes. Sorry." Trikon pulled out a chair for the psychic, then one for himself.

Shownae eased his body onto the seat. "If you put your hand on my arm, and keep it there, I will connect you mentally with Moohri. He will answer all your questions. Is that fair enough?"

Trikon looked at him pointedly and said nothing.

"Look, you know him better than I. Ask him something only the two of you would know."

Trikon's eyes narrowed suspiciously. "How do I know you won't just pull it from my mind?"

"I can pick up your feelings in general. But unless you open up to me, I can't read your thoughts, much less your memories," Shownae fudged. He leaned forward, willing Trikon to understand. "There is much more going on here than you know about, but there's no sense me telling you; you'd never believe me. That's why it has to come from Moohri."

Trikon regarded him silently, and finally nodded.

Quickly, before the Spacefarer could change his mind, Shownae sent out his focus.

Did you get to him? Moohri asked at once.

Yes, though as you said, he is not happy about it. I am weak, so please convince him as quickly as you can. A tremor traveled the length of Shownae's body, adding its own sense of urgency.

I will.

Shownae extended his arm. "We are ready. All you need do is place your hand on me."

Trikon hesitated, then with obvious reluctance, grasped the outstretched arm.

Greetings, Trikon. Shownae cannot hold this long, so we must be brief. What will convince you I am me?

Trikon's grip tightened painfully, further reducing Shownae's ability to hold his focus steady.

When I broke my arm, and you were driving me to the hospital, what did we talk about?

Your mother's leg never healing right, Moohri replied promptly. *And I told you I thought you had two breaks, but it turned out I was wrong.*

Shownae could feel belief and incredulity battle it out in Trikon's now-open mind. *Where are you?* he asked at length.

On an atmosphered planetoid on the other side of the sun. It is in a synchronous orbit to Orowa. He paused. *Trikon, I have always trusted you fully. Can I still?*

If you really are Moohri, yes, always.

What happened to me in the rocket was no accident. The thruster cables were cut and reverse-spliced.

Trikon gasped. *You cannot mean that!*

Yes, I do. When I opened the console, I just looked at it; I haven't touched anything inside. I want to send you the whole unit for testing, but you'll have to keep it secret till the results are in. Shownae must teleport it to the isolation chamber in case it is contaminated. I asked Klyfin to let me live in the chamber until we could prove I am disease-free, but he refused. Moohri was talking fast, covering as much ground as possible, for which Shownae was infinitely grateful.

You suspect Klyfin. It was not a question.

He had the most to gain.

No mention of Ablakan's picking up on Klyfin's smugness, Shownae noted with approval. It would only have led to more questions and more incredulity.

"And my house was rigged to kill me," Shownae said aloud. "I teleported out of there an instant before it succeeded, but I was still injured."

Again suspicion colored Trikon's mental tone as he said, "Klyfin told me you had somehow made an object materialize. He didn't say you moved it there."

"I will explain when we finish here," Shownae promised. "I cannot hold this contact much longer. Have you heard enough for now? If I demonstrate teleportation to your satisfaction, will you let me 'port the console into the isolation room?"

"If you can convince me," Trikon said. "Although I don't see how I'd be able to keep it from Klyfin."

If he's responsible for the thrusters malfunctioning, and he does find out, he could go after you, too, Moohri pointed out. *Don't agree to this unless you're certain you can keep it a secret. I would rather live out my days here than get you killed trying to help me.*

Shownae gritted his teeth as a wave of vertigo besieged his mind. He felt himself tip on the chair, but couldn't tell which direction to move to right himself. A hand – Trikon's? – steadied him.

"Tell Moohri I will have you contact him when I have things set up."

His voice sounded impossibly distant. Listlessly, Shownae wondered why Trikon didn't just tell Moohri himself. Then he realized Moohri's mind was also missing. Shownae tried to find it, but couldn't focus.

"Rest, Shownae. I believe."

Believe what, Shownae wondered dully. Then something cool washed his face, carefully avoiding his bandaged eye. It felt comforting, refreshing.

Shownae sat up with a start, awareness flooding back. He opened his good eyes to a concerned Trikon.

"I am sorry – again. I didn't mean to overtax you like that."

Shownae shook his head carefully. "It did feel like someone detached me. Did you hear enough? Do you understand now?"

"Yes, although I don't know how you intend to get that console here. You must tell me what you mean by 'teleporting' – but not now. You need somewhere to rest and recover. Someplace safe. I would offer my home, but I cannot say how much longer that will be safe, either." Trikon paused. "Getting the proof tested here will not be easy."

"Not with Klyfin looking for me."

A tiny smile lifted the corners of the Spacefarer's mouth. "If he wants you so badly, why don't we tell him where you are? Someplace distant enough to get him away from here for a few days, but close enough he will take the chance to go there, to be rid of you?"

"That might work. But can you decontaminate the console and test it that fast? And what about your staff? Can you trust them not to tell Klyfin?"

"Yes to all three. If I can keep it to the couple of technos I have in mind."

Shownae placed a hand on Trikon's shoulder. "Thank you. But don't endanger yourself. If this is too risky, we will find another way."

"This is Spacefarers. There is always risk to what we do. And if Klyfin did try to kill twice, I have to know it and take action at once. But first, I must secure us a place where we will be safe." Trikon wrote down a number on his desk pad, tore off the slip and handed it to Shownae. "When you are away from here, call this number. Tell Branga you and I will be visiting for a few days. I once saved his son from drowning, and he reminds me of his debt

207

every time we meet. If he is saving our lives, perhaps he will finally accept that the debt is paid."

"I will go at once."

Trikon eyed him sharply. "Are you fit to travel?"

"I feel stronger now. Thank you."

Shownae walked a bit unsteadily to the door, giving Trikon what he hoped was a reassuring smile before he slipped through. Once out of sight, Shownae called Ablakan who, fortunately, had remained mentally close by in case he was needed.

Where can I send you? the boy asked.

There was a plaza down the street which featured a line of public listen-fars. Shownae checked his pockets and was relieved to find he had sufficient credits.

Please send me here. Shownae transmitted an indistinct image of the location, including the relative distance and direction. Before he had even finished, he found himself there. Only one passer-by seemed to have noticed his strange mode of arrival, but the individual grinned at him foolishly, his central eye not quite in focus. Shownae noted the cheap canister in the person's hand and silently thanked his fates before turning to the nearest listen-far.

Once again, fortune smiled on him. Branga, after his initial suspicion had been assuaged, readily gave Shownae directions to their new temporary home. Again Ablakan saved Shownae the fatigue of a long walk.

Shownae thanked the Shalaian, and palpated the door-alert. The portal opened promptly, and Shownae was ushered inside by a tall, bony man. In the gloom behind him, a shorter but equally slight female took a couple steps forward, as though for a closer look.

"Good fates, Shownae. When will our mutual friend be joining us?" Branga's voice was surprisingly robust. Perhaps he was not as frail as he looked, Shownae thought.

"Sometime tonight. May I speak to you in private?" Now that his eyes were becoming accustomed to the dim lighting, Shownae could see four blanas clustered around the woman's legs. The youngest could not have been more than one rotation old.

"Evening-meal will be ready soon, so please do not talk too long," she told them both. She stepped forward into what little light the foyer afforded. "I am Adron. I would introduce you to our blanas, but I can see you are weary."

Shownae risked a small bow, and mercifully his balance held. "I look forward to meeting them. Thank you for your hospitality."

Another quick smile, and Adron turned back to her brood.

Branga gestured to the room on their left. It had an accordioning door which would provide a measure of privacy.

Shownae deliberately chose the one seat which was illuminated by the setting sun, though the added light hurt his bandaged eye.

Branga gaped. "What happened to you?"

"A murder attempt that very nearly succeeded. And Trikon will be getting proof of what I was almost killed over. You must realize that if you shelter us, you and your family might run the same risk."

"I see," Branga said. His body betrayed tension though his voice was neutral. "How long would you be staying?"

"Trikon said three to four days. By then he should have the proof and be able to act on it."

Branga nodded distractedly. "Your enemy is in Spacefarers, then?"

"He runs Spacefarers."

"Klyfin? Why would – No; better I not know." Branga exhaled slowly. "If Trikon has not told Klyfin about him saving my son, our home should be safe enough for now."

"We plan to send him in a false direction, anyway. It should give Trikon time to complete the tests and turn the evidence over to Enforcement. We believe he acted alone. Once Klyfin is arrested, we will be out of danger."

Branga regarded him skeptically. "He wields much power. I would be very careful till the judgment is over. But now you must

209

rest. You should be in a hospital, but that could prove equally dangerous. I will ask Adron to treat you. She has tended the sick before."

"I am indebted," Shownae said, choosing his words deliberately. Perhaps it would go some small way to erasing an old debt in the mind of his host.

"I know what it is like to be hunted," Branga stated enigmatically. He led the way to another room, further into the bowels of the dark home. "My wife-mate will be with you shortly." He left quietly, shutting the door behind him.

A soft groan escaped Shownae, as he eased his battered body into a reclining chair. He could hear muted voices conversing not far from his room. The quiet murmur lulled him into a light sleep.

Shownae was aroused by a gentle tap at the door frame. The fabric undulated open and Adron entered, carrying a bowl and cloth.

"This will help your bruises heal faster." She began to dab at his face with the strangely-scented liquid. The mild analgesic soothed the traumatized tissue almost on contact.

"Across from your room is a bath. I will run it for you, adding this –". She pointed to the bowl. "– To the water. It will help you rest better."

"You are most kind."

It had been a long time since he had felt other than cold, clinical hands on his body. Innocent though it was, he found the touch comforting.

Soon he was relaxing in the headily-scented water. Shownae was drifting in a peaceful reverie when a quiet 'knock' sounded in his head.

You feel better, Ablakan noted with approval. *May I read, for speed?*

It took Shownae a a little time to realize what the youth was asking. *Certainly.*

A funny tickling sensation played in Shownae's frontal lobe, then he felt Ablakan's sigh of satisfaction.

It is good that you and Trikon will be safe there. Please tell Trikon if he needs it, I can 'port him where you are.

Thank you. He should be here soon. How are our human friends doing?

Tom is getting stronger, Ablakan reported, then chuckled. *Jan said they are 'on ice', which means they are being isolated in case Black had germs. That 'ice' has nothing to do with being cold. English is a funny language. I will let you rest now.* And then he was gone.

Shownae smiled indulgently. 'On ice.' He really must learn that language one day, if only to savor its wildly peculiar expressions.

The medicinal bath seemed to leech out the recent trauma to mind and body, and Shownae prepared for bed in relative comfort. Branga checked in to see if he needed anything.

"Just the name of the medicine your wife-mate used on me. It has amazing properties."

"It is of her own making," Branga said proudly. "But she willingly gives out the formula. I will ask her to write it out for you before you leave."

"Again, my thanks." Then remembering Ablakan's call, Shownae added, "When Trikon gets in, please ask him to wake me on rising tomorrow. I must speak to him."

"I will. Dream of better times."

Shownae smiled. That was a phrase he hadn't heard in ages. He fell asleep trying to remember its ancient origin.

CHAPTER 12

Ablakan tossed and turned in his huge, cushiony bed. The softly-illuminated timemometer showed that almost half the night had gone by, and yet sleep would not come. Something was disturbing him, but try as he might, he couldn't identify it.

With an exasperated sigh, Ablakan removed the coverings and got up. He thrusted his feet into his cozy slip-ons. Moonlight flooded his sleep chamber, and he looked around the room in wonderment. Would he ever get used to such opulence?

But that wasn't the source of his sleeplessness. It was something more . . . insidious. Yes, that was the word. More and more he found himself thinking in English. Although there were bad people on his planet, too, there seemed to be more shades of 'bad' on Earth than on Shalaii. At least, they had more names for it.

Insidious. He looked up the word in the dictionary Jan had sent him. Fortunately, he found English as easy to read as it was to vocalize.

'Awaiting a chance to entrap; having a gradual and cumulative effect.'

Yes, that description fit the feeling exactly. He looked around him and had to admit it could easily describe him getting used to such finery, but the niggling sensation hinted of a darker fate.

For a moment, the word 'fate' seemed suspiciously appropriate, then the impression faded. It was nearly daybreak before Ablakan fell asleep.

* * *

A nurse in an isolation suit smiled brightly at Jan through the window of her helmet. "Your husband had a good night, and is anxious to speak with you." She produced a phone and bent over to plug it in. "This is his direct number."

"Wonderful! Thanks." Again she had Jack and his 'pull' to thank for the speedy service. The phone Jack had borrowed from the guard had had to be returned and, Jan presumed, fumigated.

"Anyone looking for me?" Jack asked hopefully as he peeked around the curtain separating their two beds. It had been pushed back as far as it would go, but still partially obstructed his view of the nurse.

Jan smothered a grin as she noticed Jack openly admiring the nurse's shapely backside.

"No, sir, not that I've heard."

He hammed a pout. "Story of my life." But he soon began to smile as he watched the nubile nurse make their beds. Better still, he found her quite willing to chat with him.

This left Jan free to make her call with at least a semblance of privacy. "How's my hero this morning?"

"Feeling like a hero sandwich that's been sat on," Tom admitted. "But it's a big improvement on how I felt last night. I haven't seen hide nor hair of Black. Have you?"

"Don't worry; he's history." Jan explained the messy end the physicist had met.

Tom whistled. "That's one for the books," he said prophetically. "Anything else happen?"

"Klyfin tried to off Shownae, and Shownae had to run to ground," she reported, then smiled weakly as the nurse gave her a startled look. "I'll explain later."

"Company?"

"Internal," Jan said. "Can we get you anything? Saunders said it's on him." She couldn't help grinning, as she imagined Tom requesting a remote hook-up to his precious Hubble Telescope.

Tom sighed. "Fewer tests would be nice, but I doubt that'll happen any time soon. Oh, a bit of good news: If the doctor clears me, I'll be joining you tomorrow."

"Ooh! That would be wonderful!" Jan felt her spirits soar. Separation from her beloved was almost physically painful.

The nurse looked like she'd be around for a while, so Jan kept the topics light and uninformative. When Tom started to yawn, she took the hint and let him rest.

Eventually, the nurse departed, and Jack leaned back on his bed with a smug grin.

"Got to first base, did you?"

"Tsk, tsk. You got me all wrong, Jan. I was just on a fishing expedition, and the best bait is flattery."

"So? What were you fishing for – besides a date?"

Jack shrugged. "Unfortunately, she's married. But she was a fountain of information."

"Such as?" Sometimes with Jack it was like pulling teeth.

He ticked off the items on his fingers. "One: We are front page headlines, worldwide. Gina said she was offered a thousand bucks for any tidbits she could gather here."

"Oops." Jan remembered guiltily the nuggets she'd let little slip about Shownae and Black.

"Gina said she was chosen as our nurse because she knows how to keep her mouth shut with the press. We'll find out, I guess." Jack sounded doubtful.

"What else did she say?"

"There are 78 people quarantined in this hospital, and nowhere near that many isolation rooms, which is why we're together. Black sure got around in the short time he was at Ames. This whole wing has been turned over to us potential plague-carriers, including a whole slew of medical types."

Which was about what Jan had expected.

Around 10 a.m., Saunders called. Jan got to the phone first, but angled it away from her ear so Jack could also hear what was being said.

"I just spoke to the doctor. He promised to move Tom into your quarters tomorrow," Saunders reported, inadvertently giving them old news. "How are you two holding up?"

"Fine, sir, other than feeling like a lab rat *and* a pin cushion." Jan rubbed the latest painful spot. "But I guess it's necessary."

Saunders sounded downright cheerful as he said, "Afraid so. Since we can't keep what you've been doing under wraps any longer, with all the teleporting that went on yesterday, I'm using it to our advantage. The President has authorized a publicity campaign around the fact that Earth is now one of three planets engaged in friendly and humanitarian endeavors. It looks like space exploration will again be the darling of the press. That usually translates to an increase in funding."

Jan winked at Jack, who was rolling his eyes expressively. That explained why Saunders was in such a good mood.

"Watch what you say, though," Saunders cautioned. "Phones aren't that secure, and right now, every newshound on Earth wants an exclusive with you."

"Understood," Jack said.

Jan bit her lip. "What worries me is, what's to stop some unscrupulous type from coming here in an isolation suit? Heck, they could even fill us full of truth serum. We're getting poked all the time; we wouldn't know the difference."

"See those guards outside your door?"

Jan glanced up automatically. "Yes."

"They're mine. And they know each of the staff assigned to you by sight – ones hand-picked by the hospital's director. Anyone they don't know doesn't get in, no matter what credentials they show. Same drill goes for Tom."

"Thanks, boss."

"I promised to protect you from officialdom other than us, remember? I keep my word."

* * *

Morning light brought Shownae awake even before he heard Trikon's door open and close. When the knock came, Shownae promised to join him shortly in the eating area. His stomach could definitely use some food. Surprisingly, when he began moving about, his muscles had few complaints. Even his face looked almost back to normal. Save for the eye patch, of course.

Trikon was alone in the eatery when Shownae walked in. The Spacefarer regarded him in surprise.

"You heal quickly."

"Branga's wife-mate makes an amazing potion." Shownae sat down at the table. "What happened after I left?"

Trikon chose a bright red bamsk fruit from a bowl on the table. "I told Klyfin all about you coming to see me. You made the mistake of grabbing my arm, trying to make me listen to Moohri's voice. It took two technos to pull you off me and throw you out the door. I sent an aide to follow you, to find out where you were staying. He learned from an informant – mine – that you were headed for Ju'ule. Ever been there?"

"No."

"I doubted you would have, it is such a small village. Any stranger would be noticed. I have a friend there spreading word of a stranger of your description."

Shownae looked at him respectfully. "I am sure glad we're on the same side."

"We are only if you are proven right." Trikon's unwavering gaze left no doubt in the matter. "You wanted to see me before I left?"

Shownae let the veiled threat pass. "Last night you asked about teleportation. That is one part of something gigantic. You need to know the rest."

"I'm listening."

"Watch me closely." Making sure the door was closed, Shownae 'ported out, then a moment later, entered the eatery to stand facing an astonished Trikon. "That is teleportation. It works just as well between planets."

"What do you mean, between planets?" Trikon was sweating, though the room was cool.

Shownae sat down and told the Spacefarer about what had been happening on Orowa, Earth and Shalaii. All the while, Trikon stared at him, flabbergasted.

"And I suppose you can prove all that, too."

"Easily. And Ablakan has the added ability to split his focus. He wanted you to know he'll be monitoring you, and if you are ever in serious danger, he'll 'port you back here."

216

Trikon leaned forward eagerly. "Can I meet him?"

"He won't be awake yet. But Moohri would be, and he speaks to Ablakan every day."

"Alright. Let me talk to Moohri again."

* * *

Shownae was pacing his room, unspeakably bored with his forced inactivity, when Adron knocked.

"There is a call for you."

Shownae hurried down the hall and picked up the listen-far. It was Trikon.

"I cannot talk long," the Spacefarer said. "But Klyfin just left. He said he is going away for a few days, and I'm in charge while he's gone. It appears you were right."

Shownae's pulse quickened. "Can I 'port that console into the chamber now?"

"Yes. The technos I trust will examine it and document what they find. I must get back now, and I will probably stay late. The sooner we can get this done, the better – and safer – for all of us."

"Call me when you're ready to be 'ported here."

Shownae hung up the instrument and returned to the privacy of his room. Once in the recliner, he sent his focus to the planetoid, easily locating Moohri. *Trikon is ready for the console. Is that it beside you?*

Yes. May the fates be with us. Moohri's mental tone held considerable trepidation. So much rode on that one small box and its attendant wires.

I will let you know as soon as I hear anything. With that, Shownae 'ported the item into the chamber Trikon had visualized for him.

The listen-far rang almost immediately.

"We have it," Trikon confirmed, and hung up.

It was now in the Spacefarer's hands, and that of their mutual fates.

* * *

217

Fates again. Ablakan sat up in bed as the memory of a dream frustratingly faded from his mind. A small knock came at the door.

"Enter, please," Ablakan called out, and heard the door swing open.

Saymin's head accordioned itself around the corner of Ablakan's sleep chamber. "Good morning, sir. Did you rest well?"

"No. Something keeps pulling at me, but I can't grasp it. I hate that."

"My litter-brother's mate complains of that all the time," the valet commiserated. "Then my brother will be just falling asleep and she will awaken him to tell him what it was. He says he almost bit her once, he was so annoyed."

"I'll keep it to myself, if it comes up," Ablakan promised soberly, prompting Saymin to laugh.

The valet worked his way through Ablakan's wardrobe, choosing items of clothing with professional confidence. "Juneli will collect you soon. I had better ready you quickly." Which he did. Ablakan soon found himself dressed for the day's activities – whatever they might be.

When Juneli arrived, her smile seemed to warm the room.

"Gentle morning, vacationing sir," she teased. "Would you rather walk, or should we teleport to the kitchen?"

Right on cue, Ablakan's stomach made a melodic sound, and Juneli giggled.

"Teleport," he grinned. They joined hands and a moment later stood beside 'their' table in the kitchen.

"Good morning, sir," the Chief Morning Cook beamed as he placed a steaming plate of Ablakan's favorite breakfast before him. Juneli got her 'usual', which was meager compared to Ablakan's, but it was all she wanted that early in the day.

"You know my tastes too well already," Ablakan complained between bites. "One day I must surprise you."

Cook said cheekily, "Perhaps after you have filled out a bit?"

218

Ablakan nodded sheepish admission. He would have been robbing himself of too much in order to trick the staff. In the short time he'd been there, Ablakan had come to cherish the easy camaraderie of this morning ritual.

He was about to shovel another huge portion into his mouth (table manners were relaxed in the kitchen), when a knock sounded in his mind.

"Someone is reporting in," he announced. He put his utensil down and shut his eyebanks to open up to his visitor. He didn't notice his and Juneli's platters being quietly withdrawn and placed in the warming oven.

It was Shownae. *Klyfin's taken the bait, as you call it. I sent the console to Trikon, and told him of your offer to 'port him here if Klyfin tries anything. He really began to believe once he saw Klyfin leave 'for a few days'.* There was satisfaction in Shownae's mental voice. Ablakan knew he had suffered much from being suspected and disbelieved, and was pleased that the Orowan's credibility was being restored.

That is good news indeed. How long before they have the proof?

I am told the technos are working as fast as they can in the isolation room, testing the console. Trikon thinks they may be finished later today, if the fates are kind.

Juneli, watching Ablakan, saw him suddenly go catatonic.

"Sir, are you alright?" No response. Throwing caution to the wind, she began shaking him, trying to get through. "Ablakan! Can you hear me?"

Ablakan swallowed convulsively. "Not now, Juneli. My friends are in danger."

What's wrong? Shownae was asking, adding his consternation to the terror Ablakan was experiencing.

I just realized, Klyfin left something behind in the isolation room. Something small and – insidious. I don't know what it is, but it will kill the technos and anyone who is with them.

No! Shownae groaned. *I'll call you back.*

219

* * *

The door to their room opened, and Tom's bed was wheeled in. Jan and Jack rushed to greet him.

"Well, if it isn't the man of the hour!" Jack crowed. "How are you feeling?"

"Now that I'm here, a lot better."

And he looks it, too, Jan noted. She was too busy kissing him to have much to say at that moment.

"I missed you," Tom smiled, his eyes warm with unexpressed feeling.

Jan longed to hug the stuffing out of him, but that would have to wait. As would certain other things, Jan thought wistfully. She settled for scowling at him in mock severity. "I want you to promise me you'll never, ever try to get yourself killed again!"

"Try?" He squeaked, his expression a study of injured innocence. "I was trying to *not* get us all killed!"

"Avoiding the bullet would have been better," Jack pointed out.

"Well, if you want me to do it the *easy* way . . . "

Jan nodded emphatically. "I do. Heroism is not worth the price if you don't live to enjoy your laurels."

Soon after, the nurse finished hooking up his I.V. bottles and left the room. They immediately dropped the light-hearted banter.

"What's the latest?" Tom asked, looking from one to the other.

"Trikon's trusteds are testing the console from Moohri's ship; Ablakan's on vacation *sans* interfering mother; Shownae was injured by Klyfin and is in hiding, along with Trikon when the Spacefarer leaves work." She turned to Jack. "Have I missed anything?"

"Saunders is making a big deal in the media of this three-planet humanitarian mission thing. Says we're the darlings of the press right now, sight unseen," Jack contributed.

Tom wrinkled his nose. "We could do without that."

220

"Sorry, folks. You'd better get used to it. We're the 'catch of the day', and I don't think it'll change any time soon." Jack looked comfortably resigned to his place in the limelight.

Jan eyed him suspiciously. "Why do I get the feeling this doesn't bother you?"

Jack grinned coyly. "It attracts women."

* * *

Shownae 'ported himself right in front of Trikon, who was standing just outside the isolation chamber. Fortunately, no one else was present, and the technos inside were so involved in what they were doing, they didn't notice.

Trikon gaped at him. "What are you doing here?"

"Get them out of there, fast!"

"Why?"

Shownae grabbed Trikon's shoulders. "Trust me. Do it now."

Trikon rapped on the special glass enclosure. The technos looked up, and he motioned them out with sharp gestures before turning back to Shownae. "Now explain yourself."

Shownae lowered his voice as the technos headed for the door. "Ablakan just picked up that Klyfin put something in the chamber that will kill them. He used a human term he couldn't translate, but the feeling I got was it is something that compounds itself."

Trikon's eyes enlarged. "Then Klyfin knows what we are up to."

"Not necessarily. It may have been meant to kill Moohri if he were 'ported into the chamber without Klyfin's knowledge. Not that it will do those poor technos much good." Shownae had a terrible feeling it was already too late for them.

The examiners removed their flimsy protective garments and sealed them in bins.

"What is wrong?" the taller individual asked as he approached them.

Both Trikon and Shownae took an involuntarily step backward.

221

Trikon said unsteadily, "We have just gotten word that Klyfin may have poisoned the chamber."

They looked at each other in horror.

"How?" the shorter one asked.

Trikon didn't respond at once, considering the possibilities. When he spoke again, there was a tremor in his voice. "Ara waves. Scan for ara waves."

The shorter techno was closest to the equipment room. He removed the appropriate instrument and turned it on. The scanner crackled loudly.

The color drained out of his face. "The readings are at lethal levels. We will not survive." He checked his partner, whose readings were identically extreme.

"I am so sorry," Trikon whispered, reaching a hand ineffectually towards his stricken crew.

The shorter techno was the first to recover. With the instrument in hand, he walked determinedly back into the death chamber.

As Shownae and the others watched, the techno measured the levels at both sides of the room. Then he checked the console and signaled a negative response. Evidently, the source of the ara waves wasn't the console itself, which meant Moohri had not been contaminated. Not with ara waves, at any rate. He would have succumbed to this cumulative poison long before now, had he been exposed. The realization gave Shownae some measure of relief.

The techno inside the chamber scanned the room visually till his eyes settled on the small grill which led to the self-contained air circulator and purifier. He ran the wand across the grill, then stepped back as if bitten. He turned toward them and nodded firmly.

"I'll get the container." The techno outside the chamber trotted to the equipment room. He emerged to quickly wheel the heavy unit into the chamber. It no longer mattered whether he had additional exposure. The damage was already done.

Shownae opened his mouth to warn them not to destroy any fingerwhorl evidence on the canister, then shut it again. There would be none. The only reason Klyfin may not have taken such precautions with the rocket's console was that there should have been no way to recover it.

The technos pushed the container into the storage room, with the deadly substance now back inside it. The cosmic remnant had been part of a meteor shower the week before, and was being held at the Spacefarer complex until a more suitable location could be found.

The technos approached, taking care to keep their distance from the others. How much distance, if any, was safe, Shownae had no idea.

Trikon sealed the isolation chamber, using his acting Lead Spacefarer status to change the code to something only he could now open. Then he turned to his technos, compassion and regret etched on his face.

"Please report to the isomedic lab. I will tell them you're coming. I'll be there as soon as I can."

The taller techno said bitterly, "All I ask is, get him. Promise me you won't let him win."

"You have my word," Trikon vowed.

He picked up the listen-far and instructed the isomedic techs to bring in the best radiation doctor available.

Shownae was still trembling with reaction. "There must be something we can do for them."

"Check with the Shalaians and humans. See if they have a cure."

"Right away." Shownae called Ablakan first. The youth opened to him before he had finished knocking.

Did you find it? the youth asked breathlessly.

Yes. But it is too late for the technos, unless your people or the humans know something we don't. Shownae described as precisely as possible the substance which had poisoned his crew.

I will check with my Primary and Jan. Do not give up hope yet.

223

To Shownae, the encouragement sounded like a death gong. Listlessly, he tried to make sense of it all. Their one piece of hard evidence was now too contaminated to show anyone. There was no proof who had placed the radioactive chunk behind the grill, for if the technos had the combination to the equipment room, so must many others. Klyfin would have received minimal exposure in the short time it would have taken him to place the fragment in the slot. By now, no ara waves would be detectable on him. And when Klyfin came back, he would surely have them all charged with sabotage or treachery of some kind.

Shownae shook his head dejectedly. Trikon had promised he wouldn't let Klyfin win. But from where Shownae stood, it looked like the Lead Spacefarer already had.

* * *

On Earth, in a different kind of isolation chamber, Jan received the terrible news from Ablakan in stunned silence.

I'll call Saunders at once.

"What now?" Jack asked, looking like he didn't want to know. Jan told him and Tom, then reached for the phone and punched in Saunders' private number.

"I'm sorry, but if they have that level of exposure, they're finished," Saunders confirmed. "Unless the Shalaians have some wonder drug. And if they do, I want it – badly."

"Ablakan said he'd check with Tweno. We should know soon."

* * *

"We had better leave this room, too, and seal it off for now," Trikon said. "The ara levels aren't deadly, but they are well above what is recommended for prolonged exposure."

Shownae was only too glad to comply. From the hallway, Trikon pulled the heavy doors closed and reset the combination lock as he had with the one on the isolation chamber.

"Would you 'port us to my office?"

224

When they were seated there, Trikon grimaced. "Forgive my pessimism, but I don't believe there is anything in the universe that can save those two."

Shownae sighed heavily, having reached the same conclusion.

"Which means Klyfin now has two murders to add to the two attempted ones we know of. He has to be stopped, and fast. And I don't think either of us has the means to do it, with him being Lead Spacefarer."

Again Shownae agreed, waiting for Trikon to make his point.

"I propose bringing Administrator Wiltanus into this right now."

"How?" Shownae knew there were too many levels of bureaucracy shielding the commoner from the hereditary leader of Orowa. They would never get an audience unless they teleported in. But then they'd be summarily arrested.

"I am the top-ranking Spacefarer here at present. As such, I can contact the Administrator in a time of crisis. Once Klyfin returns, that opportunity will be lost. This may be our only chance."

"A dangerous one."

"Lately, it seems everything we do is."

Which was painfully true. "I am willing if you are," Shownae offered. They had certainly been putting their fates on the line of late.

Trikon reached for the listen-far.

"Wait," Shownae said, restraining Trikon's hand. Someone was calling in.

A morose Ablakan said what didn't need saying. Shownae thanked him and closed the connection before turning toward Trikon.

"Primary Tweno and Jan send their regrets. Their people have no cure, either."

Trikon's shoulders drooped. But when he gazed at Shownae, his eyes held determination. "Maybe we cannot save my technos, but we can avenge them. And I swear to you, I will."

225

Savagely he stabbed the buttons on the listen-far.

"This is Acting Lead Spacefarer Trikon. I have news of the utmost urgency and gravity. I must speak with the Administrator at once. Can you arrange it?"

An interminable delay followed, then Shownae saw Trikon stiffen.

"Administrator, thank you for taking my call . . . Yes, Lead Spacefarer Klyfin is away for a few days, but this could not wait. Can my colleague and I see you, please? I swear to you it is imperative, for the good of Orowa . . . We do have a way, unbelievable as it sounds. It is part of what we must show you. May we come now? . . . Thank you, Administrator." Trikon hung up, looking flushed.

"He agreed to see us?"

"Yes." Trikon grabbed hold of Shownae's arm, and a moment later, they stood before their astonished ruler.

* * *

"Are you Lead Spacefarer Klyfin?" Trikon's friend Yanch asked, as he approached the stranger in Ju'ule.

"I am. Have you news of the traitor Shownae?"

"Yes. Your aide just called to say he is now at Spacefarers. He refuses to leave your waiting room, insisting it is *you* who wish to see *him*. That was the message." Yanch walked away, again a disinterested bystander.

There was one public listen-far in the whole village. Klyfin made for it, snorting contemptuously. Shownae was coming to him like a calwa to slaughter, too much the fool to realize it was Klyfin who had tried to kill him. Unfortunately he, Klyfin, was a half-day's hard drive from his office.

"This is Lead Spacefarer Klyfin. I am in Ju'ule. You know where that is? Good. Send a spanner to get me at once. Yes, highest priority. . . . Of course it is me, you fool! Check my voiceprint if you must."

Under his breath, Klyfin cursed the suspicious underling. "Satisfied? Then do my bidding, and do not ever challenge me again!"

He slammed down the instrument with explosive force and stalked away to salve his wounded ego at the only spirits dispensary in Ju'ule.

Some time later, a commotion outside the window drew his scattered attention. A spanner was landing on the dusty street. He stared at it uncomprehendingly, then lurched to his feet. *His* spanner! How could he forget?

He ran unsteadily to the streamlined speeder. Taking care to avoid the multi-level rotors overhead, he let himself be helped aboard.

One of the many privileges of office, he smiled to himself. Soon he would have Shownae in his clutches. And this time, the fool would die; Klyfin would make sure of that.

His smile grew wider as a delicious image took form in his soggy brain: Moohri, shriveling up in the toxic radiation, having unwittingly traded his life for the chance to see that homely wife-mate of his and his squalling younglings. But perhaps that was too much to hope for. Still, when you set a trap, you know sooner or later you will catch prey.

* * *

"Administrator!"

The doomed technos bowed deeply, overwhelmed by the honor of such a visit.

"I wished to meet you in person," Wiltanus said through the speaker to their isolation room. "And to thank you for your enormous sacrifice. I have had Orowa's three top specialists check Lead Spacefarer Moohri's console, and they all confirm that Klyfin's fingerwhorls are inside. But I am afraid there is no cure for the poison he has inflicted upon you. All I can do is ensure that your families are well cared for."

They bowed in unison, and the shorter techno murmured, "That is most generous."

227

"There is one more thing I can do. Considering the extreme discomfort in the later stages of your illness, I am sanctioning a lethal sedative be administered to you if or when you decide you want it."

Shownae, who was standing a short distance to one side of the Administrator, stared at him in surprise. This form of compassion had been hotly debated for decades, and to this day remained outlawed. Surely the Administrator realized what a dangerous precedent he was setting. For all his peculiarities, Shownae knew himself to be a traditionalist, hopelessly wedded to the old ways.

The taller techno regarded their ruler with such naked gratitude that Shownae had to look away. But in that moment, Shownae understood what a rare gift the Administrator had bestowed on them, risking global censure in the name of mercy. Despite his own views towards suicide, Shownae's esteem for Wiltanus rose to unprecedented levels.

Wiltanus took the charts the medics handed him and wrote down his instructions. He signed his name to the bottom of each with a flourish before handing them back. They bowed and left the room.

"Klyfin will be here soon. Come, we must prepare," the Administrator said. He and Trikon placed their hand on Shownae's arms and were 'ported into the Lead Spacefarer's waiting room. Klyfin's aide sat at his desk, pasty-faced. It didn't take a psychic to know he thought he'd also be charged with his employer's crimes.

"Can you open Klyfin's door?" Wiltanus asked.

The cowering aide hurried to comply. Inside, every scrap of paper was locked away.

"Did you touch anything in here since he left?"

"N-No, Administrator. He said to leave it as it was, so I did." He was sweating profusely, but Shownae could detect no deceit.

Wiltanus turned toward Shownae, a silent question. Shownae nodded almost imperceptibly.

The ruler raised his voice. "Hesh."

A nondescript-looking fellow detached himself from the back of the waiting room. Shownae could have sworn they had been alone. Perhaps this was one of the Administrator's famed 'shadow-guards'. Rumor had it they could blend in so well you might look right at them and swear later you saw no one.

"Go through everything. I want to know what he's been up to."

The individual nodded, looking pleased with the assignment. On Wiltanus' orders, the aide unlocked every cabinet and drawer in the room, as well as the strongwall.

Wiltanus regarded him pointedly as the strongwall opened to his code. The aide flushed guiltily.

"I never looked," he said. "But I have sharp ears."

"Thanks to our friend Shownae, you are cleared of any wrongdoing. However, you will not wish to be here when your former boss returns. Come back tomorrow."

"Thank you, my Ruler!" He scurried from the room as though chikla were nipping at his heels.

Wiltanus smiled sadly. "That is how it is with underlings. They lead a worryful life, under the wrong boss."

* * *

The spanner touched down softly, and a ground minion hurried to open the door. The cool air had done Klyfin good, and his head felt reasonably clear. Which was fortunate, for he could not afford any mistakes.

He strode into the building and nodded curtly at workers who hastily sprung to attention. When he entered his waiting room, there sat Shownae, all alone.

Klyfin frowned, though secretly he was pleased. "Where is my aide?"

Shownae looked bored. "He kept coughing. Trikon came by and sent him home."

"That is Acting Lead Spacefarer Trikon to you," Klyfin said coldly. "Why have you come?"

"We must speak in private," Shownae whispered dramatically.

Klyfin's lip curled. "We *are* in private." He sighed expansively and locked the door. "There. Satisfied?"

"Yes, thank you."

"Now, what is this about?"

The psychic's body appeared insolently relaxed as he lounged back in the chair. "I thought you should have a chance to defend your actions before I have you charged with attempting to murder me."

Klyfin regarded him carefully, trying to decide if Shownae was that much of a fool or if this was some sort of trap. "Remove your clothes. All of them."

"No. Why should I?"

"Because you are trying to trick me into admitting to something I didn't do, and I won't have it," Klyfin snarled. "If you want a *private* chat, you shall have it, but not with any recorders around. Those are my terms."

Shownae pointed a digit at him. "You are in no position to dictate terms. I have one friend left: Moohri. If I do not call him by a certain time, he will know you killed me. And there is another who can bring him home. When that happens, you, too, will die. No, Klyfin, my clothes stay on, but you have my word that there are no recorders anywhere in this room."

"Your word." Klyfin made sure the phrase dripped with his contempt for the psychic.

"Yes, my word. Considering you tried to kill me, it is worth a lot more than yours is."

Klyfin glared at Shownae in silent hostility. Abruptly, he swiveled towards his office and unlocked the door. He swung it wide open and stepped inside. Much as he hated to admit it, he believed Shownae. So if there were no recorders in his waiting room, perhaps Shownae had teleported something – or even someone – into his private office. But no one was there, and everything looked exactly as it should.

With a shrug, Klyfin closed and re-locked the door before facing Shownae again. The one small difference was the syringe carefully clicked inside a holder in Klyfin's right sleeve. Shownae had once told him he could only read people's minds if their mental shields were down. It had better be true.

"Alright, I believe you. So what makes you think I tried to kill you?" Klyfin pulled his chair close to Shownae before sitting down. The drug would prove fatal injected anywhere in the body, but the closer to the heart, the faster it would work.

Shownae rolled his eyes upward in thought. "Let's see –." At that instant, Klyfin struck.

And gasped, for the hand which had a moment before held the syringe was now empty.

The door to his office opened, and Administrator Wiltanus, Trikon and two security guards strode into the suddenly-crowded waiting room. Wiltanus was holding a cushion on which lay the incriminating syringe.

Klyfin gawked at them, uncomprehending. "How could you be in there?"

"Ablakan teleported us in and out as needed," Wiltanus said with a tight smile.

Klyfin felt the room begin to spin. He fell back onto the chair with an unceremonious thud.

"Former Lead Spacefarer Klyfin," Administrator Wiltanus' voice echoed above the ringing in Klyfin's ears. "You are hereby charged with two murders and three attempted murders. If found guilty, you will be put to death."

* * *

A jubilant Ablakan called Jan just before dinner.

Klyfin has been arrested, and Trikon is now head of the space department on Orowa. He is asking that you tell him, through me, how to test for alien diseases. They are building another isolation chamber, and as soon as they can make sure Moohri has no diseases, they will let him come home.

Oh, how wonderful! Jan cried. *We'll find out from Saunders how to get this information in a form they can understand and*

231

use. Maybe we can send them sterilized equipment to speed things up.

Although Saunders would be off work now, Jack agreed that for such good news, he probably wouldn't mind being disturbed at home. They had only been given the number two days before and admittedly, the privilege was burning a hole in their collective pockets.

Saunders grunted when Jack told him, but at least he didn't chew them out. By the next morning, a specialized team was already being assembled to fulfill Trikon's requirements. As part of the process, DNA, blood, urine, skin and several other informative samples would be extracted from Shira, Trikon and Shownae and transported to the lab Saunders was setting up at Ames to test for offworld diseases. Equipment and instructions on its use were 'ported to Moohri so he could provide similar samples for testing.

For the first time since they became involved, Jan and Shownae had little to do but wait.

CHAPTER 13

During the rest of the three-week isolation period, Jan had numerous conversations with Primary Tweno. For the first few days, Ablakan was kept hopping, 'porting himself from the palace to Tweno's old office in Tabix to let Tweno talk to Jan. In part the chats were an exchange of information, but they also served to improve Tweno's burgeoning command of English. The ruler was eager to speak to Saunders, but that would have to wait until Jan was released, since Saunders would require physical contact with her to connect mentally with Tweno. It had not escaped the Primary's notice that high-level human interaction with Shalaii was politically blessed at this time. Tweno assured Jan he intended to make the most of it, in the interests of both worlds – a goal she heartily shared.

On the day the Offworld Disease Lab became operational, Jack couldn't wipe the smirk off his face, for 'his' rat had just been sent to Moohri. He kept bugging Jan for updates on 'Fido', despite the fact it turned out to be female. Moohri and Fido seemed to hit it off well, and Jan humored Jack by making up tales of the rat's cute antics.

* * *

When the Primary returned to the island, he brought with him Ablakan's mother. Jan could feel the boy's frustration even before he spoke.

Mother has been here less than a day, and already she is demanding things and telling everyone they must bow to me and call me 'First', even though I will not be one for many prilks. And she wants me to walk tall and talk down to everyone.

Why don't you tell Primary Tweno? Jan suggested. *I'm sure he could find a way to get her off your back.*

He is too busy for me to bother him with such small things. I am supposed to take work away from him, not give him more.

An idea occurred to Jan. *You speak to Tweno daily, don't you?*

Yes, usually several times a day. Ablakan sounded surprised at the question.

233

Then why not ask him what is the proper way for you to handle a bossy underling?

Mother – an underling? There was silence for a few seconds. *Perhaps you are right.*

At some point, she will have to accept that, while you are her child, she is your subject, so to speak, Jan continued, warming to the topic. *My guess is, the sooner it is brought to her attention, the more likely she is to accept it. Everything is new for her right now, and she'll have many adjustments to make. One more may slide in without too much resistance, if it is presented the right way.*

But instead Tweno did become involved, for Ablakan reported the following day that his mother would be setting up and running a small gift shop in the palace. It was thought that since the palace staff would be her main clientele, she would have to treat them with respect to stay in business. All in all, a perfect solution, Jan decided.

During the same conversation, Jan realized she hadn't heard anything much about what Ablakan was doing.

Are you keeping up with your Learn-more?

Yes, I have a tutor who is teaching me much between my contacts with you and Shownae and Moohri and helping the Primary learn English. After work and learning and evening meal, I go out for exercise and have fun with the other children.

Sounds like a busy schedule, Jan said. *Have you made friends your age yet?*

Yes. And there is a nice girl. I think she likes me. We ride hurrymaries and run on swimmers together, he said rather breathlessly, sounding for once every bit his young age.

Jan smiled at Tom. "First love?" she mouthed.

Tom, who liked to be included in these exchanges, nodded. 'Their' little boy was growing up.

* * *

Two days after Moohri received the rat, Jan called Saunders with disturbing news. Shownae had reported through Ablakan that

234

Moohri was feeling ill. The symptoms sounded suspiciously like an allergy. When told to keep his distance from the rat for a couple of days and to not wear anything that the rat had touched, the symptoms abated.

Jack was heartbroken, and when the rat was 'ported into an isolation room for examination, he insisted that the rat's life be spared. He planned to keep it as a pet when he got out. Of course, not having seen the rat, Jack never knew if he got Fido or a substitute. To everyone's relief, Moohri's health quickly returned to normal.

* * *

When the quarantine period passed without anyone having had so much as a sniffle more than they arrived with, and no alien pathogens could be found in any specimens, they were declared safe for release. That day, Saunders announced that the government would be footing the hospital bills for all concerned. Jan could almost hear the collective sighs of relief throughout the isolation wing.

Saunders himself arrived mid-morning. Security into the isolation ward was as tight as ever, but entry into individual quarters had been relaxed, as their impending release was common knowledge. Saunders flashed his card to the guards and was let in.

"Hiya, boss," Jan grinned, heady with the prospect of leaving medical prison. "Come to spring us?"

Saunders shook his head. "Even NASA can't override medical protocol."

Jack looked at him quizzically, obviously not believing that.

Their boss pulled up the one vacant chair in the room, to sit facing the others. "The magic hour, I understand, is 11:30. Which gives us time for a little chat on how to handle the media. I've decided to let the press interview you at Ames' Public Affairs office, where numbers can be more easily managed."

"Home ice advantage." Tom nodded his approval.

"Exactly. As you can imagine, everyone wants a piece of you – magazines, talk shows, the works. You've seen our press releases, which were approved by the White House beforehand, so you know we've made most of the details public. They'd have come out sooner or later anyway."

"Good. I hate keeping secrets," Jan smiled.

But there was no trace of humor on Saunders' face. "Jan, you're in daily contact with your offworld counterparts. Anything not in these releases is not to be disclosed until Public Affairs or I have okayed it, understand? That's important. You have no idea how quickly things can get twisted around by the media. And what people see, read, hear, they believe." He looked at each of them in turn. "Right now, we have public opinion on our side, as well as the press. I intend to keep it that way." When they all murmured their agreement, Saunders relaxed a little. "So all of you, just talk about your personal experiences surrounding what we've released, nothing more.

One thing we'll have to watch out for is a backlash against teleportation, especially in light of Black's misuse of it. To date, the 'porter on each planet has protected and stood in for the anothers. I'd like to see that continue, as it minimizes vulnerability. Now that people know it can be done, everyone'll be trying to learn it. We'll need some sort of control set up to protect us from the the 'Ryan Blacks' of every world. Congress is scrambling to get something on the books in case it blows up in our faces. Jan, we could use your input on this."

"I'll talk it over with Ablakan and Shownae, as well as between ourselves," Jan promised, her gesture taking in the others in the room.

"Good. With the spotlight on you three, I want a security detail with you at all times. You're too hot a commodity, and I don't want any 'incidents'."

Although this didn't sit well with her, Jan realized the necessity. She just hoped it would be a temporary evil. If she had

236

to 'port herself and her colleagues away from every gate-crasher, they'd never get any work done.

Saunders left soon afterwards to handle a few last-minute details, but he promised to be back in time for their release.

"Chatty, wasn't he?" Jack observed.

Tom smirked knowingly. "Cat about to catch the canary, I would say."

"And we're the bait," Jan added, not liking it at all.

When finally the magic hour arrived, the group was escorted to a waiting limousine. Jan's suggestion she 'port them all to Ames was vetoed by Saunders, who wanted to avoid antagonizing the media at all cost. Extra security kept the onlookers and reporters in line. Saunders let the photographers get in a few shots, but refused to answer any of the questions shouted at them. He promised the reporters they would have their chance at the press conference scheduled for 1:30 that afternoon.

The group disembarked at the front entrance to Ames' main building. There again they had to run the gauntlet of the eager newshounds, but security was up to the challenge.

Jack exhaled gustily when they got inside. "Whew! I thought they would eat us alive."

"They'll try to this afternoon," Saunders warned. "So be prepared. Heroes – that's you folks right now – make a tasty meal."

Their boss led them past offices and labs of all sorts. Although no one left their stations, all eyes were on the procession, and many people smiled, waved or gave them a 'thumbs up'.

Their journey came to an end with Saunders holding a door open to let them enter a sizable cafeteria which had obviously been reserved for the occasion. An enticing cold buffet was laid out on one table.

"Thought you could use some human food after three weeks of hospital fare," Saunders smiled.

Jan feasted her eyes on the spread. "Oh, yes, indeed!"

"Most thoughtful, sir," Tom murmured.

Jack looked like he might attack the offerings with both hands.

The door opened, and a tall man with bushy white hair and a slight limp entered the room. Saunders strode toward him, hand outstretched.

"Good to see you, Eric." Saunders shook the older man's hand warmly before turning to the others.

"Jack Foxworth, and Jan and Tom Brody, may I introduce your new boss, Dr. Eric Rhodes. Effective immediately, he is Director of Interplanetary Relations."

Jack looked deeply impressed. "I always wanted to meet you, sir, but by the time I'd climbed high enough to have a shot at it, you had retired." He turned to the Brodys. "This is *the* Eric Rhodes, who developed the theory of the hydrogen ion drive for space travel. Would have won the Nobel Prize for it, too, but that was the year Bardeen, Cooper and Schriffer advanced the theory of superconductivity."

Rhodes chuckled. "Good of you to remember, son. Lesley here asked me to ride herd on you folks. It was more than an old space jockey like me could pass up."

"I'm supposed to be retired, too," Tom said, somewhat wistfully.

"Well, Tom," Rhodes said with a conspiratorial wink. "I'll take excitement over retirement any day."

Tom rubbed his chest reminiscently. "Too much excitement can kill you."

"Hmm, yes. We'll try to keep it to a comfortable level for a while. Are you sure you're up to this media thing? We can excuse you, if you like."

"No, I'm alright, as long as they're not carrying guns."

Rhodes clapped Tom lightly on the shoulder. "Good man. Well, I don't know about you young 'uns, but I'm hungry."

Without further ado, Rhodes picked up a plate and started shoveling food onto it. The others quickly followed suit. As they ate, Rhodes chatted them up with the ease of a senior talking to the grandkids.

"Tell me about Ablakan," he urged at one point. "Is he special for that planet, too – a child prodigy?"

Jan had to think about that. "Well, certainly the telepathic, teleporting side of him is. But other than that, I don't know. He's the only Shalaian kid I've met so far."

"Someday I'd like to let Zach talk to him. My grandson's crazy about aliens – er, offworlders. Been hounding me something fierce since he heard I'd been offered this assignment."

Jan smiled, thinking what fun that might be for the Shalaian as well. "I'm sure we could arrange it. Ablakan would probably enjoy meeting a juvenile human. So far, he has only spoken to adults."

Rhodes turned his attention towards Jack. "I understand you've talked to Tweno a couple times."

"Actually, four times now." Jack glanced furtively at Saunders.

"Good, good. What's your slant on him?"

Jack paused, picking his words carefully. "I'm no empath, of course, but he comes across as having a lot of integrity. Very fair, but nobody's fool. The kind of a man – er, guy I like to deal with: a straight shooter. What's your opinion?" He looked at Jan.

"Yes, very much so. And Ablakan respects him a lot and isn't afraid of him any more. I would trust Ablakan's judgment on anyone."

Rhodes nodded. "And Wiltanus?"

Jan shrugged. "He's just come on the scene. I'd have to say, at the moment he's an unknown quantity. Although, Shownae was impressed with him and how he handled Klyfin and the doomed technos."

"I look forward to a meeting of the minds, then," Rhodes commented drolly. He pointed his fork at Tom. "I understand you're the one who started all this, picking up on life in that star system. Impressive."

Tom looking embarrassed but pleased. "It was more a feeling than anything substantial, but I'm glad it worked out."

Rhodes glanced at his empty plate, then at his watch. "Well, folks, now that we've gotten to know each other a bit, I guess we'd best go meet the press."

Jan was shocked to realize it was 1:20. The interview would begin in 10 minutes, leaving her barely time enough to freshen up.

"Would you excuse me?" she said. "Got to make pretty."

They took their places on stools set on a raised platform behind a staggering array of microphones. To Jan it seemed redundant, as they were each wearing cordless microphones. A podium had been pushed to one side, to lend an air of informality.

Flashbulbs exploded from every direction. For some reason, her initial nervousness seemed to disappear with the flashes. She looked at Tom, and he gave her hand a little squeeze. She could feel him going formal, his defense against this necessary intrusion on their privacy. Jack appeared excited and overwhelmed. Dr. Rhodes settled back, looking at ease and grandfatherly.

When the last of the reporters had been seated, Saunders stood up. "Thank you for not pestering my staff too badly the last few days." That drew a few derisive snorts, for security had made certain they couldn't. "I know you have a lot of questions for these folks. But before you start, I am delighted to announce we have successfully conned Dr. Eric Rhodes out of a well-earned retirement to head the newly-formed Interplanetary Relations Department."

That drew widespread murmurs of approval. Saunders waited for silence before resuming. "Now, I realize it's these three you're most anxious to grill. But just remember, they've been cooped up in isolation for three weeks, so if they exhibit a bit of cabin fever, don't take it personally. Please ask your questions one at a time, and give them a chance to answer it fully."

A balding man near the front raised his pen. "Jan, how long have you known you could teleport?"

"Only about a month."

"How did you do it the first time?"

Jan hesitated. She'd been expecting the question, but not right away. "It's hard to describe," she replied, hoping she didn't sound too evasive. "You don't really realize what you're doing until it's done, and then you wonder how in the world you did it at all. Over time, you get use to it, of course."

"But now that you're used to it, how is it done?" The reporter's pen was poised over the pad, eager for details.

Saunders interjected. "Sorry, that's classified."

"Then how did Dr. Black learn it?" a woman wanted to know.

Saunders shrugged. "Hard to say. He had been working on it for years, I understand. Presumably, seeing Jan do it gave him the clue he needed."

"Jan, do it for us now, will you?" a portly man in a blazer requested. "Just in here."

Jan looked at Saunders, who nodded. Jan focused inside herself, effectively shutting out all those around her. She placed herself in the only vacant spot in the room, which was in front of the fire exit. She was rewarded with loud applause. Then she 'ported herself beside the chair she had occupied on the stage seconds before.

"These aliens you talk to, what can you tell us about them, besides this?" The sharp-faced woman waved a press release dismissively.

Jan's face softened. "Ablakan, the Shalaian boy, is the type of kid we'd all like to call our own. He's strongly empathic, and feels deeply for others – that's not the same thing, by the way. He comes from a poor family, I understand. His father died a couple of years back, and his mother worked hard to keep them fed and clothed before his psychic skills, in part, won him his present position as First-in-Training. He's resourceful and kind, and always ready to help – sort of like a Boy Scout." That got a few smiles. "I – we all – consider him a dear friend." Tom and Jack nodded emphatically on either side of her.

"Shownae – he's the Orowan psychic – I haven't known as long, and I can't talk to him directly. As the press release explains, no human who's tried so far can."

"Why is that, exactly?" One man's voice boomed above similar queries.

Jan considered. "Their imagery is so foreign to our way of thinking that we can't translate it into human terms. Ablakan tells me the Orowans have much the same trouble with many of the images I send. Ablakan translates between us, although he sometimes draws a blank on what Shownae or Moohri – that's the stranded Orowan astronaut – is saying and has to ask them to put it another way."

"How do you know he's telling you the truth about what he translates?"

Jan was careful to keep her expression neutral, but the question rankled.

"Well, for one thing, all three of us are empaths as well as telepaths. We can tell when a linked mind is open or closed to us, or hiding something or lying. All three of us are always open to each other when we talk, and there's no way we could lie without the others knowing it immediately. And none of us would want to," she added. In fact, a couple of times lately she had – she thought – successfully fibbed to Ablakan to help him through a rough spot, but she wasn't about to admit that to this bunch.

"What about their governments? How do you know they won't make your friends send invaders or plagues or bombs?" That drew many comments of agreement.

Jan actually relaxed, now that the dreaded question was out in the open.

"In the first place, neither Ablakan nor Shownae would comply, any more than I would if I were told to do so by our government. Anyway, Shalaii doesn't even have a word for 'war'; Ablakan was quite upset when I told him what it meant. I don't know about Orowa, but from the feelings I've picked up from Shownae and Moohri, violence doesn't seem to be a large part of

242

their makeup the way it is with humans. One thing I've come to realize, in dealing with these people: if any planet is a threat, it's ours, not theirs.

"I'll give you an example: I had told them Dr. Black had to be stopped, no matter how, and when the crunch came – even after he shot Tom and we didn't know whether or not Tom was still alive – all three of us 'ported him back to Shyr instead of spacing him or throwing him into the sun or something. They both tried to buy us the few seconds' time we needed to escape, rather than do him harm. That in itself should tell you something about their character."

"So you really trust them?" came from someone in the back row.

Jan nodded. "Absolutely. Ablakan and I have trusted each other with our life on at least one occasion, and Shownae has come to our rescue as well." She paused, making eye contact with the woman who had posed the question. "Please try to understand. Ablakan and I just started out as telepathic penpals. When Moohri's rocket crashed and we heard his psychic scream, Ablakan didn't have to try to help, any more than I did. But he has repeatedly put himself in danger by telling powerful people on his planet about it in an effort to help Moohri get rescued. If he were human, would you hesitate to call him brave, compassionate, a hero? Why does his being an offworlder make that any different? Shownae risked Black going after him for his efforts to save us, too. And he was badly injured at the time. Ablakan and Shownae are just plain good folks. I'm proud to call them friends."

The balding man who had asked the original question looked unconvinced. "Okay, but even assuming their intentions are good, you said yourself Ablakan is just a kid. You can't expect him to defy his government, if they decide we're a threat or something. I'm sure every planet has its version of brainwashing or coercion."

"Maybe so," Tom said, speaking for the first time. "But it's that 'get them before they get us' attitude that has sparked or fuelled countless wars and atrocities here. We have a chance to be part of something unprecedented – a cooperative galactic community. For heaven's sake, let's not blow this one, too. If there ever is a change in one of the three telepaths, it would be picked up by the other two; you can bet on that. So for now, let's not borrow trouble we don't have, okay?"

Jan smiled gratefully at Tom. "I couldn't agree more. Can't we just this once live up to our highest potential instead of down to our basest instincts? Don't forget, the crux of this initiative is to rescue Moohri. It's up to the planetary leaders to decide among themselves where they go from there."

Apparently, that satisfied them for the moment, for the reporters took a different tack, one Jack obviously could have done without.

"Mr. Foxworth, why did you wait so long before letting NASA know what was going on?"

Jack cleared his throat, glancing guiltily at Saunders' poker face. "Well, I really didn't have any hard evidence. The most compelling proof was my own experience of talking with the offworlders, and that could have been put down as hypnosis or just about anything. By then it was a foot race to get food to Moohri before his body shut down on him. And then we – that is, I – brought Dr. Black into it, and we had to deal with the trouble he was causing. It just never seemed the right time," he finished lamely.

"Did you get demoted for it?"

Jack flushed. "I don't exactly know." This time he looked at Rhodes – rather beseechingly, Jan thought.

"No," Rhodes stated. The relief on Jack's face was almost comical.

A tall, well-dressed woman spoke up. "What will he be doing?" Jack flashed her a grateful smile and turned eager ears towards his new boss.

Rhodes cleared his throat. "Understand, I just arrived this morning, so there are many details yet to be worked out. However, Mr. Foxworth will remain the Brodys' immediate supervisor, reporting directly to me. From what I gather, the three of them have done remarkably well so far working as a team. I see no reason to change that."

Several pens raised in the air. Rhodes pointed to the one in the fourth row on the right.

"It says here that Tom will be trying to pick up on other life forms in the universe. Isn't that dangerous? Just because the Shalaians and Orowans seem peaceful doesn't mean every other species will be."

"That's true. If Tom believes a planet is occupied, we will add it to the database of 'possibles' we're compiling. We have no intention of making new contacts at this time."

"Would you tell us before you do?" the same reporter asked.

Rhodes turned toward Saunders. "That decision would not be made by this office. It would be a United Nations-level decision, wouldn't you say?"

"It would pretty much have to be," Saunders agreed.

Again a flurry of pens rose in the air. Saunders pointed, and the owner of that pen asked, "What about space exploration in general? Now that Jan can teleport, will you be looking for planets to colonize?"

Saunders' lips held a hint of a smile, suggesting to Jan that she wasn't the only one who had harbored that particular dream.

"Such a decision has yet to be made. But now it is at least possible. Correct me if I'm wrong."

This last was directed at Jan, and it caught her off guard. Could she?

"I don't know; I've only ever picked up on people. Without someone to focus on . . . " her voice trailed off uncertainly. Jan resolved to give it a try at the earliest opportunity.

Again the subject changed abruptly.

"Speaking of 'people', how about letting us talk to Ablakan?" said a well-known columnist. The room erupted in support for that idea.

Jan regarded her employers. Saunders' expression was carefully neutral, and Dr. Rhodes only shrugged. Apparently, neither had any serious objection, but the feeling Jan got from the reporters made her think of a feeding frenzy.

"I'll have to ask him," she said. "If he agrees, be gentle, okay? Remember, remarkable as he is, he's still a kid." She paused to let that sink in. "If he agrees to talk to you, you'll all have to hold hands –" Chuckles and various comments rippled through the crowd at that. "The closest of you to Jack will take his hand, and he'll connect to Tom, who will hold mine. I'll be monitoring what goes on very closely. If you start hounding or upsetting Ablakan, I'll let go of Tom's hand and that'll be the end of it. So I mean it; be nice."

Jan made eye contact with several people, and got the impression the admonishment was being taken to heart. She quieted her mind and sent out the call.

We are out of the isolation ward, she informed Ablakan. *And talking to a roomful of reporters at our space department. They would like to meet you, if you don't mind.*

A roomful – that is a lot? he asked.

Yes, indeed. But I warned them if they didn't act nice I'd disconnect them. If you agree to this – and you don't have to, you know; it's completely up to you – I'll make sure they keep it short.

Ablakan's mental voice turned quizzical. *I have never talked to many people at once. It might be interesting.*

Jan blinked. *It might at that. I'll get them set up, then. And thanks.*

She raised her voice. "Ablakan is ready. If you'll join hands, we can begin. You'll have to ask your questions one at a time, like you've just been doing, only mentally. And please don't use too big words, okay?"

Obediently, they all joined hands, and Jack and Tom completed the link to Jan.

We're ready at this end, Ablakan, Jan said. "And you folks – don't shout.". A few people tittered, and it set the tone for the interview.

Ablakan, how old are you? one woman asked.

I am 14 prilks. I think that is about 10 Earth years.

How long do your people live? another one wanted to know.

Most people die when they want to, but some wish to see how long they can live even when they don't feel well any more. That started the media off on a tangent, and at length Jan intervened, asking if they had questions on other topics.

One reporter cleared his throat. *I do. Since you teleported Dr. Black, can you teleport yourself as well? Like to here?*

I have practiced teleporting myself around the palace and this island. And I did to the Primary's old office for a while. But now that Primary Tweno is here, he doesn't want me to leave the island unless he knows I will be safe where I'm going, Ablakan explained. *I could not go to Earth because I may bring Shalaian diseases or bring back Earth ones.*

I know. But if you didn't have to worry about diseases, the man persisted. *Would you come visit Jan?*

Yes, I want to more than anything, Ablakan said with such deep longing that several sniffles were heard from supposedly hardened reporters.

Another asked, *What do you have to learn to become a First?*

I do not know yet. The Primary is learning to be a Primary, and doing his work as First also. Mostly, my job right now is talking to Jan and Moohri and Shownae, and teaching English to Primary Tweno, so he can talk well to Dr. Saunders and others on Earth. It is a very good language – easy – and he is learning fast.

That triggered the inevitable question, *What does your language sound like?*

247

Jan winced in anticipation of the discordant sounds soon to assault their mental ears. She reminded him hastily. *Volume, please.*

Okay. There followed a lengthy sentence that made Jan's head spin, even at the lower 'sound' level. The reporters reacted with a variety of exclamations, some rather crude. Jan hoped Ablakan wouldn't ask her to translate them.

At length, one man said, *I understand your people didn't know there was life on other planets, either. How are they taking the news?*

Some are happy, some afraid. Like you, they wonder if Earth or Orowa will try to hurt us, Ablakan explained.

What do you tell them?

Jan and Shownae are kind people. We three will not let anyone hurt anyone, he declared resolutely.

Jan shook her head vehemently. *No, we certainly will not.*

The questions that followed mostly dealt with life on Shalaii. Ablakan answered them easily. When people started casting about for more questions to ask, Jan ended the interview. She thanked Ablakan for his time and broke the link to the crowd.

Beautifully done, dear, she told him quickly. *I'll talk to you later, if that's alright. I'd like to follow up on something you said.*

Any time, Jan. And I did enjoy that. Ablakan projected a grin, and severed the connection.

Saunders got to his feet and said, "Any final questions before we call it a day?"

"What will Jan be doing, now that it's all out in the open?" a young woman asked.

"For now, it will be business as usual. As you know, we're helping the Orowans set up a lab to test for alien diseases, so they know whether or not it's safe for Moohri to be brought home. There are several ideas we're considering, and we'll let you know what they are as soon as they become more than pipe dreams."

He evaded a few more leading questions, then brought the session to a close. As the trio filed out, Saunders shepherded them towards a waiting limo.

"I think that went pretty well," Jack said, glancing at Saunders for his reaction.

"Acceptable. But you never know how they may twist things." Saunders consulted his watch. "I didn't want to tell you beforehand – you had enough on your minds with the press – but we're due at the White House this afternoon."

Jack looked startled. "*The* White House?"

"Indeed. The President and the Secretary-General of the United Nations want to brief us – Jan especially – on 'what now from here'."

As he turned away, Tom raised a querying eyebrow, having caught the guarded look in Jan's eyes. Jack noticed it, too, and nudged Tom, who gave the smallest of shrugs.

Jan was unusually quiet for most of the short ride to Ames' airstrip where they boarded a private jet for the trip to the Capitol. Once the plane leveled off, Jan claimed to be tired and shut her eyes. Only Tom, who was sitting beside her, could see the telltale flutter of her eyelids as she sent out her psychic call. Saunders was seated in front of Jan, scanning a report. Dr. Rhodes had stayed behind to finish reading Jan's notes on the telepathic conversations to date.

Ablakan, can you get Shownae to join us, please? Jan asked, after the boy answered her 'knock'.

When Shownae entered the link, Jan had Ablakan fill him in on recent events before she explained why she had requested the 'conference call'.

We are on our way to meet the President of our country, and the head of our largest group of allied nations, she informed them. *I don't know what instructions I'll be given, but I want to suggest something to you both.*

Jan outlined her idea, and the three of them discussed it in great detail, fine-tuning it as they went. Ablakan wrote out the

English words to make sure he had down verbatim what they had agreed on.

I will tell a short version of this to our President and the head of the United Nations, Jan said at last. *I don't know how they'll take it, but if we stand firm, I don't think they'll have much choice but to agree.*

I will do the same with our Primary, Ablakan said.

He then translated for Shownae, who replied, *So far, I can only talk to Trikon. But he has been speaking to our Administrator, and I am certain Trikon will discuss this with him.*

Jan felt the tension in her mind ease. *Thank you, dear friends. We will never let anyone turn something this wonderful into a tragedy.* They both heartily agreed.

Jan 'hung up' and yawned. Before she could decide what to do next, she had drifted off to sleep.

* * *

The change in air pressure awakened Jan. A look out the window confirmed they were beginning their descent. Having never been to Washington DC, she watched the cityscape below her with interest.

Tom gave her a tentative smile, and Jan realized her 'chat' had not gone unnoticed. She winked at him, but said nothing. Now was not the time.

Jan didn't pay attention to much on the limousine ride to the White House. She kept going over their plan in her mind, looking for hidden flaws and trying to anticipate how it would be received. For that matter, she had no guarantee her counterparts' bosses would be receptive either. Jan took a deep breath and tried to calm herself. Furtively, she wiped her sweaty palms on her new outfit. You handled Black's attempt on your life, she reminded herself. You can handle this, too.

At the White House, they were escorted to a beautifully-appointed waiting room and informed that the President would be along shortly. The door opened not five minutes later, and the

President and U.N. Secretary-General strode towards their little group, hands outstretched.

The President seemed genuinely pleased to meet them, but the Secretary-General was more reserved. She could feel his uncertainty. Evidently, something wasn't sitting well with him.

After exchanging pleasantries, the group followed their host to a small meeting room, the tone of which was informal and inviting. Beverages were laid out beside a gleaming silver tray of pastries on a rich-hued, redwood coffee table. Six deep luxurious chairs fanned out on either side of the table. Once seated, they were urged to partake of the offerings. Then the President cleared his throat.

"People," he began. "You sure know how to set the world on its heels. This meeting is pretty informal, so please feel free to speak your mind." He turned his head slightly to address Saunders. "Lesley, we'll be leaving the day-to-day stuff in your court, but I –". He glanced at the Secretary-General. "That is, we – think it's important to agree on the basics. How we handle this could determine much of Earth's future direction."

"Yes, sir," Saunders agreed. "I have been following this very closely. I've spoken to Jan's contacts – although the Orowans I couldn't understand directly –"

"I know," the President said, indicating a report which lay on the coffee table.

"– And it is my considered opinion that they are pretty much as they seem. Jan and the other two telepaths have faithfully pursued their primary goal of rescuing Moohri. I have no reason to doubt their sincerity or integrity, sir, and it forms an excellent basis for friendship between our three species."

Jan fidgeted uncomfortably. She only hoped he would not regret voicing his opinion after she had had her say.

The Secretary-General addressed Saunders. "Once this Moohri fellow has been returned home, are Shalaii and Orowa interested in establishing trade relations with Earth? Has this been discussed at all?"

251

Saunders regarded Jan, his eyebrows raised in silent query.

Jan nodded. "Ablakan, Shownae and I have talked a little about how wonderful it would be to exchange information and technology. When I spoke to Tweno – he was still First at the time, but now he's their Primary – he was quite keen on it. As I recall, he's the one who brought it up."

The Secretary-General pursed his lips. "Did he mention anything about weapons, that sort of thing?"

"Oh, no. He wants some equipment for surveying a few of the other planets in their solar system. And technologies to help them cure some diseases they still don't know how to handle. I understand they've got most of them beat. My guess is they may be a lot more advanced than we are in disease control."

The President asked, "Anything else come up?"

"Tweno's hoping – as is Trikon, the new head of the Orowan space department, at least until Moohri returns – to have a decontamination chamber on each world so we can visit each other in person."

The President looked pleased. "Yes, that would facilitate things. How is Primary Tweno's English coming?"

"Very well, actually," Jan said. "I spoke to him a number of times while we were in isolation. He must have a real gift for languages because he's already almost as skilled as Ablakan, and it's been just under three weeks."

The President absently tapped an appointment book with his pen. "Excellent. We'll need to get the legal boys in on this, and find suitable ambassadors. And linguists to try and decipher the Orowan's language –."

"Mr. President," Jan interrupted, trying to calm her pounding heart. The time had arrived. "You said earlier we could speak our minds. May I speak frankly? *Very* frankly?"

He seemed taken aback, and eyed her briefly before saying, "Go ahead. This is strictly off the record."

Jan glanced at the others. Their faces held varying degrees of wariness, no doubt wondering what she was up to.

"On our way here, I had a long talk with Ablakan and Shownae at my request; I initiated it. I have kept it to myself, so if you get mad at me, don't take it out on anyone else, because they know nothing of what I'm about to say."

She stopped to take a deep breath and calm herself as best she could. No one moved or said a word.

"As you of course realize, without us three 'porting telepaths, there is no communication or interaction between the planets. That puts us in a very strong bargaining position – if we don't end up in jail for it." She smiled weakly at her own joke.

She had their undivided attention, though no one spoke. "Because of the uniqueness of our position, we could ask almost any wage for our services and be reasonably certain of getting it, am I right?"

The President nodded. "Presumably."

"In each case, we are offering to forego that. We'll work for a normal basic living wage, in exchange for our planetary leaders' agreement on the following:

Ablakan, Shownae and I have formed an alliance – we might call it the Teleporter's Guild or some such. Although we'll continue to work for our own planet regarding communication and teleporting of things back and forth, we will be responsible to each other first, and our planet second. What that means is none of us will let our world do anything to gain at the expense of the others. And we'll help and protect each other as we've been doing all along.

In essence, sirs, we intend to police all interactions and make sure everyone treats each other properly and plays fair. That's the bottom line. You may call this treason, but it is our way of making sure the three species remain friends."

Before the President could respond, Jack and Tom were on their feet.

"I agree wholeheartedly with my wife," Tom declared. "And I add my possibly inflated salary into the pot, if need be. I'm supposed to help find other planets with sentient life on them," he added, to the President and Secretary-General.

"And I'm with them, every inch of the way," Jack said impetuously.

Although annoyance flashed across Saunders' face, when he spoke it was with conviction. "Although I regret that Mrs. Brody did not see fit to inform me beforehand of her little manifesto, I would strongly recommend their plan be accepted, sirs. I believe history will speak well of us if we deal with our new associates with integrity."

The President turned to the Secretary-General. "What are your views?"

The older man chose his words with care. "Before giving an opinion, I should like to speak to Shalaii's Primary, get a feel of the, uh, man. And we might as well speak to the Orowan space director, too, even though we'll have to rely on Ablakan's translations."

Jan wasn't certain whether he was casting doubt on Ablakan's honesty or his abilities as a translator.

"Can you arrange that for us?" the President asked Jan.

"Yes, sir." The tension in her neck muscles eased a bit. At least she hadn't been summarily arrested.

Ablakan must have told Tweno of her upcoming meeting with the President, for she achieved contact at once. He and Tweno were eager to speak to the human dignitaries. Apparently, Shownae had been hoping to as well, for he opened to Ablakan on the first mental 'knock'.

Once the introductions were over, the President took the floor.

Primary Tweno, please accept our gratitude for the timely assistance your First-in-Training rendered our telepath.

Humor flowed through his words as Tweno said, *Mr. President, my English is getting better every day, but would you please use smaller words? I think you thanked me for Ablakan's help, is that correct?*

254

Yes, it is. And my apologies. I appreciate your efforts to learn English. I could not learn a language in such a short time. The President hesitated a moment before continuing. *Primary, has Ablakan spoken to you about the suggestion Mrs. Brody made?*

All attached felt Tweno's confusion. *Mrs. Brody – that is 'Jan'?*

Yes.

Tweno's mental tone went carefully neutral. *He has told me of it.*

May I ask your opinion of that? the President asked.

They hold all the – cards? – yes, cards. We play their game or we do not play at all. I think their game is good and fair. Speaking for Shalaii, I would be very happy to agree to this, if Earth and Orowa will as well.

Mr. Secretary-General? the President inquired formally, awaiting his response.

Of course, I do not speak for the United Nations; I merely report to them and it is accepted or rejected by majority vote. But yes, if Shalaii and Orowa agree, I would push for acceptance.

Tweno projected a feeling of pleasure. *Thank you, sir. What is your opinion, Mr. President?*

The President hesitated. To Jan, he seemed to be considering the advisability of what he was about to say. *Primary Tweno, have you been told anything about the history of our species?*

Yes, Tweno replied sadly. *I am so sorry. These 'wars' must be very hard on all your peoples.*

The President nodded. *They are, sir. And the heads of our many countries change quite frequently, so good intentions from those governing now may not be shared by those who come to power later. I just want you to understand that.*

Tweno projected a nod. *And I believe that is why Ablakan, Jan and Shownae have put in these guard safes.*

Uh, I believe you mean 'safeguards'. And yes, I am relieved that they have. I personally intend to do everything in my power to 'play fair', so long as the other planetary leaders do the same.

I am pleased to hear that. How much tie is there between your government and your space department? Tweno inquired.

The President waffled a hand. *There is some. Mostly, it's through program funding.*

That is good. I understand on your world friends and old enemies all now work together for space exploration. Could your space department handle most day-to-day contact with other planets?

Yes, they will be, the President said. *It is one area in which most nations are working cooperatively – well, those who have space departments.*

There was a slight lull in the conversation. Ablakan inserted, *Sirs, if you will wait a minute, I will tell Shownae what you said.*

The flash of images that followed had the President and Secretary-General exchange looks of surprise, but neither commented.

Presently, Ablakan said, *Shownae thinks their space department will gladly agree to our plan. Shownae, Trikon and Wiltanus, Orowa's leader, want to learn English from me as soon as I finish teaching it to our Primary.*

The President radiated pleasure. *Well, I believe I can persuade Congress – that's the group of people I report to, to some extent – to expedite – uh, hurry up agreeing to exchange information between our peoples. Starting, of course, with how to build equipment to scan for diseases. Perhaps in the not-too-distant future, we may meet in person.*

That would be most welcome, Tweno said.

Good-byes were expressed all around, and contact was broken.

The President sighed contentedly. "That was most encouraging. And although I'm not empathic, they did seem quite genuine. Did you get that impression?" he asked the Secretary-General.

"I would say so."

The President started to rise. "Would you excuse us now for a few minutes? Lesley, please remain."

The others returned to the waiting room, except for the Secretary-General, who turned down the hallway in the opposite direction.

"You did great, hon," Tom said, giving Jan a quick hug. "But you about scared the wits out of me. Nothing like playing hardball with the President of the United States to get the old ticker going." He placed a hand over his heart.

"If I go off on stress leave, it'll be because of you," Jack informed Jan. "And they try to call *space travel* hazardous!"

The balance of the evening was spent socializing with the President and his wife. The First Lady was the gracious hostess her position required of her, but Jan got the impression she was naturally outgoing. Shop talk was strictly forbidden, although Saunders, the President and the Secretary-General did disappear somewhere for a short time. Aside from feeling self-conscious in such company, Jan thoroughly enjoyed herself.

After a sumptuous dinner, they were offered rooms for the night, but Saunders begged off on behalf of them all, citing early-morning meetings.

The trip to the airport was uneventful. However, once they were left to themselves in NASA's private jet, Saunders had a few things to say.

"First off, Jan, I'm most pleased by the way things turned out back there. But if you ever pull a stunt like that again without clearing it with me first, I'll have Rhodes work you into the ground – and he'll do it, too. Don't be fooled by his 'grandpa' act; he can be a mean cuss if you run afoul of him. Do we understand each other?"

"Yes, sir," Jan said meekly, hiding her pleasure at his first statement.

"Good. And as for you, Foxworth, you're supposed to keep these two in line, not join them like some space-age D'Artagnan. Now that Rhodes is on board, you're no longer indispensable."

Jack stared at him, stricken mute.

Saunders let out a long sigh. "However, you have played a part in Jan's successes to date. But if you want to remain their supervisor, *supervise!* Understand?"

"Yes, sir, I will, sir," Jack promised, considerably shaken. Jan suddenly realized just how deep the attachment between the three of them had grown.

Having got his staff in line, Saunders chatted with them relaxedly about the prospects of goodwill and trade between the planets, and the possibility of having in-person negotiations.

"I'll be able to visit Ablakan!" Jan exclaimed, delighted her dream might come true so soon. "And Shownae and Moohri and Trikon."

But Saunders shook his head. "Jan, I can't think of anyone who deserves it more. But you three links are essential. As you pointed out today, without you, there is no contact between the planets. You can't be risked. I think you'll find the other leaders feel the same about their links. I'm sorry."

Jan looked at him in dismay. She realized he was right, but the thought of never hugging Ablakan or meeting her Orowan colleagues hurt terribly. Everyone else in the world – worlds, actually – could, but not she, not the three of them. Her fondest wish withered, grieving.

Tom leaned over and placed a gentle hand on hers. "I'm sorry, hon. He is right, you know."

Jan nodded numbly. She turned away to wipe tears of disappointment from her eyes.

"Perhaps someday there'll be a way," Tom tried to console her.

Jan's lip curled in bitterness. "When the need is great?"

"Pardon?" Saunders looked from her to Tom and back again.

Tom explained, but it sounded hollow to Jan.

Saunders nodded, but offered no platitudes. "Right now, I'd say the greatest need will be for patience. The next stage – getting those decontam routines set up – will not happen overnight."

And of course, he was right.

CHAPTER 14

The Brodys took a few days off to permanently close up shop in Maine. Jan phoned the lady who was tending her plants. That was when she learned that their beloved house had died of arson. The time and date left no doubt who was to blame.

"That bastard!" Jan stormed, feeling as though part of her had been destroyed. "I'm glad he's dead." She immediately regretted the sentiment.

"He got what he deserved," Tom stated calmly, but his eyes were flashing.

So the plants remained with the sitter, as did their old car, and Maine became a bittersweet memory.

Black earned himself posthumous distinctions in the annals of history as the first human to teleport, and be teleported, between two celestial bodies.

Jan was given a spacious office at Ames which was redecorated to her tastes. When finished, it resembled a den and library far more than an office, which suited her perfectly. Her state-of-the-art computer sported every program her heart desired, and an entire wall was devoted to now-indispensable star charts.

Dr. Rhodes – Eric – was the gentlest of taskmasters, thereby eliciting maximum effort from his employees. Behind his back he became known as Dr. Conscience, as effective in his absence as he was when present. And he did enjoy his little surprises.

Their first payday, he called all three into his office and closed the door. "You might want to sit down before you open these," he cautioned as he waved the envelopes in front of their collective noses.

"That good or that bad?" Jack wanted to know.

"You'll have to open it to find out."

Jack tore the stub off his and gave an appreciative whistle. "This is biweekly?"

"Yup."

"I don't know what I did to deserve this," Jack exclaimed. "But I hope I keep it up."

Eric leaned back in his chair with a knowing smile. "Oh, you'll be earning it in spades. Saunders and I have some interesting plans for you, if things turn out the way we expect."

"What kind of plans?"

"All in good time." Eric motioned for Jan to open her packet.

Gingerly, she complied. And stared. Something was definitely wrong with the zeroes. There were way too many of them.

"Uh, I think someone goofed here," she said. "All three links agreed to a basic living wage, remember? This can't be right."

"President's orders, no less. We have to keep our link happy. Can't have you defecting to Shalaii or God-knows-where."

She couldn't resist deadpanning, "Yes, that would make me the Missing Link, wouldn't it?"

Jack groaned, and Tom rolled his eyes, then leaned over to see the cheque for himself, nearly slipping off his chair in the process.

"But that's . . . " He did some quick calculations. "That's over thirteen million dollars a year!" he said hoarsely.

Eric nodded. "And she'll earn every penny of it, too, I guarantee. You might as well open yours."

"I'm almost afraid to." Tom's stub revealed a flat rate of $18,000 per month. A separate page informed him that he would receive a $250,000 bonus for each confirmed sentient species he located.

Tom shook his head in amazement. "Talk about rags to riches!"

Eric interlaced his fingers, resting his hands on his trim midriff. "As you know, Tweno and Wiltanus refused their link's offer of a reduced salary. We could hardly insist on it for ours, now could we?"

Jan stared at the figures, overwhelmed. "But if we're working the kind of hours we've been doing, what in the world could we do with it all?"

"That's your problem. I've my own inflated booty to worry about. If I get too rich I'll be worth more to the kids dead than alive. Too tempting."

261

Jan looked at Tom for help. "We don't even have anyone to leave ours to, really."

Eric said with a slight smile, "Then leave it to my kids. It'll buy me more time."

"And speaking of time," Jack swiveled his head toward Tom. "It's high time I pony up the money and dinner tickets I owe Carstairs. He's the botanist I called about the plants where Moohri is, remember? And I also promised dinner out for my old boss and his wife. Remind me when we get home, would you?"

Tom said, "Let me get those. You were helping us out at the time, so there's no reason you should be out-of-pocket on this."

They were still haggling over who would pay, when Eric shooed them out of his office.

* * *

A week-and-a-half later, another interesting development came about, this one quite by accident. Ablakan had been excused for the afternoon to give Jan a mental guided tour of the parts of the palace he frequented and points of interest on the island.

On this occasion, Jan twinned with him, so she could see through his eyes. She had only developed the skill a few days before, and found it quite remarkable. Through him, she felt the exhilaration of flying across the water on swimmers, of bouncing along aback a hurrymary and of gazing 'first-hand' at the beautiful alien landscape. Jan found she couldn't drink in the sights fast enough. Everything was so unfamiliar it often took some time to translate into human terms what she was seeing, and by then new sights were filling her vision.

"And this is what we see from the largest banquet room," Ablakan told her at one point.

As Jan looked down on the manicured aqua lawn stretching across perhaps 125 acres of countryside dotted with brilliantly-colored trees and frequent small ponds, it looked to her like an otherworldly golf course.

Ablakan, what is that large area used for?

Tweno said this land is kept looking nice, but is not used. It is to grow more food, in case the palace is ever again home to a large number of royals. He thinks it will never happen. But it is peaceful, is it not?

Yes, indeed. But it gives me an idea. I won't say anything more till I talk to a few people. Now, no fair peeking at my thoughts.

Ablakan promised, then mischievously pretended to pry a little, just to get a rise out of her, which she dutifully provided. Jan enjoyed his occasional gentle teasing.

When they finished their tour and Jan took her leave, she made a few calls to round up the others. Soon she, Tom and Jack were lounging comfortably in Eric's office. Jan described the visual tour to which she had been treated, and the acreage she envisioned as a golf course.

"I think the Shalaians, and likely the Orowans as well, would enjoy golf. Any chance we could explain how it's played and send them the equipment? Just a little gift from us?"

"Now, there's a thought." Eric's eyes got a faraway look. "A decade from now, the PGA could be galactic. Can you imagine some of the more bizarre hazards?"

That produced chuckles, for according to Ablakan, the island's harmless fauna displayed more curiosity than a house cat and tended to get underfoot every chance they got.

A flurry of phone calls located the equipment, and Jan was subjected to intensive training. Eventually, she was deemed ready, and all that remained was to make the offer.

What is a 'golf course'? Tweno asked.

Ablakan, Jan said, by way of answer. *Can you help the Primary – with your permission, of course, sir – observe through me, and you do so, also?*

It took some doing, but eventually they both shared her vision. Starting at the first tee on the course on which she had been training, Jan played a couple holes while describing the nature of the game. Afterwards, she used the golf cart she had been loaned to give them a quick tour of the course layout.

"Catch!" she grinned to Ablakan, and 'ported him a jump drive. "This has a video of how it looks from above.

Jan was gratified to feel their interest continue to grow as they experienced through her the enjoyment of hitting a long drive and of putting into the cup.

It takes practice and sometimes luck, but it's great fun and enjoyed on Earth by people of all ages, she told them.

Tweno admitted, *It does look very pleasing. And you wish to give us information and equipment for no trade?*

Yes. It's just a little gift from the four of us, not from any government, Jan explained while she was angling the cart around a grove of trees. The clubhouse came into sight.

Four? Ablakan asked.

Eric – Dr. Rhodes – insisted on contributing to this, too. He is really a very nice man, but don't tell him I said so, okay?

Ablakan nodded solemnly. *I promise.*

Tweno's words were formal but his mental tone was warm as he said, *We would be most grateful for your generous gift. What causes that small machine to move?*

It runs on electricity from batteries, but we could send you ones which are solar-driven, if you prefer.

I think the solar ones would be best for our use. And we do enjoy walking, Tweno added. *So when there is not much light, it would not be a problem for us.*

Jan was glad to be asked a great many questions about golf, for it not only indicated Tweno's genuine interest, but gave Jan the rare opportunity to be a teacher rather than a student of the game.

Wiltanus also accepted the gift with alacrity. It seemed that new forms of recreation were always in great demand on Orowa.

Some time later, Jan watched through Ablakan's eyes as he and Tweno tried out their new golf course for the first time. The clubs had been modified to meet Shalaian physical requirements. After a few wild shots on both their parts, they got the hang of it and did remarkably well for novices. Jan wondered if Shalaians had an innate sense of distance and trajectory. On several

264

occasions thereafter, her Shalaian and Orowan contacts were on their golf courses when Jan put through unscheduled calls.

For the most part, though, the Brodys' work routine became just that – routine. Five days a week Jan started at 9 a.m., improving Ablakan and Tweno's English comprehension and writing skills, especially in legal and business contexts. Jan was being coached on the side, as her own legal knowledge had been quite lacking. But the Shalaians needed it to level the playing field between them and their human markets.

At 10:30, after a short break, Shownae, Wiltanus, Trikon and Moohri would come on-line. Ablakan had insisted on working double-duty for a while, teaching the Orowans basic English while helping Tweno polish his language skills. Now that the Orowans were fluent enough for Jan to take over, she tutored them till noon, her time, each workday.

Afternoons were split between basic negotiations with one or both planets and the transfer of goods which could withstand the rigorous decontamination process they had to undergo before leaving or arriving on Earth. By evening, Jan was exhausted. Noticing this, Jack had a talk with Eric, and an afternoon nap became a mandatory part of her routine, which helped immensely.

Tom almost wet himself with excitement the first time he used the Hubble Space Telescope. He was allocated one hour, twice a week. The other nights, he toggled between the 200-inch Hale telescope at Mount Palomar in California, and the 120-inch telescope at the Lick Observatory. Tom was given the earliest possible shift so Jan would not retire too late, for she had to 'port him back and forth.

To his surprise and disappointment, Tom found he received no 'feelings' from the scans coming from the Hubble Telescope. When he realized he required direct contact with a telescope in order to pick up empathic information, Tom reluctantly gave up his time on the Hubble.

Within the first four months, he averaged one 'hit' per month of sufficient empathic strength to justify adding it to the database of 'possibles'.

Near the end of the fourth month, Shownae called Jan, bursting with excitement.

"Decontamination procedure is finished," he said. "You send a rat for us to test, please?"

"Oh, Shownae, how wonderful!" Jan cried. "Uh, do you want one we know is free of disease, or a sick one?"

"No, a well one first."

NASA, along with various disease control agencies, had poured intensive efforts into decontamination procedures which would not only identify disease-causing germs but eliminate them as well. Shalaii had quite advanced viral control technology, and the two planets put these to good use.

That afternoon, Jan 'ported the rat over, and to the delight of all, he endured the procedures with no sign of distress. Forty-eight hours later, he was returned to the Ames lab and extensive testing concluded the rat had been in perfect health.

There followed rats with a variety of contagious Earth diseases, and in each case the animal was returned to Earth healthy. The time had come for the big test. Moohri, who had been following the experiments with growing excitement, was transported off the planetoid into the chamber and subjected to a grueling barrage of tests following the decontamination measures. All the test results were 'ported to Ames and Shalaii for confirmation. Ablakan called in the good news from their laboratory first. Jan hung around Ames' lab, trying not to look as eager and impatient as she felt.

After what seemed like hours, the head technician looked up from her microscope and announced, "If Moohri ever contracted something on that planetoid, he doesn't have it now."

The lab erupted in whoops of jubilation, and Jan was whirled around by an ecstatic labworker half her age. Quickly, Jan connected to a breathlessly waiting Shownae.

He comes up clean as a whistle here as well, Shownae. Give him a hug for me.

Thank you, thank you, Jan! Shownae cried, then gave a joyous command in the ululating tones of his language.

Jan was about to disconnect when Moohri clasped Shownae's arm, thereby also making contact with her. Tentatively at first, then with great gusto, Moohri gave her a mental bear hug. Jan felt herself dissolve in tears of joy and laughter. Then he was gone. Shownae began sniffing loudly, and after an embarrassed apology, severed contact.

* * *

When Moohri stepped out of the chamber, the person closest to the door was Shownae, whose unwavering encouragement and teleporting of parcels from home had kept him fed and sane these long, lonely months. Moohri grasped his arm in a clasp of deep friendship and was surprised to feel Jan's presence beside Shownae's mind.

Jan, who had worked so tirelessly to send him food before Ablakan taught Shownae to teleport. Jan, to whom he owed his very life. Uncertain how to do what he most desired, Moohri nonetheless found himself projecting to Jan a hug so profound in its unspoken gratitude that he enveloped her with his whole being.

And then his eyes met Shira's and she flung herself into his arms. Moohri embraced his life-love as though he would never let her go, and she whispered again and again, "I missed you, Moohri, how I missed you!"

"And I you," his voice trembled. "To be away from you was the worst pain I have ever endured. And away from our wonderful blanas. Are they here, Shira?" he asked, trying to see through the throng that pressed forward to greet their returning hero.

She held him closer still. "Forgive me, my love. I dared not in case something went wrong. It would have destroyed them."

"Of course," Moohri said, chagrined. "It was too risky. Thank you for your wisdom, Onliest."

267

When at last they separated, it was because the exultant crowd of well-wishers and newspeople were upon them. Moohri and Shira were lifted onto strong backs and deposited on a platform that had been hastily erected to one side of the room. There a beaming Trikon hugged Moohri and, taking a step back, undid the Lead Spacefarer pin he was wearing and placed it on Moohri's collar.

"Welcome home, Leader," he enthused, clasping Moohri's arm so exuberantly he bruised the flesh. "You cannot imagine how happy I am to see you."

"Dear friend," Moohri said, his voice husky with emotion. "Your loyalty and strength will live forever in my memory." Moohri removed the Spacefarer pin and carefully split it in two before handing one half to Trikon. "Together, we will share the wages and duties of both our titles."

"Thank you, Leader, but our Administrator may have other ideas. A few days ago, he gave me a pouch, to be given to you on your return. I do not know what is in it, but he seemed very pleased."

Trikon handed the cloth envelope to Moohri, who opened it and read the message within slowly before giving it to Trikon with a smile.

"What does it say?" an eager reporter asked, and his query was echoed by numerous people in the audience.

"The Spacefarer's budget has been tripled," Moohri told them, grinning broadly. "I am to remain the Administrative Leader, and Trikon becomes Head of Operations. These are parallel positions," he informed the amazed Trikon. "As I said, we are partners. And there is one other mentioned in here," Moohri said, raising his voice. "Shownae, Orowa's own 'porting telepath, will you join us?"

The crowd erupted in cheers, and before Shownae could respond, he was lifted aloft as the onlookers parted to let his carriers through.

The psychic flushed in embarrassment. "I am not much for the spotlight," he admitted.

"Sorry, my friend." Moohri clapped his shoulder fondly. "You no longer have the luxury of anonymity. Besides your psychic and 'porting duties, you are Spacefarer's new Second – Administrator Wiltanus' orders. And a wonderful team we shall make."

Shownae gasped, "I am speechless."

"Not for long," Moohri laughed. "Notice how the newspeople draw closer. Let us speak to them quickly, that I may go home with my Shira to our blanas."

* * *

After Shownae abruptly closed the link, Jan opened her eyes to see half the people in the room smiling in delight and the others pretending not to notice Jan's tears of joy. Many an embrace were exchanged, and Jan thanked them with all her heart for their tireless efforts to make this day a reality.

As soon as she politely could, Jan excused herself and hurried down the hall. She stopped at each office to announce the wonderful news.

Eric stuck his head out a conference room door. "What's all the commotion?"

Tom and Jack stood just behind him They regarded her expectantly.

"Moohri's clean! They just released him."

"Already? Excellent! I didn't think the lab would finish that fast." Eric rubbed his hands together. "Well, this calls for a celebration. Book the cafeteria and get Sandra to call the caterers. I want a buffet here in two hours."

Self-consciously, Jan gave Eric and Jack a quick hug, and bussed Tom soundly before excusing herself. "I've got to tell Ablakan and Tweno."

"I'll call Saunders," Eric smiled. "It'll make his day."

Jan rushed off to find a quiet spot, for a contagious merriment was spreading through the building like wildfire.

269

Ablakan, she cried, when he answered. *Our tests had the same results as yours. Moohri is in perfect health. Trikon just let him out.*

A yelp of delight echoed in her mental hearing. It was too loud for comfort, but she hardly noticed.

I am soooo happy! he bubbled. *I must tell Tweno at once. Thank you, Jan, thank you.*

You folks helped make it possible, Jan reminded him. *It took all of us working together. Eric is so pleased he's throwing a party. Take care, dear, and please thank Tweno for us also.*

In his excitement, Ablakan forgot to say goodbye. Jan smiled indulgently. She felt like dancing for joy herself.

By next morning, the euphoria of the previous day was replaced with determination to get Shalaii's decontamination chamber operational. The isolation room was complete, but everything else had been put on hold till the results of the Orowan experiment was known. Now the equipment could be sent over and assembled by the awaiting technicians.

In less than a week, it was ready. But when an ailing Shalaian wopux was put in, with full expectation of it emerging healthy, the poor animal quickly died. An autopsy revealed a massive internal hemorrhage had occurred.

After a bull session in the Ames lab came up empty, they turned to Jan.

"We need tissue samples from healthy Shalaians of all ages," the chief technician said, and Jan passed the request along to Ablakan.

The next day, the samples arrived. They were 'ported into a small isolab where the researchers were clad in protective suits, as the samples could not withstand current decontamination procedures. Similar tests were conducted as had been performed earlier on the Orowan samples. Under identical conditions, the Shalaian cells ruptured.

That day Jan went home disheartened.

"Shalaian cells are so different from ours and the Orowans'. How are we supposed to find something that'll work for all three, yet be safe?" She grazed on a Caesar salad without tasting it.

"I don't know if we will," Jack said gloomily. "But if we do, we'll run into the same problem every time we add a new species to the mix."

Tom nodded. "We may need separate decontam procedures for different species. It doesn't necessarily have to be a 'one size fits all' solution."

"I hadn't thought of that, but you're right," Jan agreed, feeling somewhat better. Realistically, there was nothing she could do about it, anyway. It was up to the labs on each world to find a solution.

In the end, the Ames lab isolated the culprit. One of the chemicals was making the cellular membranes brittle while causing the cell's nucleus to expand. The resulting increase in pressure ruptured the cell wall.

A massive quest began for replacement chemicals. Of those that were tried, from all three worlds, only two were found to have no negative side effects. One of them, however, did not destroy the disease pathogen in a sick wopux.

The other seemed the perfect solution, at least for humans. A number of volunteers with viral illnesses emerged from the chamber virus-free. Now all that remained was to ensure the new chemical would also work for the other two species.

On that day, Eric found Jan pacing her office like a caged animal.

"Impatient, are we?"

"I'm sorry," Jan groaned. "I've got a big stack of 'porting requests, but I'm just so afraid to miss the calls." So much rode on those test results.

Eric nodded as though he had expected as much. "You're sure they're both that close to completion?"

She distractedly mauled a thumbnail. "Today. They both said they'd know today."

271

"Alright. Keep your mind clear till you get the results." Eric patted her shoulder encouragingly. "Don't sweat it, Jan. If this doesn't work, something else will."

"Thanks."

Jan waited till he had left to resume her pacing, though with less urgency. Eric was right; eventually they would find the answer.

Shortly after lunch, a frantic knocking in her head heralded the presence of Shownae. His knocks were always louder than Ablakan's.

Jan, it worked! The process, the chemical, everything.

She just had to be sure. *It's effective and safe?*

Yes to both, was Shownae's jubilant reply. *Any word yet from the Shalaians?*

Not yet. When he disconnected, Jan told Eric and the rest of her team, then went back to pacing.

It was nearly quitting time when the knock came. It was so loud at first Jan thought Shownae was calling back.

Success! Ablakan sang out. *The researchers said to tell you no matter what the disease, it was destroyed by the process, and the people came out clean.*

Jan was smiling like a hyena. *That's it, then. Orowa got the same results, and so did we. Why don't you call Shownae?*

I will! Bye, Jan. And Ablakan was gone.

Several minutes later, the happy foursome sat in Eric's office, talking on the speakerphone to Saunders.

"And once enough chambers are built to handle the need, we might be able to make viral diseases extinct," Jan was saying.

She felt giddy with the possibilities the chambers represented. She had to admit the glass of bubbly in her hand might also have something to do with how she was feeling.

"We can start interplanetary travel. Right now! Today!" Jack cried.

Jan smothered a grin. Jack had wheedled a second glass of champagne out of Eric. He didn't usually drink, and the excess was beginning to show.

Saunders cleared his throat, his voice sounding tinny over the speakerphone.

"Eric, please shut the door, if it's open."

"Oh-oh," Tom said. "That sounds like trouble."

Eric closed it. "Done."

"Good. I don't have to tell you people this is a milestone in human progress – and, I expect, that of Shalaii and Orowa as well. The President has been anticipating this final development. He wants you, Jan, to extend an invitation on his behalf to Tweno and Wiltanus' representatives to visit Earth as his guest. At the same time, the Vice-President and the United Nations Secretary-General request permission to visit Tweno and Wiltanus respectively." A muted buzzer sounded over the speaker-phone. "Got to go. I'll touch base with you later." The line went dead.

"Wow!" Jan said, impressed. "Talk about starting at the top."

Eric nodded. "Appropriate, though. And we want to discuss with you, not the pros but the cons of what happens next. Trade is about to take on a whole new dimension. I have a list here of over 70,000 companies and individuals who are chomping at the bit to pitch in person to the offworld markets." He waved a sheaf of papers at them. "Of course, they want you, Jan, to 'port them back and forth as a matter of routine.

Now, this brings up two major problems. First, we obviously haven't the manpow- – uh, peoplepower – to do that. Second, the moment they're over there, we lose control over their behaviour and how they conduct business."

Tom grimaced. "So we're talking about a sales feeding frenzy. And probably a repeat of every scam concocted since that infamous beads for Manhattan Island swap."

"Precisely. Two fresh killing grounds for human predators of all kinds. For that matter, it could work the same in reverse, with every riffraff on Shalaii and Orowa looking to ply their trade here."

Jack heaved an exasperated sigh. "Boy . . . you sure know how to take the joy out of a celebration, boss, but you're right. So how do we prevent it?"

"In part, that's what this high-level talk will be for – to warn our 'neighbors' of the dangers and look for joint solutions."

Eric leaned forward, with a grim expression on his face. Something told Jan the worst was yet to come.

"And having ruined the party, I have another little bomb to drop. Remember, I didn't cause it; I'm just the messenger."

The trio exchanged worried glances.

"Alright, let's have it," Jack said, as usual anxious to get it over with.

"Congress just finished their recommendations on stringent controls to be placed on 'porting and 'pathing. I've read the preliminary report, and it looks pretty good." He picked up a thin publication and handed it to Jan. "Some light reading for you."

Jan turned it over in her hand. "Then what's the problem?"

"I got a confirmed report this morning of a man 'porting himself out of jail. He was recaptured and is being kept lightly sedated, so he can't do it again. But this is just the tip of the iceberg. We have no way of knowing how many people can learn this sort of thing. Besides the havoc they could wreak here on Earth, just think of the money they could make as black-market 'porters to Shalaii or Orowa. Or ripping off treasures from any of the three worlds, for that matter, or as saboteurs or assassins. And again, we have to assume the same thing could happen in reverse. As they say in the movies, we've got a situation."

No one seemed to have anything to say. Jan just sat there, overwhelmed by the possibilities.

"It was bound to happen," Eric pointed out. "With Tweno and Wiltanus in the picture, we're more likely to find a solution than if we were on our own. And let's not forget: Today, between our planets, we basically conquered viruses. At least people predators are easier to see."

"But not to catch," Jan said morosely.

Jack changed position in his chair. "Actually, it may not be as bad as it seems. You've been able to 'port for just over 10 months now, and three worlds have known about it for nine. That's about *10 billion people* who knew, and only one person besides you three links and Black has managed to do it so far."

"Anyway," Tom added. "Only a few of us know we won't be sanctioning blanket visas to visit the other worlds, even if their governments agree to it. Until that's known, the sharks will try to get there the easy way – namely, through Jan."

Jan gulped. "Oh, great!" But they were right. There might still be time to avert wholesale chaos.

It took a few minutes to set her concerns aside long enough to extend the President's invitations and requests through Ablakan and Shownae. She received the replies in less than an hour: Yes, to all four suggestions. Plus an offer from Tweno for a round of golf. It seemed both offworld leaders had been planning to suggest a get-together at the earliest opportunity, so arrangements were finalized with uncharacteristic speed. So fast, in fact, that Jan, Ablakan and Shownae had to put everything else on hold so they could practice sending volunteers to each other's decontamination chamber.

Three days after the invitation was made, Eric awakened Jan at 5 a.m. to say that Saunders would arrived mid-morning, and that the President, Vice-President and U.N. Secretary-General were also on their way. Jan headed for the shower, her heartrate increasing with excitement.

She was summoned to Eric's office at 11:45. Everyone turned as she entered, giving her a moment of embarrassment.

"Ah, there you are, Jan," Saunders said. "Please come in. You remember the President, I'm sure?"

"Of course! Nice to see you again, sir."

The President extended his hand, smiling. "Always a pleasure. Are they treating you right?"

"Oh, yes, very well indeed."

"Good day to you, ma'am," the Secretary-General interjected, before he could be reintroduced. He inclined his head an eighth of an inch. Jan privately wondered if he, with his highly conservative nature, was a wise choice as a goodwill ambassador.

"Vice-President Matheson, may I present Jan Brody, our very own 'porting telepath," said the President.

The lanky second-in-command grinned down at her. "Good morning, Jan. You have my utmost respect, especially since for a brief time my life will be in your hands."

"I assure you, you will be perfectly safe."

The President chuckled. "He simply hates to fly."

Matheson effected a shudder. "Scared to death, to put it mildly. It's funny; I've twice been shot at, and it barely ruffled me. But flying? White knuckles all the way." Morbid curiosity got the better of him. "Will all my particles come apart, like on Star Trek?"

Jan let out a hoot of laughter. "No sir, nothing like that. I don't know the scientific principles behind it. All I know is I focus on the person, then on where they want to go, and they're there – in one piece and just fine. But I won't send you till you tell me to, alright?"

Matheson watched the Secretary-General closely. "You don't seem worried."

The older man shrugged. "I am somewhat of a fatalist. I will die when I die, so until then, I shall live."

"Can't argue with that," the President remarked. He glanced at his watch. "Jan, what time are Trikon and First Lisham due here?"

"In about twenty minutes, sir."

"And emissaries from Shalaii and Orowa are being exchanged?"

"Yes. First Konapi is going to Orowa, and the Orowan Sub-Administrator – I can't pronounce her name – will visit Shalaii."

276

Vice-President Matheson sighed deeply. "Well, I've had my little panic attack. I guess I'm as ready as I'll ever be. Better send us now, Jan, before I lose my nerve."

Jan said. "I'll tell Ablakan and Tweno you're ready. And sir, please give Ablakan a hug for me," she blurted out before she could stop herself.

She was shocked to hear the naked longing in her voice. Jan's peripheral vision caught Eric's eyebrows as they shot up in surprise.

Matheson nodded. "Doesn't seem fair, does it, that you of all people can't go? If he is willing, I will give him your hug."

"Thank you," Jan said, blushing furiously. She turned toward the Secretary-General. "Are you ready, too, sir?"

"Yes."

On the way to the decontamination chamber, Jan called Ablakan and Shownae, letting them know Earth's delegates were preparing for transport.

The chamber had deliberately been made to look as benign as possible, but the Secretary-General still regarded it with suspicion before opening the door. He sealed it firmly behind him. The technicians initiated the sequence, and a short time later announced that the procedure was complete.

At Saunders' nod, Jan 'ported the Secretary-General into the duplicate chamber on Orowa, then confirmed to those present that he had arrived intact.

Matheson looked almost disappointed. "That's all there is to it?"

"Yes, sir. You're here, then you're there. There's no in-between."

"Then let's go!"

Matheson strode into the chamber and in due course was transported to Shalaii.

"He also arrived safely?" the President asked.

"Yes, sir."

"Good. Now, about Lisham and Trikon. How is their English coming?"

Jan smiled proudly. "They're doing excellent, I think. All the delegates on both worlds are learning it as the universal language, because it's the only one all three species can vocalize."

"Quite the bonus for us, that," the President noted. He turned to Saunders. "The arrangements I requested are in place?"

"Yes. I saw to them myself."

"Good. And security?"

"Airtight but unobtrusive. I've scheduled the press interview for 4:00 to 4:20. The media grumbled, of course, but it should give the reporters enough to keep their editors off their backs. And them off ours."

Ablakan's knock came right on schedule.

First Lisham is ready when you are.

By all means, send him over, dear.

An instant later, Lisham popped into the chamber, his expression rather terrified. He looked down at his body, as though reassuring himself he was all there. He then let out a grateful sigh and smiled hugely at his hosts through the glass. Jan grinned back.

To his credit, the President did not gawk at his highly alien-looking visitor. As soon as Lisham was cleared to leave the chamber, the President stepped forward with his hand extended.

Measured against the photograph Jan had of Ablakan, she estimated Lisham was half a head taller than the youth and much stouter. Jan noticed his eyebanks were slightly oval, whereas Ablakan's were square. As well, the pigment on Lisham's arms and face were a few shades darker than Ablakan's.

The President shook his hand warmly. "It is a great pleasure to meet you, sir. I have dreamed of this day ever since I learned of Jan's abilities."

"As have I," Lisham said. "We are all better for the friendships we make."

"That is how I see it, too."

The other introductions were no sooner complete than Shownae called, confirming that Trikon had cleared decontamination at their end.

The Orowan arrived promptly. He waved at those outside the chamber, beaming in exhilaration. When he emerged, the Spacefarer turned unerringly toward the President.

"I have wanted to get here ever since Shownae told me about Earth," he said. "I am so happy to meet you all in person."

He shook hands with everyone in the room, eyes gleaming. Formality crumbled in the wake of his infectious enthusiasm. Jan, who was watching from the sidelines, privately seconded Shownae's comment on the change in Trikon since Moohri's return.

"And I am delighted to meet you," the President assured him, rescuing his slightly crushed hand from Trikon's eager clasp. "There was great celebration on Earth, too, when we learned Moohri was back on Orowa and in good health."

"Thank you," Trikon said. "He is my best friend, and I worried off many weights in his absence." He patted his portly belly. Then he turned a radiant smile on Jan. "My friend, I cannot thank you enough for saving his life. You are a great hero to our people. Shyr will be renamed in your honor, if you will permit it."

"Oh no, please don't do that! Shyr is a beautiful name. But thanks for the enormous compliment." Jan's voice trailed off.

Eric rescued her from further embarrassment by saying, "Are you gentlepeople daring enough to try a few Earth dishes? We've put together foods Ablakan and Shownae thought you might enjoy."

"I am – game?" Lisham said, uncertain he had the correct term.

Trikon grinned mischievously. "I have never been known to refuse food."

"In that case, let's not keep the goodies waiting."

Jan edged towards the door, having finished her part in the proceedings. But Saunders noticed and motioned her over. "Where are you going?"

"I brought my own lunch."

He shook his head. "Jan, you're not just a glorified skipper, ferrying people back and forth. You're part of the human delegation."

She frowned, confused. "But Jack isn't here, and he's my supervisor. And Tom is the one who picked up on Shalaii in the first place."

"That's true. But Trikon and Lisham have dealt primarily with you, not with Jack or Tom. They think of you as an ambassador, language tutor, local hero – you name it. Aside from the President, you are the person they most expect to see. And you're their communications link to their world."

Jan couldn't argue with the last statement. Besides, her stomach as, as usual, grumbling. So as Eric ushered the group towards a small banquet room which had been brightly decorated for the occasion, Jan fell in line behind the others.

The fare was artistically arranged on each platter. Jan noticed there were no meat dishes, although both species ate small game on their homeworlds. Perhaps alien animal proteins were considered too chancy.

"Your staffs tested each of these foods to make sure they were healthy and pleasant to Shalaian and Orowan palates," Saunders said. "But since individual tastes differ, please leave aside anything not to your liking. I promise, no one will take offence."

Lisham reached for the tossed salad while murmuring, "That is most kind."

"I have never found any food not to my liking," declared the irrepressible Trikon.

The offworlders took a little of everything before sitting down opposite the President. Jan was pleased to note that the chairs at both ends of the table had been removed, so that the seating for the President and his offworld guests were of equal hierarchy. There was little doubt as to who would sit where, for Shownae and Ablakan had each 'ported a chair from their homeworld suitable to their delegate's physical requirements.

Lisham bowed slightly toward Saunders. "This is most delicious. I understand it is polite to say you should not have bothered, but then I would never have tasted these."

"I'm delighted you like them," Saunders said. With his eyes he directed a silent query to the President, who was not slow to pick up the ball.

"I've been told your soils are not that different from ours. Would you like to try growing some of these items?"

"Mmmmmmm," Trikon said, trying to empty his mouth to answer. "All of them would be very popular on Orowa, of that I am sure. It would not be trouble for you?"

"No, not at all. I'll arrange for our botanists – plant specialists, that is – to contact your specialists, if you wish, and they can decide which Earth plants your people would like the most."

Trikon exclaimed, "If they are like these, probably all of them." Then he waved his fork about hastily. "I did not mean give us everything. Just – I am much impressed."

The President guffawed. "There's nothing we love more than having someone enjoy our food. And frankly, I can't wait to try some of yours, if they ever let me visit."

Trikon agreed sympathetically. "That is true. The leaders and 'paths cannot be risked. But they cannot have the adventure, either."

Jan tried to suppress the painful longing that welled up inside her.

"I will make sure foods from Orowa you can enjoy in good health are sent to your home. And I will have Shownae 'port food seeds and plants to your plant specialists," Trikon promised. Lisham made the same commitment as soon as he had swallowed the wedge of tomato he was savoring.

Before long, the conversation turned to golf and not surprisingly, a game was scheduled for the following day.

Now that's a match that would be worth watching, Jan thought. She was tempted to volunteer as a caddy.

Eventually the banquet ended, and Eric arrived to provide a tour of the facility for the President and the delegates. Saunders begged off, saying he had a few loose ends he needed to tidy up.

Jan was excused until 2:00, when they would get down to business. As soon as the group was out of sight, Tom and Jack appeared, demanding a full report.

"Oh, you know, it was just the usual three-planet luncheon," Jan said airily, and started to walk away.

The men exchanged pointed looks, and each grabbed a wing, lifting her clear of the floor.

"Hey!" she protested, as they hustled her into the closest office, which happened to be Eric's. She was unceremoniously deposited in a chair.

"Talk," Tom ordered.

"Details," Jack specified.

"I wouldn't want to bore you boys." Jan gave them her most innocent look, enjoying their impatience.

"*Jan!*" Jack wailed, so she relented and gave them as close to a verbatim account as she could remember. When she finished, they were both smiling.

"That Trikon's quite the character, isn't he?" Tom remarked. "In a way, I'm surprised, especially after what Shownae told us through Ablakan about their early conversations."

Jan agreed. "But remember, at the time he was still working under Klyfin. That couldn't have been easy. Now he's very disarming – the perfect diplomat, I'd say. Lisham's not as comical, but he's easy-going, too. I like them both. Of course, I already did from before."

"Sure wish I could be at this afternoon's bull session," Jack said wistfully. "I'd love to see how their minds work when they're told about the problems we all face."

Tom added, "And what Tweno'll have to say about it in his discussions. I get the feeling he's pretty sharp."

"He is," Jan agreed. "Personally, I doubt anything major will come out of this round of talks. It's too complex for a snappy answer."

Two o'clock brought a profound change of mood in those now gathered in the executive boardroom. It was time to get down to cases, and everyone knew it.

The President cleared his throat. "My friends, each of us can see the wonderful opportunities that await our peoples through the friendships and trade associations we are building."

Both delegates nodded.

"But there are others on our world – and I am guessing on each of our worlds – who see great opportunities also, at the expense of others. Just here on Earth, I am certain many countries and special interest groups are going all out to find or produce their own teleporter."

Over the next few minutes, the President elaborated on the threats Saunders and Eric had brought up. "We are hoping to find solutions between us before things get out of hand." He looked from one to the other.

Lisham grimaced. "We also have been wondering how to stop 'ported lawlessness. Primary Tweno, with Ablakan's help, is creating – legislation? – not unlike what you read to us. But what good is it on paper if people can 'port themselves in and away in seconds? Ablakan has told us only another 'porter could stop him. To show us how hard it would be, he told the guards he would attack Tweno. Four times they tried to stop him, but each time Ablakan 'ported in, 'killed' Tweno with a mushicake and left before the guards could reach him. The possibilities are . . . terrifying," he finished.

Trikon pointed out, "And our 'porters may not be safe, either. There are those who fear 'porting and would wish to destroy them." There were nods all around.

Jan shuddered. She had secretly been worrying for some time now about just such a possibility, but to hear it voiced made it somehow feel more imminent.

Trikon glanced an apology at Jan. "Also, when others can teleport, they may wish to make themselves more valuable by removing anyone else who can. Or, some may try to kidnap our 'porters or their families, to force the 'porters to commit crimes for them."

Jan had the eerie sensation there was a target painted on the back of her vest.

The President heaved a sigh of relief. "I was afraid you wouldn't believe there were dangers. I am so grateful we're all in agreement. Let's see what we can come up with. And please don't worry about how anything sounds. One idea leads to another, and right now we need ideas, badly."

Trikon asked, "Sir, is there much anger or fear on Earth about teleporting? Jan has not mentioned any." He looked at the President solemnly, then at Lisham, who nodded slowly in understanding.

The President took a moment to respond. "No. And I have been expecting it. I don't know whether to be grateful or worried."

"*I* am worried," Eric said firmly. "When kids are too quiet, they're up to something."

Lisham looked perplexed. "Kids?"

Saunders explained, "He means things are going on in secret. That usually means big trouble ahead." Then he added, "Powerful people are looking for their own teleporter."

Lisham's exhaled forcefully. "And in time they will find or create one."

The President regarded each person, until his gaze settled on Jan. "So how do we keep all the 'thems' out there from succeeding?" Within moments, everyone else in the room was staring at her.

"We can't," Jan replied. "It would be like trying to stop people from building airplanes after the Wright Brothers showed it could be done. I was thinking maybe we could try to enlist every potential 'porter we can find, but still, all it would take is one bad

284

apple out there to pick us off, one by one. 'Port us into the sun or something. They could be anywhere on any of the three planets, but as long as they could get a 'lock' on us, we'd be finished."

Trikon groaned. "What have we started?"

"Our future," Saunders replied dryly. "And if we don't shape it, others will."

The President pursed his lips. "Truly said. So how do we forewarn the 'porters. Precognition?"

Jan considered the idea. "Certainly it would help. But we have to realize that whatever one person can do, others will soon learn. It's like new technology; it doesn't remain that way for long. No matter how talented I might try to become, I'll eventually run out of one-upmanship tricks."

Lisham agreed. "The unscrupulous do not follow the rules that we must, so eventually they will win. No, our safety does not lie in power." He stopped there, his eyebanks blinking rapidly. "Perhaps it lies in purpose."

"In what way?" the President asked.

"They want one thing. Offer them another," Lisham suggested.

"Redirect their focus," the President nodded slowly. "That might buy us some time, at any rate."

Trikon added, "Give them – give *everyone* – something that will feel like a wonderful opportunity."

Eric summed it up. "Give them a new planet to colonize. It would appeal to the greedy, the hungry, the homeless, the curious, the adventurous, the business community and anyone not satisfied with their lot."

Lisham said, warming to the idea, "And we could make the first one a planet to be jointly colonized by our three species. A home for those willing to live as one, if we can keep people from dividing into groups."

"One of the sorting criteria would have to be a lack of prejudice," the President contributed.

Trikon remembered, "On Orowa, we used to have separations. We did not cause them and did not want them, but people did it

285

by themselves. So after that, every new town we started, we made sure the firefighters, police, doctors, all those the public must depend on, were an even combination from all sides. Then we made a rule that, whenever possible, each professional helper must assist only people from factions other than the one he belonged to. That way, the public learned to trust or at least depend on everyone, not just on those from their own side."

"What a great idea," the President marveled. "I guess the first order of business, then, is to find a large, healthy, fairly safe planet that will support all three of our species. If we can find it, this will be a huge undertaking, even with the resources of our three worlds. But I think I can sell it to our people, once a suitable planet is found. After all, one of our biggest problems here is overcrowding."

Saunders leaned forward in his chair. "That would give a new direction for people's energies. But it wouldn't stop predators and why they seek a 'porter."

"No, it wouldn't," Eric agreed. "There will always be that element, and they will be hard to control, as the criminal element always is. I think each of our worlds must also concentrate on finding and training as many 'porters and 'paths as they can, and have them police their own kind. It won't stop the rogues, but the more we have on our side, the better chance one of them will come up with a way to identify fledgling 'porters before they get too strong."

Jan pointed out, "We need more of us anyway, just to handle the workload."

"I will speak to the Primary at once," Lisham said. "If you agree and Jan is willing."

It was decided that both offworld leaders would be contacted so that they and their visitors could consider the suggestions which had just been discussed on Earth. The other humans left the room, then, to let Jan link the offworlders with their respective telepaths.

When the calls were over, the delegates followed the human contingent to a makeshift lounge where they could catch their breath or finish their notes. The visiters smiled happily when they caught sight of the snacks and beverages from their homeworld which Ablakan and Shownae had 'ported over for them. Their unique chairs had also been brought into the room. Eric appointed himself 'bartender', and served each the beverage of his choice.

"I leave you in good hands," Jan told Lisham and Trikon unoriginally. "And I'm just a call away, if you need anything."

"Thank you, Jan," Trikon tried to say through a mouthful of food. Lisham just smiled and waved.

Eric said, "Meet us back here in half an hour, okay? I'll need to brief you before the press conference."

"Will do."

Jan left, and predictably ran into Jack and Tom. "What do you two do, just wander the halls till I get out?" she demanded.

"Most of my job right now is supervising you," Jack reminded her. "With Tom it's easy; he follows instructions. You're the one who gives me ulcers."

Jan glared at him in mock indignance. "I do not! And you mean to say, when I'm tied up in these multi-world meetings, you've nothing to do?"

He shrugged. "Well, Eric did hint he had big plans for me, but he still hasn't told me what they are." He didn't seem in a hurry to find out, either.

Jan batted her eyes at Tom coquettishly. "How about you? You're off-duty. Were you waiting around for l'il ole me?"

"Yes, ma'am. Seems the only time I get to see you these days is between luncheons and meetings."

Jan winced. That wasn't far from the truth. "I've got half an hour."

"What have you in mind?"

Jan thought Tom sounded unreasonably suspicious, which gave her ideas, now that she thought about it. She smiled wickedly.

287

Jack guffawed, shook his head and left.

"What, now?" Tom tried to sound long-suffering, but the glint in his eye gave him away.

Jan grabbed his hand and 'ported the two of them into their bedroom. Pointedly she closed the door and they made short work of her half-hour break.

* * *

The group reconvened promptly at 4:00 on the stage where Jan had faced her first press conference. Scanning the throng of reporters crowded into the room, Jan recognized many faces from her previous interview. Most of these gave her a smile or nod when she made eye contact.

The President sat in the center chair, with an ornate table in front of them. Glasses of water, pads of paper and writing utensils were positioned in front of each person. Lisham was on the President's immediate right, with Saunders beside Lisham. On the President's left sat Trikon, then Eric and Jan.

The President gave the photographers a chance to get off a barrage of shots before he raised his hand for silence. The buzz of quiet conversation faded. All eyes watched him expectantly.

"Ladies and gentlemen, we thank you for joining us here on this momentous occasion. Without further ado, let me present, on my right, First Lisham from Shalaii, and on my left, Lead Spacefarer Trikon of Orowa."

Lisham and Trikon stood, waved to the audience, and sat down. To Jan it looked a bit choreographed, but the President thanked them and continued.

"We have been discussing common challenges facing our three worlds and have made headway in finding workable solutions for some of them."

He held up a hand when questions were fired at him from the audience. "We can't go into them at the moment, but I will say this: As First Lisham so accurately pointed out this morning, we are all better for the friendships we make. It was thanks to the collaboration between our three worlds that we now have the upper hand against viruses. We are working on another cooperative milestone, and as soon as the details are finalized, we will issue a joint communiqué.

But now, I am sure you are eager to quiz our distinguished guests." The President smiled towards Lisham and Trikon and sat down.

"What do you think of Earth so far?" a woman asked.

Lisham and Trikon exchanged glances, and Trikon stood up.

"Most that I have seen of it is from your picture books, and a little through the windows of Ames. It is very different, very alien-looking to my eyes, but most delightful. It must have felt this way to your explorers when they discovered new continents here."

A gaunt, sharp-nosed man asked, "Do we seem like savages to you?" He spoke quietly, but there was no denying the bait in his question.

Trikon flushed. "No, sir. I have learned a bit of your history, and I think I understand your question. Humans are more advanced than Shalaians in some ways, and we have developed skills you have not, but these came from adaptation to conditions on our planet which do not exist on yours. I consider all three of our species complete equals."

"So do I," Lisham confirmed. "It took the ingenuity and knowledge of all three of our peoples to develop decontamination procedures which work equally well for all of us and our diseases. We make a wonderful team, when we work together."

"First Lisham, does it frighten you to be on Earth, where we have so much war and crime? I understand you don't have a word for 'war'."

Lisham shrugged. "Not really. I am among friends who have lived here all this time and are still alive. So I trust to their wisdom to keep me safe while I am here. I am sure your Vice-President and Secretary-General are depending on their hosts on our homeworlds for their safety."

"Do you think your governments would issue visas so humans could visit your planets, like we do between countries here?" The enquirer sounded as though she had a personal interest in the answer.

Trikon waffled a hand. "I do not know. The ability to travel healthily between our planets has only become possible a few days ago."

"But surely it's been discussed."

"If so, it has not been mentioned to me," Trikon said firmly. "But I, too, am eager to vacation on other worlds with my family, if the opportunity arises."

Jan smiled to herself. Although the answer gave no further details, he had subtly aligned himself with the questioner's desires while effectively closing the door on that line of questioning. Or so she thought.

"What about your government, First Lisham?" the woman persisted.

"Yes, we have spoken of it. But I suspect much groundwork will be needed on all three planets before it becomes a reality. Everything from determining what foods are edible to other species, to how to treat a visitor who becomes ill or gets hurt. Our internal biologies are probably as different as are our shapes. And that, too will need to be accommodated, including suitable furniture."

The President interjected, "That is a very good point. Also, none of our people know your languages, and very few of you know ours. The language barrier would be a major stumbling-block at the moment."

Several pens raised in the air, but the President eyed his watch significantly. "I'm afraid that's all the time we have for now. I will make a statement at the end of the conference. Thank you all for coming."

As one, they stood and filed off the stage. They ignored the questions being hollered after them. The President, Saunders and the delegates walked ahead, chatting relaxedly.

Eric slowed down to accommodate Jan's shorter legs. "I think they're calling it a day. Not much else to do till the conferencers on the other planets give a thumbs up or down to our suggestions. I understand the First Lady and a few bigwigs will be arriving shortly. Are you and Tom up for some high-level socializing?"

"Thanks, Eric. I'll check with Tom, but I'd just as soon give it a miss. I'm not much of a party animal, and it's been a very long day for me." Which was true, but Jan also had the germ of an idea she wanted to think out.

"Wish I had that option. My dogs are killing me. If you're not here by seven, I'll give them your regrets."

Jan turned to leave. "Thanks."

"Oh, and Jan, I need you here by eight tomorrow. Might be a briefing, if the party turns to shop talk and anything more comes of it."

"Will do." Jan smothered a yawn. "Been a good day, though, hasn't it?"

Eric smiled. "Yup. I wouldn't have given us a hope in hell of finding any kind of workable solution. Still got my doubts, but we do have a starting point."

"A promising one, I think. G'night, Eric."

Naturally, Tom and Jack just 'happened' to be coming around the corner as she walked towards the exit.

"Give me a ride, lady?" Jack leered, faking a pronounced limp.

Jan indicated a smirking Tom. "Only if he can come, too."

"Oh, well, if he has to," Jack grumbled. They placed their hand on Jan's arm and left the building.

Some time later, the trio were settling down to a makeshift dinner when the phone rang. Jack was closest, so he punched the button to activate the speaker. They now had a speaker phone in every communal room they used.

"Sorry to disturb you," Eric said briskly. "But we just got a call. That inmate who 'ported himself out of prison just got sprung by three men with a lot of fire power. Six dead, and none of them the bad guys. Someone wanted him real bad."

Jan looked at her companions in dismay. The race was on.

CHAPTER 15

"Ideas?" Eric sounded understandably tense.

Jan pushed her plate to one side, her appetite gone. "A couple. I thought of them during the meeting, but I didn't want to say anything till I could try them out. I still don't want to – especially over the phone."

"Alright. Let me know as soon as you've got something concrete. And Jan, I don't have to tell you, we need it yesterday."

"No kidding!" Jan pressed the button to end the conversation.

Tom looked at once hopeful and wary. "What ideas?"

"Let me talk to the other links first." Even to her, the notions sounded pretty far-fetched. But then, so had teleportation a year ago.

Jack gave Tom a meaningful glance and got up to leave.

Jan sighed gustily, trying to purge the fear from her mind. So 'they' now had a novice 'porter. He had been kept lightly sedated to deny him the strong focus required to teleport. How long before his mind would be clear enough to try, she wondered.

Jan calmed herself as best she could before sending out her call. She linked first with Ablakan, then with Shownae, and filled them in on the bad news.

Already? Shownae gasped.

To Jan, Ablakan felt equally distressed, but all he did was ask, *Can you find him, Jan?*

I don't know. I have a couple things I want to run by you both, see if you think they're feasible.

Right now, I would listen to anything, Shownae declared.

Jan took a deep breath. *Alright, here goes. Ablakan, remember when you were trying to find Shownae near where Moohri had met him, and he wasn't there?*

I remember.

Then you said you found him on another continent. Think back. Exactly how did you go about looking for him? Or for Black on Shyr, for that matter?

293

Ablakan seemed taken aback by the question. *By his mindprint, of course – how Shownae's mind felt to me when I accessed Moohri's memory of talking with him. But you don't have this 'porter's mindprint.*

No, but we know what it feels like mentally to teleport. Let's try an experiment: Ablakan, would you 'port yourself a few feet away, while Shownae and I stay connected to you? I'd like us all to take turns 'porting. If I'm right, we each have an individual style, like a fingerprint, but we all use basically the same process.

Shownae brightened. *So we could pick up on someone else who is trying to 'port. It's worth a try.*

Ablakan's mental state abruptly changed. *I'm about to 'jump'. Are you ready?*

Yes, Jan had only time to say, before the boy relocated a handsbreadth away. Quickly she reviewed her experience of the event, committing it to memory.

Did you both feel that? Ablakan asked.

Shownae replied. *I did. But it happened so fast . . . Can you do it again?*

Alright. Here we go. He repeated the process, and this time, Jan was able to predict the sequence of mental/feelings permutations, rapid though they were.

Got it, she said. *I'll go next.*

Jan gave them a few seconds to focus on her mind, then 'ported herself beside the stove. *And again.* She was back at the table.

Now me, Shownae said, and Jan easily followed his twin 'ports.

You were right, Ablakan concluded. *Each person does it a bit differently, but I would know the 'porting thought-and-feeling anywhere.*

Jan smiled in satisfaction. *Me, too. Now I should be able to locate him when he tries to 'port – at least, I hope so. Maybe I can suppress it, then when they leave him alone, 'port him to Ames. I'd better talk to the others here first.*

Be careful, Ablakan cautioned. *If he is stronger than we believe, he might try to send you to your death, like Black was planning to do.*

Jan snapped her fingers, remembering. *That's the other thing I wanted to talk to you about. I'd like to try something else. Let's start with something inanimate – not alive, I mean. Do you have something nearby you wouldn't be too upset if it got destroyed?*

Ablakan sounded doubtful. *Perhaps my browakki. I'm getting a bit old for that now.*

Good. Touch it, please. Jan waited till she felt Ablakan handle a strange object, then zeroed in on it. *Got it.*

Mentally, she imagined first Ablakan then Shownae trying to 'port it away from that spot, but the object remaining in place. Then she 'keyed' it to her personal 'fingerprint' and, to make sure it would move for her, transferred it to the other side of Ablakan.

It is now beside my other hand, the boy said. *I was following your thoughts. Let me see if I can move it now.*

Jan watched in her mind his efforts to reposition the object, and was gratified to see him fail. Shownae fared no better.

They spent several minutes each practicing with various objects. As a final test, Jan removed her 'lock' on the browakki, and the object readily moved for all three of them.

But will it work with people? Shownae voiced the obvious next step.

Five minutes later, flushed but happy, Jan knew that her plan had worked. Locked by Ablakan, Jan could still 'port herself around, but Shownae couldn't move her, so presumably, no one else would be able to, either. That was the final test. After Ablakan removed the block against Shownae 'porting Jan, they locked each other so that only the three of them could transport each other without express permission. Rogue 'porters could still endanger them by placing deadly items near them, but at least the links wouldn't find themselves spaced or inside a volcano.

That will protect us a bit, but not our families or bosses, Ablakan pointed out. *They could be targets, too.*

Jan sighed. *You're right. We'll have to lock down almost everyone we know, and still they won't be really safe.* She rubbed her forehead in frustration. *This is getting crazy.*

Shownae paused. *Unless . . .*

Jan could feel his thoughts, but not interpret them.

Do you suppose, he continued. *We could set our minds to automatically scan for 'porting fingerprints other than our three? That way, as soon as someone started developing the skill, we would become aware of it.*

That would be ideal, Jan admitted. *But I'm not sure I can do that in the background. Heck, I still don't know if I can pick up on that rogue beginner. But I'd better talk to my bosses pretty soon, find out what they want me to do if I locate him. For all we know, he might not ever be able to 'port again. It could have been a one-time thing, a fluke.*

Ablakan pointed out, *Even a fluke can be repeated, with enough practice; Black proved that. I think we must consider him a 'porter, either way.*

I guess you're right. Jan thanked them for their help and broke the connection. She opened her eyes, feeling her companions' presence in the hallway.

"I'm finished," she called, and two heads popped around the corner.

"Any luck?" Tom asked.

"Yup, and we have a lot to talk about. Can you reach Eric and the others, Jack?"

He looked doubtful. "If they're in the midst of high-powered entertaining . . . "

"Never mind." Jan turned her full attention on Tom, batting her eyelids, then hamming a pout. "You never take me anywhere. And there's this big shindig tonight that we've been invited to, and I feel like dancing and all –"

"Say no more, m'dear," Tom made a dramatic gesture. "It's off to the fancy ball for us."

296

Jan broke her personal 'land speed record' getting ready, and fifteen minutes later, she 'ported the dashing trio into the vast cafeteria which had been transformed into a ballroom for the evening.

Saunders was the first to spot them, as they made their way toward the V.I.P. table. He waved them over. "Glad you could make it."

"Thank you, sir," Jack answered for them.

Lisham beamed. "You see? I told you they would be back. How could they miss the first interspecies party?"

"I am delighted to lose that bet," Trikon smiled gallantly. "And very glad you have come."

Jan was feeling decidedly guilty by then. "Thank you, but . . . "

"We saved you a spot, just in case." Saunders indicated three empty chairs beside him. Obediently, they took their places.

Jan noticed the President and his wife on the floor, slow-dancing, and wondered when the First Lady had arrived. Eric seemed to be missing. Perhaps his sore feet had gotten him out of that engagement.

"Eric's not much of a night-owl," Saunders said, following her gaze. "You didn't just come here to hobnob, did you?"

"No. There have been developments, and I need decisions quickly."

The First Lady noticed Jan and gave her a big smile. The couple edged toward the table as they danced, the melody being nearly at an end, anyway.

"How wonderful to see you," she greeted them. Jan and the First Lady shared a quick hug, and Tom and Jack had their hands warmly shaken. "I was so disappointed when Eric said you wouldn't be coming."

Jan was feeling guiltier by the second. Saunders cleared his throat.

"Actually, I had asked Jan to let me know if there were any important developments. I understand there have been. Would it be unspeakably rude to steal your husband away for a few minutes? I promise we'll keep it short."

"By all means," the First Lady replied graciously. "It'll give me time to get to know Tom."

Jan whispered loudly, with a wicked grin, "Mention the word 'telescope' and he'll love you for life."

Tom glared at Jan as she turned away, chuckling. The last thing Jan heard was the First Lady asking, "What do you think of the Hubble Telescope?".

Saunders led the President, Jack, the delegates and her down the hall and into Eric's office. He closed the door and turned expectantly toward Jan. She gave them a brief account of her conversation and experiments with Ablakan and Shownae.

"Just in case, I'd like permission to 'lock' you against unauthorized 'porting," Jan told her bosses. She motioned toward Trikon and Lisham. "Your 'porters would like to do the same for you, if you don't mind. I can call them now, let them do it while I'm 'locking' the President and Dr. Saunders. I could take a chance and 'lock' Dr. Rhodes, too, for tonight, until I can get his permission in the morning."

Both delegates agreed, and Jan put through the calls, leaving their links to handle the details.

"Are you ready, sirs?" she asked the President and Saunders. Both nodded consent. She concentrated, performed the procedure, then relaxed. "Done."

"My wife and children would be obvious targets as well," the President pointed out. "But I don't want to worry them. Can you 'lock' them without their knowledge?"

That accomplished, she asked, "Are your children at the White House?"

"Yes."

She accessed their mindprints from the President's memory, and effortlessly located them in their beds. Within half a minute, they, too, were protected from mental abduction.

The President heaved a sigh of relief. "That's a load off my mind. Thank you, Jan. Once again, we owe you a debt of gratitude."

Jan squirmed uncomfortably and mumbled, "Glad to help."

"You said you needed some direction?" Saunders reminded her.

"Oh, right." Jan faced her boss, grateful for the change of topic. "That rogue 'porter who was sprung today? If he tries to 'port, I may be able to pick up on him, using that 'signature process'. If so, should I try to bring him in? And if I do, where do I put him? I'm sure the lab people could sedate him enough to keep him from 'porting. But then maybe those who sprung him would try to take him from here. They left a lot of bodies in their wake last time – and that was inside a hospital."

The President turned to Saunders. "Do you know what he was in for?"

"No, but I can find out."

"Please do. And Jan, I think you'd better bring him in if you can. Lesley, how quickly can the labworkers get ready for him?"

"Pretty fast, I expect. I'll alert them immediately. We'd have to keep him in the security area and monitor him around the clock to make sure the sedative is holding. At least until we decide what to do with him."

The President asked, "Jan, can you 'lock' him down so he can't 'port?"

"No. Ablakan and I tried that with each other, but it only works for others trying to 'port you after you've been locked down. You can still move yourself or other people or things; it doesn't change that."

The President seemed lost in thought for a handful of seconds. "Alright. As soon as Lesley has things set up, see if you can find this guy and bring him in. And dump his abductors in his old cell. Leslie, better give the warden a heads-up on that at the same time you're checking what this guy was in for. They'll probably be armed."

"Yes, sir," Jan and Saunders said in unison.

"When you have the 'porter here, I'll talk to him personally. Maybe we can convince him to work for us."

Jan didn't much like the idea of recruiting a convict as her first student, but admittedly, she didn't know what he had done. Perhaps it was something they could overlook, like creative bookkeeping. She fervently hoped she wouldn't have to deal with another Black.

The President and delegates returned to the party, promising to give the First Lady their regrets and to have Tom join Jan and Jack in Eric's office. Saunders was already on the phone, making arrangements with Security and the lab for their prospective guest.

When Tom arrived, Jan 'ported the three of them home, and the men left her alone to concentrate. With a deep sigh, she closed her eyes and began her search, hoping not to fall asleep in the process. Her day had begun very early, it was now considerably past her bedtime.

* * *

Frederick Samual Bradshaw, alias 'Hard Luck Freddie', frowned in concentration. It didn't help to have two burly men with smelly armpits and evidently no brains breathing down his neck. The diminutive pickpocket wrinkled his nose distastefully as he got another whiff of the closer one's body odor. Where the hell was he, anyway?

At some point in the last few hours, he had been drifting pleasantly in and out of reverie. He had found the hospital bed far more comfortable than the one in prison. It still rankled that he had been so close to freedom, only to have it yanked away through yet another rotten turn of fate. After many long months, he had finally succeeded in teleporting himself out of his stinking cell, only to land too close to the gates and be spotted by one of the guards. He'd been so rattled by the resulting commotion that he had been unable to concentrate. After that, no matter how hard he tried, he couldn't hold a focus. Damned sedatives!

The next thing he knew, there was the sound of gunfire, and much shouting and running. Then two men burst in wearing medical masks. These two men, he felt certain. They smelled the same – bad. He was grabbed and a hood pulled down over his head. When he protested loudly for such unwarranted treatment, he was told to 'shaddap' or they'd slug him. So he shut up and went where they led him. He was pushed into the back seat of a vehicle, and immediately the car lurched forward, so he assumed a third man was involved.

And now that his mind was clear, they wanted him to teleport a pebble from the table at which he was seated to the table where the well-dressed man with his face in darkness sat waiting.

"But, y'see, I never tried to teleport anything but me. And I only did it once."

Silken-voice in the shadows didn't seem disturbed. "Then you can do it again. Only this time, it's just a little rock. Take your time and do it right. We will wait."

Freddie glared at him in frustration. "It's not that simple."

"I understand that, and I can be patient – to a point. All I ask is that you practice diligently. If you succeed, you will have a very lucrative position in our firm, a job with security and a great many benefits, Freddie."

"What if I can't do it?" He was sure he knew the answer, but he just wanted to hear Mr. Suave over there say it.

"Then we would have no further need of you, would we?" No menace, no threats, but Freddie knew the drill: produce or die.

His Adam's apple bobbed spasmodically, and he forced his mind to concentrate. What had he been thinking, feeling, just before he 'ported himself out of jail?

* * *

Jan had spent an unfruitful hour scanning the continent for that 'signature'. Her brow throbbed from the effort. She opened her eyes, got to her feet and stretched taut muscles.

Tom and Jack emerged from the unlit hallway. They must have been watching her all this time, she surmised.

301

Tom asked hopefully, "Any luck?"

"No." Jan realized she was feeling decidedly petulant. You're getting spoiled by all your successes, she told herself severely, and sulk when you don't get your way.

"Wow, are you tense!" Tom exclaimed, as he placed his hands on her shoulders. He began massaging them and her neck.

"Mmmm, that feels good." She must have been scrunching her body in an effort to find the man. It didn't help any that she wasn't sure she wanted to find him.

Jack looked at the kitchen clock. "It's almost 1:00. How about calling it a night? You can start over in the morning."

"I might as well," she said, but just at the moment, she didn't want to move. Tom had magic fingers, and they were untying knots she hadn't even known were there. Jan yawned deeply, letting her head fall forward.

Funny – there was a little niggling feeling in her head, like when Ablakan had first pulled the word 'hello' from her mind.

Abruptly, she stiffened, head snapping upright. "I've got it! I found him. Call the lab – fast!"

Jack whirled around and began punching in the numbers.

In a split-second, Jan located the body that went with the focus, and projected a jumble of gibberish words into his mind to distract him and keep him from teleporting. He was so close to succeeding she wasn't sure she could stop him. Then she felt his frustration and knew it had worked.

"Hurry," she urged Jack.

Seconds eons long, then Jack's "Go!"

Jan quickly enveloped the man with her mind and 'ported him into the lab. Still mentally attached, she felt his disorientation, then dismay as the security guards and medical personnel converged on him.

"Ouch!" she yelped, feeling the hypodermic needle puncture his skin. Fear, shock, panic, and finally, the dampening effect of the sedative taking hold.

With a sigh of relief, Jan released his mind and smiled at her companions. "You can tell Saunders, 'mission accomplished'. Now for the kidnappers."

* * *

Morning started earlier than she was ready for, but Jan managed to get herself dressed in time to join the President, Saunders and Eric for a briefing. It was barely 9:00.

"I have the report on our Mr. Bradshaw," Saunders stated. He rustled the multi-page report he was holding. "Pickpocket, mostly. A few priors for having light fingers at his friends' houses as a juvenile. No apparent gang connections. Known on the streets as 'Hard Luck Freddie' because he always seems to trip himself up. Not too bright. Has a weakness for gambling and women. That's about it."

The President's face brightened. "Could have been a lot worse. He might be reformable, with the right incentives. Lead the way."

When the President strode purposefully into the lab, the little man slouching in the chair with a doughnut in his hand looked up in disbelief. Saunders and Jan stood in the doorway, letting the President have the floor.

"Good morning, Mr. Bradshaw." The President extended his hand, smiling broadly. "I hear you have had an eventful couple of days."

"Uh, yeah. Are you really –?" Freddie offered a limp hand to be shaken.

"Your president, yes."

"Where am I, anyway?" He looked around at the newcomers, eyes widening as he recognized Jan. "Is she who I think she is?"

"Jan Brody? Indeed. You're at Ames Research Center, Mr. Bradshaw and, I would like to think, among friends. Or at least colleagues."

"Did I 'port myself here?" Freddie asked weakly. Jan could almost hear him berating himself.

"Actually, I gave you a bit of a hand," Jan supplied. "But you almost had it. Did you know, you're only the third human to 'port

303

by design? Pretty impressive." She gave him her most admiring smile.

He scowled. "Lemme guess. You want me to teleport for you, like Jan does."

"Well, she is overworked, and the pay is rather good," the President admitted.

Freddie stuck out his weak chin belligerently. "That's what that other guy said, too. Then they threatened to kill me if I couldn't deliver the goods."

"Killing is strictly forbidden around here," Jan assured him. "We didn't even try to kill Black when he was after us."

"But he ended up dead anyway, d'in't he?" Freddie pointed out.

The President cleared his throat to recapture the man's attention. "The important thing here is, we want to hire you, train you properly. You would become a very important man, Mr. Bradshaw. And extremely wealthy. And we provide the best overall protection from those who would wish to kidnap or harm you. In fact, those who did now occupy your old cell." He paused significantly. "Of course, you would have to turn, shall we say, respectable. Think you could do that?"

"Maybe." The wary eyes were greedy. "How much wealth are we talking?"

The President looked a query at Saunders.

"As a trainee, you would pull ten grand a month, clear," Saunders supplied. "As your skills develop, that would increase substantially based on your level of expertise."

"How much?" the little man demanded. "As much as Jan makes?" Her salary had become common knowledge a long time ago.

The President nodded firmly. "If you become as skilled as Jan is, and provided you keep your nose clean, then yes, you would."

Freddie stuck out a sticky palm. "You've got yourself a deal." This time, there was firmness in his grip.

Unnoticed, Jan stepped out of sight in the hallway, closed her eyes, and added Frederick Bradshaw to the roster of 'locked' teleporters.

* * *

The morning went by quickly. The conferencers closeted themselves in the boardroom for another session, this time focusing on trade and commerce. Jan's presence wasn't needed, so she spent the time catching up on the backlog of goods which needed to be sent to other worlds. She had barely made a dent in it when Tom stuck his head through the doorway to say it was lunchtime.

"The President asked if there's been any word from Ablakan or Shownae yet."

"No. But then, I've been 'porting stuff around solidly since 9:30. They may not have been able to get through. I'll check now."

Jan quieted her mind and called Ablakan, only to receive a 'busy signal' – their code for being already mentally engaged.

But Shownae was free. He reported Wiltanus and his visitors were making good progress, but had nothing to pass along just yet. When she tried again, Ablakan responded, but like Shownae, there was nothing new to report.

Jan and Tom stopped by Eric's office to deliver their no-news message on their way home for lunch.

"Whew! Quite the morning," Jan exhaled when they got there. "I sure hope Fred works out. I really need the help."

Privately, she had her doubts, although he had felt ingenuous enough when he agreed to take the job.

"Shrimp salad?" Tom offered.

"Oh, sorry, Tom. I was just thinking about Fred." She absent-mindedly reached for the bowl.

"One morning, and she's already thinking about another man," he quipped.

"No, seriously. What do we do with him if he won't change his ways? We can't keep him a prisoner and sedated forever."

305

Tom frowned. "I know. I've been wondering the same thing. Once he can 'port well, it'll be a great temptation for him to heist whatever he wants."

"Well, I'll not worry about it for now," she resolved. "It was nice of Eric to give us the afternoon off. I guess just about everyone will be watching the golf game."

"No doubt, with it being the first tri-species game ever. I might wander over there for a while myself. Care to come?"

Jan yawned, propping herself up with her elbows on the table. "No, thanks. I'm zonked. You go watch. I need to sleep."

Soon afterwards, Tom kissed her as she lay snuggled in their bed, then closed the door quietly behind him.

CHAPTER 16

Jan was unceremoniously yanked out of a deep slumber some time later. She sat bolt-upright in bed, staring across the room at nothing. She could feel the hair on her neck sticking out like porcupine quills. Nothing moved, but Jan tentatively projected her mind to search for an unauthorized consciousness within the house. Her scan came up empty.

Must've been a dream, she thought, annoyed at herself. She turned on her side and tried to get back to sleep, but the sense of imminent danger persisted.

With a groan, Jan gave in and slipped out of bed, still in her lounging pajamas. She wasn't sure where she was headed until she found herself approaching the Reading Room. The comfy chair she had used for 'pathing when they first arrived at Ames was seldom occupied now. Instead, she and her counterparts on Shalaii and Orowa simply transmitted or received as needed, wherever they happened to be.

For some reason, this time the chair beckoned and, not certain why she was doing so, Jan sat down in it. Something – or someone? – was mentally tugging at her. There was fear involved, and danger. It was not nearly as nebulous as it had felt moments before. Jan cleared her mind and sent her focus out in a broad, highly-sensitized search.

And found her. A young mother, by the terror her mind held for a child. The toddler was fighting the strong current which inexorably carried him further downstream, and the frantic mother was inadvertently transmitting her verbal cries for help.

Using the mother's focus as a locator, Jan plucked the child from the waters and set him down beside the astonished woman. The mother clutched the squalling child and cried in her mind, *Angel, whoever you are, thank you!*

I'm not an angel, just a teleporter, Jan replied, startling the woman so deeply she nearly let go of the toddler.

Are – are you Jan Brody?

That I am.

The woman seemed only then to realize what they were doing. *How can you talk in my mind?*

Same way you've been yelling in mine, Jan replied, amused now that the danger had passed.

What do you mean?

Jan considered the situation, and threw caution to the wind. *I would be easier if we talk in person. Mind if I drop by?*

Uh, no, I guess not.

Jan placed herself beside the woman. The mother gulped, then blurted out in surprise.

"Gee, you're as short as me! – Oh, I'm sorry, I just meant . . ."

Jan laughed and lightly touched her arm. "Don't worry; you're not the first person to give me that bit of bad news. My, what a handsome young man you have there! What is your name, dear?" The child buried his face in his mother's leg.

"This is Billy, but he's a bit shy." She stuck out a somewhat free hand. "I'm Brenda Hancock. We just moved here." Brenda motioned towards a rundown apartment complex across the road. "Billy wanted to go feed the ducks. He must have seen them from the window, but there weren't any when we got here. Ducks, I mean. Anyway, I just turned around for a second, and I heard a splash and a scream, and the current had him." She didn't seem to want to let go of Jan's hand. "Thank you, Mrs. Brody, for saving my boy. He's all I have left, now that my husband's gone. The cancer just spread and spread." Tears welled up in her eyes. The memory was obviously still too fresh.

"I'm so sorry, Brenda. And please call me Jan."

Jan noticed how shabbily they both were dressed. It didn't take a psychic to realize whatever money they may have had was long gone – probably for medical bills. The woman was almost destitute.

"Brenda, is this the first time you've spoken in someone's mind?"

She drew back. "Of course. I wouldn't do that on purpose. That'd be like . . . like breaking into someone's house."

308

"If you force yourself in against their will, certainly it's wrong," Jan agreed, remembering guiltily a certain forced entry into Plaka's and, more recently, Freddie's minds. "But sending out a call – be it an S.O.S. like you just did or asking permission to talk to someone – that's quite different, don't you think?"

"I guess." Brenda sounded unconvinced. She shook herself. "Where are my manners? Jan, can I offer you a cup of coffee or tea? I've got the kitchen unpacked, at least. Or maybe you'd prefer something cold. It's pretty hot already. See, Billy's hair is almost dry."

For the first time, Jan noticed she was in a completely different part of the country. It was uncommonly hot, and there was a dry breeze blowing. As they crossed the street and walked towards the building, Jan said, "Forgive my ignorance, Brenda, but what State are we in?"

Brenda squinted at her. "Why, Georgia, of course. I don't understand. How could you come here if you didn't know where 'here' is?"

"I just plunked myself down close to your mind. You don't come from these parts either, do you? I mean, you don't have a Southern accent or anything."

Brenda's voice turned listless. "No. Dan heard of a healer down here who was supposedly doing great things, so we came. But he turned out to be a fraud. He left town just before we arrived. The sheriff was after him or something. But the trip was too much for Dan. He had to be hospitalized, and he never came out."

She turned away to unlock the rickety ground-floor apartment door, and to hide the tears that refused to stay bottled up. Billy clambered inside ahead of her. He grabbed a rusty toy fire engine and trotted down the hall to play.

"I'm sorry, Jan," Brenda said in a quavering voice. "You didn't come here for a sob story."

"Perhaps not, but sometimes you just have to let it out. I've got three planets full of people who'll listen to my every whimper and

309

whine. But not everyone's that lucky. And what Granny Jan would prescribe right now is a good cry and some tea."

Brenda smiled wanly. "Tea and sympathy?"

"Why not? You've got to clear it out sometime; why not now? I suspect you've spent a long time being brave for Dan, and now you have to keep Billy from seeing how you feel, am I right?"

Brenda nodded, her mouth quivering, as more tears overflowed their banks.

"Then let it out, dear soul," Jan breathed softly, drawing the brokenhearted woman into her arms.

Together they shared a good old-fashioned cry, till Jan remembered she might be called on at any time and couldn't afford puffy eyes. She stilled her tears of empathy, but let her feelings of comfort and sympathy flow to the woman sobbing on her shoulder.

At long last, the woman's pain eased and the tears subsided into occasional showers followed by hiccups. That triggered giggles, and soon they were both laughing helplessly.

"Oh, Jan, you've no idea how good it feels not to have that – that pressure-cooker inside me always threatening to blow. Thank you for being so kind." She dabbed at her eyes with a tissue. "I must look a fright."

Jan grinned. "I suspect we both do."

"Please, sit down. Can I get you that tea I talked about – oh, years ago?"

Jan pulled out a rickety chair and sat down, and Brenda did the same. "Thanks. I'll need to head back soon. But before I go, would you humor me a bit? I'd like to try a little experiment."

"What kind of experiment?" Brenda didn't quite recoil, but that was the impression Jan got. The woman transmitted like blazes whenever her emotions were engaged.

"Nothing bizarre. Would you trust me, just a little?"

"I guess so." Her body language suggested the opposite.

Jan pretended not to notice. "Good. Would you close your eyes? I'll stay right where I am. I just want you to try something."

Brenda obediently shut her eyes. They immediately began to flutter, signaling a change in brainwave patterns.

"Think of Billy. He went down the hall a while ago with the fire engine. Where is he now?"

Brenda started to shift in the chair.

"No, don't look. Go there with your mind. Find him from here."

Brenda's eyelids flickered rapidly. "He's not in his room any more. He's gone toidy – I mean, gone to the bathroom."

"Okay, we'll give him a minute, then."

Brenda opened her eyes. "I didn't realize how easy it is to see someone that way," she whispered, awed at what she had done. They heard a muted flush.

"Were either of your parents psychic?"

"No, but my uncle was. Tarot cards and such. I used to think he was crazy. Oh, and my grandmother, before she died, thought she saw an angel, only it turned out to be her grandniece dressed up for a school play," she finished awkwardly.

"Believe it or not, Brenda, I only started dabbling with psychic stuff about four years ago. Out of boredom, mostly. I couldn't get into soaps and talk shows," Jan grinned, trying to put the woman at ease.

Brenda nodded. "Me neither, especially these last few years." Her face lengthened.

"Well, Billy must be out of the bathroom now," Jan said brightly, not wanting Brenda to slip back into melancholy. "Let's see what he's up to, shall we?"

Brenda sighed and closed her eyes. Rapid eye movement began promptly. "He's hugging Boo – that's his teddy," Brenda reported in a faraway voice.

"Good. Would you call him out here, please? With your mind. Just say his name, and ask him to come out here to you, just as you would verbally."

Jan held her breath while the younger woman complied. Almost immediately, Billy trotted around the corner, Boo clutched tightly in his arms.

"Yes, Mama?" he asked.

Brenda stared at him for a moment. "Um, do you want cookies and milk?"

"Yes, pease."

Jan followed Brenda to the cupboard and said in a low voice. "Ask him mentally if his hair is dry."

Jan turned around to watch the response.

"All dry," the boy nodded, rubbing his head.

Brenda stared at Jan, incredulous. "He thinks I'm saying it out loud," she whispered.

"It's hard sometimes to tell the difference between what we hear with our ears and with our mind. You have a rare talent, you know."

"You really think so?"

"I know so. Much too much talent to waste out here. We need people like you very badly, in case you didn't know. And it pays mighty well." Jan's eyes fell on the toddler who was now cramming a cookie into his mouth. "You could make a wonderful life for Billy in California."

"That's where you work, isn't it? At Ames?"

"Yup. They work my tail off, but they treat me great, so I don't mind. Besides, it beats the heck out of working in a bank."

Brenda chuckled. "I'll bet."

Encouraged, Jan decided to press the point. "Would you think about it? I'm really serious about this. I need back-up something awful. I'd like to talk to my boss about you. I'm sure he'll want you to come."

Brenda looked around the shabby little kitchen. "And leave all this?" she mocked herself.

"We all have to make sacrifices. For the common good, you understand," Jan grinned. "So, with your permission, I'll call you mentally when I've had a chance to talk to him."

312

Brenda shook her head incredulously. "Do you always do that?"

"Do what?"

"Swoop into someone's life, save their child, offer them a job and a new life? And all before breakfast?" She looked pointedly at Jan's pajamas.

Jan said sheepishly, "Oh. Actually, I get 'afternoon naps', since I have to stay up late to 'port my husband to and from telescopes in different States. And no, this is my first time playing Wonder Woman."

Brenda stuck out her hand. "Well, I'm ever so grateful for all you've done – and are doing – for us. I'll be listening for your call."

"No problem there," Jan assured her. "I'll just 'knock' inside your mind. Mentally open the door, and then we can talk. It's easy. Or give me a 'busy signal' if you're occupied."

Brenda's eyes shone with hope. "Okay. And thanks again."

"My pleasure. Talk to you soon. Bye, Billy."

"Byebyebye," the child responded, opening and closing his fingers in lieu of a wave.

Jan stepped outside the door into the shadow of a magnolia bush and, reasonably certain no one was watching, 'ported to her kitchen. There she was nearly run down by a startled Tom. Jack had returned home while she was gone. He let out a yelp at her abrupt appearance.

"Where've you been?" Jack demanded.

"Um, Georgia." Which inevitably led to a detailed description of her afternoon adventure.

When she had finished, Jack asked, "How strong a telepath is she, d'you think?" It was hard to understand him, as he was munching a hamburger on the fly.

"Unpracticed and untrained, she's a lot further along than I was before I 'met' Ablakan. And I think she has the potential to be a stronger telepath than me."

Tom whistled.

"How am I supposed to ride shotgun on two ladies who can run – and maybe 'port – rings around me?" Jack asked plaintively.

"Don't ask me. And if I knew, I wouldn't tell you."

Jack grabbed a random lock of his all-brown hair. "See these gray hair? You're the cause, y'now."

"Oh, pooh. All this excitement keeps you young," Jan scoffed. "You should thank me for rescuing you from your old dull, boring job."

Tom raised a hand to interrupt them. "Much as I love to watch you kids squabble, I think we should be there when the golfers finish. Which could be any time now."

They easily picked out Eric at the front of the crowd waiting behind the ribbon on the 18th green.

"Any news yet?" he asked when Jan approached. It took her a second to realize he was referring to conferencing reports from Shalaii and Orowa.

"Um, no. I turned in early for a nap. Actually, it's a good thing I did. I had a little adventure of my own."

"Oh?"

"Had to break your little rule about not 'porting myself outside of the area," Jan confessed, citing threat to life and limb.

Eric's jaw muscles tensed. "Go on."

So she did. When she finished, Eric regarded her doubtfully.

"She's a natural, Chief. What's more, she's fairly bursting with compassion and integrity. And I am willing to bet she could be taught to 'port like I do in no time. I'd be glad to train her, on my own time if necessary."

His expression was markedly skeptical. "You're sure she's that good? You're not just feeling sorry for her?"

"No, Eric. She *is* special. You should see – hear, I guess – the way she transmits. You'd swear she's speaking out loud. Let me bring her in. Then you can see for yourself. I can teach her at the same time I train Fred. Besides, you said it yourself: We need help, and fast."

314

"Heck of a coincidence," Eric noted. "But I'm not about to turn down a gift. Okay, the President wants you to 'port him and the delegates to the White House for dinner. When you're through, bring her to my office."

"Thanks, boss. I'll let her know."

He leveled an admonitory stare at her. "Do it mentally. No more 'porting unless it really is life-and-death."

"Understood."

Jan stepped away from the crowd and placed the 'call'. Brenda answered at once and quickly agreed to the meeting, though the time was left open, as Jan didn't know when she'd be called upon to 'port the dignitaries.

A ball landed impressively close to the 18th cup and a beaming Trikon came into view. A minute later, he handily sunk the putt to win the day. A burst of applause acknowledged his victory, and he bowed deeply towards the crowd.

The President came in second, with Lisham and Saunders tied for third place. They gathered around Trikon, shaking his hand.

"How did you learn to play so well?" the President marveled. "Or are all Orowans so gifted?"

Trikon laughed, "This is the first game I have won. I usually finish last!"

"Whew! It's hot out here, isn't it?" Saunders remarked hopefully. "I could sure go a cold drink."

The President admitted, "Me, too. How about you gentlemen?"

Both agreed that they were thirsty, so Jan took the hint and 'ported the party to the cafeteria. The room was empty save for three people sitting together across from the cashier.

Saunders treated his contingent to their choice of frosty beverage and a snack, then Jan placed them in the conference room to chat in private.

"Any word from Ablakan yet?" Lisham looked at Jan expectantly, but she shook her head.

315

"Neither Ablakan nor Shownae will tell me a thing, but I keep picking up guarded pleasure or optimism or something. I'd sure like to know what's going on."

Trikon muttered, "They should tell us, even if it is not finished. We shared our progress with them."

"Not all of it," Jan said, glancing at Eric.

"Oh?" Saunders shifted his gaze to her.

When Jan finished her report, Saunders said, "Gentlemen, I have to wonder how many more 'Brendas' there are out there on all our planets – people who have no idea what they can do. I'd recommend we set up an advertising campaign to draw them in, have our links test them."

The President cautioned, "We'd better get to them before the 'special interest' types do, like the ones who snatched Fred Bradshaw. When will Brenda arrive, Eric?"

"I'm interviewing her after you leave."

"Good." He turned toward Saunders. "If she works out, I'd like to be kept informed of her progress, too."

"Certainly, sir."

Jan gulped. She hadn't realized the President was getting progress reports on her.

A gentle 'knock' heralded an incoming call.

"Someone is reporting in . . . It's Shownae. He says Administrator Wiltanus wishes to speak to all of you. Primary Tweno and Ablakan are also linked with Shownae, along with the delegates to each planet. Whatever's going on, looks like they're ready to let us in on it."

Once she had the Earth contingent firmly linked, Tweno took the mental floor.

My friends, we apologize for the long delay in getting back to you. Ablakan was trying to locate a suitable planet but could not because he needed a consciousness there to focus on. And of course, if he had found such a consciousness, it would mean the planet is already occupied, so we couldn't use it for our purposes.

That was the point we were at when Administrator Wiltanus came up with his wonderful suggestion.

Wiltanus said, *Yes, we suspected that would be the case, as Shownae found the same problem when he tried. What we do have, and now offer for your consideration, is our forested moon, Shyr.*

We would keep ownership of the moon, of course, since it is a satellite of Orowa. But it could become a recreational and vacation spot for all peoples, with permanent facilities for inter-species negotiations, trade and commerce. Your Dr. Black demonstrated it is a healthy and safe place to colonize, so that gives it an advantage over any undiscovered planet.

The President exclaimed, *Administrator, I can't tell you how moved I am by your offer. It seems the perfect choice.*

Tweno added, *Indeed it does. We would be delighted to provide as many people and any materials you need from Shalaii to help transform Shyr.*

I am certain every member nation would want to contribute according to their ability, the U.N. Secretary-General stated, showing no reservations.

Congress would go for this, too, I'm sure of it, the President added. *We could provide building materials and manpower, although our people would have to be trained how to construct things to Orowan standards.*

Jan remembered the pictures Shownae had sent of Orowa's version of the Seven Wonders of their world. Weird more nearly described them. Although Jan had no idea how they could remain upright, given their configurations, they had outlasted the oldest human structure by thousands of years.

A mental image of a pristine forest being leveled assaulted Jan's sensibilities. *Would much of the forests be left standing?* she asked timidly.

All structures would be placed in natural clearings, Wiltanus assured her. *And we believe there are many. Forests do not make way for people. People live among the trees, or in open spaces, if*

317

that is their desire. The forests were there first, and they shall remain always.

That is wonderful to hear, sir, Jan breathed.

Wiltanus projected warm approval as he said, *It is good of you to care. With your permission, colleagues, Let us submit ideas for each other's consideration. Each species will have different insights, and we can combine all those which would work best together.*

Excellent idea, the President enthused. *I will arrange for a team to draw up plans and suggestions for you and Primary Tweno to look at. When would you like the first draft sent to you?*

Perhaps we see each other's first ideas in one of your months.

Everyone agreed. After an exchange of appreciation and goodwill, the mental conference ended.

The President slapped the table in an unusual display of excitement. "That was just what we needed! Now, if we can only pull it off with everybody working together and staying on good terms."

Trikon smiled, "We must all choose builders and planners who have large skills and small egos."

"Good point," Saunders agreed. "If we must make use of talented zenophobes, I suggest we keep them here and make them work through channels."

Lisham added, "We will bring back anyone who does not work well with the others."

The President said, "If we all do that, and those being sent to Shyr know it's a requirement of their employment, it should keep conflict to a minimum." He looked at his watch. "There's still an hour before dinner. What say we get down a few notions while we're here?"

Once they got into it, ideas and counter-suggestions came thick and fast, with everyone making copious notes. Only one contentious issue came up, but it was a big one: competition in the marketplace.

318

"That is like fighting. It makes enemies of friends," Lisham objected, looking most upset at the prospect.

"Much of our world's societies – whole economies, in fact – run on the free enterprise system," the President pointed out. "And yes, it could definitely be considered adversarial. But usually there is no ill will among competitors, just renewed efforts to gain a bigger share of the market."

Trikon asked, "How can we be friends while trying to take what the others want and need? That is a contradiction, is it not?"

The President rubbed his chin. "We're so used to it here, I never gave it much thought. Looking at it from your point of view, yes, it is a contradiction. But it's also the cornerstone of how we do business. I'm not sure we could change to any great extent how our entrepreneurs operate – not and still let them do their job."

Saunders leaned forward, considering. "The bid process might ease that," he said. "We could set up a panel of an equal number of business representatives from each planet to consider blind bids. Since they wouldn't know whose bids they are until afterwards, the panel would be judging them on merit alone. And if we come down hard on any company that tries to cut corners in goods or workmanship, it should level the playing field."

That mollified the offworlders somewhat, and the actual mechanics were tabled for a future date.

By the time they were ready to leave for the White House, the room looked as if it had been hit by a cyclone. Paper was strewn everywhere, but the meeting ended with much optimism on all sides.

Trikon sighed in satisfaction. "I shall dream happily of these days for a very long time."

"It certainly does get the mind working," Lisham agreed. "I feel like I am back in Over Learn-more."

Jan translated to the President, *soto voce,* "Like university."

Saunders was actually smiling as he said, "I look forward to seeing what they came up with on Shalaii and Orowa," then added hastily, "If I am privy to it, that is."

"You are," the President assured him. "We are all in this together. I would like to have all involved now see it through to the end, if their schedules permit."

"I know of nothing more important than this," Trikon assured him.

Lisham was quick to say, "I am 'in', as well."

As they bunched together, ready to be 'ported, Jan realized this was the first conference she'd ever attended in which no arguments or ego clashes had arisen. Perhaps that was the best omen of all.

* * *

Brenda, it's Jan. Got a minute? Jan 'pathed.

Sure do. Is the meeting still on?

Indeed it is. But I thought I'd best tell you a few things first, so you're not having to walk in 'cold'. The President and a couple of high-level delegates from Shalaii and Orowa were just here, conferencing. You probably saw it on the news.

Oh, yes. There was a query in Brenda's voice.

I just thought I'd tell you because they may want to meet you, if the interview goes well.

Brenda squealed in consternation. *Me? Oh, no; I couldn't!*

They're all just people, Brenda. This is a high-profile job. We deal with folks like that all the time. You'd be amazed how quickly you get used to it.

There was a lengthy pause. *I have nothing suitable to wear for the meeting,* Brenda said in a small voice. *Do you think your boss'll understand?*

Jan chuckled. *I know how you feel. It was my first thought when I was told we were going to the White House. Say, we're about the same height and build. I could delay the interview a few minutes, and let you try on a few of my things.*

Brenda radiated relief. *Jan, that would be great.*

How about now? Are you and Billy ready?

Um, Billy is just eating a sandwich. Can you teleport me and Billy and the sandwich all at the same time?

Jan chuckled. *No problem. I've 'ported hundreds of items at once, although they were all in a box at the time. Just hold onto Billy and the sandwich, and I'd bring you here as one 'package'. Or better yet, why don't we let Billy finish eating, and in the meantime I'll talk to Eric – Dr. Rhodes – and buy us some extra time?*

Okay. Thanks.

Jan sprinted to Eric's office to explain the delay.

"Women and their wardrobes," he grunted, then put up a conciliatory hand when Jan glared at him in mock outrage. "Okay, just don't take too long."

Ten minutes later, Jan checked with Brenda and learned they were ready for transport. With great care, she enveloped them in her focus, and an instant later they stood in front of her in the Reading Room where she had just 'ported herself seconds before.

Brenda looked around her in surprise. Billy just blinked and hugged closer to his mother.

"Hi, Billy, remember me? We met yesterday." Jan smiled brightly at the befuddled child. The toddler nodded.

As a test, Jan thought but did not project, "I bet your mother would like a hug from her young man."

Billy showed no signs of having heard, suggesting the boy wasn't himself telepathic. So the talent was all Brenda's, Jan was pleased to confirm.

"Billy, here's some paper and crayons, if you'd like to sit over there and color while your Mom and I chat." These were eagerly snatched from her extended hand, with a small 'tanku'. Brenda helped him up onto the chair behind the oversized desk.

"I'm surprised you'd have crayons around here," Brenda remarked.

"I borrowed them from one of the receptionists this afternoon. She keeps playthings in her desk because her grandkids come by sometimes."

Jan heard the front door open and close, then the sound of footsteps approaching. Jack stuck his head around the corner, wearing his most disarming smile. "Eric said you'd be here. Mind if I come in?"

" 'Course not, Jack. These are the nice people I was telling you about."

"Hi, Billy. Welcome to California, Mrs. Hancock." Jack stuck out his hand.

"Hi," Brenda said shyly, but Jan could see the handshake she gave Jack was surprisingly strong.

"Brenda, this is my immediate supervisor, Jack Foxworth. He was a propulsion engineer, but now he's working here at Ames and trying to keep my husband, Tom – you'll meet him later – and me from running amok."

He rolled his eyes, softening the effect with a grin. "And what a hopeless task that is!"

Brenda suddenly pointed her finger at him and exclaimed, "You're the man who helped Jan learn to teleport! I read about you in the papers. It's a pleasure to meet you, sir." Her eyes were big with wonder. "I don't understand how you could teach someone to do something you can't do yourself. That's just amazing."

Jack beamed at the unexpected praise. "I did rather surprise myself at that," he admitted immodestly.

"Broke." Billy held aloft a crayon. The colored tip lay on the paper.

Brenda sighed and turned towards the toddler.

"I'll take care of it," Jack offered. "You gals go ahead and talk behind my back. I'm used to it." He sniffed, laying it on thick for Brenda.

Jan could have hugged him for putting the young mother at ease and tending the child. And it gave her an idea.

322

"Brenda," she said quietly, "Mentally ask Jack where he's from."

"Colorado. Most beautiful mountains in the world." He smiled at her just as Billy tugged at his sleeve.

"I know for a fact that Jack's not telepathic," Jan whispered. "So it looks like you can project into anyone's mind without physical contact. I can't do that, you know."

"Really? You're not just saying that to build me up?"

"No. I can communicate with other telepaths and link them to non-telepaths who touch me. But to speak directly in anyone's mind without contact like you do, and make it sound like you're speaking verbally – right now, I can't. But I'd love to learn, if you're willing to teach me."

"I'm not sure how I do it," Brenda looked sheepish. "But sure, I'd be glad to tell you how, if I can figure it out."

"Thanks, dear. Let's go see what we can find for your interview. Maybe Jack could tend Billy while you try things on."

"That'd be great."

Jan turned to her boss. "Jack, would you mind entertaining Billy? Brenda and I have some girl-things to tend to before she meets Eric."

"No problemo. I used to play with my nephew in D.C. about once a month, but of course now I can't, being stationed here. This is a treat for me, actually."

Thirty-five minutes were spent transforming the shabbily-attired young widow into the beautiful, self-possessed creature she had probably once been. Jan handled the physical part. But it was Jack's open admiration that rekindled the woman self-confidence. Jan made a mental note to buy Jack the world's biggest pizza.

* * *

At 6:30, Brenda strode into Eric's office wearing Jan's favorite outfit and a quiet air of professionalism. After the description Jan had given him of Brenda, Eric was deeply impressed.

323

He stood up and shook hands, smiling at the vision before him. This lady was worth delaying dinner for. He motioned her to the most comfortable chair.

"Mrs. Hancock, Jan has spoken highly of you. And although I would not like it to get back to her, I have a great respect for her perceptions. Can you describe in your own words what you do that has Jan so excited?"

Brenda ensured her mouth was firmly shut, then said in Eric's mind, "I seem to be able to talk to people in their minds."

Both eyebrows raised in surprise. "Impressive," he said. "Most impressive. Can you do that with anyone? How far can you project like that – to non-telepaths, I mean?"

"I only just found out about it yesterday, when Jan brought it to my attention. But she had me speak to Jack – Mr. Foxworth – that way when his head was turned, playing with my son, Billy. He answered my question as though I said it out loud and I don't think he realized I hadn't." She paused for a moment before adding, "I have no idea how far I can project, but I'd love to find out."

* * *

Eric pressed a button on his phone.

"Hi, Eric," Jan replied.

"Would you come in a minute?"

Jan been expecting his call. "On my way."

When she was seated, Eric said, "Mrs. Hancock –"

"Please call me Brenda, sir."

"Thanks. And to you I'm 'Eric'." He turned back to Jan. "You were right about her skills. It would be a great help to us, especially if it works over distance. I'd like you ladies to try a little experiment. Jan, please put her through to the Vice-President. He's visiting on Shalaii right now, Brenda. Then, Jan, you bow out. I want to see if she can chat with him on her own."

Brenda gulped, then squared her shoulders. "I'm sure willing to try."

Jan contacted Ablakan and told him about Brenda and the experiment they wanted to run, if the Vice-President was willing. In due course, Matheson joined the conversation, his hand on Ablakan's arm.

Telepathically, and aloud for Eric and Brenda's benefit, Jan said, *Ablakan, let's make this a better test: Please tell him I'll just let Brenda feel his mindprint, so she can locate it again. Make sure he stays where he is for now. I'll break contact and Brenda can locate the Vice-President on her own and project to him like she's doing here.* Jan winked at Brenda, mouthing 'piece of cake!'.

Okay, Ablakan said.

Jan could feel his keen interest in this new method of 'pathing. Being able to connect non-telepaths without physical contact would be enormously helpful. Moohri had been lucky indeed that he possessed just enough telepathic ability for her and Ablakan to reach him.

"Brenda, just place your hand on my arm and I'll put you through."

Brenda shut her eyes and complied.

Good day, Mrs. Hancock, the Vice-President said cheerfully.

Good day, sir.

Jan interrupted, deliberately wishing to minimize contact between them through her for the purpose of the test. *Sir, I'll cut contact now, but please remain where you are for a few minutes, if you don't mind.*

No problem. Take your time.

"Okay, Brenda. You can let go my arm now. Do you remember what his mind felt like, and where to find it?"

Brenda nodded, but looked uncertain.

"Good. Just let your mind return to his. Tell me when you're there."

A slight delay, then another nod.

"Ask him when he wishes to return home."

A few seconds passed. "He says tomorrow after dinner," Brenda told Jan in surprise. "I heard his mind say it."

"Did you hear it in your mind or his?"

Brenda said promptly, "His. We're both there now, but I can chat with you here at the same time. I don't know how, but geez, this is fun!"

"Great, Brenda. But keep your emotions calm for now."

Jan gave them a chance to talk for a bit, then tapped Brenda's arm to get her attention.

"Please have the Vice-President ask Ablakan to contact me in about three minutes and tell me the gist of the conversation you just had."

Another delay, then Brenda physically relaxed and focused back into the room. "I didn't even know that was possible."

"I'm so happy for you – for all of us, really." Jan gave Brenda's hand a little squeeze. "Can you give Eric a quick rundown of the conversation you just had?"

Brenda had barely finished when Ablakan called, right on time. Eric inclined his head toward Brenda.

"Eric and Brenda, would you place your hand on my arms?" Once they had, Jan said to Ablakan, *Please tell us what they were talking about.*

Ablakan gave an identical synopsis of it, then added, *Brenda, I am Ablakan, and you are a wonderful telepath. Would you teach me your way sometime, too, please?* His young voice was high-pitched with barely-contained excitement.

I would be honored to, if I can figure out how I do it. And I am delighted to meet you.

The boy projected a smile. *Thanks, Brenda.*

Jan interjected, *Sorry to 'test and run', Ablakan, but Eric's interviewing her for a job, so we'd better go. Please thank the Vice-President for us.*

I will. Talk to you soon, Brenda. Goodbye, my friends.

"That was so exciting," Brenda exclaimed, eyes glistening.

"It was indeed. Jan, would you excuse us now?"

"Sure, boss." Jan left the office, closing the door behind her.

But even before she got to her office, Jan was grinning hugely. Brenda was a shoe-in. It did Jan's heart good to know the young widow would no longer have to worry about money. And with an exciting new career, perhaps the pain of the past few years would fade away.

Twenty minutes later, Eric and a radiant Brenda entered Jan's office.

"Here's your protégé," Eric announced. "Although who will teach who the most is anyone's guess."

"That's for sure! What about accommodations?"

"The delegates will be back here tonight, so space is at a premium. Would you mind if she bunks in with you folks? I understand the bedrooms in the main house aren't in use right now."

"Capital idea! Would you mind, Brenda?"

Her face turned pink with pleasure. "If it won't inconvenience you, no, we'd really appreciate it."

"Then that's what we'll do. And Eric? Thanks!"

"Glad it worked out," he acknowledged with a smile. "Oh, and Jan, tell Jack I need to see him first thing in the morning."

* * *

Nine a.m. the following day, Jack settled into his favorite chair in Eric's office. He regarded his boss expectantly. Jan had been adamant the night before that it wasn't bad news. Still, much as he enjoyed surprising others, Jack hated being on the receiving end.

"A few months ago, I promised you'd be earning your salary in spades," Eric reminded him.

Jack looked sheepish. "I've been busy, but I sure don't have much to show for it."

"Well, you will from now on." Eric made a tent with his fingers. "I asked Jan to keep the contents of the last interspecies session quiet, because I wanted to tell you myself."

Jack whistled appreciatively when Eric told him the news. "Shyr! What a perfect place to start."

"Indeed. And in a sense, that's where you come in. Even with Brenda on the payroll, we'll need more help, if we can find it. So in addition to your supervisory functions, which now includes Brenda and Frederick, you'll be overseeing Earth link recruiting, training and policing. That should keep you busy," Eric smirked.

"No kidding!"

"Jan and Brenda can help you set it up." Eric's expression turned pensive. "I don't know how much you should involve Fred at this time. I want you to keep an eye on him, bring him along slowly."

"I intend to," Jack nodded. "Do we have funds to cover a hefty advertising campaign?"

Eric's features relaxed somewhat. "The President said to give it top priority, and it's getting a budget to match. Get yourself an assistant. You're going to need one."

CHAPTER 17

If Jan thought the preceding months were busy, they seemed like a vacation compared to the hectic pace she and her counterparts were forced to keep. The pressure didn't come from Eric or Saunders, but from the massive push to transform Shyr into an interspecies trade and recreation center. Estimates put substantial housing construction at least a year down the road, but that in no way reduced the feverish traffic of ideas, preliminary negotiations or the number of schematics and tentative contracts which needed to be 'ported to and fro.

Fortunately, electrical modifications soon permitted leaders and businesses on Shalaii and Orowa to run computers imported from Earth, and vice-versa. Mountains of information, schematics, proposals, etc. could now be exchanged on jump drives and the like, and on the offworld equivalents. That cut down the links' workload, but not by much.

Brenda and her son Billy fitted into the Brody/Foxworth household like an old glove. Even when the delegates left for home, three days later than originally planned, no one hastened to change the arrangement. Eventually, it was simply taken for granted that they were a team at work and a family at home. Chores were performed by whoever happened to be there at the time. That included minding Billy, who blossomed in the happy chaos which surrounded him.

As Eric had predicted, Jan and the other links learned as much from Brenda as she did from them. Before long, Jan and the other 'paths were as adept at Brenda's form of telepathy as Brenda was herself. For her part, Brenda soon mastered teleporting.

But Frederick Bradshaw was a different story.

Jack said, his brow furrowed by the effort to pin down his feeling about the man, "I can't put my finger on it. He's learning quite well, and does everything I assign, but I don't know. It just feels like something's missing. Are you picking up anything?"

"No, he keeps himself tightly closed, even when 'porting," Jan replied. "I've tried to get him to join in 'pathed conversations, but he stubbornly refuses. Says he's a 'porter and that's all he wants to be."

Tom tone was ominous. "You know what I think? I bet he's sending other things on the side, maybe black-market stuff. That's why he won't let anyone pick up on him."

"It's possible, I suppose, but I don't see how." Jan had done everything she could to draw the man out, make him feel part of the team, but to no avail. "We're always tracking in the background. If he were 'porting when he's not supposed to, we'd know about it."

Jack looked skeptical. "Maybe it's just me. I can be standing there watching him, and he's doing his job – not fast, but he does get things where they're supposed to go. Maybe all he's doing is slacking off. Still, I suppose we should be grateful to have the extra talent."

Shalaii, Orowa and Earth had massive ongoing campaigns in place to locate natural telepaths and, where possible, train them to 'port. Orowa found two on the first go-round, but so far none had been located on Shalaii. Jan knew that Ablakan was tiring under the workload.

Late one evening, Jan placed a telepathic social call to him.

Any luck yet? she asked.

No, but I haven't had time to look today.

To Jan, it seemed improbable that Ablakan could be the only one on their entire planet with such abilities. *I just don't understand why no one has come forward yet who can do it.*

Until you sent me your message, no one here even knew telepathy existed, Ablakan pointed out. *It is not like your television shows, where this happens every day. On our world, even the thought of it had not occurred. But I will keep searching.*

Jan cast about for something encouraging to say. *Perhaps there are some, but they don't know how to recognize it.*

Ablakan said doubtfully, *Perhaps. I have tried sending out messages, but no one who has come claiming to have heard them can correctly tell me what I said.*

330

As overworked as he was, Jan could imagine how discouraging it must be for him to squeeze in these interviews, only to come up empty.

An old memory surfaced. *This may be a long shot, but remember me telling you I couldn't pick up on you, the first time I tried? I started to project an image, and then you picked up on it and completed the connection. Maybe you could try something like that.*

Ablakan perked up instantly. *You mean have people send me messages, and see which ones I can receive?*

Why not? In a sense, instead of trying to find them, let them find you – mentally.

That could work, Jan, Ablakan exclaimed. *I will send the request to our media as soon as Tweno approves it, which I am sure he will.*

I wish you the best of luck. I know how badly you need back-up.

It is true, he admitted ruefully. *Even the energies of a child has its limits.*

Jan told him with mock severity, *Child you aren't, young man! I'd put your maturity up against any one of us any day.*

Ablakan sighed. *Thanks, Jan. But sometimes I wish I could be a regular child, even just for a day.*

Jan felt a wave of empathic weariness wash over her. *Well, I won't keep you now. You've a notice to write and, I suspect, a bed to get to before long. You sound bushed.*

Jan felt his confusion, as he repeated, *Bushed?*

Tired.

There was a sigh of agreement. *Tweno says I work too hard, but there is so much to do, and we must keep up with the other planets. Our business people are counting on us.*

Then you go write that note so you can get yourself some help. Let me know if there's anything I can do.

I will, and thanks, Jan. Ablakan signed off with a quick mental hug.

With Jan's idea fresh in mind, Ablakan scribbled down a hasty note to Tweno, outlining the proposal. Late as it was, Tweno was closeted with yet another group of financiers wanting the ruler to approve a proposed business venture on Shyr.

Ablakan shook his head worriedly. Tweno was at least four times his age, and working even harder than he was. Ablakan didn't know how long the Primary could keep up such a bruising pace and remain in good health. Even Tweno's beloved games of golf had fallen by the wayside under these unreasonable pressures.

Ablakan simply had to find others who could handle some of the more commonplace 'pathic and 'porting traffic so he could relieve Tweno of the jobs he, Ablakan, had originally been hired to do.

After placing his note in the middle of Tweno's desk, Ablakan sent himself to the kitchen for a quick bite, thanked his servers and went to bed.

The next morning Ablakan awakened refreshed, and at the appointed time presented himself to Tweno. The Primary smiled and motioned him to a chair.

"I like this idea. I think it has possibilities. Here, read this and tell me what you think." Tweno pushed a handwritten page toward him.

The draft advertisement encouraged those who thought they could, to transmit a mental message to Ablakan at a given time. Each province was assigned a different window of opportunity.

Ablakan nodded at Tweno appreciatively. That would keep Ablakan from possibly being inundated with incoming 'calls', and not knowing how to separate them to find their owners. At least if there were several at once, he'd know which region they came from by the time slot.

"Anything you would like changed?"

No, this is perfect. It hadn't occurred to me that many transmissions might in at once."

332

"Perhaps wishful thinking, as the humans say. But we could be that lucky."

The media eagerly spread the word, offering a prize of their own for whichever region produced the most confirmed telepaths. Privately, Ablakan was surprised by the press' unusual show of optimism.

A few days later, as the time approached for the first attempts to be made, Ablakan became more and more agitated. He imagined himself being bombarded by hundreds of messages, unable to sort out which came from whom. Or worse, that none at all would come in.

Tweno arrived, armed with a muchipans and a tallyboard. Each of the regions were represented by amusing diagrams, with their names underneath in the Primary's handwriting. The muchipans was plunked down before Ablakan with comic ceremony.

Ablakan grinned at Tweno, feeling again the deep affection he had for the ruler. "Sir, you may not be telepathic, but you are one true empath."

"Got to be, to run a planet properly." He placed a hand on the boy's shoulder. "Relax, my friend. If this does not produce results, we will try something else. There is never only one way, you know."

"I know." Ablakan scratched his cheek distractedly. "But I have been with you for almost a year, and still I have taken no work from your shoulders."

Tweno shrugged it off. "We never expected all the trade and interactions we are enjoying, either. Life produces change, and we must change with it. You have just enough time to eat that before maybe becoming a receiver."

Muchipans were irresistible to Ablakan, and he unabashedly wolfed it down to the last golden crumb. He opened his mouth to thank Tweno, and stopped dead, mid-word, as the image of a Shalaian welder holding above his head an ornate welcome-shell filled his mind.

'Kyollan, Welder' was written above the doorway in the background, and the communication code for the lodging strongly impressed itself on Ablakan's mind. He grabbed his stylus and feverishly committed the code and other details to paper as the image faded away.

"Already?"

"Yes," Ablakan whispered. "And a very strong one"

Though he waited eagerly, no other messages came through. Still, having another telepath would help enormously. And it also proved that he was not an oddity. There was at least one more like him on Shalaii. Ablakan could hardly wait to make contact.

"I'll have to interview him first," Tweno said. "Skill is important, but so are intelligence and integrity. We must ensure he has all three before we accept his services."

"Of course, you are right." Ablakan was taken aback at the possibility that he might not have found his Shalaian 'other' after all.

They discussed the testing process candidates should undergo. Finally it was time for the next region to 'call in', but all Ablakan got was emptiness. Just before the deadline had passed, though, a picture of a hand-scrawled house, evidently drawn by a child much younger than Ablakan, floated in front of his mind's eye. Then it was gone. Ablakan did everything he could to backtrack the image, but was unable to do so.

"How old did the child seem to you?" Tweno asked, when Ablakan described the brief contact.

"Perhaps four, maybe even three. No discipline, but much strength and hope. I would very much like to find her."

"Her?" Tweno sounded surprised.

"Yes. It was definitely a feminine mindtouch."

None of the other regions produced results like the first two, although a few weak attempts entered Ablakan's mind almost as shadow images. Perhaps in time the authors would emerge as true telepaths, but not yet.

Tweno returned to his office to send for the welder. Ablakan used every mental trick he could think of in a vain attempt to locate the child.

Inside of a week, Kyollan joined their ranks. He was a pleasant individual, easily taught and guided, but when it came to 'thinking on his feet', as Jan called it, he was totally inept. Nor could he master teleportation. Still, Kyollan was able to shoulder much of the linking of businesspeople. He also was a quick study when it came to languages. Before long he had taken over the tedious job of teaching English to what seemed like the half of their planet's population intent on involving themselves in interplanetary trade.

With heartfelt relief, Ablakan presented himself to Tweno and insisted on shouldering the less critical aspects of the Primary's workload. Between the three of them, there was now occasionally even time for golf.

* * *

"Brenda, did you see that?" Jack exclaimed. Billy had finally succeeded in throwing a foam ball in the general vicinity of Jack's leg, close enough for Jack to score a catch.

"You're getting much better," Brenda assured him, deliberately misinterpreting Jack's remark.

Jan bit back a chuckle. It didn't take an empath to see how close those three were becoming.

Tom came up behind Jan and put his arms around her. "Jack's smitten, you know," he whispered softly in her ear.

"Uh-huh. And that pink in her cheeks isn't from the nip in the air, either."

"They make a nice couple."

"A nice family," Jan corrected, and felt him nod.

It was Sunday. Brenda and Jack would be back at work tomorrow. Jan and Tom had been given the week off, with strict orders to get some R&R. Sixteen-hour days had taken their toll, and Jan, for one, was only too happy to rest. Not that she didn't love her work, but the grueling pace could only be kept up for so long. She suspected that embarrassing episode of her falling asleep during a conference call had twigged Eric that her energies were flagging.

They had found one more confirmed telepath who would be coming in for training the following week. Of course, Eric wanted him brought up to speed as quickly as possible. The pressure from the business community for 'air time' with their markets on the other planets was becoming worse every day. With only Jan and Brenda to connect them, there just wasn't enough time to go around.

At least Fred was taking up the slack, doing most of the routine 'porting. To Jan, his skills seemed slow and plodding compared with Brenda's. Almost like he's always got something else on his mind, she thought, then shook her head. She was on vacation; this was no time to think shop. But her mind stubbornly refused to listen, for now another image presented itself. She acquiesced with a shrug. And stared in amazement.

A crazily-shaped house, not unlike the one in Ablakan's initial message, danced before her mind's eye. Under it were a series of symbols which she recognized as Shalaian, painstakingly drawn in colored pencil. The image wavered a bit, then faded away.

Jan bolted out of her chair and into the house, grabbing the first scrap of paper she could find. Only a marker pen was handy; that would have to do. As rapidly as she could, Jan reproduced the symbols, for already they were becoming less distinct in her memory. Finally, she redrew the house as nearly as she could remember it.

Tom appeared at her elbow and peered over her shoulder at the sketch. He looked at her questioningly.

"This just popped into my mind. I'm guessing it's from a Shalaian child, very young, but, oh, Tom, is she strong! If Ablakan could find and train her –"

"– he might not work himself into an early grave."

Jan temporized, "Well, with Kyollan there, he's got a bit more time off, at least."

"Probably about as much as we have," Tom muttered.

" 'Scuse me. Got to call Ablakan." Jan hurried to the Reading Room. It was the only place in the house, save their bedroom, that was off-limits to Billy and consequently free of toys and game pieces. He's becoming one spoiled kid, Jan told herself severely, knowing she'd continue to cater to him at least as much as the others did.

Ablakan, she said, when he answered. *I just got the strangest message. Catch.*

Ablakan grabbed the slip of paper as soon as it appeared in front of him. He gave a whoop of delight. *It is her! This is from the child I told you about two months ago. I have been trying to locate her, but could not, until now.*

That's wonderful! What do those symbols mean?

They are part of an address. They should be enough to help me find her. Thank you, Jan. You have made my day.

He logged off in his eagerness to seek the young imager.

* * *

It took less than a minute for Ablakan to access her mind, intent now on a new drawing. How he longed to 'port himself there, but he knew that he must not. As the only teleporter on Shalaii, he could not afford to take any chances, however slim.

Ignoring protocol, he plunked himself down in the Primary's office. Tweno looked up in surprise as Ablakan breathlessly leaned over his desk in his eagerness to impart the news.

"She contacted Jan. On Earth. Gave her a partial address. And I found her."

"Found who?"

Abalakan beamed. "The little girl I told you about."

"The four-year-old?"

"No, she is three," Ablakan said. "But her mind is so strong, so determined. Please, Tweno, can we send for her right now? Here's the address."

337

Tweno expression turned humorous. "The last time you were this excited, you woozed. You are not planning to wooze again, are you?"

Ablakan grinned at the gentle ribbing.

"No. But she is so special. She could not get through to me, probably because I was so busy 'porting, so she projected to Jan. How she knew where to find her, I have no idea. But can you imagine her doing that – at three?"

"You don't have to convince me. I will send for her and her parents at once."

"Thank you."

As Tweno reached for the hear-other to inform First Konapi on Enaxat, where the child lived, he said to Ablakan, "Of course, you realize she is too young to help you for a long time yet."

"Yes, but if she is this strong now, think what she may be able to do when she is older!" Ablakan just had a feeling about her.

"That may be, but don't pressure her. Remember, she is barely out of infancy."

"I won't," Ablakan promised. "And I will make anything telepathic that she does a game. We'll stop when she doesn't feel like playing any more."

* * *

Richard Ironhorse officially became Earth's fourth resident link the second week after the Brodys returned to work. He required virtually no training, having developed skills and self-discipline through his decades as a First Nations shaman. Given to laconic responses and droll understatements, he nicely complemented his more verbose co-workers.

Jan found herself finally able to cut back to a mere 10-hour day, five days a week. This is heaven, she thought, getting home with the sun still up for the first time in ages.

Tom arrived not long afterward. He would have to leave after dark for his stint on the Hale Telescope. As he came in the door, Jan noticed his eyes were inordinately bright.

"Saunders said the President called. The U.N. gave us the go-ahead to contact one of my hits. Eric'll be telling you tomorrow, but I can't wait that long."

Jan glanced at the star chart taped to the fridge door. Eight stars were neatly circled in three colors: red for those he felt the most feelings from, green for the middle-of-the-roaders, and blue for those he considered iffy. Four red, two green and two blue circles represented a vista of possibilities.

"That's great, hon. But it's been a while since I've had to use imagery. I'd better practice."

"Good idea."

Jan thought she knew, but she asked anyway, "Got a particular one in mind?"

"This one." He pointed to the star most nearly in the center of the cluster. "I've been pulled towards it several times when I've focused on nearby stars. This one's the strongest by far."

"Okay, then, I'll run it by Eric tomorrow. Do you want to be in my mind when I make 'first contact', assuming I succeed?"

Tom's eyes lit up like a Christmas tree. "Would I!"

The next morning, Eric called her into his office. He took one look at her eager face and grunted. "I didn't think he could keep it to himself."

"Can you blame him? He's had to wait almost a year. Anyway, I needed to practice imaging again."

Eric gazed at the celestial map. "I suppose he wants you to try that big central star?"

"Yes, he's quite excited about that one. I offered him to piggyback on my focus – that is, if it's alright with you," Jan said.

Eric shook his head, giving her an apologetic look. "First contacts can be dangerous, Jan. You're forging a pathway that perhaps more than thoughts could travel down. It's just a guess, mind you. But still . . . no sense risking two valuable people if we don't have to."

Jan bit her lip. "Tom will be awfully disappointed, but I guess you're right."

"If you do find beings, as soon as you're certain they're benign, by all means put him through," Eric offered.

When Jan told him, Tom came as close to sulking as Jan had ever witnessed. He sat in the room, silently watching her as she prepared her mind and emotions for the trek into unfamiliar territory. Jan swallowed, fighting down apprehension as she remembered Eric's warning. If they're nasty, just break contact, she told herself sternly. You're not a novice any more.

Jan closed her eyes and projected her focus out beyond Shalaii and Orowa, along the curving arm of the Milky Way. As she neared the target star, her pulse quickened. She felt a consciousness waiting for her, urging her onward. Luring me in, she couldn't help but think. Resolutely, Jan pushed the thought away and concentrated instead on the visuals. The star was a giant by Earth standards, and 14 planets revolved around it. But which one – or more – held life?

Before she could choose, a large green-and-white planet drew her like a magnet. A multiconscious presence sent waves of joy cascading into her. In an instant, her mind was laid open like an oyster. She watched in dismay as every thought, feeling, action and bit of knowledge in her memory were twinned and sent back to the planet.

Thank you, Jan, the presence said at last. *And now you may have ours.*

Her mind expanded into eternity. Snippets of data and perception dopplered by her awareness and flowed into her in a seemingly endless stream. When she felt her mind must burst from the overload, the stream became a rivulet and finally ceased.

Wh– What have you done? Jan gasped, when she could think again.

Your brain does not have the storage capacity ours has, so we have had to choose what we felt would serve you best.

Jan shook her head gingerly. *But I don't remember a thing.*

340

As you need something, it will come to the forefront of your thoughts, the multiplicity assured her. *And you have given us much to think about as well.*

Is that what you do? Amass knowledge?

Exchange is more accurate. Data shared helps us all. That is how we learn and progress.

Well, that is what humans were after, too, Jan realized.

Do you have space travel? They had taken the initiative away from her, but this was still first contact.

A sensation of amusement danced in her mind. *We do not have movement. We travel with our minds.*

Oh. Jan was unsure what to make of such a creature – or group of creatures.

Do not worry, Jan. We do not go after minds, but we are quick to welcome any who approach.

If I brought others, would you have to do the same thing with them, since most of the information would be the same?

Yes. Each being is unique, with individual thoughts, feelings, experiences, knowledge and understandings, she was told. *And we would give each person different information, based on what we think they could best use.*

Jan digested that. *I will tell the others,* she said at last. *Thank you for meeting me and for the exchange.* Jan was uncertain how grateful she actually felt, but at least she could be polite about it. As an afterthought, she asked, *How should we address you?*

You may call us 'School', if you wish.

Is that a translation of your name or that of your planet?

She felt the humor which accompanied the reply, *We have no name for either – or for anything else. But you name everything, so to you we can be known as School. Come back soon. We will not need to read you further, and we can talk about many things if you wish.*

Thank you. Jan projected a deferential bow and broke contact.

Tom was staring at her, eyes wide with a mixture of curiosity and anxiety.

341

"What happened?"

For once, Jan didn't know how to answer. "I'll tell you in Eric's office. And I think we want all the 'paths in on this."

"That interesting, huh?"

It took half an hour to round up everyone physically and/or mentally. Only Fred turned down the invitation. The link included the three-year-old Shalaian, Tix, who was being allowed her first contact with humans, now that she had assimilated a child-level knowledge of English.

When they were ready, Jan explained in detail what had occurred.

Tix piped up before anyone could comment. *I call them Brika.*

You mean you've met them? Jan asked in surprise.

Yes, but they think too much.

Ablakan's mindprint was equally taken aback. *How did you meet them?*

Mams forgot me in bed, so I went to play in my mind. I found them, but they are old.

Jan chuckled. *Even older than us?*

Much, much older. They do not know how to die, she astounded the group by saying.

Do they want to? Shownae asked.

No. But they know everything else. She excused herself then, and wandered off to play.

The group explored the pros and cons of continued contact with 'School'. The prospect of having one's whole life copied and assimilated by an alien species was unpopular with everyone, but the potential for advancement was also unparalleled.

Jan, Eric asked at one point. *Let's see if we can retrieve anything you learned. Jack, ask her a question about something she wouldn't have known before.*

How far is it from Earth to School?

199.346 light years. The others felt Jan's surprise, as she exclaimed. *I didn't know I knew that. Is it right?*

342

Jack confirmed, *I had it rounded off to 200.* He mentally and physically rubbed his hands together in mock glee. *I'm gonna have such fun pumping you for answers. Get my work done in half the time, go home early.*

Not on my watch, you don't, Eric grunted. *I intend to get your fat salary's worth out of you.*

Jack winked at Jan. *Oh well. It was worth a shot.*

Afterwards, Moohri opted to visit School, with Shownae's reluctant help. It would act as a test of sorts. School would be invited to exchange information with Moohri, but to leave Shownae untouched. How they handled this request would determine what future interactions there would be.

To everyone's relief, School honored the Orowans' wishes to the letter. When Shownae waffled, half-deciding to participate, School recommended he think it over first and return if his desire became stronger.

After that, carefully selected people on each planet were encouraged to attend School, to the mutual benefit of all. That included Brenda and Richard Ironhorse, but Fred flatly refused to upgrade.

That night, when Fred had left for home, the gang convened a meeting in Eric's office.

"Well, what do you think he's doing, then?" Eric demanded in exasperation.

"I don't know. I can't catch him at anything, but I just know he's doing something." Jack thumped the chair arm for emphasis. "I'd wager anything you like on it."

"Specifics, man. Is he stealing anything? Slacking off? Gambling on the job? What?"

Jack turned toward Jan and Brenda for assistance, but all Brenda could do was shrug helplessly.

Jan stirred in her chair. "There's nothing concrete, Eric. But we all have the same feeling. Like –" She tried to identify the elusive sensation. "It feels like he's doing one thing on the surface, and something entirely different underneath."

Jack exclaimed, pointing a finger at her. "Yes, exactly. Could it be like a carrier wave or something?"

Eric scowled. "If he is, I want proof, and fast. What we're doing here is far too sensitive to risk. If he's a mole of some sort, I want to know it, and now."

A mole. Something entirely different underneath. It didn't sound quite right to Jan, but the nucleus of an idea began to form.

She said to Jack, "He's still a lot slower than we are at 'porting, right? I mean, number of 'ports-wise."

"He has his eyes closed nearly twice as long as you do, no matter what he is 'porting or where to," Jack confirmed. Then he caught sight of the glint in Jan's eyes. "What?"

"Let me check it out. I'll tell you later, if I'm right."

Tom pointed out, "That's what the victim always says in mystery novels, just before she gets offed by the bad guy. Tell us now."

"Nope. Nor will I get offed. But if he's doing what I think he is – or rather, *how* I think he's doing it, we'll have to figure out what to do with Freddie-boy."

"Tom's right, Jan. Spill it." Eric said it lightly, but it was an order nonetheless.

"Okay, but only to you, Eric." Jan raised her voice over the objections being directed her way from her indignant companions. "If I tell the rest of you now, you'll all be watching him like a hawk. He'd be bound to pick up on it. Let me do this my way. I promise I'll fill you in afterwards if I'm right."

* * *

The bogus list of items to be 'ported lay negligently in Jan's lap the next morning. She used a feather-light touch to follow Fred's mind as he sent a shipment of wire ropes to an Orowan warehouse. His back was to her, and she checked her watch. Mental activity from start to finish: 3.5 seconds. That beat her usual five seconds by a handy margin. Yet his head was still bowed in feigned concentration. After a bit, he lifted his head and sighed before reaching for his clipboard.

344

Twice more, Jan followed Fred's mind as he more than doubled the apparent time of 'porting. She was beginning to think he was guilty of nothing worse than goldbricking when she felt his feelings change.

The man began exuding tension and excitement, intermingled with a touch of nervousness. Jan made a show of consulting her roster as Fred sent a furtive glance in her direction. Satisfied, he turned away and lowered his head. Jan cautiously placed her focus in the slipstream of his and waited.

In her mind's eye, she saw a crateful of produce arrive at the main dining facility on Shyr, and moments later, a second item – a small cardboard box – appeared at the feet of a fair-haired man in the back of the warehouse. Instantly, he grabbed it and rushed through the back exit. Jan didn't have to wonder; Fred's mind leaked a momentary image of bags of a white powdery substance. Drugs.

"Back in a bit," Jan said as nonchalantly as she could manage, and left the room. Once outside the door, she sprinted to Eric's office. He looked up at her.

"And?"

"Drugs to Shyr. Bags of white powder." Now that she was out of Fred's presence, she permitted the disgust and outrage she felt to pour out in full measure. "I'd like to wring his scrawny little neck!"

Eric reached into his top drawer and extracted a syringe. "I had the lab boys prepare this, just in case. Inject him with it and keep him from 'porting for five seconds. That's all it'll take."

Jan stared at him. "I could have been wrong."

"You haven't been yet," he countered. "Security will be standing by."

Jan reached for the syringe, holding it gingerly despite the cap which was securely in place over the needle. She wasn't cut out for this cloak-and-dagger stuff. Unfortunately, she was the obvious choice since Fred expected her, and only her, to be in the room for the next two hours.

She took a deep breath to calm her nerves, then walked back into the room. Fred gave her a look of indifference, then turned back to his work.

Jan marched past him to the water cooler. He took no notice. She let a small amount of fluid dribble into her cup and drank it down before placing the empty vessel back on the table. It took all her concentration to keep her emotions neutral as she walked by again. He turned his head away from her, and she chose that moment to pounce, plunging the needle deep into his upper arm.

"*AAAAAA!*" he screamed, trying to wrench himself out of her physical and mental grip. Jan hung on grimly, all the while flooding his mind with conflicting words and feelings.

"*Noooo,*" he moaned, as the sedative began to take hold. Still Jan bombarded him with interference. She didn't stop until she saw his eyes glaze and go out of focus.

Jan fell back, emotionally shaken, as four burly security guards strong-armed the erstwhile trafficker out of the room. Eric strode purposefully toward Jan, slowing as he noted the expression on her face.

"Your first bust," he quipped lightly.

"And my last. Damn it, Eric, he had it all – tons of money, respectability, a great future –"

Eric squeezed her shoulder gently to stop the tirade. "I know, Jan. But some people aren't happy unless they think they're getting away with something. They're just hard-wired that way."

"What do we do with him now? We can't keep him tranquilized forever."

"No, we can't. I'm calling a meeting for 10:30, but I have something I want you to do before then."

Jan eyed him mistrustfully, but her doubts faded when he outlined his plan.

* * *

"I thought so," Tom nodded, when Jan told the group about Fred's illegal activities. "How did you cotton onto it?"

Jan shrugged. "We were all pretty sure he was pulling a fast one, but he wasn't doing it outside of authorized 'porting times. So he had to be doing it at the same time as his regular sends."

"Seems obvious now," Jack admitted.

Brenda asked, "How long can they keep him doped up?" She and Richard Ironhorse had been off-duty during the last meeting, but Jan had since brought them up to speed.

"We may not have to. Jan?" Eric prompted.

"Eric had me call School. He figured, if School can copy the contents of someone's mind and implant data in it, maybe they can also erase memories."

"And can they?" Richard was leaning forward eagerly.

Jan could only shrug. "They don't know; they've never tried. But since we can't make Fred go to School, they've agreed to access him here, just this once. They will try to remove all knowledge of teleporting and everything he's done and learned since he came here."

"Then dump him back to jail," Jack said.

"Can't do that," Eric said. "He'd have no memory of trafficking and so couldn't defend himself against the charges. We either leave him his memories and he does time for it – if they could keep him in jail that long – or we try to get the whole thing wiped from his mind and let him go."

Jan frowned. "Well, when he was sprung from prison, he was doing time for something else."

"He received a pardon – from the President, no less – when he agreed to work for us. Like it or not, he's a free man." Eric's expression left no doubt he wished that was not the case.

Although it didn't sit well with any of them, erasing the whole affair seemed the most practical solution, if it was even feasible.

School's multi-mind presence arrived an hour later, sending shock waves through the small telepathic community at Ames. Jan desperately tried to shield herself from the overwhelming presence. But as before, her mind fell open, laid out for the picking, had that been their intent. True to the agreement, School

347

only zeroed in on Fred. They successfully excised every memory from the moment in prison when he first contemplated learning to teleport.

After School left, Jan 'ported Fred to a spot just outside the prison walls. She placed a suitcase in front of him. In it were the bare essentials for starting over, and an envelope containing $1000 in small bills. Knowing Fred, he would not give much thought to where the money had come from or how he had gotten out of jail. He would just disappear as fast as he could. It seemed a small price to pay to be rid of the man.

* * *

A week after Fred was unceremoniously purged from their ranks, Eric said to Jan, "I have a special assignment for you." His eyes sparkled mischievously, but he refused to divulge what that job might be.

Tom and Jack seemed to be smirking a lot lately, too. Something was definitely up. While trying to guess what it might be, Jan suddenly realized her birthday was three days away. Well, that explained it. Jan resolved to be 'surprised', no matter what they came up with.

And surprised she was when, after sleeping in on her birthday, she was summarily called in to the office. Jan had booked the day off and made delightful plans in no way related to work. She arrive at Eric's office feeling decidedly put out.

"What is so important that I can't have my birthday off?" she fumed as soon as she opened the door.

Then she noticed Jack and Tom draped casually in their usual chairs, but the looks of utter innocence on their faces were a dead giveaway.

Forgetting her earlier decision to feign surprise, Jan demanded, "Alright, you guys. What are you up to?"

Eric smiled benignly. "We figured, if you have to work on your birthday, it might as well be something you'd enjoy. We have an offworld buddy of yours who just came in this morning.

348

He's got a whole week's vacation, so we're assigning you as his guide."

"Really? Who?" Jan thought she knew. Moohri had been talking about a visit for some time.

"Follow me." Eric led the way down the hall to her office. He opened the door with a dramatic gesture and motioned her inside. As she stepped through the doorway, the others crowded in behind her.

Jan stopped dead in her tracks. She felt her cheeks redden in thrilled disbelief. Then she flew across the room to crush a grinning Ablakan in her arms, as this dearest of dreams came true.

"Oh, Ablakan, I've wanted to do this for so long," she breathed, beaming at him through ecstatic tears.

"So have I, Jan. You have been more of a mother to me than my own ever was. I love you. Happy birthday, dearest friend." He embraced her again, his eyebanks closed in deep contentment. "And Eric promised, no work at all for you and Tom and Jack."

Jan clapped her hands in delight, as Eric added, "Yup, I don't want to see hide nor hair of you lot for a week. Go show him the best Earth has to offer. Just keep Friday night open for dinner at the White House. You'll have to take a security detail along, of course, but they won't get in the way."

"Oh, thank you, thank you! You're the best!"

Eric harrumphed as he became the victim of an enthusiastic Jan-hug.

She wiped a happy tear from her eye as she turned back to Ablakan. "But how did you ever get permission to come?"

"Kyollan asked School for help. Now he can 'port like the rest of us and think for himself. When Tweno said I could visit you, I was afraid it would leak out. I so wanted it to be a surprise."

Jan squeezed his hands, trying to convey the profound affection words alone couldn't say. "It's the best gift you could ever have given me . . . all of us, actually."

"You got that right!" Tom exclaimed.

Jack waved his hand in joyful impatience. "C'mon, you guys. There's a whole planet to explore, and only a week to do it in. Let's go!"

Grinning like a hyena, Jan led Ablakan towards the happy conspirators eager to entertain Shalaii's favorite son.

And now, a sneak preview of . . .

When the Need Is Great

Hell Holes

"OWWEEEE!"

Ablakan sucked his punctured finger and glared in mock severity at the long-haired calico kitten.

"No, Shnook, don't bite." He shook a finger from a safer distance at the unrepentent furball. She twitched her tail in response, fever-bright eyes never leaving the long digit just beyond her reach.

Ablakan grinned fatuously at Shalaii's one and only feline. Schnookums was a birthday present from his dearest human friend, Jan Brody. From the moment he laid eyes on a tricolored domesticated cat, during a visit to Earth, he'd dreamed of having one of these magnificently independent creatures come live with him. Of course, he could not inflict such a destructive whirlwind on a palaceful of irreplaceable treasures. But now that he was on Pantai, he could indulge his desire.

Ablakan opened the cleanser door in the anteroom and extracted a suitable-sized dressing to cover the tiny punctures. The wide mirror reflected his beige leathery arm, the skin crisscrossed with tiny lines from the quilted cushion on which it had rested. The handmade gift was from Earth's second 'porting telepath, Brenda Foxworth. He noticed that his sun-gold mane, which flowed from its apex at the back of his head to halfway down his spine, at the moment resembled the tangleweed he had removed from the garden path yesterday. Shnookums found his mane almost as irresistible as fingers.

Ablakan cast an indulgent smile at the troublesome cat before brushing his mane back into place. He carefully checked his eyes. Fortunately, the kitten's claws had not left a mark as they attempted to capture the tiny pupils which moved independently of each other in his eyebanks. The breathing slits underneath had not fared as well, and he dabbed at a small bead of half-dried blood. As a final check, he opened his ovoid mouth baring his twin rows of sparkling teeth.

Satisfied at last that the features of his horizontally-oblong head were still in place, Ablakan re-entered his sleep chamber.

A gentle knock on his door sent the kitten scurrying toward the sound.

"Come in," Ablakan called, and the door opened a crack.

"Is *she* inside?"

As if in reply, a small paw, needle-sharp claws extended, insinuated itself into the gap and tap-tapped around the corner in an effort to reach the body that went with that voice.

"Shnook, no!" Ablakan scooped up the protesting feline before it could get into more trouble.

"I've got her, Saymin," he assured his valet, who opened the door gingerly.

His elder by three decades (that he would admit to), today Saymin wore notably incongruous attire. His uncharacteristically short leggings had been rolled down to expose the bottom third of his legs. The right one, just above the ankle, sported an enormous bandage held in place with seemingly leagues of tape. Saymin deposited his load of clothing on the bed and walked toward the closet with a decided limp.

Ablakan had seen the damage Shnook inflicted on him the day before — three miniature scratches which only just succeeded in breaking the top layer of skin. But if Saymin needed to feel like a martyr, Ablakan wasn't about to deny him the pleasure. At least while distracted by the cat, his valet wasn't trying to matchmake

352

for Ablakan. Being a boy one day and Shalaii's most eligible bachelor the next was pretty disconcerting.

"How is your leg?" First Ablakan of Pantai inquired, knowing Saymin would expect a fuss to be made over his 'war wound', as he called it.

"I have learned to ignore the pain, sir." The valet favored the kitten with an aggrieved scowl. "The medic assured me it is not life-threatening."

"I am relieved to hear that. Are you settling into your quarters well? Have you everything you need?"

"It is beautiful," Saymin smiled. "Primary Tweno was indeed generous in the arrangements — well, mine, anyway. I have not seen anyone else's yet. And such a view!"

"I'm not surprised. We are so fortunate to have him as our ruler."

Ablakan blinked rapidly and turned away, his eyebanks becoming sodden. Despite the magnificent surroundings and plush accommodations Tweno had arranged for him and his staff, Ablakan was feeling overwhelmingly homesick.

As usual, Saymin noticed the mood change and placed a hand on his employer's shoulder.

"I miss them all, too, sir, and you can be sure they miss you as well. There is still much daylight left. I am certain you would lift his heart if you 'ported over and challenged the Primary to a game."

"They won't be eating for a while yet," Ablakan agreed, cheered by the prospect.

"Why not give him a call right now?" Saymin quietly left the room as Ablakan closed his eyebanks to mentally 'knock' in Tweno's mind. The Primary opened to him instantly, unable (or perhaps not trying) to hide his pleasure.

"I was wondering if you have found replacements willing to let you beat them at golf?" Ablakan needled.

"No, they're all poor sports here. They don't want to look bad when I beat them, so they refuse to play. Use all sorts of lame excuses, like family or having to work — you know how it is. Are you offering?"

"I need the exercise," Ablakan smiled, then honesty got the better of him. "And I miss the company."

"Then let's not waste any more time."

A moment later, Ablakan appeared before him. They grinned at each other knowingly, for each had felt the loneliness in the other during that brief contact. Tweno was now barely taller than Ablakan, who stood 6'6" (according to Jan's measurements), but Tweno doubled him in weight. Ablakan hoped in time to also would put on weight to offset his gangly length, but everything he ate seemed to translate into height.

Carts in hand, Ablakan 'ported them to the first tee with the offhandedness of old habit. Ablakan watched as Tweno, who had been to him more surrogate father than ruler over the years, sent his ball in a devastatingly accurate trajectory to land three feet from the cup.

"Are you sure you haven't been practicing?"

Tweno grinned but said nothing.

Ablakan's shot had a slight curve to it, and his ball stopped at the far edge of the green.

"The first week is always the hardest," Tweno told him as they sauntered towards their respective balls. "When I moved into the skyzone tower in Tabix, I almost quit. The honor of governing our largest continent just didn't make up for the homelife I had left behind, even after my mother died. I wasn't much older than you when I took on the job."

He grinned at his protege to take the sting out of his next comment. "And I didn't have the ability to 'port myself home when the loneliness got too sharp."

Ablakan felt his skin pink, but not because of Tweno's remark. He had only just remembered someone he should have been missing even more.

"How is my mother handling it?"

Annoyance flickered across Tweno's face. "She is playing the heartbroken mother to the hilt, and the staff are flocking to buy her wares out of sympathy. But when I went to see how she was feeling, she almost brushed me off when she saw I hadn't come to buy. I certainly wouldn't worry about her."

"It was generous of you to let her continue running the palace gift shop, now that I'm no longer there." Ablakan felt his gratitude stronger than his words conveyed. The alternative would have had Epash living with him, probably trying to run Pantai instead of letting her son do his job.

"The staff have grown surprisingly fond of her," Tweno murmured, as he pulled the putter from his bag. He neatly sunk the ball in one tap.

Ablakan sunk his in two strokes. With a sigh of contentment, he retrieved his ball and waited his turn at the second tee.

It was as they approached the second hole that a hole of a different sort appeared, no larger than a pin prick in the fabric of space. Nearby particles of cosmic dust abruptly veered toward it, to disappear an instant later. The vortex grew, and more debris, this time from further away, fell prey to its growing appetite.